FIASCO

OTHER BOOKS BY CONSTANCE FAY

Calamity

FIASCO

CONSTANCE FAY

BRAMBLE

TOR PUBLISHING GROUP
NEW YORK

FIASCO

Copyright © 2024 by Constance Fay

A Bramble Book
Published by Tom Doherty Associates / Tor Publishing Group
120 Broadway
New York, NY 10271

www.torpublishinggroup.com

Bramble™ is a trademark of Macmillan Publishing Group, LLC.

The Library of Congress Cataloging-in-Publication Data
is available upon request.

ISBN 978-1-250-33045-1 (trade paperback)
ISBN 978-1-250-33046-8 (ebook)

Our books may be purchased in bulk for promotional,
educational, or business use. Please contact your local bookseller
or the Macmillan Corporate and Premium Sales Department
at 1-800-221-7945, extension 5442, or by email at
MacmillanSpecialMarkets@macmillan.com.

First Edition: 2024

Printed in the United States of America

0   9   8   7   6   5   4   3   2   1

To Frank Harris,
who is never afraid to look upward and dream.

FIASCO

CHAPTER 1

The *Mirror* is a preposterous spaceship. The soap bubble of plasglass coated with iridescent finish doesn't look like it could survive an emergency landing, an impact with a piece of space trash, or even a kick with a moderate-weight boot. It looks like exactly what it is, the pipe dream of a society woman possessing more money than sense.

My ship—the *Hermit*—floats just outside radar range as I assess the points of entry to the *Mirror*. The bounty for Geni Etienne, recent ex-wife of Sarah Etienne, flashes on a console in my peripheral vision. This is supposed to be an easy retrieval—fools aren't difficult to track down—and Geni is a fool if nothing else. After a mutually agreed-upon divorce, the woman got absolutely shitfaced, broke into her ex's private dock, and stole the pleasure ship and everything within it—including Sarah's prized genetically engineered flying lizard.

Goes to show, it never pays to trust. Either you wind up stealing a ship from your estranged lover or hiring a bounty hunter to track your lover down.

I'm Cyn Khaw, said bounty hunter.

When I get within range, the sentinel-override protocol provided to me by Sarah will deactivate the thrusters and the security system, leaving the *Mirror* helpless in the void. All I have to do is enter the ship, locate and restrain Geni, and plug in coordinates to take us back to Sarah Etienne's private dock—where a tidy sum of credits awaits me. Research indicates that Geni wouldn't know a blaster from a bouquet, so she's unlikely to be armed or dangerous. Only vapid.

She was a foot model before she met Sarah. I'm sure a lot of foot models offer things besides excellent pedicures to society, but Geni isn't one of them.

I should be able to take on one socialite with a grudge. I've certainly faced worse. You don't work as a bounty hunter unless you're mostly inured to violence and some kind of desperate.

I'm less inured than I'd prefer, but more desperate, so it evens out.

The desperate part will only come into play if the sentinel-override code doesn't work. If the code *doesn't* work—because Geni was unexpectedly clever enough to change it—then I have to break in. Which means I'll set all the alarms off and lose whatever element of surprise I have.

I really hope she didn't change the code.

I brush a hand through my newly cropped blond hair. I grew it out for my last mission—embedding with a cult on a desert planet so I could approach and retrieve one of their members for deprogramming. I managed to get her off-planet safely despite a few hiccups, including the meddling of an irritating scouting crew who insisted on trying to save me from myself.

No time for reminiscing, though—I have a bounty to retrieve.

I zip up my space suit, close the secondary-seal flap over the zipper, and slip my blaster-belt around my waist. It fastens snugly and the thigh strap ensures that nothing flies around if I go zero-g. The blaster fits perfectly in its holster and my helmet locks into place with a solid click.

A shiver works its way through me, but I shake my head once, a sharp negation of the sensation. This is a precaution. I will not be untethered in space.

I *won't*.

I flex my hands in their gloves, familiarizing myself with how they slow my reflexes. I probably won't need fast reflexes. Geni seems like the type to wallow. Probably she's watching holos of her wedding ceremony and weeping into the scales of her ex-wife's luxury lizard.

I nudge my ship into range, activate the sentinel override, and grimace as I wait for it to work or fail. It takes a bit. Long enough that I start to wonder how likely I am to get dead in the next few minutes. Eventually, I am rewarded by a whole array of sensors pointed at the *Mirror* registering dead signals and the happy green light of a successful connection on my ship's display. Go time.

I've never been so happy to have a lazy bounty.

Instead of a boarding ramp, I have a flexible connecting tube, which is exactly what it sounds like. It'll shoot out from my ship and, if I'm both very skilled and very lucky, will attach in a clever little airtight seal around the *Mirror*'s hatch. It's only failed twice in the last standard year, which makes me *fairly* skilled and extraordinarily lucky.

Today is not attachment failure number three. My luck continues. The tube locks against the *Mirror*'s hull and the memory-metal floor stiffens to support it. With the memory-metal structure activated, the link between ships will even withstand towing force. I breathe a heavy sigh of relief that I expect to fog the faceplate even though I know my suit is calibrated to prevent that sort of thing.

I provide the verbal command to open the air lock and unholster my blaster as I step inside, thumbing down the intensity to stun because people frown on accidentally shooting holes through spaceships—or through bounties. Sarah wants her ex returned to face justice alive, not riddled with laser holes.

Who knows? After all this they may get back together. Stranger things have happened.

The air lock is larger than the one on the *Hermit*. No different than any other air lock, with the exception of the ridiculous crystal chandelier that some overachieving designer placed smack in the middle of the ceiling. It's . . . a choice. I close the exterior hatch behind me and cue the pressurization sequence via my backdoor remote access. As the room equalizes with the rest of the ship, I grip my blaster, preparing for a hatch to fly open and a squadron of cheaply purchased security to shoot at me and test the resiliency of my armored space suit.

It isn't all that resilient. My credits aren't unlimited, and I have to eat and pay off family debts as well as invest in armor. So when the door finally slides open, I'm pressed against the wall alongside it, waiting to see a blaster nose its way inside. Nothing. I breathe a sigh of relief as I step out of the lock. Still nothing.

Maybe this job will actually be as easy as it seems.

The ship continues its ludicrous opulence on the inside. An opalescent sheen coats the rounded white walls, ceiling, and floor. I'm sure *everyone* likes living inside an iridescent egg. I don't know why people say the wealthy are out of touch with the common person. Seems totally normal and easy to keep smudge-free.

At first, I think the ship is filled with surreal sculptures. A collection of spindly legged half-hatched shells perch in a corner, gleaming in the golden ambient light. Fragile scales line a wall, flaring at waist height.

It's furniture. Wildly impractical furniture that will break the second you try to use it, but furniture, nonetheless.

I creep through the quiet ship, blaster out, waiting for someone to pop out and try to murder me. According to the schematics Sarah provided, the orb is subdivided on the inside. The hall I'm following now should open on a large central chamber that mirrors the shape of the ship itself. Three bedrooms surround the central chamber, and a staircase winds its way around the dome to a hatch in the top that accesses the helm. I came in via the hold, which is beneath the central chamber—and large enough to contain a small personal vessel as well as random supplies. A backup chandelier, maybe?

Good design if you want your ship to be difficult to secretly infiltrate. Rotten design if you're the secret infiltrator.

Essentially, I must traipse through this whole vessel just to steal it. Rude.

As I approach the central chamber, noises start to filter into the hall. Wet smacking noises. The kind that are only fun to hear if they're coming from you and even then not if you stop and really listen to them. It appears Geni has moved on romantically. I calculate the odds that I get all the way up that staircase while they're distracted and I come up short. By the pace of the panted breaths, this little interlude is nearing its climax. Pun intended.

I hate to kill the mood. Then again, people are rarely armed while in the heat of the moment, so they're less likely to kill me in retaliation. Besides, if I wait around, it smacks of voyeurism, and I really don't want anyone to think I was creepily watching them prior to making a capture. Despite the oxygenated ship, I keep my face mask down as I round the corner, blaster raised, and nearly shit myself.

Geni has, indeed, moved on. She's presently *moving* on a prone male form, hands in her hair like she's posing for an advertising campaign instead of enjoying herself. That's not why panic is poking little spines into my guts. It's *who* she's moving on. Carmichael Pierce. Not the current Pierce in charge, which would be catastrophic, but his heir, which is just *short* of catastrophic. Carmichael works as his father's head of security, which means me popping up will be extra humiliating. He is the face of the Pierce Family, their bright new future.

I guess all that luck had to run out sometime.

Also, this is a very stupid choice for Geni if her goal is to remarry rather than just get her rocks off. Someone placed that highly can't afford to marry someone like her who doesn't bring any political clout. Pierce has their hands in all sorts of quasi-legal shit and makes alliances to keep it on the quasi side rather than fully illegal. If it's energy, its pulse is Pierce. Solar, wind, nuclear, atomic, algae, fission, or anything else.

They've gobbled up star systems like a particularly gluttonous stray cat does mice. At this point, Pierce territory includes eight star clusters, at least thirty additional planets of value, one binary system, a research pulsar, and approximately two-fifths of the trading lanes. Maybe three-fifths now that Nakatomi is gone. And I have to interrupt his sexy-time to serve a warrant.

No one likes that. Powerful people even less than normal people, I imagine.

Pierces are brutal, ruthless, and—apparently—quite well-endowed, which I discover when Carmichael tosses Geni from his lap to the plushly upholstered bench seating—in an iridescent white, of course—and reaches for a blaster that's been left on a side table. His hair is long, wavy, and blond. His eyes are dark. His face is rodenty despite the clear signs of facial surgery that arched his cheeks, strengthened his chin, and angled his jaw. Something about the eyes and the shape of his nose, maybe.

I put on my big-bad-bounty-hunter voice. It's mostly my normal voice but less scared sounding. "That would be a bad idea. My bounty is for everything present *except* you, Carmichael. Geni Etienne, formerly and soon to be Geni al Astal, there is an open warrant for you in Pierce-Etienne border territory and I've been contracted to retrieve you. If you come with me without resistance, no harm will come to you."

I'm smart enough to not give my name. Families love to hold grudges but there are a lot of bounty hunters out there. I sidle to the side table and retrieve Pierce's blaster, tucking it in my belt.

Geni grumbles under her breath like I'm an inconvenient paparazzi. Her blue-greenish hair is still perfectly styled, draping over her shoulder. As I watch, the roots shift to a brilliant magenta that slowly makes its way down the rest of her strands. Optical-coating dye. No wonder her hair stayed in place. Her eyes are wide, hazel, and lacking intelligence. "What is it going to cost to make you go away?"

I kick the pile of clothes slightly closer to them. No need to do this naked. We can all be civilized. I don't want to stun-blast them. For one thing, sometimes stunning has side effects. For another, stunning a Pierce would embarrass him, and embarrassing a Pierce is a great way to inspire him to make my life a living hell.

"Keep your hands in view as you dress." I snap the command while keeping my distance across the room. "You seem to be unclear about how bounty hunting works. I don't do it for the money. I do it for the glamour."

"Glamour?" Her lip curls. "I can give you glamour. I can get you admittance to all the best social clubs. Esoterica. Makewells. Thorn and—"

"Who would even want to go to a social club? What do you do there? Drink? Hobnob? Socially hit people with actual clubs?" I shake my head. It says something about Families that her only thought of glamour is some sort of location where people can view her being fancy. Also, she can't recognize a joke. "Carmichael Pierce, you are free to leave the ship in your own vessel. The *Mirror* and its contents are owned by Sarah Etienne and shall be returned to her."

Please just leave the ship. It's easy. Take the easy way.

He doesn't take the easy way.

Carmichael lunges at me with arms spread and I stun him with a shot to the torso. He flops on the floor like a dropped pile of laundry. Only without any clothes. So, I guess, the opposite of a pile of laundry.

Geni squeaks.

I'm far too professional to squeak. My nervous panic is on the inside because I just shot a naked Carmichael Pierce and watched him helplessly flop on the floor, and now I'm going to have to restrain him. A hidden security force would have been *better* because security forces, like me, are nobodies. No one gets upset if you stun them and they usually understand that the job comes first.

Fuck. Fuckity fuck *fuck*.

Yes, this is Etienne business, but that's like trying to explain to a tornado that you just had an earthquake so it will have to try again later. It doesn't give a fuck. I just shot a human tornado, and he probably bruised his very exposed winky when he fell on it.

I'm so screwed.

Instead of pacing frantically trying to figure out what to do, I turn to face Geni. I toss a pair of plastic tie cuffs to the floor. "Put the cuffs on him. Nice and tight."

When she's done locking Pierce's wrists behind his back, I throw her another pair of the cuffs. "Get dressed, then cuff yourself."

"You k-killed him." She's crying, or at least that's what she wants me to think she's doing. No actual tears, which ruins the effect. She's complying with my requests, though, which is what I really care about. She spends an inordinate amount of time fussing with her collar for a woman who's headed to prison for spaceship theft.

"I didn't kill him. Why would I ask you to restrain him if I killed him? He's stunned. He'll be just fine in a couple minutes."

Probably.

After scanning the room for possible weapons, I drape a blanket over Pierce, raise my face shield at last, and search the rest of the ship. The ship is even more blindingly white without the slight tint of the face shield filtering the light. No other living creatures are present except a chubby winged lizard, small enough that I could hold it with both hands cupped, in a cage in one of the bedrooms. It gnaws on the drool-coated bars of its cage. The aforementioned pet of Sarah's. Something smells like sulfur and, when I approach the cage, I see that slivers of metal have been pared off the bars.

Flakes of it decorate tiny fangs and the lizard belches at me. A spark flies out.

Well. That's a wildly impractical creature to bring on a spaceship. I stow Pierce's blaster on a shelf behind the cage, because if I keep it stuck in my belt, I'll probably shoot myself in the butt.

"I'm here to take you back to your mom," I tell the lizard. It belches again and sticks out a narrow, forked tongue. I'm going to assume that means "yay."

It's kind of cute. Reddish-gold scales near its spine fade to brass on its belly. Small, diaphanous bronze wings are folded tightly against its back. Brilliantly golden eyes. Black gums, which I see when it bares its teeth at me. I bare mine back. The bars look like they'll hold for a while yet, so I leave the lizard where it is and turn to the main area.

A fist comes out of nowhere and nails me directly in the nose. I stagger backward, stars pinwheeling in front of my eyes, and reflexively snap a kick to my left. I hit something, but not hard enough to stop a second blow that strikes the edge of my helmet rather than my face. I fall back against the doorframe, trying frantically to get my head back in the game, except my head is exactly the problem. You don't quickly bounce back from getting hit in the face unless you're a professional actor.

Because they don't *actually* get hit in the face.

Since my brain isn't working well enough to target anything, I focus on moving. I push off the doorframe just in time to avoid a third strike. Carmichael Pierce's fist batters into the metal frame as I dodge away, hand fumbling for my holster and my blaster.

How did he get untied? How did he wake up so quickly? Apparently I didn't hear him escaping *or* putting his pants on. Bad day for me. A stun round takes someone out for at least half a standard hour. He was out for ten minutes max. As I backpedal, I shoot a glance at Geni. Still sitting on the white furniture, restrained, watching us like we're an action holo. She didn't free him.

I may be wearing a space suit, but I'm a moderately sized woman and Pierce is a large man. Space suits are made to stop the cold or the heat—not fists. Also, he keeps aiming for my face, which isn't protected at all. I'm built and trained for ambushes, not brawls. Priap must have had a hidden blade nearby to cut his wrist ties—maybe even subdermal.

He is a chief of security, after all—I should have considered who I was dealing with. I backpedal for a moment, trying to buy time. I don't feel bad for stunning him anymore. But I'm a little concerned that stunning him may not be *enough*. Legally I'm allowed to kill while retrieving a bounty. A normal person, that is. If I kill a Pierce, his Family will come at me with everything they have, leaving me a little smudge on the ground. So I can't shoot him and I'm not going to win a hand-to-hand fight against someone twice my size who's literally been training his entire life and is acknowledged as the best in his Family, despite his rodent-like features.

I raise my blaster, but he knocks it out of my hand in a high kick that would make me applaud if my fingers weren't spasming in pain. The blaster goes spinning and we both lunge toward it. I manage to sidestep a thrown elbow, capturing his forearm and ducking behind him to lock it behind his back. I force Pierce to his knees for a split second, spinning him away from the blaster, but I don't even have time to celebrate before he bounds back up, other arm reaching back over his head to snag my suit and throw me forward over his shoulder.

I grab his ear as I fly over his head.

He screams, latching on to my wrist and, as I fall back toward him I do it elbow first. My elbow digs into his neck, but I sacrificed a graceful landing for a violent one and I crash to the floor on my back immediately after. Which turns out to be a bad location, because he manages to get to his feet before I do and kicks me in the ribs while I'm attempting to rise.

I hit the sofa, shoving it slightly forward, but manage to throw myself up and over it, putting the furniture between us. Geni moves toward the blaster out of the corner of my eye, and I bark a commanding "No" at her.

Wonder of all wonders, she listens and stops moving.

"Dumb bitch," Carmichael grunts at me as he leaps on top of the sofa like an absolute moron instead of walking around it. He clearly doesn't even think he needs my blaster to take me out. Which is presumptuous.

So instead of kicking *him*, I kick the sofa with everything I have. It slides back, knocking him against the wall, and I sprint back for my blaster. His heavy footsteps come from behind me. I stumble and dive for it, my fingers reaching for the grip just as his own fingers wrap around my ankle.

I kick him in the face. He grunts and his fingers relax just enough for me to wriggle free and finally reach the blaster. He approaches from behind, his shadow falling over me where I stretch on the floor.

I twist and point the blaster.

I can't afford the kind of enemy that he presents. I want him to forget me as soon as possible. Any smart person would. But I guess I'm not that smart of a person because instead of trying to cajole him or smooth over the situation I sneer up at his standing form, blaster steady. "Try it."

He blinks, a trail of blood dribbling into his eyes. "You're Cyn Khaw."

Carmichael says my name like it's a profanity and I feel a momentary rush of pride that my reputation is such that a Pierce recognizes me. It's immediately followed by a rush of abject terror because, if he knows me, he'll be able to track me down later. "You're that bounty hunter. The one who spaced that whole ship full of traffickers."

I adore it when people bring up that part of my history. It certainly wasn't an incredibly scarring moment in my life that

I revisit every time I close my eyes to sleep. Some people, people like Carmichael, love my story. As though what I did wasn't awful. As though it was impressive somehow.

It *was* impressive, just not in the way they think.

"You're a monster." He says it in an admiring way, like how you'd say "goddess." "I always wanted to meet you."

I stun him. Don't even think about it. It's deeply stupid of me, but why stop being deeply stupid now?

He hits the ground with a thud. Stunned again for whatever brief period of time he stays out. Not dead. I confirm by checking his pulse. I force myself to my hands and knees, breath panting and fingers shaking as adrenaline shoots through me like a comet.

Geni is half-twisted off the furniture trying to get away from me, still in her restraints. She looks at me, aghast. Like I'm the monster he named me. I point a shaking finger at her. "Don't fucking test me, Geni. We're here because you got greedy and couldn't get divorced like a normal person. You want to go boff a Pierce, have at it. But don't steal your wife's property when your prenup makes it clear it isn't yours. Especially don't steal her pet. Which, by the way is eating through that cage, you imbecile."

Her lower lip quivers and big fat teardrops pool in her eyes. Her voice breaks when she speaks. "She was so mean to me."

Maybe she was. None of my business. I'm not here to be a good guy, I'm here to enforce the law and defend my client.

I shrug—wince when it pulls at something stiff—and restrain Pierce myself this time, running my thumb over the skin of his wrists to check for a subdermal blade. He doesn't have one. He somehow snapped the ties. My credits are on some sort of strength mods, but it could be something far less common. I didn't notice it with his first strike but the thing about getting hit in the face is that it *always* hurts. I feel a little better about my lack of resiliency in this fight. To be safe, I put ten ties on him this time, loop some expanding ties around his torso and upper arms to confine him even more, and drag him into one of the side bedrooms. Not the one with the lizard and his old blaster. The furniture is all attached to the wall, and I remove anything that he could use to fashion a weapon. This time, I don't give him a blanket to protect his decency because the "what if I accidentally humiliate a superinfluential man" portion of the evening has come and gone long ago.

Geni falls into a sulky silence. Perhaps because she's considering her bad life choices. More likely because I let my hand drop to the blaster when she opens her mouth. I could stun her, too. It would probably make things easier. Instead, I lock her in one of the other rooms and confiscate her coms and datapad.

The ultimate punishment.

I take the ridiculous winding stair around the perimeter of the room until I reach the door in the ceiling that allows access to the helm. The dark void stretches over the semitransparent dome that covers the helm. I dial in the coordinates to head back to Sarah's dock in Etienne territory and activate the autopilot in the *Hermit* to follow the same trajectory.

My next stop is the room with the lizard. It's nibbled through two bars and has its head nearly all the way through, jaws working in the air as it strains for freedom. I retrieve Pierce's blaster from the shelf behind the cage and put it back in my belt. Better to keep it on me, it seems.

"Are you going to bite me?" I ask the lizard, reaching for the cage door. It makes a little whirring sound. Doesn't sound bitey—which is a thought that a lot of people probably have right before they get bitten. I let the lizard out and it extends its crumpled wings and executes an awkward flight to my shoulder, where tiny golden claws dig into my space suit. Tiny enough that they shouldn't impact suit integrity.

I tentatively reach a gloved hand up and scratch the scales

beneath its chin. It makes that whirring sound again. Still no biting. It also doesn't seem inclined to go its own way, so I move around the ship carrying the lizard like a mobile accessory.

Eventually, I tug a section of the bench seat in front of the door to the room Pierce is locked in and sit down on the floor, back against the bench. I let my head drop back onto it. He knows who I am.

I am so screwed. Again. Some more.

A smiling holo of Sarah and Geni rotates slowly in the corner. They look happy. I wonder if they were, or if it was just for the picture. I have the same kind of holos of my family. We were happy in them. Big grins all around. The holos still have the grins even though the real ones have faded. It's like looking through a window to the past, and most of the time, the past hurts.

They don't smile at me anymore but at least most of their bills are paid. They have a roof over their heads thanks to the work I do that they'll never know about. They think I'm a private investigator, working a series of small-time cases to find missing baubles. They'd be horrified to know what I really do.

The lizard bites my ear. I sigh and scratch its chin again.

Without a doubt, nothing good comes from trusting. Someone always winds up bloody.

CHAPTER 2

The sodium-yellow tunnel lights slant at an angle through the small high windows to my office. If I stood on a box to look outside—or opened the door—I'd see polished taupe rock and a selection of storefronts, connected via metal walkways, bridges, and even one or two zip lines. I don't know what dummy thought that fast-track zip lines were a convenient way to get from one side of the Burren to the other, but all they managed to do was create a hazard of flying bodies in the midst of low-budget squalor.

The Burren does squalor well. It's a small space under the surface of a domed moon that orbits Zed-7. The underground scrubbers recycle the atmosphere, and the heaters bring the rock up to habitable, if not comfortable. It's dark, dirty, and desperate, but for all that, it has a certain charm. The sort of overemphasized personal brightness that comes from having dark surroundings. Since the only material around to work with is stone, sculptures ranging from smooth and abstract to rough-hacked and lewd bedeck the space between shops and homes. The ceiling of the Burren is painted like what someone imagined a planet's sky would look like.

For all I know, there is a planet with a sky like that—bright yellow-red and traced with purply clouds. I'd like to see it in real life.

I lean back in my chair, stretching my arms over my head and wait for the vibration on my interface tattoo to tell me that my dinner has been delivered. If I don't open the door immediately, someone's going to run off with it. The lizard chitters. Yes, I still have the lizard. Sarah insisted. She said she couldn't look at it without thinking of Geni's betrayal and that it liked me more than it had ever liked her. More likely, she didn't realize that it has the capacity to gnaw through the bars of any humane cage she purchases.

It feels like a consolation prize, a little perk to make up for the fact that Carmichael Pierce is about to destroy my life.

"Its name is Vuur," Sarah told me while shoving the creature into my hands. It squirmed. "Give it a good home. I have to go on a retreat. Clean my psyche. Drop off the radar."

She's terrified of Carmichael, too. Smarter than I thought she was.

So now I have a Vuur. I pet the lizard on its chin, and it takes a delicate bite out of the metal hoop in my ear.

A key piece of information that Sarah forgot to share: it doesn't just gnaw on metal, it *eats* metal. Like, to stay alive. I knew it had a penchant for chewing on bars but why someone would genetically alter a being to eat hull material and then stick said being inside a spaceship is mind-boggling. It's already put bite marks in half of my weapons. I had to barter with the foundry down the street for bags of scrap metal.

I would have said I wasn't a pet type of person. I'd have been wrong. The little brat is endearing.

My office is no-frills. A desk, a holo podium, two chairs with a plas-synth coating. The original coating peeled off and I've patched it with available scraps from the market. They look kind of jaunty in a mismatched sort of way. A collection of twisted-twine flowers in yellow and pink, made and painted by my cousin Aymbe when she was ten and I was fifteen, long before she was abducted and murdered and my family fractured. I haven't seen twine-art with a weave this intricate outside the trawlertown where I grew up. They're a sliver of home—unique and individual—and they are strewn over the top of the small chipped dresser that holds my clothing. I straighten one of the stems and a fleck of paint chips off. Aymbe always wanted to leave the trawlertown, to see the galaxy. At least some little part of her managed it.

A heavy punching bag that's also patched in so many places it's more patch than bag rounds out the decorations in the main room.

That's about all there is to see except for the small bathroom and the soundproofed windowless closet in the back with a fold-down bed for when I can't put off sleep any longer. I've gotten good at avoiding it but stims only last for so long. The closet door locks. A lot. More locks than you could imagine a door would have. It's probably more secure than the Burren credit union's vaults. The room is a retrofitted panic room and is the whole reason I bought this place. You could break into the main office equipped with nothing more than strong intentions, but it would take a team of experts to enter my bedroom. The coverlet on the bed is rosy pink, which would surprise anyone who knows the public face of Cyn Khaw. Generally, notorious vigilante murderers don't have fluffy pink beds. At least, not the kind of vigilantes in the holos.

Luckily, no one here knows my real name. I've got a bad reputation. It doesn't make for good neighbors. My neighbors know me as C, which doesn't stand out at all somewhere like the Burren where anonymity is the rule, not the exception.

The interface tattoo on my wrist vibrates, a small signal rippling up my forearm and down into my hand. Dinner has arrived. I set Vuur on my desk with a command to leave my datapad alone. It immediately ignores that command and starts to gum the corner of the device. They could have engineered it with brains in addition to looks. I guess lizards aren't known for their smarts.

With a sigh, I dredge into the pouch on my hip for a flake of brass—lizard-nip—and toss it. Vuur clumsily catches it in midair and plops down to the desk in a slump, licking its teeth. I swing open my door just in time to watch a black cat dodge away from the noodle box with an overly innocent look on its face and a tourist scream by on a zip line.

"These zip lines are better than the holos." The craggy voice comes from next door, and I glance over to see Madrigal Alvarez sitting in a folding chair on the stoop of the retirement home, a foil bag of scallion-and-sardine-flavored chips resting on her lap. Madrigal pops a chip in her mouth with pleasure and offers me the bag. A brindled cat sitting on the edge of her stoop watches the motion with intense focus.

"I don't know how you can digest those." I wince, crouching down and picking up my red glossy box of noodles. "The last time you talked me into them, my breath smelled like dead fish for a month. Where do you even find them?"

"Wouldn't you like to know?" she says, patting the bag with a satisfied smile. I really would. Madrigal is awfully well-connected for an elderly lady confined to the house next door. "How can you eat those noodles every night?"

I pull the door shut behind me and sit outside, perched on the low wall that lines the front of my office, leaning against a support post as I unfold the lid of the noodle box. They coil within like greasy threads coated in garlic and axiole spice. Delicious. The two-pronged fork that comes with them is perfectly sized to twirl the larger noodles or scoop the smaller. "They have everything a woman can want: protein, carbs, veggies, dirt-cheapness."

"You're gonna get an ulcer." Madrigal eats a few more chips.

I shrug and scoop up some noodles. The stale-dirt tang of the axiole—or potentially the actual stale dirt that filters down from above—adds a thickness and complexity to the flavor. The yellow light makes Madrigal's skin look like crumpled brown paper. In better lighting, she'd be a beauty but that would be hard to find in the Burren. Her hair is in a thick steely knot at the back of her neck and her dress is a vibrant red. The little black cat creeps closer. I dredge out a chunk of some form of meat—better not to ask questions—wipe off the sauce, and toss it to the feline. She catches it in the air and devours it quickly with loud smacking noises.

"Howsit?" I keep shoveling down the noodles.

Madrigal shrugs. "Same as always. You're starting to look like a person again."

"As opposed to—?"

"A lady doesn't say what you looked like before." She pauses like she's considering the statement. "A fucking shipwreck."

I snort out a laugh. I didn't look that bad. I bruised for a day or so, but I heal fast. My chin-length blond hair is tightly braided in three tracks down my scalp. My pale brown eyes are unshadowed because I slept two days ago.

My mother's skin tans dark, and her hair is black as the pit at the edge of the Burren, but the one banished Pierce ancestor long ago on my father's side dominates the genetic profile. They built their aesthetic to last. It's a shame. I've always wanted my mother's petite height and delicate bone structure. Her warm skin.

I could be so much sneakier if I were built like her. This hair makes me stand out like a docking beacon and it repels hair dye. Damn Pierce geneticists. Talk about hubris.

"Glad to hear you didn't become a lady while I was gone." I scoop out some more noodles. "Are you free to play Hanjong later tonight?"

"No time like the present." She pulls the board from alongside her seat, and a pang of sympathy ripples through me. Madrigal is essentially trapped in the home, surrounded by people in a state of decline or inconsistency. I'm the only one she can play Hanjong with because I'm the only one both willing and capable. She still has at least one person on the outside. Someone keeps her supplied with *things*, but that's not the same as company.

She has never admitted it, doesn't have to, but rumor has it that Madrigal Alvarez used to run the Stix, the gang that operates every illicit smuggling activity that touches the gravity well of Zed-7 and has their tentacles in every way station and port in Pierce space. This crime maven brought the board outside, on the off chance that I would be free. Eager for the opportunity to connect.

I must remind myself that, while my lack of friends is by choice—or my basic personality—hers is by circumstance. The noodles turn sour in my stomach, and I drop the box on my stoop for the cat. She warily sniffs my fingers but won't let me come any closer than that. I understand her feelings. Trust doesn't come easily for me, either. I toe the box closer to her. Once she's fed, I leap the gap between balconies to the retirement home and settle in the chair across from my friend.

I haven't told Madrigal about the mission that left me bruised. About how Carmichael recognized me. Because that would mean telling her about the real me. The girl who fled her loving family and beautiful planet over ten years ago, saying it was in search of vengeance for her murdered cousin. Really it was because I couldn't stand the eyes of my family, the expectation that I would save everyone by marrying a nice boy and having half a dozen chubby babies to crawl around my mother's kitchen.

I mean, it was also vengeance. I can multitask that much.

"What ever happened to that boy who was floating around your office? That one with the burly build and moony eyes?" Madrigal's not really asking. This is tactics. She wants to distract me from the game.

"Nothing happened," I mutter, moving a piece. And it's the truth.

"That's disappointing."

"Not really." I don't do romance. Moony-eyed or not, that boy was not ready for the full Cyn Khaw show. It's aggressive, obsessed, driven, and an absolute mess. I've pared my life down enough that it's basically sustenance. Everything I have goes to my family or my hunt. I may track people for a living, but there's only one who matters. One whom I've been after my whole adult life. The Abyssal Abductor.

"Disappointing," she repeats, knocking one of my pieces off the board. It skitters toward the pit at the edge of the porch but is batted back at us by the cat. I pick it up.

If I told anyone who I was, it would be Madrigal. Which would mean ruining our pleasant evening-board-game tradition with the truth. Any minute now Carmichael Pierce will be breaking down my office door, smashing to pieces this small life I've built in the Burren, cutting off the trickle of money I send home to my family.

Pierce will come after *me*, I rationalize, not my neighbors, which means I don't need to tell her for her own safety. It's just my own selfishness that makes me want to talk to someone, to get a sympathetic ear.

Also, I'm pretty sure she already knows who I am. It's a game we play. I pretend she's a kooky old lady instead of a dangerous crime boss, and she pretends I'm a down-on-her-luck PI instead of a notoriously deadly bounty hunter. I sometimes pretend that half, too.

But I could be wrong. Maybe she doesn't know and then why should I burden her with the truth? I look forward to our games. Tonight, I win two and Madrigal wins three. I'd like to pretend I threw the last one to her to make her feel good, but she cut me off at the ankles and then spent some time luxuriating in my defeat before putting me out of my misery. The woman's a barbarian. When I finally jump back to my own balcony, my shoulders are relaxed for the first time in days, and I feel the pleasant numbness of sleepiness. Perhaps I won't even need the soundproofing in my room tonight. Perhaps I'll sleep peacefully until morning.

There's a first time for everything.

I wave good night—it is what passes for night in the Burren, the sodium lights dimmed long ago—scoop up the messy remains of my dinner, and enter my office. Vuur is curled in a little ball on my desk. I scoop it up, tracing a finger along the rough line of scales that mark its spine, and stare at the winking notice of new messages on my datapad. There's always more work to be done. Always new leads.

It doesn't occur to me that they may be social messages. I speak to my family once a standard month. I call them. They never call me. They did, early on, but there were too many missed connections. Too many times when I got the scent of the Abyssal Abductor and pursued it at the expense of everything else.

The literal expense. I unplug the lamp because the switch doesn't work anymore and I can't afford to replace it. The lizard huffs out a hot breath on my fingertips. It looks peaceful. I ignore the messages and retreat to my bed. I sleep for a full two hours. Not bad.

In the morning, the lights flare before setting at a level that most would call murky. Half the day passes where I visit the local constabulary androids and check the bounty screens for new jobs. Nothing worth the effort it would take to fetch them. Two of the screens are broken, the familiar shape of a fist starbursting shards over the display. Someone wrote FUCK PIERCE on the third, but I can see through the paint enough to determine that the jobs posted wouldn't pay for a new lamp, much less rent.

. . . . .

When I get back to my office, someone is sitting in my chair, her back turned to me, impeccable black hair twisted into a chic style that screams money. If she still looks like money after traveling the Burren, it implies she has as much if not more power. A large bag rests at her side, lid open, weighed down with what appears to be nothing at all. When I open the door, she doesn't turn to look at me. Instead, her head angles subtly toward my job board, where I track my trickiest bounties. There has only been one bounty featured there for years.

Vuur perches on the back of my desk chair watching her with wary avarice, little lizard eyes adhered to her jewelry. The mere fact that it is alive tells me that it hasn't made an attempt at a nibble yet. Whoever the woman is, I'm betting she takes no prisoners.

She doesn't have the coloring of a Pierce and that's all that has kept me from stunning her in the back, rescuing the lizard, and fleeing for my life. I sidle around the room until I can see her better.

"That's an impressive background you've put together, Cyn Khaw. Rather primitively assembled, though." The subtle high-class accent added to the posture that says that she could buy and sell not only me but the entire Burren several times over tells me everything I need to know about who this is. I complete my sidle and stand on the opposite side of my desk, getting the full effect of all that Family intensity. Estella Escajeda, in my office.

I've seen her on the holos because she's fucking famous. Hard to believe someone my age would be this powerful.

This can only end poorly. At least I haven't embarrassed this one while naked yet.

"You've come a long way to insult my methods. If you'd have made an appointment, perhaps I would have thrown a sheet over it to protect your delicate sensibilities." I don't know why the heir to the Escajeda Family is in my office. I don't want to know. Working for Families is bad business. I made an exception for Etienne and look where that got me.

Belatedly, I realize she called me Cyn instead of C. Of course she did. She's so powerful that aliases are probably meaningless if she really cares to investigate. Now *two* heirs know who I am. A month ago, the number was zero. I preferred that number.

I experience a moment of panic where I wonder if she's here because of what happened with Carmichael. Pierce and Escajeda are rivals. They'd never work together, but I wouldn't put anything past them. I'm a tool to people like Estella.

Estella coolly assesses me from eyes so deep a brown they're almost black. The artful sweep of her lashes is accentuated with very little cosmetic assistance. Her face has the smooth flawlessness of a sex robot and half the personality. In their quest for perfection, Families have left character in the dust. At least in my opinion.

A little weathering tells the kind of life you've led. My family's skin screams of the sun of Ginsidik, their hands pattered with the telltale scars of a life at sea. Wrinkles indicate if they smile, squint, or frown. Estella's face offers no such map. Expressions slip off it like water. The subtle glimmer of some sort of implant flashes inside the shadow of her ear. Coms are usually either more understated or more obvious than that. I can't figure out what it is, which means it's probably something deeply interesting.

I poke my finger in the apparently empty bag as I pass it. My skin brushes complicated folds of fabric. Well, shit. That explains how she got here without a trail of holo paparazzi. It doesn't explain *why* she'd use something as expensive and precious as nullifying fabric to move through a location like the Burren. Nullifying fabric fools the eyes, but more importantly, it also fools cameras— even heat-sensing systems. It isn't invisible, but it blocks signals, so it shows up as a blank point. If any constabulary androids are monitoring feeds, they'll know someone snuck around but they'll have no clue who.

The engineer from the ship I encountered on Herschel Two had something similar—the cheaper version that would fool the eye but probably not a lens. I'm not an expert, but it wasn't the kind of ship that would have much of anything expensive on it.

I could almost wish I had the toys of a Family. Almost. But they come with a price. If I was in a Family, there would probably be a reality holo about my escapades—casting them as noble or diabolical depending on who was airing it. People would know who I am.

Awful.

"If I had made an appointment, there would be a record of my presence." As Estella speaks, I notice a faint whisper of a line by the corner of her eyes. The beginning of a furrow in her brow. Not enough to mar the impression of exquisite regularity in her visage, but enough that it's clear an actual emotion is trying—and failing—to break through. That, more than anything else, tells me this is a crisis of epic proportions. You don't get an emotion out of a Family scion unless it's a world-ending moment. "Also, your reputation leads me to believe that you would have refused to meet with me."

I snort. The sound floats through the room with all the elegance of a cat fart. At least she admits it. It's enough to get me seated facing her. Vuur creeps from the back of the chair to my shoulder, nuzzling its nose under my ear in what could be a gesture of affection but could also be sniffing my earring. "With your Family's resources, I would anticipate that you could hire anyone in charted territory. What brings you to my door?"

Her mouth presses into a thin line. "My *Family's* resources will not be involved in this particular retrieval. They can't be."

That quickly, I want to know everything about it. Stupid curiosity. I just can't be presented with a question and leave it unanswered. My mother always said a curious serpent winds up as dinner. She has a lot of sayings about serpents. "I assume *someone's* resources will be involved."

"I have investments of my own. But that won't matter. This job, you'd do for free." Her face is so motionless it could be steel. Like she's bottled up tight as a vault.

A hollow pit opens within my stomach. There's only one job I'd do without pay. The hunt I've failed over and over for almost half my life. The person who took my cousin and never brought her home.

"The Abyssal Abductor has taken another ransom. Her clock started two days ago."

She's right. I'd do this one for free.

The Abyssal Abductor is a serial kidnapper who has plagued this system for nearly twenty years. In his early years, he aimed small—targeting young children of ordinary families, demanding thousands of credits. In recent years, he's moved on to stealing more wealthy children for millions of credits, and he's doing it more frequently. He can't actually *need* credits anymore, which means, I guess, that he's just doing it for the joy of crime. He's escalating, though. Which means that he's more dangerous than ever.

The Abductor is still fair, in a way. If you pay his ransom, he returns the child unharmed. Usually they've been locked in a VR pod the entire time, barely aware they were kidnapped because of their virtual adventure. Merciful. Or maybe just convenient.

The problem comes when families can't or won't pay the ransom.

That's happened four times. We were the first and I know firsthand what results from failure. He made a mistake when he took Aymbe. We weren't wealthy by our planet's standards. My father and mother were both machinists and musicians. My grandfather a blacksmith. Hard workers who lived comfortably, but hardly rich. I couldn't figure out why he'd take Aymbe over the mayor's son, or one of the algae processing supervisors'.

We didn't have many credits to our name. Half the work on the trawler is done on barter. People don't keep credits handy. We borrowed heavily to make the ransom and my father and uncle went to make the drop. Unfortunately, none of us, Abductor included, accounted for the weather. The storm that hit their ship killed my uncle and every single credit we'd saved was lost to the sea—the Abductor insists on a hard credit drop. Banks make things too easy to trace.

A kidnapped child is useless if there's no ransom to be had. I lost my uncle and my cousin in one fell swoop. Then I lost the rest of my family because that sort of thing either binds you together or breaks you apart.

We didn't go the good way.

"Why is the Escajeda heir approaching me about this in secret?" I might take this case for free, for vengeance, for justice, for heroism or guilt—but I'm not an idiot. Something is off. If it's public knowledge that the Abductor is on the prowl again, it would be in the feeds, all over the ether. It isn't.

Also, why me? I've made a stir at several ransom recoveries—

I've been closer than anyone else at catching the Abductor, but I always made sure I was gone before any reporters showed up. "How do you even know where to find me?"

I've done my best to keep that private. Having a secret identity only works if it's an actual *secret*.

"No information is a secret if a Family wants it. Your identity wasn't protected because you were cautious. It was protected because no one important cared." Her voice is clipped. Impatient.

"That's rude for someone who just suggested that I work for free. I'm suddenly feeling very expensive." Vuur's claws dig through my jacket, maybe sensing my offense. Maybe telling me to shut my mouth. Probably that one. I reach for professionalism. It's a stretch. "What can I do for you that's so important you'd sneak on-planet?"

Estella's posture is magnificent. Perfectly straight, yet somehow comfortable rather than stiff or awkward. I've seen her father in news holos and he looks like a king. She looks like an executive. Cold, ruthless, and confident. If I tried to stab her, I halfway believe that blade would snap. "You're known for two things. One, you spaced a ship of traffickers. I don't care about that except that it means you're capable of being ruthless, when necessary, which is valuable. The other is that you're hunting for the Abductor because he took and murdered your cousin. You've come the closest to finding him. With a reputation like yours—" She lets it drift off like my reputation is too unsavory to mention specifically, which, honestly, is a kindness I don't expect. "You've nearly caught him twice."

I wince. Now it just feels like she's rubbing in my failure.

She continues, taking on a lecturing tone. "Once, on a frozen polar cap right after a girl was returned to her Family in Wilk territory. He dropped her at a way station, and you managed to identify his ship and track it to an ice moon nearby. The second time after you tracked him all the way to his flophouse. That adventure resulted in a shoot-out that left five constables dead and the Abductor in the wind."

"That second time, he *baited* me into following him with a coded coms message and the threat to take another. He likes to play with me. You didn't answer my question. I didn't only ask why me. I asked why in *secret*."

Something about this—no, nearly everything about this—reads off.

She pinches her mouth together and presses the side of a smooth metal band around her index finger before speaking. "I, Estella Escajeda am entering into contract with Cynbelline Khaw for the duration of her hunt for the Abyssal Abductor. Anything pertaining to myself or my Family that she may discover over the course of this investigation shall remain indefinitely private under penalty of banishment."

Of course, she has a recorder in her jewelry. Vuur makes a leap from my shoulder to the glittering ring, jaws gaping and long black tongue extended, and I manage to catch it just a hair away. Its scaly little body wriggles in my hands as I yank it back to my shoulder with an apologetic wince. "No. Bad." I turn my attention back to Estella. "You can't banish me. I don't live in your territory."

"Perhaps I was unclear. *Total* banishment." Her voice is frigid, and her hands are poised on her knees, knuckles so tight they're nearly white.

This secret must be legendary. The kind that could ruin a Family. The kind that makes her desperate enough to come to me because, no matter the contract, if I want to hurt her with anything I learn, I can figure out how.

I lean back in my chair, elbows on the armrests and fingertips pressed together because if I don't constrain them, they'll probably be noticeably trembling with excitement. I can almost detect the Abductor's scent in the air. "I accept your stipulations. This secret better be worth it."

She presses her ring again. Back to off-the-record. "He has my daughter."

I almost don't understand the words. She's so rigid for some-one whose daughter is in mortal danger. I don't know why I'm surprised. Families are monsters. Probably she's as worried as if she misplaced a nice necklace. "You've kept a daughter hidden for years?"

"Twelve years, to be precise." Estella says it carefully, as though speaking about her child is a foreign language with which she has only passing familiarity. "I had an affair with a fellow student while I was completing my education on Idyllwood. Someone im-practical as a future partner. For the duration of my pregnancy, I arranged, with my nearest brother's help, to study remotely while researching novel mining techniques on a border planet. While there, in the company of a tiny security contingency, I had Boreal. She was given to a trusted friend to raise."

I blink, wondering if she's saying what I think she's saying.

"Have you visited her?" When I left home, I'd promised to never talk to my family again, with all the passionate drama of a new adult. I lasted about a month. It would take unimaginable strength to never speak to your daughter again.

"How is this relevant?"

Honestly, it isn't. I'm just shocked that everything I've suspected about Family parenting is true, but I pull myself together and give her a reason. A good one. "It could be helpful to know how the Abductor knew she existed."

"I see her several times a year when I visit my old friend. Boreal and her adoptive mother know that I am her birth mother, but no one else does." Her hands still haven't moved.

I grimace. "Someone does. Unless her abduction was a very unlikely coincidence."

Finally, some movement. Estella reaches into a sharp-edged portfolio beside the chair and retrieves a plas-sheet. She hands it to me.

Familiar language slaps me in the face and I forget about

Estella and her coldness. The Abyssal Abductor sends very specific ransom requests. He likes taunting his targets with their powerlessness. His message is scrawled on the sheet with heavy black font. It's addressed directly to Estella Escajeda.

"You say you trust your brother, but he's the most obvious culprit for selling this information. You're the heir and she is yours, I assume. If he eliminates her, he's closer to the top." I hand the sheet back to her. I've seen enough of it.

"It isn't my brother. Arcadio could have hurt her countless times over the years. He's seen her more than anyone else."

Arcadio. Shit. Right. I *know* her brother. In a way. He doesn't know me. Not as Cyn Khaw, at least. He knows me as Generosity the cultist, poor misguided soul who ran back to her cult at the first opportunity and probably exploded along with the rest of them. I knew he was an Escajeda, of course, but I didn't spend much time with the man. Although he looked a hell of a lot more alive than his older sister. He was made of flesh and bone instead of frigid ambition.

"My only advice to you is: pay the ransom. He returns his targets unharmed if you pay by the deadline and don't bring in the authorities."

"Your cousin was not returned."

"We didn't pay." I don't add that we never even found her body because he dumped her too deep in the ocean. "If you pay, you're fine. If you don't, he sinks his abducted target in an ocean and leaves them to die. Four adolescents have died that way. Four too many." We found Aymbe's clothes, washed ashore stained in blood, ripped from her body by time and predation. "Please. Pay the ransom."

She folds her hands tighter in her lap. "I have given you my decision. If you track him down, a ransom won't be necessary."

Fuck, are Families cold. But *someone's* got to take care of this poor kid. Clearly, to her mother and uncle, the Family's reputation is more important than Boreal.

"So I'm a contingency plan, to track him down before the dead-line?" Great, extra pressure. Not that it matters. I was always going to throw everything I have into tracking the Abductor. I always do. "Has the Abductor left any additional information?" I tap my fingers on the desk. Her sharp dark eyes watch every motion like I'm about to go for a weapon. Mostly I'm just keeping my fingers nimble in case Vuur takes a header toward her gleaming silver necklace. "I've tracked him before, or traced his steps after the fact, but it's usually a new planet—although of some significance to the abductee. Without any new information, I'm stuck searching blind, and you know as well as I do, your Family is associated with more planets than nearly any other."

She nods, face still businesslike. "I can give you the planet he was on one day ago. It meets his . . ." She swallows. A quick jerky motion of her throat. "His parameters. With one exception."

His usual parameters are locations with deep oceanic abysses. I raise my eyebrows. "How did you manage that?"

"Boreal is Escajeda enough to have the most advanced tracers implanted. Tech that he very likely has not encountered before. The problem is that he has settled on Ginsidik. I know. He never returns to the same territory. This time, he did. You have familiar-ity with the planet, I understand?" If by "familiarity" she means that I lived there from birth into early adulthood, then yes, I'm familiar. It's gorgeous. I fucking hate the place. "As you know, the ionosphere scrambles signals and, for certain tech, can cause it to glitch. Her tracer glitched after she hit the planet's surface. He has no reason to know that I could trace him to Ginsidik, so he has no reason to leave. I'm sending you along with the only other person I trust."

"Your brother. Who, conveniently, has dropped off the radar even more the past year."

"Exactly. He has taken up with a scouting crew of a ship called the *Calamity*." She says the word "scout" like it's filthy. I wince internally. I wonder if they got a new ship. Their old one had a different name. I don't remember what. Something dumb. The only good part about my time with the crew was the sparks that danced under my skin every time their medic looked my way. Micah Arora is the sort of person who sees far too much but keeps his own council. I never knew if my attraction to him was reciprocated.

Probably not. I wasn't at my best out there.

I haven't been at my best for quite some time, honestly. Micah was exactly the kind of patient and insightful that made me want to tell him more than I should. The type that made me believe he might even understand. I didn't, though. Any more than I did with Madrigal.

Estella continues, "They have been afforded access to Ginsidik via negotiation with the Pierce Family and will be picking you up at the port this evening."

I wonder what they had to give up for the docking rights. Pierce isn't known for being generous. Not my problem, though. My problem is that not only do I have to return home again, but I also have to see the crew of the *Calamity*. I had subtle augmentations for the retrieval mission where I met them. I might not be bulky, but I look like what I am, a hunter. I'm long, lean, and prone to sharp edges. To embed with the cult, I needed to look like prey. I wore my hair longer, had temporary iris tattoos to lighten my eyes and injections to change my facial shape to round. I was also five kilos lighter than normal when I went there and eight kilos lighter than normal when I left because all there was to eat on the fucking planet was mind-altering plants and grainy meat. I look delicate rather than harsh when I'm thin. I'm used to carrying some muscle. Now, with more flesh on my bones, combined with the faded injections, I might be able to enter the ship as a stranger and skip all the dramatics.

People go by the big cues. Coloring and facial structure. Change that and even a scanner won't recognize you.

I outline my standard fee for time, overhead, and danger, and she accepts the contract as if this is a routine furniture procurement, before efficiently forwarding the information that she's collected and the docking time for my meeting with the *Calamity*. When she stands to leave, her face is set in stone. With a swirl of her wrist, the nullifying fabric wraps around her, and Estella Escajeda winks out of view.

Vuur whirrs a little sound of disappointment at the vanished jewelry. I whirr a little sound of relief that she's gone. I consider sleep, decide I did it too recently to be able to drag myself back to the state, and instead spend the rest of the day researching the *Calamity*'s crew. I don't learn much because I *also* researched the crew after Herschel Two.

I paid extra attention to one very specific member of the crew. The medic, Micah Arora. I didn't find anything useful then, and I still don't. Banished from Pierce territory when he was young for some unknown slight against his family. Then he disappeared. Then he was a medic with the *Calamity*.

The engineer, Caro Osondu, appeared out of nowhere a few years ago, which means that isn't her real name. The biologist, Itzel with no second name, appeared out of nowhere about fifteen years ago. The only people with records are Temper and Arcadio, and those are so public that everyone in charted territory knows their history.

It's deeply unsatisfying research.

CHAPTER 3

■ ■ ■ ■ ■ ■ ■ ■ ■ ■ ■ ■ ■ ■ ■ ■

Madrigal is on the front porch again when I leave, hover crate at my side full of weapons and shoulder weighted down with a satchel.

"Back on the road?" she asks as she pops a chip into her mouth. This time, the flavor is anchorfruit and artichoke. The dust sprinkled on the chips is a shocking slime-green. One of the stray cats is curled on her lap, green powder bedecking its white muzzle. It languidly licks its whiskers and gives me a long slow blink that warns me not to encourage her to move.

"Bruises are healed. Means it's time to get new ones." I shrug the satchel higher on my shoulder. The lizard sitting on it chitters at the cat, who hisses back. "You sure you don't want to take care of Vuur?"

Vuur is not made for space travel. It eats ship parts. Also, apprehending bad men is dangerous and it's just a little guy.

"No pets allowed in the home. Someone might be allergic. Even though I have my own room—at great personal cost, I might add. Do you know how many roommates they've saddled me with that I had to make miserable until they moved out? Too many. Anyway, why do you think I spend so much time on the porch with the cats?" Madrigal licks green from her fingertips as she studies my crate. Probably cataloguing its value. Old habits die hard. I reach up and pet the lizard. Guess it's stuck with me a little while longer. "You have an interesting case?"

"It's interesting. Hopefully the end of a long one. One I've never quite been able to let go. The family kind, lowercased and upper, which just means it's fucking complicated and likely to end badly. I'll be seeing my kin for the first time in a decade. They want nothing to do with me. Then, of course, I can't even tackle this *alone*—I have to be a part of a crew. You know I prefer to work alone."

I'm not usually so forthcoming. Probably I'm trying to postpone my meeting with said crew. She pauses, studying me with those eyes that sometimes go predator-sharp. "I'm going to offer you some advice that you'll probably ignore." She leans forward, poking one strong finger in a gesture that encompasses my whole state of life. It's covered in green dust, which also, probably in some obscure metaphoric way, encompasses my whole state of life. "People who stand alone die alone. Look after yourself—first and always—but that doesn't mean no one else can look after you either."

I nod. More to be polite than anything else. It's surprising advice from Madrigal, but then again, a gang member without compatriots is just one weird lady with a penchant for crimes. She had a team once, even if its size has dwindled. "I'll keep that in mind."

She sees through my placatory words and shakes her head, a rueful smile curling her mouth. "I didn't think for a second that you'd listen to me. I certainly wouldn't have at your age. Maybe still wouldn't now. Knowing isn't always the same as doing." She points at me with a green-stained finger. "You know my holo-access code. Don't be afraid to use it."

I don't know the first Madrigal, the one whose name can still make people shake on the streets, and she doesn't know the Cyn who once was caught by a ship of human traffickers and was the only one to emerge alive. We're comfortable with our secrets. I smile to show her that I appreciate the sign of trust, pleased that someone cares enough to give me advice even if I plan to flagrantly ignore it.

I bid her farewell and head out toward the docks, more spring in my step than there has any right to be.

"Send me pictures!" Madrigal calls from behind me. "I want to see if that trawlertown's really as primitive as you say it is."

Depends on one's definition of "primitive." Mindsets don't translate to pixels. Some might say the trawler is delightfully simple. Quaint. Like a lot of sweet things, it's a trap. Sticky enough that it's nearly impossible to leave. It took a tragedy to get me out. And now I'm on my way back.

I wave a hand in acquiescence and continue threading my way through the crowd. Bars are always busy in the Burren—because employment is low, and everyone lives in a dirty hole underground. There are establishments on every level of the Burren, because it's dangerous to climb a ladder, much less take a zip line, once you're intoxicated.

As I climb toward the surface, I pass a sculpture of a large tree, so big that it's carved into the rock of several levels and another of some sort of collection of interlocked shapes. People wait outside the take-out liquor stores or try to get seats at the more exclusive establishments. A woman staggers out in front of me—must have had a head start on cocktail hour—and almost topples over the thin guy-wire that separates the platform from the pit. I nab her by the collar of her shirt and yank her back. As I do a man runs into me, almost tugging my bag from over my shoulders. Vuur chitters angrily at him, and I pat the pockets to ensure that nothing was stolen. We've had an influx of crime lately. Hardly surprising with the prevalence of boredom and bars. The next thing that comes after that is always anger and resentment. It's largely directed at Pierce, as though they owe us a sky. Since I look Pierce, I've been subject to a few attempted robberies.

You'd think they'd put together that I'm just as hard off as the rest of them, but I guess that's where the liquor connects dots that aren't in the same constellation.

I don't drink. This is why. The idea that I'd be so dissociated from reality that I'd plunge to my death, that my personality would change, that I'd be vulnerable is repugnant to me. I understand that many enjoy it, but it doesn't scratch any of my particular itches.

My personal vices lean toward stimulants instead of downers. Not because I like the feeling. Because I hate to sleep.

The docks are nearly empty once I make my way to the top of the Burren. A large sliding metal door and a sometimes-faulty plasma shield separates the cave from the surface and the port in the dome. A container shuttle sits against the far wall, loaded with the old goods that aren't wanted in other markets, so they've made their way here. They'll unload it in night shift, when the streets are as empty as they get. The only other ship present is off to the left, a familiar heap of antiquated machinery shaped like a fat dart with chunky fletchings. It's an old-fashioned design for ships, from back in the day when it was harder to escape the drag of an atmosphere. I suppose that, for a scouting vessel, they contend with more extreme gravity than the average ship. CALAMITY is scrawled on the side and the exterior cannons have been refurbished since I last saw them.

Same old ship with a new name. An appropriate new name. This crew means well but they almost wrecked my last mission.

I breathe out a smooth controlled breath and slightly modify my posture. I hunch my shoulders and take shorter steps than usual. Vuur's claws dig in, adjusting to my new pace. It makes a little peeping sound, as though it's concerned that I'm ill. As I approach the ship, the entrance hatch swivels open and a short compact woman appears in the opening.

The captain, Temperance, goes by Temper. Temper was formerly a Reed, banished by her own brother, who, as it turns out, was responsible for at least half of the mess on Herschel Two. Her hair is red and pulled back into a braid. She's wearing slightly oversized coveralls, and the banishment tattoo on her face glimmers brightly. I had a temporary mark for the mission on Herschel Two, designed to fade after a few months. Hers won't ever. It's scarified down to the bone.

She's the sort of woman whom you might pass by on first glance. She has none of the carefully composed, stunning beauty of most Family women. It's motion that brings Temperance Reed to life. The efficient capability of her movement, her quick tongue, and the glitter in her eyes when she verbally spars with Arcadio Escajeda.

She's joined by the engineer, Caro Osondu. Everyone acknowledges she's an ace engineer but no one knows why she's wasting her talents working for an impoverished scouting crew. I assume that it's because she's hiding from someone powerful, but even then, she could probably do better.

I assess the ship. *Formerly* impoverished.

When they see the crate floating alongside me, they open the cargo hold, a long, deep hatch in the bottom aft of the ship, and exit to meet me.

"You must be Cyn Khaw." Temper's voice is almost musical. It's a good voice. Intellectually I know it speaks of money. She probably had elocution classes as a child. Somehow, despite that example of insane privilege, I still like her. "I'm the captain, Temper. This is our engineer, Caro. The rest of the crew is inside, readying the ship for launch as soon as you're on board and stowed."

I nod to both of them. "I travel light when it comes to personal effects. The hover crate is weaponry."

"That's a lot of weapons." Caro's eyebrows go down rather judgmentally for someone standing directly in front of a top-of-the-line cannon. The engineer has dark-brown skin, short tightly curled black hair, and articulate fingers bedecked in a multitude of rings. She's a little taller than Temper and the kind of curvy that makes most men stop in their tracks. Her ears are lined with glimmering hoop earrings.

"Better safe than sorry when dealing with the Abductor. He has a lot of resources. Rich parents pay good credits to get their children back." I pat the top of the trunk, kind of like I'm reassuring myself that it's still there.

The engineer's eyes narrow like she's looking for some reason to be upset and can't find one. "That trunk better stay locked while you're on board."

"Of course. I have no need for weapons while I'm traveling with allies, do I?" I can't resist adding the last two words.

Temper rubs her temples like we're being trying—because we're being trying—and moves forward like she needs to make the peace.

Vuur takes the lull in conversation to launch from my shoulder, eyes locked on the smorgasbord of metal in Caro's ears. Just what I need. I catch it by its hind legs, scales slipping through my fingers as I adjust my grip to its fragility, and yoink it back. "Not strangers." I set it back on my shoulder.

"We weren't informed you had a . . . pet." Temper eyes the lizard skeptically. I look at it that way on the regular, so it's an easy expression to suss.

"I understand having a creature on the ship is not ideal. I will keep it confined to my bunk." I rub its chin and send it telepathic messages to look as cute as possible. It ignores them because it isn't telepathic and belches a spark. Now I want to rub my own temples. I can't wait to get in my bunk and lock the door. This has already been more than my preferred amount of human interaction.

"I have a creature of my own on the ship. I like to keep him confined to my bunk, too." Temper snickers before taking in my blank expression. "Bad joke. The security officer is my partner. Let's get your gear stowed and we can get out of this shithole." Temper's smile glows with just enough of a sharp edge that I'm reminded this particular rich girl has survived on her own in the toughest parts of space and probably shouldn't be underestimated.

A man strides through the hold and I suppress the urge to hide behind my crate of weapons. Micah Arora. He's just as compelling as he was the last time I saw him and probably just as dangerously perceptive. He's attractive enough—all the parts are in the right places and appropriately sized—but it isn't any individual feature, it's the sum of them that somehow magnifies the effect of his attention. Micah Arora is intensity personified. He's electric with it.

That energy shows in the flexing of the strong muscles in his arms, the sharp focus of his dark eyes, the tense line of his jaw as though he's always chewing on his own irritation. He's the sort of man who was designed for action—incapable of stillness and impatient with stillness in others.

The last time I saw him, he was tasked with playing my babysitter. The cranky medic clearly wanted to be in the field with the others, but instead, he ministered to my injured wrists with focused precision. Because we spent a lot of time together in the ship, he taught me to make a Chandra-region fry bread. I wouldn't call him a good teacher. No one as impatient as Micah teaches well. But somehow his effort to put a nervous cultist at ease charmed me more than polite practiced smoothness would have.

I still make the fry bread sometimes.

Not because it's delicious. Because he taught me.

Which is far more sentimental than I usually get, but the fact that someone took the time to do something so . . . *wholesome* . . . is entirely out of place in my world. And that makes it unique.

I needn't worry because Micah doesn't even notice me, striding down the ramp toward a nervous-looking delivery man holding a large box with a "this way up" arrow pointed down at his feet.

"Those are medical supplies, you fucking imbecile," the medic growls, wrenching the box from the delivery man and righting it. "You could kill someone if you handle chemicals like that."

"I didn't know—"

"There's a green star stamped right on the box, big as your face. What the fuck else would they be?"

This doesn't feel like a good time to renew our acquaintance. Temper and Caro share a glance and a chuckle. I sidle to the other side of my trunk and check that the sequenced lock is deployed as I deactivate the hover function and the magnetic slab in the cargo bay secures my weapons trunk to the floor.

Then Temper, Caro, and I leave the delivery guy to his fate. I could almost feel sorry for him if he wasn't so cavalier with package handling.

Temper disappears to the helm, likely to pilot, and Caro gives me a tour of a ship that I already recognize. She's not what I'd call friendly. More like she's trying to pretend to be friendly, but she actually hates me. The kind of pleasant smile that hides a razor.

It's a good ship. Nicer on the inside than the outside. Far nicer than I remember from before. Someone's doodled little sketches on the bulkheads. Small maintenance drones hum around the walls and the floor like engineered bugs. They're new. Maybe purchased with the credits from the planet-exploding mission. Caro's proud of them, so they may be her own creation. Her tour centers heavily on the engine room and the helm—points of interest if you're an engineer.

They actually have a phydium engine, which even I recognize. It looks like something out of the future, crouched in the center of their engine room, a thing of gleaming metal and flashing lights. It's amazing it doesn't blow the chassis apart. I have to pick my jaw up from the floor when I see it. I never thought I'd actually fly in one. Caro glows like I just admired her child. Far as I know, only the Escajeda Family have access to the fuel, which means that this crew is working closer to the Family than I thought.

I'll have to be on my guard. If the stony-eyed woman in my office was any indication, the Escajeda Family's agenda is not as simple as getting Boreal back alive, because there's an easy way to do that that doesn't involve me. I can trust that they want her back—it's probably a matter of pride, if nothing else—but I can't trust much of anything else.

While we're on the tour, Itzel, the biologist, wanders out of the small pantry attached to the mess, holding a sprig of something green.

"The hydroponic garden is doing much better after we scrubbed the filters. The lettuce tastes like lettuce again." She studies the lettuce and then notices me. "Oh. I'm Itzel." She glances around and then offers me the bunch of lettuce in her hand. "Lettuce? It doesn't taste like algae at all."

You might think that I'd like algae, growing up on a trawler like I did. You'd be wrong. Algae got everywhere. Breathing was tasting algae. The stuff farmed on Ginsidik was used for biofuel—it reproduces quickly and cheaply, which makes it the kind of renewable resource that people like for sustaining equipment that needs to operate for a long time at a moderate price. Which means most equipment, lighting, commuter ships, shuttles, heating systems. Farm domes. Algae is ever so useful and not commonly harvested—because it takes massive space for populations to survive and breed. It also requires a large source of nutrients. In the case of Ginsidik, that means sea-serpent droppings. Anyway, sometimes other strains made it in the nets and plenty of algae-based food could be found in the trawlertown. "I'm Cyn. And no, thank you."

"You have a Hynegian flying lizard." Itzel says it flatly, abstraction gone. Her eyes stab little Vuur and its claws curl into the leather on my shoulder. She's a tiny woman with slender tattooed hands, lean muscles, and a smoothly shaved head. She moves like a knife. "They're monstrosities of genetic manipulation."

Wow. Rude.

"It's a rescue." She gives me a look like she knows I'm the kind of vain asshole to buy a show pet. "I can't afford to live somewhere better than the Burren. You think I'm dropping Hynegian credits on something that eats all my metal accessories?"

"That thing eats metal?" Caro studies Vuur. "Fascinating. Keep it the fuck away from the engine room."

"Like I said, it'll stay in my bunk."

The ship shudders and I drop a hand to clutch the counter that lines the wall on the edge of the room. "Is it supposed to do that?"

The engineer looks at me like I've offended her. The biologist wanders off. "We're taking off. Ships shake sometimes. Temper wants to meet about strategy once we're underway. I hope you have a plan." She says it almost like a threat.

"I have twenty. It all depends on what we see when we get there." She sniffs. "You'll be sharing a bunk."

I'll be what? As the outside contractor, I thought I'd be guaranteed a bunk of my own. I was last time and that was when they thought I was a crazy cultist. I uncurl the fists that my fingers are attempting to form. I can't sleep if I'm sharing a bunk. I can barely sleep if I'm not. "I'd prefer not to. I'm not picky about space and I don't sleep much. I'd bother a roommate. I can crash anywhere."

"We like to keep people in the bunks. That way you don't have to burst into someone else's space if you have to use the toilet. And if we have to make a tight maneuver or take fire, you're somewhere insulated." She shuts down my protests. "Besides being our medic, Micah's the best person to bunk with. You haven't met him yet, but you saw him on the dock."

"Oh, the one who was tearing a new asshole in the delivery guy? He seems like a dream bunkie." No way. No. No way that I'm sharing a bunk with that force of nature. If I were a normal person, I'd be all over the setup (and the medic) but I'm not. I'm a person who scream-sleeps and is hyperaware of any vulnerability. I need a door that locks and for everyone else to be on the other side of it.

And he'll notice I'm not sleeping. It's his nature to notice things like that.

Caro snorts. "Okay, he's kind of an asshole, but he's a sound sleeper. No snoring or sleep-talking or anything. Better than bunk-ing with Itzel or me. But before we get there, this is the infirmary."

I'm opening my mouth to argue the whole bunking situation when she activates a door, and it slides open.

There he is.

He's still unpacking the box—correctly oriented—reaching one well-muscled arm for a high shelf as we enter. I can see those muscles because, as with every time I've met him, the sleeves have been removed from his coveralls. Smooth brown skin, thick black hair with some wave to it, eyes you could get lost in. Not that I've tried. Mostly I try to avoid those eyes because they look like a trap.

Attention is only nice if you actually want to be seen. There are few things I want less. I've been playing the part of someone else in each part of my life for a long time. The disappointing and slightly inept PI for my family, the hardscrabble neighbor for Madrigal, the violent hunter for bounties. I'm only myself when I'm asleep and myself is a hot fucking mess. He will not be seeing *that* if I can help it.

Micah lazily studies me through slitted lids. A yellow banish-ment tattoo, like a tear falling beneath his left eye, glows on his face. "This the bounty hunter?"

I'd convinced myself that his voice didn't sound that good. Low and irritable but oddly pleasing, like dragging your hand the wrong way through a cat's fur. At least when he's not yelling at delivery people. He never yelled at me.

I answer for Caro. "This is the bounty hunter."

"I hear we're bunking together. Hope you like it on top." The casual comment sends a flush of heat through my stomach. He's talking about the top bunk, of course.

Probably.

"I like it any way I can get it," I answer, which, regarding sleep, is a lie. I intend to use that bunk as little as possible now that I know I have to share. I have enough stims to get me through the whole trip with relatively few physical side effects. I'll crash on the trawler where there's more privacy, but maybe I can work out a better place by then. I don't like the idea of the medic's insightful gaze on me when I'm sleeping. I definitely don't want him around when I'm dreaming.

"This is going to be interesting." Caro sounds amused, albeit still hostile. "Micah, this is Cyn. Cyn, Micah. I'll leave you two to get acquainted. I want to be in the engine room when we go full burn." Caro snaps me out of my thoughts as she spins and walks down the hall, leaving me alone with the medic.

"Is there anything I can do to help?" I call down the smooth metal hallway after her. I don't like to be deadweight.

"Think of a good plan so we don't get dead when we go after this kidnapper," she responds without looking back.

"Shooting him in the face is an excellent plan," I mutter under my breath, and startle when Micah chuckles.

I'll attract more attention standing awkwardly in the hall, so I enter the infirmary and drop my bag as though the medic doesn't make me feel awkward at all. And by "awkward," I mean horny. I'm adult enough to admit it. Just not out loud. The door automatically slides closed behind me, shutting us in the small space together.

When I approach the table, Micah's dark eyes narrow and his nostrils flare slightly. Before I know what's hit me, I'm pressed flat against the door by the firm body of a suddenly enraged medic who has a hand around my neck, just tight enough to cut off my air if I try to yell. His eyes blaze into my own with piercing intensity. Vuur squawks an outraged squeak and abandons me to my fate, clumsily fluttering down to a desk.

If Micah actually knew me, he'd know I'm not the type to yell. I'm the type to knee in the balls and then punch in the throat.

"*Ow.* What's wrong with you? You could have hurt Vuur." I glare at him. His breath brushes against my cheekbones.

"What's a Vuur?" His fingers tense like this is a trick. Maybe it is.

"The lizard. Its wings are fragile. They don't support it yet."

He glances at the lizard, lips tensing in thought. I'm just positioning my knee to make him a soprano when he turns his focus back my way, holding me just as pinned with his gaze as with his body. His words freeze me in place.

"What are you doing back on board, Cyn? Or should I say, Generosity?"

Well, shit.

CHAPTER 4

Kneeing him in the fun zone is a good solution if the problem is an overly aggressive roommate. It's not a good solution for a perceptive medic who just realized my former identity—especially not when I'm at the mercy of the rest of his crew. Still tempting. I don't enjoy being manhandled.

Well, I *do* enjoy it in very different circumstances.

"It's not what you think." I keep my voice low and even, calm, while testing the strength of his grip where he presses my wrist against the wall. Not an easy slip, but I could probably make it.

"Oh, really? What am I thinking, Cyn Khaw?" His voice is low, almost a purr. It drags over my skin like silk, catching in spots. Warm muscles tense where they press against me. I take a deep experimental breath and shift my weight. He snorts out a breath of his own and pushes away from my body like I'm the irritating one, still holding me in place with one hand on my wrist and one bracketing my neck. His gaze rakes my body until he shakes his head sharply like he's dispelling an unwelcome coms message. How does he recognize me? I look similar to Generosity but not remotely identical. A cousin, not a twin. I could definitely kick him in the balls right now. It's tempting.

"I have no clue. I just know that whatever it is, isn't the truth. I was minding my own business, happy as a bird, and Estella Escajeda toddled into my office, hired me, and told me to board your ship. I thought it would be easier to avoid a drawn-out conversation about the last time our missions intersected."

"Birds aren't happy."

What? Are we going to delve into the mood of birds while he holds me against a wall?

"Oh, you've met *all* birds, have you? Fair warning: if you don't release me, I'm going to kick you so hard you cough out your testicles."

"I'm fairly certain that isn't medically possible." He leans a little closer, fingers tightening minutely against my skin. I shift my weight, preparing a strike. I warned him. That's all the respect he gets based on past history and yummy arms.

"I believe in experimentation. We won't know for sure unless I give it a try. Care to be the test subject?" I coo at him, twisting my wrist out of his grip and shifting my weight just enough that I can tug his face right at mine. His eyes widen minutely as his lips draw perilously close to my own. The hand on my neck loosens enough for me to shift to the side just in time for him to get a face full of the metal door that was bracing my back.

I step away, scooping Vuur up and taking it with me. There's no way to be outside Micah's reach in the small confines of the room but what I gave him was little more than a love tap. He should realize that. "I'll give you a taste of the truth since you seem to want it so much. This mission is my priority. I've spent years hunting this menace. I've spent years being one step behind. The Abyssal Abductor took my cousin. He also killed her. I've spent my entire adult life trying to keep him from doing that to other children—other families. I'm here to hunt him and rescue Boreal. You and your crew can help or stay out of the way, your choice."

"You want me to believe your presence here is a coincidence?" His jaw clenches and I ensure the table still stands between us.

"Believe whatever you want. My past interactions with your crew were an unhappy accident. I couldn't afford to tell you who I was on Herschel Two because I had a job to do, and that job was not a priority of your crew."

"And do you have another job here that isn't a priority of my crew?"

I throw my hands in the air in a helpless shrug. "I have no idea what your crew's priorities are. I've already told you mine. Is this going to be a problem?"

How suspicious can one man be?

He studies me, dark eyes hot and hand rubbing his jaw. "I thought you were going to make me cough out my testicles."

I snort. "Never tell your adversary exactly what you're going to do to them. You were worried about your balls and forgot about your head completely. Don't feel bad, it's a common fault in men."

I expect him to look angry. Or maybe a little worried. He looks intrigued instead. Like I asked him to dance instead of smashing his face into the wall. I'll never fully understand men. "Are we adversaries, then?"

"Of course not. Unless you decide we are."

He purses surprisingly full lips as he thinks about that, then changes the subject before I get lost thinking about said full lips. "You came in disguise because you wanted to avoid an awkward conversation?"

Honestly, I came in disguise because I'm rarely myself. "To be clear, I was more in disguise the last time I saw you. Facial fillers, eye mods. Sweet-innocent act. This time, all I did was slouch a little."

"You weren't very good at that sweet-innocent act. Wore it like an ill-fitting space suit."

"How dare you. I was perfect in my role. Rashahan didn't suspect a thing."

"That why he tied you to a chair with razor wire and tasked me with cutting the banishment tattoo from your face?"

"That was because I was becoming close with Charity. Building her trust so I could eventually extract her. You can't just yoink someone out of a cult. You have to earn their faith. Otherwise, they'll just go running right back. Rashahan didn't want anyone else to be close to his favorite girl." A shudder ripples through me when I say it.

Something flickers across his face. "That's what you were doing. A retrieval. Was there a warrant out on the girl?"

I chuckle, imagining what kind of crime Bianca Laitung could have done postbanishment to earn a warrant. "No. I was hired by her parents. She got involved with a bad guy. He blamed her for some of his crimes, got her banished, and then took her to the Rashahan's happy little family because he thought it might be a way to rise in power somewhere else. Her banishment didn't make her not her parents' daughter. They were worried."

Everyone else had been there longer than Bianca and my not-so-subtle feelers about escape got me chained to a chair next to Micah. Bianca, whom I thought was almost a friend, immediately dropped me at the first sign I was out of favor. In fact, she's the one who reported me. Goes to show that you can't trust a brainwashed cultist. I mean . . . obviously.

I was tempted to leave her there, if she wanted to be part of the group so desperately. The only thing that made me return for her was the tears in her parents' eyes when they knew where she'd found shelter, and their desperation to have her, if not home, then safe. I've seen that look in my own family's eyes. It's my primary weakness. That and dreaming. And prolonged hand-to-hand combat. And Vuur's treat-eyes.

I guess I have a lot of weaknesses.

"It's true, then, you do personal retrievals. Which means, if that's true, then the story about the *Iceberg* . . ."

"How did you know it was me?" I interrupt. I don't want to go where he's going. He's about to ask about the event that made me infamous. The event I try to forget every day of my life. There are a lot of tall tales floating around in charted territory. My experience on the *Iceberg*—the public story, at least—certainly sounds like it's been exaggerated, so I don't blame him for wondering. Doesn't mean I want to answer. I've shared enough with this man today.

He cocks his head, perceptive eyes taking in more than I'd like. Then he taps his finger on the side of his nose. "Olfactory mods. The goal was to sniff out disease, but it also gives me a far better than average sense of smell. You may have changed your looks, your voice, or your movement, but you didn't change your scent." A smile twitches on the edge of his lips. "Sweet, but a little more. Like candy with a hint of pepper."

It's probably the first time in my life anyone has ascribed "sweetness" as a descriptor to me. I don't hate it. It's also proof that he doesn't remotely know me. "Do you intend to share what you've gleaned with the rest of your crew? I would rather not have past history color present interactions."

I mean that in many ways. I don't want Cyn Khaw's history to come into play any more than I want Generosity's. They *know* Cyn's history, of course, but that doesn't mean that it has to play a part in our interactions. In a perfect scenario, they ignore it completely. Like professionals.

If I'm fighting against both sets of expectations, I'll never win. If Micah wants to tell the crew what he knows, I can't stop him. This is why I don't like working with others.

I brace for it.

So, of course, he's in the mood to be reasonable. "I see no need to share it if what you've told me is the truth. This doesn't mean that I trust you. It means I'll be keeping an eye on you, Cyn Khaw. Don't think you can betray us."

I'm not even sure what betraying them would look like. Siding with the kidnapper who killed my cousin? Seems unlikely. He's even more suspicious than I am, which is impressive. The jittering of the ship has smoothed into a sensation-free movement. It feels much less like we're about to fall into pieces at any moment.

The door slides open and Itzel gets two steps inside, focused on Micah, before she sees me tucked behind the table. Her eyes flick over us, cataloguing the body language. Micah's leaning toward me, arms braced on the table. Me across from him. Somehow, I've forgotten that I'm supposed to be keeping a distance and I'm right up against the table on the other side, fingers curled around the edge of the metal, lizard coiled on the table in front of me looking up at both of us.

Itzel purses her lips in speculation. "What's happening in here?"

"Nothing," Micah and I reply in unison.

Her eyebrows waggle. "Looks like you're fighting or sparking."

"What?" What's sparking?

"You don't want to know." Micah glances at me before returning his focus to his crew member. "Are you bleeding?"

"No." She sounds offended.

"Then why are you here?"

He might be pretty, but he's certainly grumpy. I wouldn't let him talk to me like that even if he was my crew. She shrugs it off and points at me. "Because everyone's waiting around in the galley for this one to give us a briefing. Good thing I showed up while the clothes were still on."

This is going a dangerous direction. I'd better correct her assumption. "We weren't—"

"I'd rather saw off my leg."

My head swings around to Micah. "Really? Your leg?"

Itzel reaches across the table and scoops up Vuur. "Don't worry about it. His legs aren't that great. He doesn't place much value in them."

I'm getting dizzy from this conversation. Itzel sweeps out of the room, lizard cradled in her hands.

As Micah and I follow her to the mess, I assure him, "I'll be bunking with Caro or Itzel."

Who will assume I'm bunking with Micah, meaning that no one will notice that I'm not actually bunking with *anyone*.

Micah grunts. Which, I guess, means that's just fine by him. I'd hate to tempt him to remove a leg. Priap.

We gather in the mess, and I'm introduced to Arcadio Escajeda for the first (second) time. His face is more expressive than his sister's and every fraction of concern that she was lacking is written across his handsome features. I don't know if that means he's a better actor than she is or if he actually cares.

He looks like he could crush the metal control panel. Temper threads an arm around his lean waist and he glances down at her, face minutely softening when his own arm finds its way around her. It's sweet, in a weird way. I'm not used to seeing positive human emotions in people born to Families. They do their best to convince us they have none.

They've succeeded in convincing me.

Introductions done, I give them a brief overview of the Abyssal Abductor's habits. A holo of Ginsidik floats in the center of the room, offering a tactical view of the location in question.

"He—we know enough to know that it's a he because there was a witness to one of his early abductions—takes children, male and female, aged between seven and seventeen standard years. He always holds them for a full month, no matter how quickly a family can access the ransom money. It gives him time to prepare for the drop. His ask varies, but it's always something that's difficult for the family of the abducted to pay. He's been targeting more well-placed children in recent years and the bounties are getting higher. He's also been targeting younger children. The first to be kidnapped were in their late teens. Now, they're preteen or early teens. Maybe they're easier."

"He always returns them?" Arcadio's face is stone when he asks the question. He doesn't have the smooth imperfection of his sister, but it's close. The coloring is pure Escajeda, black hair, black eyes, tan skin. He wears a closely trimmed beard. Although his posture is indolent, the tension of his muscles belies the laziness.

"Everyone who pays on time. This isn't personal for him. It's an investment, and abductions only work as an investment if you habitually deliver the abductee back unharmed. For those who have been returned there is no record of assault or additional trauma—beyond the original abduction, that is."

"Did the previous victim from Ginsidik offer indications about where she'd been imprisoned? Your sister, was it?" It's heartbreaking that he thinks it will be that simple. It's also unfortunate that I have to break the news about what happened to Aymbe.

I swallow again. "My cousin. We couldn't pay the ransom for Aymbe. There was a storm, and all our hard-earned credits were lost. My uncle was killed. By the time we learned what happened, the deadline had passed. Even if it hadn't, we had no way to get any more money.

"The Abductor always attaches a buoy so a body can be found if someone refuses to pay. We found her buoy, floating above a trench on the other side of Ginsidik from where she was taken. A storm ripped it from her body. Maybe the same fucking storm. The trench was too deep to properly dredge but her tattered jacket was later found washed up on one of the tiny islands in the area." I target the location on the holo and it flashes red.

It looks so small, alone in the sea like that. I do not cry. Crying would be making this moment about me, and it isn't. "This is where the buoy was found. I do not suggest spending much time searching that region. He's too smart to use the exact same location."

"If you're telling us not to scan the critical region where the last child was deposited, we're going to come to words." Escajeda's shoulders square and it's like looking down the fast end of a shuttle bearing down on me. Temper's fingers tighten minutely on his waist. I appreciate the gesture, but I'm not sure what she could do to hold him back if he unleashes himself.

"What I'm doing is giving you the benefit of years of experience. Scan it if you want."

"Then where do you recommend that we begin?" Temper edges her body slightly between us. Arcadio's hand drops to her shoulder, like he's reassuring her that he'll behave.

"There will be only one place to begin. The trawlertown is about all Ginsidik has going for it. This is the time of the year when Aymbe was taken, so it will be in the same region. It houses the Ginsidik constabulary force, rental water vessels, and any locals who may or may not have seen anything shifty."

"Let me get this straight." Caro angles her head toward the region of the map that blinks yellow for the trawlertown. "This is a literal floating city. Built atop a massive trawler that harvests algae. In fact, the same species we use for renewable energy aboard the *Calamity*. It roves all over the planet's surface. Seems optimum for a kidnapper to have a constantly moving location."

"Not really. The trawler is as insular as it gets. Everyone's in everyone else's business." One of my primary issues with it, to be honest.

"That seems like it would limit the places that the Abyssal Abductor can go, unless he has a submersible, which, given his predilection for killing if the ransom is not paid, is entirely possible." Temper has apparently decided that Arcadio and I aren't going to go to war and has moved to stand in front of the holo, body language screaming impatience. Her arms are crossed, and her foot taps a staccato beat on the floor. I don't think it's anything to do with me. My impression of the captain is that she's generally uncomfortable with inaction. Her idea of a plan was to induce a volcanic eruption.

Itzel's attention flits from me to Vuur. The tattoos on her fingers are dark and intricate. I don't recognize their origin but there seems to be something symbolic about them. Some of the ink is clearly newer than the rest and it's all done in stark black rather than the familiar gold glisten of most interface tattoos or the vibrant colors of the remote-outpost-clan tattoos.

When she finally does ask a question, it is value-added. "Has anyone done a chem-bio analysis of the returned children to see if there is something in common? They all ate somewhere. They were exposed to some environment. Did they have sunburns? Similar stomach contents?"

"They have tested when the families allowed it. It's both helpful and unhelpful. The results share nothing that can link to a singular location for all victims. Each child is held for slightly less than a month on a different planet or moon. They do not move during their abduction, but they are all held in different destinations. As the few abducted children who have not been ransomed in time were all dropped in different oceanic trenches, I believe the Abductor picks a location with a convenient trench nearby in advance, just in case. Although Aymbe's body was never recovered, her jacket was, and some particles still lingered on the fabric. They did not match the region where the buoy was left. Based on the season and the variety of algae that was blooming, we have a location to scan with drones." I point at the northern quadrant, which has a stippling of archipelagos but no large landmass.

This time of year, the red algae will be blooming in the north and the trawlertown is there, too. "We should land in the trawlertown and start there, because the Abductor is a smart and organized person. Too much planetary exploration will draw attention to our ship—clearly foreign—and might make him skittish. Skittish criminals break pattern and kill early."

"Has he been confronted before?" Arcadio's knuckles crack as he grips the console, and Temper winces at the noise.

"He has. Several times. There were fatalities. None him. There was a fucking bloodbath on Omega V when the family's hired security managed to find him. He somehow knew just before they arrived. He was prepared. That's why it's imperative that we keep our search quiet. We're on the trawler to investigate the algae for an Escajeda client who contacted me because of my familial connection. We don't tell anyone what we're doing. Anything else doesn't just risk our lives, it risks Boreal's."

Which may not matter to Arcadio at all, so long as his precious Family reputation stays intact.

"What happened with the other fatalities?" Micah's question is delivered in a low voice, like he doesn't want to ask but needs to know.

"One was a case of divorced parents. Each thought the other was faking the abduction for some sort of clout. Neither paid. Their son was found in a trench on Mariner." I clench my jaw against a surge of emotion. "One wasn't able to raise the funds. Trench on Corfu. The child on Omega V was the only one to be killed early. After the battle. That's why I told Estella to pay instead of entertaining this search."

Arcadio and Temper exchange a glance. Probably about some Family orders they have. "The search is necessary," Arcadio grits out. So fucking prideful, Families.

"If we can't search in the *Calamity,* how do you suggest we proceed?" Temper has given up the attempt at stillness and paces along the narrow confines of the room. Arcadio's eyes track her like she's his magnetic pole.

"We can use the drones," Caro inserts. "They can scan for human-sized heat signatures and habitations."

"He'll be on the lookout for drones. You'll warn him that we're here looking for him." This is a great way to get Boreal killed. No way are we using drones.

Caro's smile is smug. Also confident. "Not *my* drones. We have standard scouting drones on board, but we also have stealth drones. They have slightly fewer capabilities but enough for what we need.

There's no way he'll detect them. I've had them inside the Etienne Family vault."

I stare. Stare some more. The Etienne vault satellite is the most secure location in charted territory. I want to know everything about that particular job. But it's irrelevant to the subject at hand. The relevant part is that the Abductor is paranoid, but not as paranoid as Etienne.

Instead of arguing, I take her at her word. "He'll choose an island that is otherwise unpopulated, so you can eliminate any space with too many heat signatures. He likes being close to but not directly in populated areas. It's part of his game—the danger of being caught. If we get any information in the trawlertown, that can help. We'll rent a watercraft in town and venture out to the location in that."

"And we're just trusting you with all of this? Knowing your history?" Caro's arms are crossed now, her lips pursed. Clearly, she's been stewing on something that's about to boil over. Maybe it'll explain the glare she's been shooting me since I arrived.

I sit down at the table, instead, like I'm comfortable. The lighting in here is shit. Some pale-blue stuff with grates over it. The ship is confusing. Some systems are shiny new and state of the art and some haven't been new in tens of years. "I welcome questions. I assumed we were all working together and antikidnapping."

"You spaced a ship full of people instead of bringing them to justice. A ship full." Her words snap out with the sharpness of a whip crack.

Ah. That. It is how most know me. I'd rather be unknown like I am at home. But once you've earned a notorious reputation, it doesn't behoove you to act all regretful. It's yours either way. "I did. You're skipping the fact that they were human traffickers. It's not like I spaced a ship full of babies. Your captain gouged her own brother's eye out, but you don't see me making a big deal out of it. I'm sure he had it coming."

"I knew I liked her." Temper grins.

"It was a whole ship, Temper. What if someone didn't know what they got into? What if all the captives weren't out?" Caro looks stricken. I've heard it all before. I've *thought* it all before. "She looks just like a Pierce, and she obviously has their same casual attitude toward human life. How do we know this isn't some Pierce Family scheme? She works for the highest bidder. Maybe they kidnapped Boreal to use her against the Escajedas, their greatest rivals."

I want to point out that they just exploded a volcano on top of a cult whose brainwashed members were just as likely to be innocent as the human traffickers, but that would reveal a bit too much. Vuur scampers from Itzel's hands and up my arm, rubbing its head on the underside of my chin. Sweet little critter. "I'm not a Pierce. Some Pierce a very long time ago boinked one of my ancestors out of wedlock and their blond hair just won't go away. If I were a Pierce, do you think I'd be living in the *Burren*? I didn't space a ship full of good guys, so if you're good guys, you shouldn't worry about it. If you don't like me very much, help me catch this Viallock and we'll never have to meet again."

Itzel blinks dark eyes at me. "Viallock?"

I sigh. It's heading home that's doing it to me. I haven't even hit barge and I'm slipping into backwater Pierce slang. That's not a great point for my "I'm not a Pierce" argument.

"Regional Pierce slang," Micah drawls from his position at my side. Of course this would be the time he chooses to join the conversation.

"Viall Pierce was the original Pierce Family head." Caro provides the information like she bears a grudge at me for saying something she knew about. "Almost a deity with the Pierce Family's ancestral worship."

"Farther you get from the Family, the less the worship and the more his name is used like a curse," Micah finishes.

"Never quite understood that little Pierce quirk." Temper shifts her weight, and slightly behind her, Arcadio mirrors the gesture, like he's so committed to watching her back he needs to always be at the optimal angle. "Ancestor worship is strange when people are still living who remember that ancestor. Kind of ruins the mystique."

"Many Families do it," Caro pipes up. Does she have a textbook on Family dynamics embedded in her brain or something? "It's easy to topple an individual. Much harder to take on a deity. Pierce likes to think of themselves that way."

Her gaze sticks to me with tar-thick animosity again.

"Cyn's the best for this job." Temper's flat voice closes the argument. "It doesn't matter if she's a good person. She knows the Abductor and she knows the planet. She isn't a hobbyist or a maverick. This is personal for her. Her past isn't up for debate."

"It doesn't matter if she's a good person" is hardly a sterling endorsement. Then again, I've had worse.

CHAPTER 5

Almost a full standard day later, I'm conducting a food inventory with Itzel and Micah. Normally they do it before launch, but they were in and out of the Burren so quickly there wasn't time to check the stock. It's going shockingly well so long as we focus on the task and don't veer into the personal. Itzel tries to feed a sprig of something green to Vuur and is rebuffed. He's denied each offering she's made before that, even the juicy cube of steak.

"So unnatural." She shakes her head while studying it.

"It *is*. Therefore, it's natural." I feel strangely defensive of the little creature. It licks the exposed aluminum portion of a protein-pack wrapper. Micah makes a grumbly sound and nudges the wrapper away.

"Don't get me wrong, it's fascinating. Just sad that people felt the need to meddle."

That's like the main thing people do.

Vuur pounces and Micah nudges the wrapper away again.

"Why aren't you letting it eat the aluminum?" I ask, snatching the offending protein pack away. "It's hungry."

Probably. I'm not sure how much a Vuur needs to eat.

A smile crinkles the corner of Micah's eyes but doesn't make its way to his mouth. "It's not pure aluminum. It's mixed with other nonmetal materials. It will likely make the lizard sick."

I don't want to know what a sick Vuur looks like. I didn't even consider compound materials. I'm so not ready to be a lizard caretaker. I stack the protein pack on a nearby shelf and turn to face Micah again.

He protected Vuur. "I appreciate it."

Micah gives me an indecipherable look. Maybe he just can't turn the medic part of himself off. Maybe it wasn't any special protectiveness to the chubby little lizard. Vuur nibbles on his finger and Micah extends it, letting the lizard bite. "I didn't do it for you."

Well . . . that puts me in my place. Lower than a bloodthirsty lizard.

"Protesting a bit too much, aren't you Micah?" Itzel drops him a wink that is about as subtle as a frag grenade.

"I'm not offended," I clarify. "I prefer honesty. I know exactly what Micah thinks of me."

"Do you?" Itzel tosses a large bundle of nutrient-printer filler onto a high shelf. "Does he?"

"Leave me out of this," Micah grumbles. Itzel pats him on top of the head like he's a pet. I'll never understand these people.

When we finish, I head out, making it into the hall before I accidentally drop the protein pack I snagged for my own meal on the floor. When I pause to pick it up, I catch the trailing end of their conversation.

"Stop trying to help me, Itzel. I don't trust her." Micah's lowered voice barely makes its way to the hall.

"What does trust have to do with it? If you keep conflating trust with naked times, you won't have any naked times."

"I'm not trying to have naked times. I'll leave those to you."

A rustling of the final supplies sliding into place. "I'd never steal your woman that way. Again, I mean. Well, I suppose it's been more than once. If it makes you feel better, I've stolen Temper's man on more than one occasion. Never Caro's, though."

"Caro doesn't have men to steal, and Cyn is not *my* woman." His tone is unequivocal.

"Tell that to the hungry look in your eye when you watch her."

"That's a suspicious look. The hungry part is in my stomach."

"Ah. The way to a man's heart." Her voice takes on a thoughtful edge.

Micah makes a growling sound of frustration and I take that as my cue to leave. Itzel might have good intentions, but she has bad instincts. He's watching me because he knows I've been here before and he doesn't trust my intentions, not because he's entranced by my mesmerizing figure.

It's good.

Not *that* good.

I return to the gym, where I've stashed all my belongings. Vuur curls its tail around my neck and makes itself comfortable on my shoulder, belly full of iron shavings. Itzel suspects that it's been biting us because it needs more iron. I blink sleep-weighed eyes and try to distract myself. We still have more days in transit ahead. I can't be getting tired yet.

An irritating vibration comes from the external pocket of my satchel, tucked in the corner behind the resistance machine. It's one of the distinctive preset vibration patterns of a cheap coms with all the location data wiped. They call them gast coms. The issue is, I didn't put a coms, gast or otherwise, in the external pocket of my satchel. When my fingers brush against the unexpected slab of plas-metal, it immediately syncs to my interface tattoo with an unwelcome shudder that ripples up my wrist.

It's unmarked, no different from any other gast coms, with no indication who put it here or how it got here. My first thought is some member of the crew, but I can't figure out the angle. I go further back. A man collided with me in the Burren, right when I was rescuing the drunk woman from her untimely demise. He had an opportunity to slip something in my bag. I was distracted.

It keeps vibrating. Now that it's synced to my tattoo, the vibration is pacing up my arm as well as rattling my bag. I don't like it. I glance into the hall of the *Calamity*. No one coming toward the gym.

I activate the door, sliding it back into place silently behind me, and a male voice transmits to my personal coms unit due to proximity. It's garbled. "Cynbelline Khaw."

"Cyn," I correct through gritted teeth. This is a bad beginning. "To whom do I have the pleasure of speaking?"

"Are you somewhere private?"

"So I can facilitate whatever the fuck this is? This weird clandestine shit?"

"Yes. This weird clandestine shit." He says "shit" like he's read it in a book but never pronounced the word himself.

"I am alone." A strange little pulse emits from the phone, causing the lights to flicker and go out, leaving me in the darkness. My fingers curl around the gast coms as my breath catches in my throat. "Tell me you didn't put a tiny EMP in the coms. I could have been alone in the engine room, you priap! I could have a medical implant."

I mean, I'm *close* to the engine room. Only the fact that the usual noise echoes through the wall reassures me that taking this call hasn't killed us all.

"I don't particularly care. Electronics in your vicinity will recover shortly—that was a reboot, not a shutdown." His voice isn't muffled anymore. It's familiar in that "oh shit" way. "Do you know who this is, Cynbelline Khaw?"

"Carmichael Pierce." Is there a place to throw up in here? There should be. It's really a design oversight.

"Yes. It *is* Carmichael Pierce. The man you tased naked and delivered to the authorities the same way. The man who was paraded through a way station like a common criminal."

"It's not like I did it for funsies. It was self-defense. I'm not going to let you beat me up to stroke your ego."

"You'll do whatever my ego demands." His voice is smooth and dangerous with the sharp edge of fury threaded through it. "A ship that has ties to the Escajeda Family, the *Calamity*, was flagged for a brief docking permit yesterday evening and you were granted access to the docks. You are no longer in the Burren. We have reason to believe that you are presently traveling on the *Calamity*."

He has yet to make a request, merely stated several facts and then waited for me to fill in the blanks. I hate it when people with authority do that. I also have a completely natural thread of sheer panic running through me that he's tracked me down, because there's no way this interaction goes well for me. I listen silently. No questions have been asked. I have no reason to respond.

When the silence stretches, he continues, voice clipped, slightly drained of that false smoothness. "We have reason to believe that a crew member of the *Calamity* is traveling under an assumed identity. He is wanted for crimes on the Sunspire Way Station including drug dealing, gang activity, assault, attempted murder, and arson. His name was Micah Arora. He wore an eye patch that may or may not have obscured a mark of banishment. I will forward the bounty to you and await your acceptance."

Nothing about Micah sounds like what Carmichael is describing. "Not interested."

I terminate the connection.

Carmichael Pierce's voice continues speaking through a unit that should be turned off. "You are uniquely placed to serve the purposes of my Family. It's the only reason you're still breathing."

I terminate the connection again and start the sequence to decouple the coms from my interface tattoo before I realize it's as shorted out as the lights.

"That won't work." He's still there. Smug now. What a priap.

"I can do this all day, Pierce. Never underestimate the amount of stubborn pettiness I have in me. Find another hunter. I'm on a different job. It would be a conflict of interest."

"I can't properly express how little I care about a conflict of your interest—less even than your well-being. In a perfect universe I would be free to bring you low and all would be right again. As it is, you are in the position to be useful to my Family and that will have to sate my need for retribution."

I pinch my eyes shut. Pinch my lips shut. Swallow a gob of fear that seems to have lodged in my throat. As enemies go, Pierce is as bad as it gets. I *knew* it was a bad idea to stun him. My suddenly nerveless knees give out and I plop down on a weight bench. Vuur, my constant reptilian companion, chitters and scampers away, almost to the edge of the bench.

"I won't do it." I'm all out of volume—the words come out practically in a whisper.

Carmichael seems to—correctly—take my response as cowed terror, and he continues, "I can inconvenience you in any number of ways, but I don't want to do that, Khaw. It's too much work. Especially when all I need to do is reveal your true identity. You may not care if your neighbors know that C is the notorious Cyn Khaw. But how do you think it will go for your family when everyone knows Cyn Khaw is the same Bella Khaw who grew up in Ginsidik? When we tell them exactly what you are and when they know exactly how vulnerable they are against the very large array of enemies you've made. You've been able to stay a ghost until now. Untouchable. But you're oh so easy to touch."

My hand freezes over the coms, one brush away from attempting to disconnect again, but I'm too scared to do so. I can't risk my family. Our relationship may be complicated, but I never doubted their love for me. Cyn Khaw has made a lot of enemies. Some are locked up, but others aren't—case in point. And I'm sure at least a few would be happy to rack up some innocent victims in the name of revenge.

"And how would your parents look at you if they were to know the truth about their little girl?" Carmichael's voice oozes false sympathy.

They don't know the truth about me. Probably they don't know

Cyn Khaw exists at all, because the trawlertown doesn't exactly follow the hottest gossip in charted territory. Khaw is a common enough name it doesn't draw attention. I knew I should have changed it, but I didn't want to let go of that part of myself. Which is funny, because they're the ones who don't want me to *be* myself. They want me to be the sort of person who is all soft edges. Who plays the drums and dances and has at least two chubby children and a doting partner.

Even Aymbe didn't have that particular dream. She might have had soft smiles for friends and family, but she wanted off-trawler even more than I did. She pretended better than I ever did was the difference. Or maybe she never got old enough to push.

My family are ambivalently disappointed that I'm a struggling PI. I can't imagine how they'd react to knowing my real day job. Well . . . I *can*.

Poorly.

I don't want to turn on Micah, but I don't see a way out. Pierce runs the trawlertown. They literally hold my family's fate in the palm of their hands.

"I can't do it immediately. I need time. The *Calamity* is investigating algae for the Escajedas." I fully embrace my earlier theoretical cover for this trip. What does a Family care about beyond credits? "That could be a lot of money for Pierce. If I take him now, they'll leave the trawler to try to recover him and you won't make your profits."

He's silent. Maybe considering. Maybe contending with indigestion. After a very long wait, he finally responds. "You have two standard weeks."

That's no time at all. Boreal's clock won't even have run out.

"I need four weeks."

"This isn't a negotiation. You will get two. If you fail in your task, or abandon it, you and your family will personally make recompense to those whom Arora harmed. If you succeed and Arora is taken into custody, I will refrain from retribution." Finally, the coms goes silent without my prodding. It stays silent this time.

This is all bullshit. Pierce is not known for mercy. No Family is. He'll get any use he can out of me and then probably kill me anyway. Normally, I'd take my chances and hide. The problem is Carmichael is just petty enough to go after my family if I fail.

Exhaustion presses at my temples. Weariness weights my shoulders. I knock back a shot of premixed stims.

Maybe Micah Arora really is a monster, really does deserve to be sent to Pierce justice. I have all the time we spend tracking the kidnapper to verify the charges levied against him.

．　．　．　．　．

Micah lays in front of me, sweaty and breathing hard. It's a fantasy that I've let myself toy with several times in the wee hours of the night when my shipmates are sleeping. Except it's not a fantasy. He's really here, splayed at my feet like some sort of diabolical offering.

I should clarify: we're in the gym, and he's lying on the floor, doing crunches.

It was better the fantasy way. Although probably safer this way since he's apparently a murderer and an arsonist. Could a murderer and arsonist be this compelling?

Probably.

I pull against the resistance bands on the machine, doing my best to ignore a literal and figurative wet dream brought to life in front of me. I'm moderately successful, mostly because I've had practice over the last three days. It appears that both Micah and I find time for physical fitness after the others have gone to sleep.

I use the activity to keep awake. I don't know what he uses it for, but he works out with the same singularity of focus that it appears he applies to everything. Vuur uses the time to nap, curled up in a scaly ball on top of the resistance machine. Luckily for me, it seems to sleep cat hours, meaning I only have to keep it from eating a critical ship component for about eight standard hours a day.

Eventually my muscles are quivering and spent. Adrenaline ripples through my body, at odds with the exhaustion that the stims are barely keeping at bay. I lick my lips, then realize that somehow my eyes have dropped back to Micah, who, thankfully, has transitioned to push-ups and can't see me staring at him like an idiot. What if Itzel was right and he does find me—no. That direction leads to insanity. How can I ogle him when I may be betraying him at the end of this misadventure? Or the middle of it.

Guilt propels the words from my mouth. "I'm going to go clean the kitchen-drain filter. It's been clogging."

His shoulders tense, as though he forgot I was here, which can't be the case. He doesn't even glance over his shoulder when he grunts something that might be "sure."

Maybe I'm not so guilty.

I make my way through the quiet ship, fingers tracing the walls. Near the door to the gym, there's a drawing of the volcano on Ginsidik sketched large on the bulkhead. Each crew member is painstakingly drawn. If someone leaves, I wonder if they'll leave the drawing as is or edit them out.

The galley is cozy in the dim light that illuminates the ship at night. I turn it up slightly, just enough to clearly see the panel under the sink and open the panel to provide access to the drain-filter system. They get fussy on ships like this and it's a nasty job to clean them. I turn the valve to stop water flow, remove the filter, replace it with the spare, and turn the flow back on. That's the easy part. The harder part is cleaning the original. I lay down a silicone sheet on the mess table, put the cylindrical filter on it, and retrieve a set of tweezers and a few bins. One for biodegradable material, one for recyclable, and the last for true waste.

You don't just chuck a filter in the trash on a ship. And if you rinse it off, all the muck will just catch in the filter again as it goes through the recycler. So you carefully pick out large waste, identify it, place it in the appropriate compartment for reuse, and then repeat the process until you've gone through all the waste. The ship's algae will eat the biodegradable material. In fact, once I'm done sorting the big stuff, I'll rinse it over the algae vat and let them eat.

The hydroponic garden hums in the corner, real-food stock next to it, and the wall holds nutrient-printer refill packs and protein packs. I'm pulling a long red hair from the filter, lost in the repetitive task, when Micah appears, towel draped over his shoulder, eyes taking in everything. He pauses for a moment and I'm terrified that he'll say something snarky and cutting. Instead, wordlessly, he brushes past me into the storeroom, a wave of heat traveling in his wake. In a moment, he emerges, holding flour, yeast, sugar, oil, and salt. The nutrient printer beeps through some sequence. Judging by the sequence components, yogurt. Refrigerated items are in short supply on a ship, so he'll need to make that ingredient fresh.

His flatbread. I swallow a thick knot of emotions. He ignores me as I work on the filter and begins mixing ingredients. So I return my focus to the filter, picking pieces from it until it's as spotless as it can be. There's something comforting about him working in the galley behind me, in the smell of the oil heating on the stove and the crushed herbs sprinkled over the dough. I straighten my back, stretching stiff muscles, and drop the filter in the sanitization furnace, which will destroy anything too small for me to pick off.

A hand reaches into my field of view, holding a hot piece of flatbread glittering with salt and oil. I glance up, locking eyes with Micah. He wiggles the flatbread at me, so I take it. I consider thanking him, but it feels like any words at all might shatter this peace between us, where he isn't threatening me and I'm not betraying him.

Micah tears a piece from his own retained snack and it's difficult not to stare as his jaw works on the bread. I brush some invisible specks of crumb from the table in front of me. When I glance back up, he's watching me—something unreadable in his eyes.

"Good job on the filter. You didn't have to do it," he says before he walks out.

That's not a thank-you. It's also not a snarl.

For the future of our working relationship, I'll take it. I'll also take the bread. It's hot and soft and as mouthwatering as the man who made it.

It tastes like last year when life was simpler.

CHAPTER 6

■ ■ ■ ■ ■ ■ ■ ■ ■ ■ ■ ■ ■ ■ ▪

The ship bucks when we hit atmosphere two days later, disrupting the artificial gravity just enough to have me briefly floating in the middle of the mess surrounded by specks of stim powder that were about to get mixed into a morning refreshment. Over the trip, we've adjusted our time and circadian rhythms to coincide with that of Ginsidik's rotation.

It's a fast-spinning planet, so a solar day is only about fifteen standard hours, meaning Ginsidik goes through two solar days and two nights in about one normal standard day. Waking hours are separated into firstday, firstnight, and secondday. Secondnight is for sleeping. It might seem strange, but it's at least similar to standard time. I've encountered a planet or two that have daylight for a whole year, followed by a year of dark.

Either way, it can fuck with your sleep schedule.

A normal person's sleep schedule won't be a problem for me if I can just collect all these grains of powder before the gravity reactivates. Too late. I crash awkwardly down on the table, on top of the spilled cup of water, and the powder rains down on me like ash. Something in the ship makes a grinding noise and it jitters all around me. I clutch the edge of the table to stay in place, legs skewing over the sides. Caro runs through the galley from the helm on the way to the engine room, not even pausing to comment on my position.

I'm sure everything's fine. Totally normal landing protocol.

I'm on my last legs. My stims are custom mixed to delay the effects of sleep deprivation but I can already feel the darkness crawling at my temples. I'm growing fuzzy right when I need to be sharp.

I'll be fine. I'm always fine.

Micah hasn't commented on my sleeplessness, and I haven't commented on my new plans to betray him. So far as I know, no one has caught on that I'm not actually bunking with *anyone*. Even with that little subterfuge, he'll recognize my symptoms soon enough. Medics keep an eye out for the sorts of behaviors that endanger crews. Whatever strange attraction I have toward him, I'm confident that he reciprocates it only with the wary caution usually reserved for feral animals.

Rightfully so. He has rarely let me out of his sight on the voyage, but he hasn't exactly been chatty. More like he's waiting for sabotage and wants to be ready.

Boreal Escajeda is nine standard days into her abduction. I'm about eleven from having to betray Micah. There is no time to waste, but I will have time to sleep in privacy (even if I have to book a room on-planet) while the drones and satellites conduct their scans.

The trawlertown constabulary force is a complicated matter, or at least it was for the year I worked there. The local constables do little things well—finding lost pets, policing shoplifters, defense against the rare pirate vessels. Large criminals have large pockets and can afford to pay the connies off.

They aren't all crooked, but the highest ranked are.

I scrape the powder off the table with the edge of my hand and dump it into a refilled cup of water. The way my hands are shaking, I don't even have to stir to make the crystals dissolve. I knock back the drink as the ship jitters and shakes around me and then, so suddenly it seems unreal, smooths until it feels like we've flipped a page into a new reality. I almost stagger in the stillness.

"You ever put anything in your body that isn't a stimulant?" The medic's voice comes from the entryway to the mess.

"You ever put anything in your body that isn't asshole juice?" I don't turn. Instead, I stick the cup in the pressurized cleaner and start the brief decontamination cycle. You don't leave dishes lying around in the sink on a ship.

"I don't put it in. I produce it naturally." He reaches around me and places a protein pack in my hand. Why does he keep trying to feed me? I'm hardly underfed.

Oh. He knows I'm popping stims like candy and he's trying to keep me even—cancel out the churning acid pit that so often comes from taking stims on an empty stomach. A wash of embarrassed heat flushes my body, followed by an influx of irritation. I don't need him to take care of me.

Because I'm so excellent at taking care of myself.

I puff out a breath and open the protein pack. It tastes sweet. He figured out my favorite flavor. How can I stay mad at him? Even if he's watching me because he thinks I'm about to screw his crew over, he also noticed things that only matter for kindness. That ever-familiar clench of guilt pinches my insides. He's a good person, even if I'm not. His chest brushes against my shoulder blades in a way that makes my traitorous stomach clench. I slide out of his personal space just as he moves in.

One thing I've noticed about Micah is that my skin feels electrified when he's too close. A second thing I've noticed about Micah is that he likes to be too close. It could be his lack of trust for me overall, or a personal quirk—people get like that after too long on a ship. The lack of personal space becomes normal.

I've also noticed that Vuur is sitting on his shoulder. Little traitor.

The ship bumps off the landing pad and we go through another moment of questionable gravity where the artificial system gives way to the natural. Ginsidik's gravity is lighter than standard. Light enough that when I got to the Burren, I had to spend almost a year building the muscle it takes to function and fight in a more normal gravity. Now, it feels like weight is being lifted from my shoulders and I resent the relief. I don't *want* Ginsidik to feel like home.

I make my way to the helm because going straight to the loading dock and hurling myself from the claustrophobic confines of the ship seems rude. Also, because hurling myself from a ship is my personal worst nightmare. That, too.

On the outside, just a stone's throw away—if one is really good at throwing stones—is my family, the people I love more than anyone else but will also do my utmost to avoid completely while I'm on the trawler. They're too much. Overwhelming. After Aymbe, I became the hope of the family. I was supposed to renounce my rebellious temperament, marry a nice trawler boy, and pop out some hearty trawler babies. Ideally a dozen or so, enough to fill up the hole left in our family. Reset time until maybe, with enough babies and enough happiness, we forgot what happened.

Instead, I fled, telling them I wanted excitement and adventure. I wanted to make a difference. What they heard is that I wanted anything but *them*, anything but what I grew up with. As it turns out, with such a narrow focus on the Abyssal Abductor, all I've got is excitement and adventure. I don't have a soft place to land.

No one is in the helm except for the captain, the Escajeda, and Micah, who follows me in. Temper turns to me. "Caro is preparing the drone. Satellite mapping has begun. She and Itzel will focus on the search for any sign of Boreal on-planet. Arcadio and I have a tour set up at the algae plant to help build your cover story. I'm sure it will be riveting. Who doesn't love staring at algae?"

"Good. While they're watching you, I'll start putting feelers out for any unknown information about Aymbe's disappearance. Maybe we can glean something from the last time he was here." I throw in a jaunty little salute to add a touch of good nature.

"*We'll* put feelers out, Captain." That smooth voice joins the conversation as Micah stands by me, arms crossed over his chest, looking far too good in his ridiculous sleeveless coveralls. They're called *cover*alls, they're supposed to cover all. Vuur gives a triumphant little chirp, head aloft, nostrils flaring as the ship begins to intake air from Ginsidik instead of recycling its own. Micah's eyes spark with intensity and the corner of his mouth curls up slightly, like he's anticipating pouncing on me.

Fuckity fuck fuck. "Unnecessary. I couldn't possibly take someone so important to your crew."

"Didn't you hear? They're going to wander around the plant and look pretty. The golden scions of Families. I'm not nearly attractive enough to pull that off. They won't have any medical needs and we're fully provisioned. I want to stretch my legs a little."

Stretch his legs, my ass. Although he's right about prettiness. He's pretty like a hunting cat is pretty. In a way that's smooth and natural and viscerally terrifying. "They may not be forthcoming with an outsider."

A complete lie. People here are basically friendly. Yet another reason why I don't fit in.

Micah grunts a noncommittal response.

They'd be far more forthcoming with an outsider than they will with me. I can't tell them why exactly we're here because I can't risk Boreal, which means that I need to use a cover bounty. One with connections in town that give me a reason to have access to the constabulary station. I have the perfect case in mind. Considering I betrayed the constables once, I'm not sure they'll be amenable. Considering I haven't slept in days, I'm not sure I'll be persuasive.

My fingers shake and I carefully fold my hands into fists. Vuur dives from Micah's shoulder, almost missing mine completely, because while it has cuteness and sparks in its list of talents, it doesn't have aim, but I catch it. It squirms around and emits a little hiss, offended that I didn't let it crash to the floor, I guess, but seems mollified when I feed it a chip of iron.

I haven't figured out what a well-balanced diet looks like for a creature like Vuur, so I'm trying to vary its metals. I may not be ready for responsible pet parenting.

"I'll let you do all the talking." Micah smiles a hard grin. Must have had an extra helping of all that asshole juice when I left the room.

"Fine," I growl. "Follow me and don't fall in any of the line-cleaning sink pits. The motion of the town will suck you right under and my guess is your mods don't enable you to survive at pressure without air for long."

Mine do. As I learned the hard way.

We leave the ship and step into the vibrant blue-clear light of Axios, the system's sun.

After the dry air on the ship, the wet stickiness of Ginsidik slaps me in the face. It's summer in this hemisphere and the soft heat is like a damp blanket. The trawlertown moves south when the seasons change, staying in perpetual summer. Algae reproduces in the heat—not because that's an ideal condition for the algae itself, but because that's when the sea serpents gather and breed, meaning lots of delicious serpent excrement for the algae to eat—and the town's sole purpose is harvesting algae for Pierce energy plants.

Micah hisses in a breath and slips a pair of dark glasses over his eyes. The sun is bright on Ginsidik and it reflects from the top of the rippling ocean that surrounds us. I can almost feel my pupils constricting to tiny points. Luckily, my cornea mods tint naturally under the light. They just need a moment to activate.

"Too hot for you to handle?" I jibe. The heat bakes my skin, and both my shirt and jacket stick to my back in a wash of sweat. Yes, wearing the coat is uncomfortable in the heat, but it covers the scars that map my skin, and it blocks the sun until I can buy some of the special sea-mud mixture that locals use to protect their flesh.

I can't exactly see his eyes under the glasses, but I imagine they're narrowed. "I've never found something I couldn't handle."

Well. I can't decide if that's a threat or a promise. Maybe both.

I have no response. Many in my head. None that I feel like saying out loud.

Two dockworkers watch us as we cross the bridge from the landing platform to the border of the trawlertown. The clay on their skin cracks in tiny flakes, sharp edges casting shadows. My mother knows a wise woman who tells your future based on how your clay cracked.

When we went to her, she stared at the skin under my eyes, across the forehead, and down the nose before shaking her head sadly and claiming that she couldn't see anything. Then she asked me to leave the room so she could speak with my mother in private. I spent the rest of my childhood assuming that she saw something horrible in my future and didn't have the heart to inform me. After Aymbe was taken, I assumed she'd seen that instead, that my cousin's future had been intertwined with my own.

As it turned out, my mother had been selling odds for the weekend's tub-fighting tournament and the wise woman wanted to place a bet.

She lost. Guess she wasn't so wise after all.

The streets of the trawlertown spread before us in a comfortable haphazard disarray. The broad base of the trawler barge stretches for many full city blocks, interspersed with holes for engine access and net retrieval or repair. It gives the feeling of a city traced with canals, rigid bridges linking sections together and ensuring a consistently sized egress between solid sections. When it was initially floated, the town was a meshwork of grids of small homes that wouldn't catch the wind. Windows could be shuttered in the rare summer storms and the external trawling equipment protected the habitations from wild swells. A town that is constantly mobile, subject to the seas, is a challenge of engineering. It must be flexible enough to never break, but rigid enough to not be crushed by the forces of nature.

I include the leviathan serpents that populate the sea amongst the forces of nature. I take out my coms and snap a picture of the town for Madrigal.

The original construction was delicate and intricate, decorated with fine-metal filligree and etamarine stone-set murals. In the subsequent years since the trawler was first floated, the population has boomed and busted several times over. Habitations have been expanded and demolished. Blocks have merged and been spliced. Now the trawlertown is an energetic chaos of buildings and platforms. It looks like a jewelry box half rifled through.

"You grew up here?" The careful neutrality in Micah's voice is almost tactile. My pride crests in response.

"It was a lovely place to grow up." My childhood was idyllic. I grew up under the sun's light, on the water, with the wind in my hair. With the stability of home but a different view out the front door every day. It was adulthood when everything went to shit.

He lifts his hands like he's surrendering. The wind ruffles his hair against his brow. The sunlight plays across all the tantalizing little dips and valleys that appear in his forearms, biceps, and shoulders. I can only imagine what his back looks like.

But I won't. Because a million reasons, starting with the fact that we're tracking the criminal who destroyed my family, who has an innocent girl right now whose Family isn't willing to pay her ransom, and ending with the fact that I have to betray him in under two weeks.

"I simply meant that you seem very cosmopolitan." He insists on walking on the street side every time we cross a bridge and enter a new neighborhood. I didn't notice it at first, but it's unmistakable the farther we walk. It could be seen as a protective impulse. More likely, he doesn't trust *me* to protect him, so he wants to be the first person to encounter any trouble.

"And this is outwater?" I shrug and turn, walking around the periphery of the trawler. Gantries stand like pillars on shipside, the cranes swooping above us and the fine-mesh nets draping on the water side. It looks hazardous, but this is actually the safest place to walk if one is unfamiliar with the town. No unexpected holes. No street racing on the small three-wheeled vehicles that are the only form of transportation on the narrow twisted walkways of the town. The constabulary station is at midships, port side. "Maybe it is rustic, but you gain a different sort of confidence being a big serpent in a small sea. Means you know what it's like to be big and it doesn't frighten you."

He considers me, face still. "I can't imagine much of anything frightening you at all."

It startles a laugh out of me. Vuur shifts on my shoulder, giving me a dirty look with its little lizard eyes. Because I laughed at Micah, I feel obliged to offer some truth. "I'm frightened of nearly everything. Fear is just like anything else: if you ignore it hard enough, you function just fine."

Kind of. The slight twitch in his cheek tells me that he's biting back a comment on the quality of my functioning. Instead, he studies a street musician. "I know what you mean."

"Something you should know before we get to the station. Most of them are far more interested in a payday than in justice." I hope to take care of this little information sharing session on my own, but if he's going to prove difficult, he deserves the warning.

"If it's common knowledge that they're crooked, how do they stay in power?" The tone of his voice implies that he thinks I'm probably a criminal who just doesn't trust connies. And, in that, he'd be about three-quarters right. "And how do *you* know about any of this?"

"Because I used to be one of them." I don't feel like sharing much more. The dishonorable discharge from the force still stings even though I understand the truth behind it. The only way to be free of them was to be discredited.

It is, perhaps, a repeating pattern in my life.

Micah sends me another appraising look, like this tells him something about me that he already suspected. Since he believes I merrily spaced a ship full of people on a whim, I imagine that the picture of the puzzle was already fully formed before this little piece slotted in. His judgment shouldn't bother me, but it does. Reputations cut both ways and my own has been working against me just as hard as it works for me.

It's as exhausting as staying awake for this entire trip. Probably about as crazy-making. But as with sleep, it's still better than the alternative. I try to swallow a gigantic yawn and, when I fail, hide it by looking toward the sea.

"Why did you leave?"

Well. That's deeply personal and deeply none of his business. I wish we could go back to the same growly Micah who worked out with me completely silently every night. "It wasn't that I had to leave. It was that I couldn't stay."

I wait for the inevitable question. A thin cloud moves over the sun. One of the leviathan sea serpents thrashes off to the side, disrupted by the arc of the nets. I manage to capture a video of it to send to Madrigal. She loves a predator.

I keep waiting.

It doesn't come. I can't decide if he's polite or disinterested. I also can't decide if my irritation is larger than my relief. If I brace myself for a collision and it doesn't happen, sometimes I feel cheated. The trawlertown's large enough that I don't feel the pitch and yaw of the sea beneath my feet. This time of year, the seas are fairly peaceful, despite the rare summer storm. The truly bad weather hits between summers, when the town moves from hemisphere to hemisphere and passes through the equatorial typhoon zone.

The constabulary office looms in front of us, a half-block long, low and squat as the rest of the buildings. Since I was last here, they've erected the fun new addition of an open-air prison on top of the building. Bars frame a long row of cells, two of which are occupied by sunbaked and morose individuals. One has a thread-bare mattress propped like a lean-to against the barred wall, the prisoner within huddled beneath it, hungry for shade. Must be at least two people in town didn't have enough bribe money to get overlooked.

It's inhumane, cruel, and a new low for this department. We didn't torture people. We barely locked them up. I can't imagine that crime has grown so bad that these cells are justified. A low grumbly noise comes from the man at my side, and I glance over to see his eyes locked on the prison. A muscle twitches in his jaw. "They always had those cells?"

"They're new." I wonder what else has changed.

CHAPTER 7

■ ■ ■ ■ ■ ■ ■ ■ ■ ■ ■ ■ ■ ■ ■ ■

"Get out." A large man blocks the door to the constabulary office, arms crossed over his barrel-shaped chest.

"I already *am* out," I very helpfully point out as I study Mo Anaspian. Also known as the captain of the constabulary force. My old boss. A real charmer. He's applied streaks of sun-blocking mud to his cheekbones and the bridge of his nose. His brown eyes are small, like someone pressed them too deeply into his face.

If he was a nice person, they might make him look intense or focused. Since he's a priap, they make him look like a priap.

"Out of the fucking planet." The look on his face says he'd enjoy escorting me there. Which is fair. I tried to take him down once, a long time ago.

I missed. He's good at sucking up to people in power. He just doesn't waste the charm on people beneath him. Pierce loves him. Something I wished I'd known before I tried to take him down.

He turns his attention to Micah. "I don't know who you are, but you've partnered with the wrong woman." The constable captain's face beneath the mud is a livid shade of red, like the thin-skinned fruits that grow on the narrow isles to the south. "This woman never met a lie she didn't want to snuggle right up to."

The propaganda begins. I shake my head. This would have been better if we'd encountered literally any other connie. He used to work secondday. I thought I'd avoid him by visiting early. I could have beat him into the station and accessed the updated maps and schematics of the trawler and the surrounding area before he knew I was here. It would have been faster than waiting for an upload on the *Calamity* and it would have been more likely to be accurate. "Feeling sad that I never tried to snuggle up to *you* instead, Mo?"

"Cynbelline. Little Bella the Bought. Always talking tough. You aren't really that hard, though, are you? Breakable as a fine-thread net and just as twisted," Mo sneers. He glances behind himself into the station. I can see silhouettes but I can't identify the connies behind him. Apparently they're people he wants to impress, because he raises his voice slightly. "Couldn't quite hack it when you had to work in the real world. Had to make yourself look important."

Micah makes a gravelly noise in his throat that I can't quite decipher. This is why I didn't want him here. It's embarrassing enough to be personally dragged through my history. I don't need an audience. But then he shifts his weight so that he's standing more solidly behind me. Like he's offering me backup. I'd be flattered if I wasn't so infuriated.

I have a problem with every sentence Mo uttered. He absolutely knows I hate the name Bella the Bought because *I* was the only one of them who wasn't bought. If what I said to him was a gentle poke, his response was a slap with all the power of his shoulders behind it.

Everywhere else I go, when people learn my name, they shut up and step back like I'm a deranged murderess. Only at home do people still see me as a child. It gives me hope, though. If he knew Cyn Khaw the bounty hunter existed, he'd assuredly throw it in my face. Mo's probably the best-informed person on the trawler, which means that my largest secret is still safe. One of my largest secrets. They're getting harder to categorize.

Before we left the *Calamity*, I set up my interface tattoo to carry my access. Now I swipe my middle finger along the fine gold sensors and pass the information on to the station database. He gets that distant stare that people have when their interface lenses pick up a message, and his lips twist into a scowl.

I can't resist a smug smile that I haven't remotely earned. If you don't get victories often, something victory-adjacent can be good enough.

"I'm escorting an Escajeda Family member to the planet. They're interested in algae power for one of their Family stations. While here, I want to check on a friend who may be on-planet. They know Etolla Hancha."

I doubt Etolla has ever been off-planet, but as a mystic, she does some readings from a distance. It's plausible someone from outside reached out to her. What's more, although Mo is a big serpent on Ginsidik, he's *also* never been off-planet. I could tell him everyone's wearing soup on their heads, and he'd have a sliver of doubt that it might be true no matter how crazy it sounds.

"I don't know what you offered Escajeda," Mo spits as he continues to block the door. "But this is Pierce territory. This string of code gives you access. Not assistance."

I can almost see the cogs turning in his brain, coming up with new ways to make my life difficult. Lucky for me, Mo's cogs always turned at about half the rate of a normal person's. I interrupt before he can get there. "I'm not requesting assistance."

"You step one foot over the edge, Cynbelline, and I'll have you roasting in the sky cells for the rest of your natural life," Mo growls, and then retreats into the station. The door slams behind him.

I wipe my hand over my face. I could have handled this better. In a lot of ways. Probably if I appeared humbled, he would have been more open, just to have the chance to lord it over me. This isn't about me and my history as much as it feels like it is right now. It's about a little girl who's undergoing something frightening, and about stopping a predator.

I can't tell anyone that's what it's about, but if I could sneak into the station when he isn't working, I could probably get more useful information. Then again, I could also end up in one of those sky cells. I'll save the breaking-into-the-station part for my last effort, if everything else fails.

Micah's brow is furrowed. He studies me like I'm written in a foreign language.

"Well? Aren't you going to ask for the full story?" My shoulders tense, waiting for it.

He simply shakes his head. "Do I look like a fool? That sort of man is eighty percent bluster and twenty percent mean. Not a fraction honest."

A woman passes us in the street, with a halo of curly dark-brown hair and a multicolored dress. She glances over her shoulder and eyes me. Pauses. Eyes me some more. Then she taps her finger against her chin before turning and continuing on her way.

Micah snorts a soft chuckle. "Welcome home, Cynbelline."

I'm in his space, jabbing a stiff finger in his chest before I even think about it. "It's Cyn, to you. Not Cynbelline. Not Bella. You don't get to name me, Mikey. There are a lot of places to hide a body on Ginsidik." Micah looks vaguely stunned, like he thought we were playing and I bit him instead.

It occurs to me that I'm being a trifle unreasonable. Sure, I'm home after so many years it's barely recognizable. I just relived one of the worst moments of my life by facing off with Mo and I'm way overdue a night's sleep. The person who changed my childhood into the before and the after has taken another child. I must betray Micah to ensure my family's safety.

He only knows about two of those things, though. My sudden reaction to his mild comment must seem unhinged.

"Bella?" The voice from behind me is as familiar as a thousand sunset calls to come home from the edge of the trawler and as powerful as a thousand ice spikes to the gut.

I freeze, finger still dimpling the hard pectoral muscles of the man in front of me. Lips curling into a grimace. Maybe I can disappear. Maybe if I will it hard enough, I'll discover this is a dream and wake up.

Maybe if I burst into tears, I can just float myself away.

"Are you going to threaten to hide her body, too?" Micah isn't smiling anymore, but his eyes miss nothing. He looks handsome with the wind playing in his black hair.

I would never threaten the woman behind me with a watery grave. I would never knowingly say those words in her presence. It's her worst nightmare. A fate she's imagined night after night since years ago, when I came home and her sister's daughter didn't. Since she lost a girl who was the next thing to a daughter—the youngest of our extended family unit. I shrink, something within me going fetal and soft and guilty. I just can't get it right today.

"Hi, Mom."

Cygna Khaw stands behind me, statuesque as ever with her burnished bronze skin, thick black hair threaded with white, and polished gold eyes so bright they could illuminate a dark room. I haven't seen her in ten years, but she looks almost exactly like the day I left. Wary. Nervous. Deeply disappointed in her daughter's foolishness. Wondering why I'm so disheveled when the firstday isn't even over. I brush my hands over my coat and dust floats from it. Sweat trickles down my neck.

"You're back." Her voice is flat, controlled, but I can hear the tiniest thread of hope in it, and that hope crushes me into an even smaller speck than I already was. The very fact that I'm here means she may think I've changed my mind. That I'll take up some trade and pop out babies and float from north to south for all the remaining years of my life.

Also known as one of my worst nightmares. Only one of them. I have a lot. If you don't have a lot, your imagination isn't working well enough.

"I'm not staying," I blurt out. The second-worst thing that I can say at this exact moment. A thin line presses between her eyes, but that's all the emotion she shows. I feel the need to explain my presence. My mind goes completely blank of any gentle placation. So, horrifyingly, honesty comes out. "The Abductor is back. On Ginsidik."

Which is the first-worst thing I can say. And something I shouldn't even say out loud, but this is my mother, and we all say stupid things in front of our mothers.

She flinches like I hit her, eyes flickering around like he's lurking behind the nearest gantry; the shanty across the street from the connie station that sells hot yeasted bread, serpent skewers, and flavored stim water in both first and second mornings; the man at my side. She pulls herself together quickly. The Abductor didn't break my mother. He distilled her into a crystal-clear and rock-hard version of herself.

She's still looking at Micah, with eyes that have turned calculating. Then she stares at my abdomen, which is notably bump-free. "Is this your—"

"No." Micah and I blurt the word at the same time. Which is a little offensive. It wouldn't be *that* awful to be considered my partner. I continue, in a softer voice, "This is Micah. He's a medic. Part of the crew that's with me. We have a lead on the Abductor. We can put an end to this, Mom. We just need to finish some scans and we'll have him. That's why I didn't tell you I was coming. Because we have to hunt him."

A flat lie. I didn't tell my family I was coming because I can't bear the thought of going to that house where I last saw Aymbe. The home where I grew up and where my extended family lives now because they're still playing catch-up from the ransom we lost on Aymbe. We took a lot on loan, and desperation meant that we took loans from people whom it isn't smart to take loans from. The terms are monstrous. At this point, we've paid the full ransom at least five times over in interest. My contribution helps to keep them afloat, but I haven't done enough to allow them to sprawl again.

My mother's face says she knows exactly what I'm doing. Micah's does, too. Even my honesty is a tool to distract from the bigger conversation of what became of our family. A frantic piece of bait thrown to the sea for chum.

"Don't you need to finish some scans? That means you have time. Come with me, it's nearly firstday meal. Everyone needs to eat." On the trawlertown, meals are split into firstday, which is at the end of the first lit day, and then morning and night on the secondday. It's considered bad luck to eat in the midday dark. I open my mouth to make an excuse. To say I'd love to come home but I have to stay with Micah since he's new in town. She's on to that argument before I can even make it. "Bring your medic. He looks like he could use a good meal."

I silently beg Micah to refuse. About a second too late, I realize that I should have protested the fact that she called him *my* medic. I hide another yawn behind my hand.

"I'd love a meal." I can hear the grin without even looking at Micah. He's having fun with my awkward family reunion.

"Good. My name is Cygna. My rude daughter didn't bother to introduce me." Mom looks us up and down. Puffs out a breath like something new disappoints her and turns. "Follow me. After this long, you probably don't know your own way home. We thought when you finally came back, you'd be bringing your partner and your family. Maybe looking for a place of your own."

Zing.

I trail behind her, immediately regressed to childhood, doing my best to suppress the hunch that tries to press my shoulders up around my ears.

Micah mutters something into his coms. This is fine. It's just firstday. I've eaten thousands of firstday meals. I can handle one more.

Why *not* introduce my family to the man that I'm soon to betray to ensure their safety?

The home I grew up in isn't far from the connie station. It's cylindrical, like most homes on the trawler, with a smooth arced roof that deflects the force of storms. The walls are painted a brilliant green—as though humanity hungers for the color so much that even on a water planet, we must put it somewhere. They're near the center of the trawler, a wrought-iron bridge connecting their segment to another right next door. It's desirable property. Even in storms, you can hardly feel the pitch and yaw of the water, but sometimes the canal wavelets make it through the first-floor windows. Watermarks line one half of the cylinder of their home, a natural landscape of waves and aged colors. It smells mustier here than on the edges—the inescapable scent of wood rot.

When we step inside, it's the same familiar juxtaposition of old and new. The trawlertown's construction is fairly organic. None of the glistening screens that you see on way stations. No glossy chrome. Smooth-sanded pale-grained wood harvested from an island chain in the southern hemisphere dominates the building materials. A tiny stain of mold flecks a baseboard near the door. In such a wet humid place, it's impossible to keep on top of mold.

My father sits at the small bar on the edge of the kitchen, crouched over a disassembled blaster, the lasing crystal perched alongside a mirror and lens. I freeze in the door at the sight, and Micah collides with my back, hands dropping briefly to my waist to keep me from ricocheting forward. His fingers press for just a moment, hot brands that I can feel even through the coat, and then he releases me.

My father is fixing a blaster. My father *has* a blaster. They're nearly impossible to get in the trawlertown. Only the connies have them. Maybe some of the very worst criminals.

And my father. The one who taught me that a punch is more effective if you wrap your fingers around your thumb. It's not, by the way. It's a fantastic way to break your thumb. It appears his martial training has progressed since I left. Part of me wants to be disappointed. A good man has grown hard.

All I want is for them to go back to the happy people I re-member from before Aymbe was taken. From before everything changed and their focus homed in on me. Something like that can dissolve a family. Broken things can be mended. Dissolved things are simply gone.

. . . . .

"You've barely touched your soup," my father chides as I stare at the bowl of green algae with snails floating in it. He's big about firstday. About any meal. Believes in cleaning your plate or, in this case, bowl. We always butted heads about it.

"I ate before I left the ship." Stims are like food, and Micah gave me that protein pack.

"You're wasting away," my aunt Mygda snorts, and then points at my face before looking at my mother. "Look at how pale she is. No good sunlight off-planet. Unhealthy. No one's going to marry her looking like that."

Um. Good? Also, I don't look *that* bad. Dark circles under the eyes are stylish some places.

Micah, seated beside me, is plowing through his second bowl of soup as though it's the first meal he's ever eaten. I wonder if he'd be as enthusiastic if he knew that the snails are harvested off the stomach armor of sea serpents by little aquatic drones—symbiotic sequins on the leviathans of the deep, sucking down serpent-skin juice.

I gave everyone the cover story of our presence on-planet before the meal and impressed upon them the necessity of keeping it quiet. We know more than anyone what happens when something goes wrong with a ransom. They won't talk in public.

"What have you been doing with your time?" my mother asks, an edge in her voice that says she's rehearsed this conversation in her head and there are only a few right answers. She used to be spontaneous and lively. I miss that version of her.

Unfortunately, I don't know what the right answers are. Or maybe I do but I can't honestly provide any of them.

"I get out and about a lot. I saw a neat ship the other day. It was shaped like an egg." Not going to go into what work actually looks like. That I stunned a naked man on my last job. That he thinks he owns me now. That he may be right. That's not conversation for the firstday table. Much like Madrigal, they think I'm a PI. "Work's good. Pays the bills."

"Pays the bills on some distant moon," Mygda snorts. "What use is that? You weren't the one who wanted to get away from us, Aymbe was. I knew that girl wouldn't stay. But somehow, you're the one who ran away. Your parents talk about you all the time. About how you could have taken over your mother's place on the machining floor, your father's spot in the drum platform."

We aren't even done eating and she's already at it. I stare blankly, sleep-deprived brain unable to dredge up any sort of rebuttal.

"Children need to roam free," my maternal grandfather pipes up from the far end of the table.

"What about trees?" my half-deaf paternal grandmother hollers from the other end. "We're not talking about plants."

"You know what, the shallow-kelp is blooming now. You can see the first flower-spikes off the port side with binoculars," my father offers to his mother. He expertly removes a snail from its shell with one of the wickedly sharp knives my grandfather makes in his smithy.

"I carried those flowers in my wedding bouquet." My mother shoots a pointed glance in my direction. "I always imagined my daughter with a bouquet of her own."

And we're back.

I clumsily attempt to change the subject. "The connies have gotten worse, looks like."

"I told you what they were," my mother sniffs, and then turns to Micah. "This one couldn't wait to be on the force, joined the second she left school. Thought they were a shining example of heroism. Didn't want to follow our path and actually make something with our hands. Didn't even last a shift until she saw the truth."

"Not that she did much good during that year," my aunt snips. "Maybe she would have made a difference if she hadn't meddled and gotten kicked out. We might have had help hunting that priap down."

As though we didn't all discuss it at the time. Aymbe was taken right after I was kicked out of the connies. I was so green I could have been growing in a seabed. With me in disgrace, we decided it was too dangerous to tell the connies. The Abductor told us not to in his letter. He said that he'd know.

While Aymbe's death made my mother grow hard, it made her sister bitter as bruised fruit. She blames everyone around her. Probably blames herself the most. It must be horrible to be inside her skin, but it doesn't make her easy to live with. "We all agreed not to tell the constables."

"Anyway, she got kicked out after a standard year for trying to make them better than they were," she continues in that voice I never heard the first twenty years of my life. The thorny one that hides poison. My mother winces.

"What do you mean by that?" Micah leans back in his chair, broad shoulders at odds in the tiny kitchen. His face says that he thinks it's impossible that I would ever strive for someone's personal betterment. That he knows better. That he knows *me*, somehow.

"He's an awfully strapping one," my father's mother says to my father in what she might think is a whisper but is barely short of a scream. "Our Bella found a man who can haul in the nets, if you know what I mean."

I—don't know what she means. Is that innuendo? What is a net in this scenario? I rub at my temple with my fingers. Maybe I'm asleep. Maybe this is a really weird dream.

"I used to tie my own nets, you know." My grandfather leans toward my aunt. "Fiber fine as a baby's hair. I sold them to traders in the far north, up by that dump."

"She tattled." My mother ignores the other conversations going on, her voice implying my actions were impossibly naive. She's right. I *was* impossibly naive. I'm sure that, in her mind, the noble course would have been to resign. Maybe to go public to the press before they had a chance to smear me. "Instead of trying to actually change things from the inside, she gathered a whole file of evidence—more than a drive of their various illicit activities—and sent it up to the head of Pierce bioenergy, the managing authority of the trawlertown."

"They knew, of course." I take over this little story. I can't handle the mixture of pride and disappointment that comes out in the retelling. Or listening to my grandmother continue to catalogue Micah's outstanding features. She seems quite smitten. The familiarity of the audience and my own exhaustion makes my answer more honest than it might be otherwise. "Or they didn't care, at least. They sent the whole thing to Mo—charming man you met earlier today—who was my commanding officer and one of the most crooked of the lot. Before I knew it, I was kicked out of the force on drummed-up charges of taking kickbacks and stealing evidence for my own use."

"Bella the Bought." He repeats the title in a considering tone as he licks the spoon. I've never been jealous of a spoon before.

Well. That's certainly an insane thought. I blame the sleep deprivation. "Propaganda always goes down smooth if there's a kicky little nickname associated with it."

"After she got herself kicked off, she couldn't get help when he took my Aymbe." My aunt brings the conversation back around to how disappointing I am. The side conversations go quiet at the mention of Aymbe. You could hear a snail drop. They aren't loud . . . make little ploppy sounds.

"Remember her first dance at the sunset circle?" My grandfather's voice is soft. "The sun lit her hair like water."

"She was such a good dancer." My mother sets her spoon gently in the bowl. "Found the beat like it matched her heart."

My aunt blinks abruptly, staring down at her own bowl. "Everyone watched her. That's how it always was. All eyes on Aymbe."

And it was. She was beautiful. Lively. Attention-seeking in the way so many teens are, before they grow up enough to learn that attention can be dangerous.

"And you walked up to those Markosi brothers and told them that if they kept staring at your cousin like that, you'd shove them off the ship." My father points at me, laughing. He glances at Micah. "She was always looking out for Aymbe. We raised her to be brave."

For a brief moment, we are who we once were. What we could have become.

"Except she didn't look out for her when it actually mattered." My aunt's voice sours again.

And just like that, we are who we are again. Who my aunt is is hurtful. Who my parents are is a darker version of who they once were. They used to be so happy. Now my father has a blaster and my mother is hard. Maybe they wouldn't be if I'd stayed.

I accidentally drop my spoon and it clatters on the floor. I duck down to retrieve it, like maybe having an instant where no one is staring at me will help me come up with a better way to handle this situation. My fingers collide with Micah's, already wrapped around the lost utensil. His face so close to my own we could almost kiss. His eyelashes are a dark fan against his skin. They look soft. I freeze for a moment, struck dumb by the sheer proximity, mind going blessedly empty. He places the spoon into my hand and, with a small quirk of his lips, returns to an upright posture.

"Stop it, Mygda." The edge in my mother's voice, directed to her sister for the first time, is enough to make me sit straighter in my chair. My mother is polite to a fault—until she isn't. My dad loves to tell the story of when she was young and broke into the distillery to take a bottle of booze after one of the workers there refused to sell to her because, as he put it, she was "too pretty to drink the hard stuff." Hard to believe that young harridan is the same woman at the table today.

Mygda's mouth snaps shut, and she storms off to one of the bedrooms, the door slamming behind her.

"It still hurts her like it's fresh," Mom says by way of explanation. I've been around a lot of people in pain, and I generally judge a person by how they remember empathy even when in their own crisis. So instead of agreeing or saying something placating, I simply nod. Micah makes one of those grumbling noises. Maybe regretting coming over.

I can pull this together. I'm working. This isn't all disastrous rehashing of history and my grandma commenting on the pertness of Micah's hind end. "Have you heard anything strange? Any place where we should start our search?"

"No one talks about it anymore." My mother adjusts the placement of her water glass. "There's a whole new generation that barely remembers it."

There's one person in town who remembers everything. Luckily, she's also part of my cover. On the trawlertown, people like Etolla, who tell fortunes, are about as close to spirituality as we come. She tells us our future, and because of that, people assume that she's seen all their bad parts already. They feel the need to tell her things she hasn't seen. She keeps quiet about it. Likely because people take it really poorly when you spill their secrets, even if you never asked for them in the first place. But there's no official expectation of confidentiality, so if she heard something in the subsequent years, she might talk.

I stand up, wiping my already clean hands off on my still-dirty coat. "Thank you. For the meal. We should probably check back in with the crew. Please remember that no one should know that the Abductor is on Ginsidik."

"We aren't fools," my mother sniffs.

No, they aren't. I am, maybe.

Shockingly, Micah stands without me yanking him out of his seat, smiling politely to my mother as he makes the Pierce Family genuflection of respect, a smooth wrist-flick upward until the palm faces forward.

She turns a far more approving expression in his direction. "You should rethink this one, Cynbelline. He's respectful."

"And that behind!" my grandmother chimes in. Micah chuckles.

Not touching that with a pole the size of the gantry. He may be respectful. I'm not.

"It was . . . good . . . to see you," I say ineffectually, as I back toward the door. "I—"

I what? Miss them? Love them? Wish I could be what they want? That this house didn't give me hives because of all the expectations? All of those together combined with a heathy dash of not wanting to encourage them too much, because even if I could, I'd never come back here permanently. Leaving may have been Aymbe's dream, but it's my reality.

I've seen how big charted space is. I can't ever settle for small again.

"I'll see you again. When it's all done. When we've caught him." A child's promise, but it's all I can offer at the moment. My father's disassembled blaster reflects the sunset as I open the door, the light glinting from the mirror and creating a small speck on the wall. It looks like a sniper's target.

CHAPTER 8

"How long has it been since you talked to them?" Micah asks in a very casual voice.

"We talk all the time," I grumble. We do. About inconsequential and, in my case, largely fictionalized things.

He makes a humming noise of disbelief. "I don't talk to mine."

My eyes flick to his banishment tattoo and then away. People's banishments are public record, so he came up in my research. His parents banished him. "Do you wish you did?"

"Maybe. If they were more like yours."

If he thought that was a fun lively conversation, then he has a low bar. Then again, they wouldn't be so intense if there wasn't love there.

I drop Micah off at the ship to give the others an overview of our day, find out their progress on the Boreal front, and download updated trawler schematics before I question Etolla. For one thing, she's the rare person here who *is* more likely to speak to me than to an outsider. For another, I don't really want her telling him any intimate details from my past. Firstday dinner with the family was enough.

And I'm superstitious enough to think there's a chance she really does have some prognostication ability and it would be just like her to give him a warning that I'm about to turn him in.

Etolla lives in a lofted home on stilts, smack in the middle of the trawler. The fact that it survives storms probably lends to her credibility as a mystic, but mostly it's good construction in a stable location. The stilts aren't high enough to put it taller than most of the surrounding buildings, they just lend it an air of uniqueness.

Also unique is the fact that the house is covered in copper sheeting. The shine has long since faded, but the glorious blue-green tarnish is expensive as a gemstone. Probably more.

I climb the twisted metal staircase outside her door and rattle the knocker—a coiled sea serpent. A touch on the nose, if you ask me, but no one did. It rattles and she cracks the door enough for the inside light to leak out into the twilight. "Cynbelline. I foresaw this meeting in your mother's clay."

Lie. She's the curly-haired woman I saw outside the connie station. I wasn't thinking about her then, and she's changed the way she dresses, so it didn't occur to me immediately. "Etolla. It's good to see you."

She cracks the door open and ushers me into a cozy space draped in vividly patterned fabrics, glistening with sea-glass crystals and overstuffed cushions. I've been on a lot of worlds, and mystics have a consistent aesthetic. On occasion you'll find a techno-teller of some sort, who reads your electrical output, but even they like accessories more than the average person. Perhaps part of collecting stories is collecting clutter. "I'm always happy to speak with you, Cynbelline."

"I need to ask you some questions. You may not have answers. If you don't, please be honest." A vague introduction serves no one.

She pinches her fingers in a jar of masking clay. "I see you with a handsome man and many children."

"Not exactly the kind of question that I—wait, how many is many?"

She lets the clay fall and gives me a knowing look. "Enough."

How many is enough? I can barely take care of a lizard—as evidenced by the fact that it's currently confined to Micah's bunk, so this handsome man better be pretty nurturing. "I meant questions about the past, Etolla, not the future. After Aymbe disappeared, did anyone speak with you about anything strange? Anything at all. Could have been something you heard years later."

She nods as though she knew I was going to ask that. She nods a lot, though, so I think that's probably just a trick of the trade. "You're the first to bother to ask. Once they knew it was the Abyssal Abductor, they didn't really bother to investigate, did they? People visited me a lot then. To see if he would take another child. To see if Aymbe would show up. Your aunt herself came to visit me."

Perhaps not the referral she assumes it is. "Did anyone seem to know something that others didn't?"

Her lips purse as she thinks, and clay squishes between her fingers. "Tally. Enderson Tally. I didn't speak to him but to his mother, before she up and left the trawler for good. Said her son saw your cousin talking to someone. Apparently he swore it was the middle Wetzacohl boy. I thought it was just Tally spreading lies. You know how he was as a teen."

Tally was something of a stalker. Aymbe complained about him. She told me he was following her, that he wouldn't leave her alone.

The kidnapper wasn't him. He had an alibi for the time of her disappearance.

Etolla leans forward, pinning me with an intense stare. "Maybe four babies."

"Four!" I yelp. "That seems excessive by any standard. I've got a career. I've—kind of—got a lizard. I'm a busy person."

"Maybe five."

"Maybe none," I argue, as if this is a negotiation.

She raises her eyebrows and shrugs in an exaggerated gesture that's clearly meant to placate me.

"Do you believe Tally really saw something, or that he was just talking big?" No matter what she believes, I'll follow up, but I want her opinion. Etolla is good at reading people. It comes with the territory. Not good at reading me and my increasing number of future children, apparently, but at *most* people.

"His mother was confident. But she was confident in everything her sweet boy saw and did. Never believed a bad thing about him. She always said your cousin was taking advantage of his generous nature, was setting him up and then spreading tales about him."

I have a flicker of memory, Aymbe giggling about Tally's infatuation and how she'd try to use him to get the answers to the previous year's exam because their teacher reused tests. Not exactly flattering behavior. Well, she was just a kid.

I give Etolla some off-world gossip in exchange for her honesty. Tell her about the growing anti-Family sentiment that came from Nakatomi's power grab but also about the new bathroom hand dryers at Prism Way Station, which have a suction so hard it feels like they could remove your skin. As I prepare to leave, darkness presses on the edge of my vision, I'm so exhausted. Must be the stims wore out. There's only so much they can do, and they do less for each day without sleep. Etolla daubs a smear of her clay on the back of my hand.

"I didn't come for that, Etolla."

"Everyone comes for this. Even when they don't." She holds my wrist in a gentle grip and blows on the clay. It dries quickly, in a cobweb of pale cracks.

"Make it quick, then." Rude of me, but I might topple over in the middle of her home if I don't get out soon.

Her thumb swipes over the clay, and when she looks up again, there's a worrisome furrow between her brows. "Your future is your own. You simply have to choose it."

Guess destiny is too busy with other people to waste time on me. It doesn't feel like my future is my own, though. Maybe she means that I'll have to choose to betray Micah in order to have a future at all. Otherwise, my future is so overshadowed by Carmichael Pierce I can't believe it'll ever exist. "Thanks, Etolla. I'll keep that in mind."

On my way out, I swipe my interface tattoo to deliver her standard fee for a reading along with a little extra for the lead on Tally.

I need to get back to the ship to crash. A group of revelers, off-shift and celebrating their evening, bounce into me, or maybe I bounce into them. One of them sneers down her nose at me. Light-emitting diodes are embedded under the skin of her cheeks in a glowing purple line. Her hair is threaded with gleaming optical fibers. Her fellow youths are similarly bedecked. Clearly, I am not nearly illuminated enough for this party.

Good thing. I'd hate for someone to accidentally invite me to a party.

I give her the half-flick version of the Pierce salute that indicates polite avoidance and step around the group, stumbling like a wave hit me, but I'm fairly certain it didn't. A strong arm wraps around me.

I twitch, looking up, and stick in Micah's gaze. His arm is warm, his body like a harbor in wind-tossed seas. Ah. So the delirium has set in.

I lose a moment. Flicker in and out and find us standing in front of a serpentmonger selling snake flesh harvested from nets. Chunks of meat sizzle on sticks, glistening white and brown, striped with pinkish seasoning. They smell as tempting as anything here ever has but can't deflect me from my course.

"Why are you here? Is there news about Boreal?" I mumble. The crew should be out tonight, enjoying the excitement of the trawler, catching the sense of the community while drinking fermented seaweed juice and sun beer—asking people questions and trying to gather information as they do it. That's the whole reason I'm making a beeline for the ship, hoping to crash and snag a few scant hours of sleep before they return.

"No news. You think I trust you enough to let you roam alone?" That again. If I didn't need the physical support he's offering so much, I'd wrench myself away. Except—it's not just that. I don't know Micah well, but I know him that well. He's here because he was worried about me. Because he caretakes by nature. I glance back toward Etolla's house. She's watching us out the windows. She holds up five fingers.

Not going to happen.

"He came back here. There must be a reason he came back," I mutter, more to myself than to him. "Something that ties Boreal and Aymbe together."

"Hmm," he hums a noncommittal noise that tells me he thinks I'm beyond the point of normal conversation. Fine. I can dismiss him, too.

"I'm going to the ship. You should socialize with your crew. Meet the locals."

"I met the locals at your parents' house."

That was probably enough to put him off locals completely. "They're good people. They've had a hard time since Aymbe. Things like that break some families. They stuck together."

Except for me. He gives me a considering look. I could read something into it if I had all my faculties in order, but I don't, so I just appreciate the way the light show in the ionosphere plays across his high cheekbones. He nudges me away from the busy street and into a calmer side lane, keeping between me and the revelers.

Then, somehow, we're back at the ship. I disentangle myself from him and pat him solicitously on the shoulder. "Thanks, but I'm fine. I'm just going to check on Vuur. Have fun out there."

His mouth opens like he intends to say something, but I flee before he gets the chance. Maybe he'll go join the rest of the crew. I hope he does. I stumble to the sliding door to his bunk. Of all of them, Micah knows my identity. I can't risk sleeping in anyone else's bunk. Vuur flutters happily right at my face and I catch it just at the last moment. I spill my small bag of brass chips on the desk and clamber up to the untouched top bunk, stretching across a foam mattress that feels like a warm embrace. The lizard ignores the flakes and curls its little body within the cradle of mine.

I'm asleep before my head hits the pillow.

. . . . .

I wake on a spaceship, pressed behind a wall panel, a vent near my head. It's dark. Cold. I'm drowning in the kind of long terror that settles in until your bones become brittle as ice. Footsteps drag on the other side of the wall. Limping ones—somehow all the more terrifying than if they were fit and spry. I hear the sawing of breath. I smell nothing at all. Feel a tap-tapping reverberate down the smooth metal of the wall as he plumbs it like a depth gage. Testing to see if the bulkhead is as hollow as it should be.

It isn't.

(This is not real. I didn't wake up this early in real life. I woke up when he yanked me out of my hiding spot. I woke to stark white light and a toothless mouth leering down at me. I woke to the terror. I didn't sink into it slowly.)

Jump forward.

Dragged by a foot. I kick with the other. Panicked. Ineffectual. Try to grasp a wall. A table. Anything. My fingers wrap around a doorframe. Not a doorframe. An air lock. My hands freeze on it so hard they're stone. Steel. My heart is in my throat. I'm blind to fear and a whole crew of traffickers are watching. Laughing. I'm a joke. A bounty hunter who arrived too late to rescue anyone—after all the slaves were sold. Who had to hide in an air vent to avoid detection because her timing was off. One of the men yanks at my leg. Feels like he's going to pull it off. Another kicks my hand where it grips the air-lock frame. I don't let go. He kicks again. Once more. My fingers don't work right, and I slide right into the air lock.

Jump forward.

The air-lock door is closed. Port full of faces. Horrible laughing faces. The air lock is tiny. Grated floor. Smooth pale walls. Massive sliding hatch that opens into absolutely nothing except a horrible death. Being spaced isn't a particularly painful death. Nor a long one.

It could be considered merciful except for the space between heartbeats when you fully and completely consider the void as you drift into nothing at all. As you become nothing at all. I scream. I beg. I pound on the door.

(I didn't do any of those things. I was frozen in terror. Still in denial. I only scream in the dreams. Because I know what's coming.)

Jump forward.

The hatch slides open at the same instant that I jam my hand into the grated floor, cramming the buckle of my coat sleeve so tightly that even the sudden violent expulsion as the pressure equalizes with nothing at all cannot eject me from the ship.

Cold.

Panic.

Terror.

Nothing. Nothing at all. Everything in me grows empty. The saliva in my mouth effervesces. A rime of frost coats my skin.

My eyes.

My mind.

I am dying. This is what the end feels like. Complete powerlessness. But then, it keeps going. My vision narrows to a pinhole. My brain narrows the same way. Turns in on itself. Folds like Hanshang petal crafts. Erupts like a volcano.

Changes.

(I don't know if this is real. The frost part probably isn't. I lost a lot of this time, whether due to oxygen deprivation or trauma. I don't want that time back. Ever. Some mysteries should remain that way.)

Jump forward.

The hatch to space slides shut, and pressure pumps in so fast it's a new kind of pain. The door to the ship slides open and a lone man enters. The others wandered away. Disinterested with the floating body in their air lock. It's so boring to murder a woman. So dull. He thinks I'm dead. I should be dead. No one lasts that long in the vacuum. It kills you over and over in every possible way. The antithesis to life. When he wrenches at my coat, a layer of ice chips off my face. My nose clears. Air slips inside.

He works my arm out of my coat. His chuckle is spiny enough to cut the rest of the ice from my mind. I have no weapon. No strength. All I have is a moment before he closes that door and spaces me a second time, now that I'm unstuck. Discarding me like trash.

I use his own shoelace to tie his boot to the same grate that I used to hold myself in place. It's a wonder my fingers work well enough to do so. I roll away before he notices, keeping limp and boneless until I bump against the door. He's so busy going through the pockets of my stolen coat that he doesn't notice I'm gone until the hatch closes and I look at him through the same window he used to study me.

Jump forward.

I stagger through the ship to the helm, whole body shaking so hard it may come apart before I reach the helm. Mind shaking. Psyche shaking. The blow that takes the captain in the back of the head is pure luck. I hit him with his own navigation tablet. An asteroid belt shines on the fancy screens above. I drag him out. Seal the helm.

The tablet falls from boneless fingers. I'm about to lose it again. Maybe forever. I won't let them be the ones to dispatch me. When my knees give out, my hand is already poised over the color band that controls the air locks. The safety measures are already stripped everywhere but the helm.

I open the ship to the void of space, and as I fall to the deck, I hear the meaty thud of bodies ricocheting through the hallways as the pressure sucks them into the black.

. . . . .

A hand presses over my mouth and I'm still there. I'm still in the *Iceberg* with the feel of the void all the way down to my atoms and the empty sound of death surrounding me. Still paying the price for trusting a source who swore that Aymbe wasn't dead—that she was on that ship, awaiting rescue. Sold to a higher bidder, which made a sick kind of sense. I don't even realize I'm screaming into the hand until my tongue scrapes at a broad palm. A knife is in my hand before I think about it, arcing toward the dark form hovering above me.

No one will catch me in my sleep again. No one will drag me, vulnerable and stunned, to a horrible fate. No one.

Another hand captures my knife. I hurl myself off the bed at my attacker, tumbling to the floor in a tangle of limbs and sweat. I bite his palm and taste blood when my body crashes down on his own. He grunts and pulls it away. I rear back my leg for a kick, and the light finally plays across the sharp features of his face. The bare arms, wrapped in sturdy muscle.

I'm lying on top of Micah Arora, sleep-fogged brain collapsing like a holo as I stare blankly into dark eyes that see far too much.

■ ■ ■ ■ ■ ■ ■ ■ ■ ■ ■ ■ ■ ■ ■

"What are you doing in here?" I come out of sleep physically turgid but mentally flaccid. As demonstrated by the fact that I'm lying on top of Micah and *those* were the two words that came to mind. My mind can't leave the horror show but my body is focused on the warm form spread beneath me.

"I came in to wake you up. The others are coming back to the ship and you were doing a lot of screaming." The slash of brilliant light coming through the door from the toilet area illuminates half his face in a stark swathe. The priap looks like a painting with the light caressing the angles of his cheek and jaw. I'm also still lying on top of him, chest to chest, my hands pinning his shoulders down, my legs straddling one perfectly proportioned thigh.

My brain plummeting directly to the gutter.

"Also being bitten. You're half-feral." He shakes his hand, the movement tensing muscles throughout his body and, because of our proximity, throughout my own.

"More than half." I shove backward and lurch to my feet, stepping back as far as the tiny room allows. "There's a door. Perhaps you could try knocking before you started shaking me."

"I did knock. You didn't wake up." He's still lying on the floor, levered up on one elbow and studying me with that dark gaze like I'm a bomb about to go off. "I was with you all day. I saw how close to the edge you were. Knew you couldn't have slept more than a moment since we started this whole adventure. It'll kill you, you know. Even with the best stims. Body needs sleep."

I churlishly offer him a hand up off the floor, which he accepts. I let it go as quickly as I can. Not because it's unpleasant. It's entirely too pleasant. His fingers dragging against my palm when he releases me send tingles up my spine. "What fantastic advice. I've never heard it before. Clearly, it's referring to exactly the kind of sleep I get. I sleep fine most of the time."

Lie.

He cocks his head like he's trying to translate a foreign language. "What was that all about?"

I don't respond. My nightmares are none of his business.

He continues, as though I might be confused. "It happened the last time you were here, too. The screaming."

"Don't worry about it," I jab back. "It won't be a problem anytime soon. I slept."

He shakes his head, a dry chuckle escaping. "It's like you're a whole woman sewn from red flags. Fascinating."

I resist a witty retort—mostly because I don't actually have one. Vuur is still curled into a warm little ball on the trunk at the foot of the bed, little rib cage moving up and down like a steady bellows. Little traitor didn't even defend me. I should have gone to the inn, but some part of me felt like the ship—this bunk in particular—was safe. "What time is it?"

"It's still not quite morning—firstday morning. The rest of the crew lost track of time at the drum concert on the stern. They forgot nights are short here." He follows me out of the ship and into the bright spark of dawn. We leave the little lizard to its sleep. Micah holds up a palm to block the rising sunlight. "Why does the time matter? Shouldn't we wait to update the crew before they hit the bunks?"

My brain is finally working for the first time in days, and I know where to start. "No time to wait. I have a lead. Last night, as you know because I'm sure you were lurking outside to make sure I wasn't buddying up with kidnappers or something, I spoke to the local mystic. She indicated that there may have been a witness just before Aymbe's abduction."

Micah catches my arm and pulls me backward. "And no one questioned him? What if she wasn't even taken by the Abductor and this man did some sort of copycat thing?"

I look pointedly at his hand on my sleeve and back at him until he releases my arm. Boundaries. I need to keep boundaries between us. No matter the fact that I could almost pretend he's offering emotional support. I shouldn't want that. Not from him. "I did question him. Both quietly when she was kidnapped and later when the rest of the constables became involved. Enderson Tally had a solid alibi. And there's no way he could have gone halfway around the planet to drop a buoy. He was a fool—probably still is—but he wasn't a killer."

"That's his name? Tally?"

"Yes. Did you get the updated schematics of the ship?"

He waves my own datapad in front of me. I snatch it from his hands and enter Tally's name. We updated our systems to the most recent local maps yesterday. A little light shows where Tally lives. I blink. That's interesting.

Somehow Tally found himself in the large vista-homes in the steady stern of the ship. From the picture Aymbe painted of him, I thought he'd still be in a drunken stinky heap in his parents' home—which was far from the prestigious stern.

The *mayor* lives in the stern.

I briskly stride across the deck of the trawler, enjoying the buoyancy of the gravity. Each step devours the deck beneath me and my coat flares very dramatically. I step extra vigorously because I enjoy the drama. It isn't quite so humid this morning, so I feel mostly powerful instead of mostly sweaty. The water moves smoothly and sparkles dance on its surface.

I also feel fully awake, despite the shaky-pale sensation I get after I dream.

Micah strides at my side, staring mistrustingly over the side at the quick-moving water in the canals. "So what's your plan?"

"I'm going to pump him for every piece of information he has and then—and I'm just tossing around the idea—maybe punch him a few times in the ear for funzies because he was creeping on my cousin."

Homes get bigger near the stern. Some even have something resembling landscaping. Trees and flowering vines. One even has a small pool containing tiny ornamental serpents. Very strange in a ship that floats above leviathan serpents. Maybe aspirational for the little ones: someday they, too, can terrorize us in storms. If I ever find a planet with gigantic flying lizards, I'll have to take Vuur. It would be so excited to see its cousins.

We approach one spectacular home. It's painted a warm white tone and it has a yellow-tiled roof. Vibrant dark-pink blooms climb the side, and a half moat of a canal separates it from the rest of the homes in the region. There's a frame of polished sea glass around the carved wood of the double-wide front door. It smells like flowers and money.

Also a little bit like the fertilizers necessary to keep all this plant life thriving on a boat. Mostly flowers and money, though. Money always smells a little bit like shit. It takes dirty hands to hoard it, after all.

I knock on the door. I usually like to kick doors in—take people by surprise. But this particular door looks like it's constructed too well for me to get very far. Micah stands slightly behind me, leaning back to gaze at the round porthole-styled window on the second floor above us.

A man opens the door. His Pierce-blond hair is combed back from his face in a clean sweep and the dark tan of his skin matches that of most denizens of the trawler. His face is broad, his nose is straight, and a narrow line of script is tattooed under his ear. I can't read it from where I stand. Enderson Tally, in the very clean and well-maintained flesh.

"Can I—Bella Khaw! I haven't seen you in ages." A broad smile spreads across his face. I wince at yet another person using the name I've tried to bury. It reminds me of failure. Bad move, stalker.

"Hello, Enderson." I do my best to keep cool and professional. I'm impatient. Even more knowing that Enderson knew something and didn't bother to tell anyone. "You probably know exactly why I'm here."

He blinks, confused. "Not really."

"You saw Aymbe with someone. After you stalked her for the better part of a standard year, always breathing down her throat. If you hadn't been passed out in an obvious heap later that night, right in front of Stinky Stu's Serpent Shack—so close everyone had to step over your body to get their food—I'd have thought you did it yourself. You didn't see Wetzacohl. We all know that by now—he was in lockup. Why did you say it was him?"

Sometimes I just dive into it. When you ease someone into an interrogation, you give them time to erect their defenses. It's always better when someone is defenseless. The entryway behind him has a mosaic sea-glass floor in the shape of a compass. In the center of the star, a narrow delicate table supports a sculpture of a wave caught in the wind—also made of sea glass. It's an entryway that screams wealth and taste.

Tally blinks, like he's stunned, and then a flush works its way from his neck to his cheeks. I brace myself, expecting a blow. Micah shifts his weight behind me. But nothing happens, and instead of lashing out, Tally's head drops. This is shame, not fury. He *should* be ashamed. It's all I can do not to reach down his throat and yank the truth out. If his guts come with it, well, mistakes happen.

"I—I'm not proud of who I was back then." Tally's voice is soft.

"I was deeply unhappy and your cousin, well, she didn't make it any easier for me. I wasn't interested in her—not like you think."

I *know* he followed Aymbe. She told me about it. She was terrified and she was certain it was him. I even caught him watching her sometimes.

I open my mouth to press the issue further, but Micah interrupts me. "We're not here about that. We're here because you saw something, and you didn't tell anyone."

Okay, that's more critical than belaboring Tally's history.

Tally stares at Micah like he just noticed he's here. "It *was* Teramo Wetzacohl. She smiled when he came over. Like she knew him. Why would she smile like that if it wasn't him?"

I don't know why she'd smile. Maybe because she was a seventeen-year-old who saw an attractive boy. Maybe the sun was in her eyes, and she made the same mistake that Tally had. Maybe she was practicing the deadly efficacy of her grin. She practiced it a lot. I do know, for sure, that Wetzacohl wasn't there that day on account of how I saw him being arrested myself. He managed to take off his pants while on a gantry and threw them into the sea before the connies could coax him down.

A serpent ate the pants. Aymbe never had the best taste in men.

"Describe him for me. In detail." I prepare to enter the information in the datapad. Tally brushes his fingers through his hair, realizes that he's still holding the door open, and gestures for me and Micah to enter the glass-floored room. Micah gazes around the room with unveiled interest.

"He was big. Taller than the first spar." Tally stops as though height is the only descriptor needed.

"Hair color? Skin color? Interesting features?" I nudge him.

Micah picks up my list and adds a few items of his own. "Did you hear his voice? Was there an accent?"

Tally yammers off a description that sounds nothing at all like Teramo Wetzacohl beyond height if any thought is put into it.

"Was there *anything* that was unique about him? Style of cloth-ing? Dye used to color his clothes? Tattoos?"

Interface tattooing in the trawlertown tends to utilize solar-powered inks, because sunlight is never in short supply. People from space stations have movement-generated energy ink, which is funny because space stations are so confined that sometimes people don't move as much as they need to and you'll see them outside a locked door, frantically waving their arm until they get enough power to open it.

I've seen all kinds of ink. They all say something about where you're from. My own original glossy-black solar-ink interface tat-toos now have gold threads running through them, allowing me solar and motion-generated power. The Burren doesn't offer much in the way of sunlight.

"Yes . . . I didn't think of it. His tattoos looked greenish. Like seaweed, that stuff we have to drag out of the nets near that island chain with the rock that looks like a needle."

Green means solar powered but photosynthesizing solar power. Not common because most people don't like plant blood injected under their skin. It also sometimes gives you a particularly herbal smell in the rain and tends to die if you don't eat the exact right diet.

Which is a weird choice for a serial kidnapper because people who smell like wilting greens draw attention. It's not that I don't trust Tally—although I absolutely don't trust Tally. It's that I don't understand why he'd come up with that particular lie. Which means, improbable as it is, it might actually be the truth.

"Dark green or pale?" Micah interjects with the question, and I glance over, gaze skittering off his intent face. It's a good face. And a good question, although I've only ever seen dark-green ink.

Tally taps his chin with one well-manicured finger. "Kind of me-dium green? Like, when it's not quite dead yet. Halfway-dead green."

I'm sure the color is a huge selling point. Micah isn't giving away any significance that might have at the moment, so I continue my follow-up questioning. "She reacted like she knew him. Did she realize her mistake? Did they go anywhere?"

"I wasn't watching her like a stalker or something. She was trouble. That girl was always trouble. I helped her in school and she spread rumors about me and then blackmailed me with more rumors if I didn't give her test answers. I was worried about her. I thought she was going to get someone hurt."

Another man enters behind him, a toddler-aged girl in his arms, and presses a kiss into Enderson's cheek. Armor Gillis, the mayor's son and, apparently, Enderson's husband. That explains the house. Armor's hair is also blond but is long, gathered in a loose knot on top of his head. He has one of those faces that is instantly likable. A streak of what looks like batter under his high cheekbone adds to the approachable affect. He's also exceptionally tall—which perhaps explains why Tally was so struck by the height of the man he saw with Aymbe—Tally has a type.

A type that, upon new information, doesn't seem to include my cousin. Maybe he was young and confused and wasn't handling things well. Maybe I've judged him too harshly for too long.

Armor glances over at us and dismisses us as beneath his notice immediately. Rightfully so. "Enders, Myllie wants her firstday soup the special way you make it. Apparently I don't know how to stir it right."

"Big swoops." Myllie waves her small arm back and forth, miming a spoon.

Enderson scoops Myllie from his husband's arms and she chuckles in joy. Everything about this is wrong. I expected to find him half-drunk in some flophouse, abandoned by all. Instead, he's in a loving family, in a beautiful house. A mature and functioning member of the trawler society.

Probably more mature and functioning than I am, truth be told.

He bounces Myllie slightly and turns his attention back to me. "She was a little startled when she saw him up close. But it didn't last long and then she did that smile thing she used to do. You know the one, where it was like her whole body did it and she played around with her hair?"

Aymbe called that her "mantrap" smile. They all thought it was naturally inspired by their own amazingness, but she spent years practicing it in front of a mirror to maximize its effect. Every single guy who experienced that smile turned to jelly. It was very effective, if also very manipulative. She was a vain kid, but who amongst us isn't? Most of us get the opportunity to grow out of it.

"Anyway, he gestured to something over the side of the boat. I couldn't see what exactly. It was far away. Aymbe said something about a necklace."

Necklace. We were close to a chain of islands that is properly named Merias' Teeth. A moniker that Aymbe and I always found horrifying. Back when she was a little girl and I babysat for her, we called it the Necklace and named each island after a specific stone. "Did she say anything about a particular stone?"

"That she wanted some guy to buy her? I don't know. She noticed me then and called me a—" He glances at his daughter and then covers her ears for a moment. "—fucking weirdo, so I went back inside."

That tracks. It might sound foolhardy, but I believe that Aymbe might have been just naive enough to leave with a handsome stranger if she thought it was her ticket off the trawler. She always thought she was meant for bigger things than this place and she was impatient to get there.

The Necklace. Her body was found far from there, and to my knowledge, no one investigated that particular island chain. It's a place to start.

After all this time, a new lead is tantalizing.

"Thank you." I'm far more polite than I intended to be upon

entering, because I'm still off-balance by Tally's dream life. "We'll leave you to firstday."

Enderson bounces his daughter slightly. "Good, because we need to get Myllie fed and ready for the Pierce shuttle. Today is vaccination day."

Micah precedes me to the door and Tally follows us. "Bella, one more thing. You said that I didn't tell anyone. I did. I told Mo Anaspian the first day we were informed Aymbe was missing."

It's almost like Mo is awful at his job. I never thought he'd deliberately withhold evidence. Not about something like this. Maybe he decided it was too late to do any good. Maybe he investigated in secret.

Maybe he didn't do a thing. It's too late to call him on it, and I doubt there's any proof. I wave a farewell to Tally.

Micah waits until we're out canal-side before speaking. "You seemed surprised by him."

I sneak a picture of Tally's beautiful home for Madrigal. "I am. I didn't personally know him back in the day. He's younger. He was a small-time troublemaker. Lots of public intoxication. General creepy vibe."

"You sound like a constable." It's clear from Micah's tone that it's an insult.

"I was one." The sun reflects brilliantly on the lapping wavelets of the sea around us. I shake my head, bewildered by everything I just saw. "But really, I was an older cousin. Aymbe said he was stalking her. That he was in love with her. That he wouldn't take no for an answer."

"Some young men are like that," Micah says noncommittally, shading his eyes with a hand as he studies the horizon. I like that he's not prodding, not pushing his own opinion on me. I suddenly have a vivid flash of what it would be like to be on a traditional hunt with him. Chasing a normal scofflaw without the specter of Pierce floating over my shoulders.

We'd make a good team. He doesn't try to force himself in when I'm questioning someone. Doesn't imply he knows best.

Maybe that just means that *he* makes for a good team and also I'm here.

I get to the root of the issue. "Does the man you just met seem like he was like that? He was a mess, for sure, but I don't see any malevolence there. Aymbe was frightened, but that doesn't mean there was an actual threat. Maybe he saw that she was trouble—she was—and kept an eye on her like he said. She was making his life difficult. And then when he watched her, she saw something else in it."

"He said she was trying to blackmail him, though, no? For test answers. Does that sound like her?"

I'm immediately defensive. I wouldn't let someone speak like that about Aymbe when she was alive, much less now. But she wasn't *just* an innocent girl. She was a person. Whole and tarnished like the rest of us. "I don't think so. I believe she tried to get answers from him, but not that she blackmailed him. Maybe he misinterpreted her. Maybe she threatened him because he made her uneasy and he took it as blackmail."

"People are complicated."

That they are. "We got a clue, though. The Necklace is a nearby island chain. We might not know which island, but we have a new location to search. If he took Aymbe there, he might have taken Boreal."

"Then it's a good day." Micah bumps his shoulder against mine. It could be a mistake, but I've never seen Micah move with less than extreme grace. I bump his shoulder back.

Supportive gestures with plausible deniability. Exactly my sort of thing.

CHAPTER 10

■ ■ ■ ■ ■ ■ ■ ■ ■ ■ ■ ■ ■ ■

"He shouldn't be here," I mutter under my breath to Micah as Arcadio strides past us to stand in the prow of the rented boat, nearly vibrating with his desire to increase our speed. "It all gets fucked when the family is there."

"Aren't you here hunting your *cousin's* killer?" The medic isn't taking me seriously, which wouldn't be a change. He's presently distracted by the looming storm clouds sweeping over the chain of islands in front of us. Another excellent point I made was how we absolutely should not be making this trip this late on secondday because if we all drown in the storm, no one would be rescuing Boreal Escajeda and her cheap-ass mother would be forced to pay for her.

"How do you think I know that it gets fucked?" Everyone assumes they know more about my planet than I do—an unsurprising state of affairs given the crew of the *Calamity*. Their intentions are good. They could maybe do with a touch less self-confidence.

I stare toward the horizon for the first sign of the islands. Merias' Teeth is a beautiful island chain, studded with waterfalls and glossy green or pale-yellow leaves, deserving of a more beautiful name than it has. Lumpy rocks create formations that tower over the water and offer both expansive views and great surfaces to dive from. School kids traditionally sneak off to the islands whenever the trawlertown pulls within range and pretend they're land-bound instead of aquatic. Living on the earth seems strange and exotic. The stillness of the soil almost dizzying.

As someone who now lives beneath the surface of a planet, it's lost some of its charm.

I stopped going to the Necklace at some point during my adolescence, but I was a supervisor on one of Aymbe's school trips there, so I know which islands she liked. Of course, back then she liked making sand towers and flower crowns. I had no idea that apparently teenaged Aymbe was saving the verdant islands for scenic boffing retreats. Makes sense. Privacy is hard to come by in the trawlertown.

Aymbe was—let's face it—a little heedless when it came to sexual decisions, but I never knew her to be dumb. She started young, like a lot of people do on the trawler. So she meets this tall man. She likes the cut of his clothes or the way his breath smells or just the fact that she's never seen him before and invites him off the trawler thinking he's her chance to leave this planet for good. The Abyssal Abductor can't believe his luck. His target is abducting *herself*. It would explain why he chose her, of everyone. He didn't. She chose him.

The real question is if they lingered in the Necklace and if things took a turn while they were there. If so, maybe Aymbe left a sign—something to indicate what happened to her and where she would be taken next. I don't know for sure which island she would choose for romance, but my personal preference would have been the one we called Opal. Its beaches glow with iridescent white sand and bowers of tall thin trees shade grottos lined with bright-pink flowered ground cover. The rented boat is autopiloting its way to Opal.

Micah stands, unexpectedly clumsy as the boat rolls beneath his feet. He meanders up to the prow to stand beside Arcadio, awkwardly patting the other man's shoulder in that method of silent communion that men share on occasion. Silence is my preferred sort of communion as well, but everyone assumes I want to talk things out. Temper takes the opportunity to sit next to me, looking a bit green in the face when we hit a particularly choppy swell.

I don't know what to think about Tally's revelations. He's hardly a trustworthy source—despite being married to the mayor's son—but at the same time, a part of me believes that Mo might have had information he chose not to share. I just don't know why he *wouldn't* share it. He might hate me, but that shouldn't trickle down to the rest of my family. They deserved any news they could get.

"I could have scouted the area on my own," I remind Temper, because I find it difficult to miss an opportunity for a jibe. I squint over the water. The familiar sensation of sun-resistant mud cracking on my face is a memory I never intended to revisit. "Now I'm going to have to spend half my time keeping everyone alive and I won't be focused on the task at hand."

"Perhaps. If it was just scouting. But we might need to perform an immediate rescue and *that* you might not be able to do alone." A vibration buzzes against my hip, urgent and aggressive. None of my coms are set to that frequency. I reach down and my hand brushes the outline of the special Pierce coms, tucked in the side cargo pocket of my pants.

I don't know why they're contacting me, but it can't be for any good reason. My clock hasn't run out. I still have about eight standard days. I ignore it. A cold sweat blooms under my coat, nerves ratcheting even higher. I can't see a way out of this mess.

Temper seems to be a normal person—or at least as normal as someone from a Family could be—so I decide to take a risk and try to get an explanation for something that's been bothering me. "I get that you're invested. That no one cares more than her family. But Estella seems to be driven more by pride than desire to get Boreal back safely. If she wanted her back safely, she would just pay the ransom and not risk this hunt alerting the Abductor."

Temper narrows her eyes, and her jaw goes a little hard. Perhaps it was a bad choice speaking bluntly. "Because things with a Family are never that easy. This actually being the Abductor is the best-case scenario."

I blink, shocked. And a little offended. She does understand that the Abductor is fully capable of killing children, right?

Temper continues, "Estella's models indicate a not-insignificant probability that it could be someone else, someone manipulating the situation to put the Escajeda Family under their thumb. If so, they'll collect the ransom happily but refuse to hand Boreal over. They realize they have her on the hook. Estella has proven that she is desperate and they can extort almost anything from her. The secret to phydium, access to the Family's vaults, political favoritism. A blind eye turned for activities like the Nakatomi Family was trying on Herschel. I'm sure you saw that in the feeds. In showing that she'd do anything to save her daughter, she could sacrifice millions of lives of her Family's vassals."

My head spins. I remember the thin lines of tension in Estella's impassive face. The white jut of her knuckles. I thought her cold, but more likely, she was frozen. Angry and terrified and sick with the danger. "Surely that sort of thing doesn't happen these days."

Temper all but rolls her eyes. "Of course it does. Family children are incredibly vulnerable to kidnapping. We're trained in how to handle being kidnapped and also in how to handle retrieval. It's never simple and everyone wants a lever they can use to control a Family.

"It's not that they don't care. They care deeply. It's that, for a Family, showing that you care can be a death sentence."

The buzzing against my leg finally stops. I'm quiet, digesting what she's said, reevaluating the situation. My stomach tightens. No wonder the crew is on edge. The stakes are even higher than I thought.

What if it's Pierce?

A silly thought. Why would my personal enemy also go after Boreal? There are lots of Families or not-quite Families out there who'd love to manipulate the Escajedas.

But Pierce are at the top of the list. They're ruthless and

opportunistic, and when I told Carmichael where we were going, he didn't blink.

I nod my head in Arcadio's direction. "How come he hasn't talked to me after that first argument? There some sort of issue that I don't know about?"

She shakes her head, a shadow falling over her face. "I'm sure any other time you wouldn't be able to get him to shut up. I certainly can't. Unfortunately, right now, you remind him of himself. Someone who lost a loved one. He dealt with something similar recently—but at least then it was an adult in danger. Family is everything to him. His sister is one of the most important people in his world after he left his Family. She didn't cut him off like the rest of them did. Don't ask me why—I certainly don't understand how functional sibling relationships work."

The boat lurches under us. As we spoke, the waves picked up energy, white-licked and growing as the storm eats the sky. I grimace. "That's going to be a problem."

"They let us charter the boat. They wouldn't have if they thought it was risky." She taps the back of her life vest where a very small single-person-sized inflatable vessel is carefully folded. It's a security measure. Judging by the state of the rental office, my guess is that only one in three of the vests will actually inflate if emergency strikes.

I snort. "They don't care if you drown. You're from off-planet. Something happens to us, they'll exact payment from Caro and Itzel, buy a better boat to rent. If they can't pay, they'll confiscate your ship."

"My whole ship for this piece of shit?"

"I know. It's a terrible deal for the boat vendor."

She snickers, so I guess I hit the sweet spot of insulting someone's ship without insulting them personally. Because we can't have one nice moment without an interruption, the ship shoots nose-first into a trough between waves and Temper turns an even deeper green color and throws a hand over her mouth. I grab a bucket for her and leave her tucked inside the cabin as the rain starts to hit the deck in sheets. I remove the coms from my ear and change its setting to waterproof. This type of device doesn't function while fully immersed or drenched, but it can at least be made watertight and activated again later. Arcadio and Micah are still up in the prow, wind shoving their hair back as they perch at the most dangerous portion of the ship with no idea that they're one bad wave from tumbling into the ocean.

People who are unused to the sea are always cavalier to its dangers. With a groan, I push my way forward as the boat tips and tilts and the two of them finally realize that their location has become perilous. Water pours over the deck where the waves overrun the rails. The rentals from the trawlertown all have autopilot and equalization control that should make it as safe as possible to ride out any storm, but that's assuming everyone is tucked away belowdecks.

"You need to get inside the cabin," I scream into the wind.

Arcadio tilts his head and Micah taps his ear to tell me they can't hear me. I emphatically gesture to the cabin, and they finally get the message and start forward until a wave pushes us directly into another trough and then continues to push until the boat is flipped nearly on its side.

I lock my feet and capture the rail out of old habit. Arcadio and Micah have nothing to grab.

Micah reaches for Arcadio, captures the back of his coveralls, and both scramble for something to keep them on board. Micah clasps a loose line and holds them stable enough for Arcadio to reach the rail.

I breathe a sigh of relief.

Too soon.

The line in Micah's grip snaps. A wave crashes over the deck.

When the wave clears, there is no more Micah.

I'm over the edge after him before I think about doing it, slic-ing into the water in an efficient dive as a new wave crests and topples the ship in the other direction. The sea churns around me, froth and cold and thick mineral taste so overwhelming that I'm disoriented until I pop to the surface and scan the waves for a sign of the medic. The fast-changing topography of waves does not aid the search until I see a winking red light in the distance. His safety vest.

I carefully stroke through the water, letting the storm do most of the pushing until I finally collide with Micah's flailing body. He elbows me in the cheek, and I try to get a better angle as he thrashes, my face throbbing.

It's cold. That tells me that we're still in the deep water, which means that the storm, frustrating as it is, is not our primary problem.

"Stop struggling!" I yell into Micah's ear.

He does not stop struggling. I take my only option and wrap myself around him tight as a cleated line, my legs twining with his and my arms hugging his broad torso.

"You look like bait." I try again, clamping down on his limbs with all the strength left in my body and trusting our vests to do their jobs. A wave sweeps us up and then back down. The rain beats on my face.

"Taking your opportunity to kill me?" Micah snarls, face so close to my own that I can make out every shadow in the darkness of his eyes. Tension makes his features sharp. His eyes stare right through me. "Were you biding your time, waiting to betray us?"

I open my mouth to reply, a wave tries to drown us, and then I spit and cough for a few moments as I try to get that awful briny taste out of my mouth. "Why would I try to kill you? I'm trying to save your life, you priap."

He attempts to reply. One of his arms slips free of my grasp and he captures the back of my vest and starts yanking. Except all that tugging activates the small raft attached to my vest, which deploys and miraculously does inflate. It also catches the wind and flies away from us into the storm, tumbling end over end atop the waves.

Well, shit.

I cling all the harder and speak over him. "You've seen the serpents off the side of the trawler. Some grow huge and all of them hunt based on vibrations. You spasming around like this is basically ringing a dinner bell for a leviathan serpent. Hold *still*."

He blinks, eyes finally going clear. I wonder whom he saw a few moments ago. What memory he was battling. Because I am a polite person, haunted by memories of my own, I don't ask.

"Is the boat coming for us?" He spits out a mouthful of water and stops trying to drag me off of him.

I shake my head. Boat rescues during a storm aren't a part of the programming. The rudimentary AI of the vessel won't risk its current passengers for us by deviating from its course and they can't override its path until they reach their destination. There is usually a rescue drone attached to the hull of the ship, but I'm guessing this one was damaged or nonexistent because we'd have seen it by now. "That's what the safety vests are for. Thanks for that, by the way. Stop *moving*!"

"Why?"

Must he have a question for everything? In the heat of the moment? "You are thrashing around like bait. The leviathan serpents get frisky in storms and tuckered out after. Would you rather face a frisky or a tuckered sea snake?"

"I'd rather not face a sea snake at all."

Now that he isn't wriggling around like a nice juicy piece of prey, I disentangle myself and activate the safety vessel in his vest. It inflates into a sleek body-sized oblong canoe that wraps around him until his body is half-cocooned safely above the water. My assumption was off. Both of the vests kind of worked. Except mine is probably floating somewhere far far away by now.

I guess I'm the bait now.

Micah's hand wraps around my arm. "We can share."

"They're only made for one person. It might not be seaworthy for both of us."

His jaw hardens. "Do you think I'm the kind of man who floats in comfort while someone else is vulnerable?"

I barely know what kind of man he is. I'm not the kind of woman who sinks someone's vessel just so she can be safe.

"I'll be fine."

"Get in the fucking canoe."

Impatient. Grouchy. That's the kind *he* is. I wriggle over the edge and the whole thing sinks until each wave nearly swamps us. At least the movements as we frantically bail seawater out are masked by the flimsy vessel around us.

Micah glances at me, hair soaked and flat to his head, one rogue curl stuck to his forehead. The glow of his banishment tattoo reflects on nearby water droplets. "Maybe both of us together won't fit down a serpent's gullet."

"They have very large gullets." For a long while, all we can do is bail our tiny craft as the rain beats down and the waves do their best to drown us. It's not altogether unpleasant, perhaps because I've found the one circumstance that forces him to keep his mouth shut and stop asking me questions I can't answer.

A wave tilts the small boat up, tumbling me toward Micah. He catches me before we collide, hands tightening around my shoulder, my ribs, pulling me back into the present. Pulling my mind directly back to the sewer, because his grip on my skin, the heat of his hands, the strength in his arms all dial my brain to a very specific frequency and it certainly isn't survival mode. Maybe repopulation mode.

Not five-children repopulation. No matter what Etolla thinks. At least I made the smart decision to leave Vuur in the safety of the *Calamity* with Caro and Itzel. It's looking more and more likely that I don't have the lifestyle for a high-maintenance pet, much less children. Maybe a lichen of some sort.

I force my mind to our current situation.

Storms on Ginsidik are violent but fast-moving. The water has smoothed somewhat and the sky, while still ominous, is dribbling rain instead of spraying it like a throat-cut murder victim. The islands are visible in the distance once again, small humps against a flat-gray sky. Sapphire is taller and pokier than some of the others and I can make out its familiar spike-front face, closest to us.

If Aymbe didn't take him to Opal, she would choose Sapphire. Two islands away from Opal and much smaller. If Merias' Teeth were real, Sapphire would be a canine to Opal's molar. Sapphire has a chain of waterfalls with caves behind the curtains of water. Great for privacy, but if you're the only people on the island, privacy isn't really an issue, and the caves are damp and clammy. Still, it's a showier island, especially at night, and Aymbe liked showy.

"What is your appetite for risk?" I want to explore Sapphire, but he might not be up for it. Even if we wash ashore there, the safe prudent plan is to hunker down, be quiet, and wait for backup.

He raises an eyebrow and his breath fans warm across my face. "Are you challenging me?"

The response surprises a chuckle from me. "No. You'll know what a challenge looks like because I'll have already won. This is just a question."

He bares his teeth in a smile. "So certain."

I posit my theory about Sapphire, doing my best to be scrupulously honest. Seeing as I've been scrupulously honest about nearly *nothing* since I met him, this marks a first in our relationship.

"We should investigate," he agrees immediately, twisting his neck to observe the island over his shoulder. "Also, I don't fancy spending any longer in serpent-water than I need to."

A man after my own heart. I really don't want to betray him. The Pierce coms weighs down the pocket of my pants like an anchor. I want to be the sort of person this man *trusts*, and I don't even fully know why.

We carefully activate the small motor at the back of the craft. Before, with the waves as they were, we couldn't move without taking on more water. As it is, we're taking on water but slowly enough that we can get rid of it almost as quickly as it flows in. As we creep forward, I slide the large dagger strapped to my thigh from its sheath and hold it ready.

When the water lightens, I know we've entered the shallows. Which means the leviathan serpents are no longer a concern. The smaller yet still predatory breeds are present but at least we won't be swallowed whole.

I don't know if that's better.

A large curved shape pokes the side of the boat, denting it inward into my knee, and the breath sticks in my throat. "Stop moving."

"But we're— What the fuck is that?" He freezes, arms and legs braced within the canoe, tension bracketing his mouth. We continue to creep forward as the motor tries to push an overweighted craft through the water.

"We have a curious serpent. Moderate sized but it could take a limb."

"This is objectively the worst planet we've ever been to. What kind of people float above giant hungry serpents? This explains everything about you."

"I know that's not true. The last planet I saw you on was riddled with iffy soil, lunatics, and was, when you left, in the act of exploding. That's far worse than this."

"Wrong. There were no snakes. I'll take exploding over snakes any day."

I absorb that in silence as the snake continues its slow exploration of our incredibly fragile vessel. One particularly aggressive bump lifts us half out of the water. Shit. Shit shit shit shit. It should be going away by now. We haven't wiggled. It hasn't bitten. Which means it's feeling playful, which is the next worst snake emotion after hungry and frisky.

Honestly, they're all bad.

Sleepy is probably okay.

"It's not getting bored." He grits it out through clenched teeth.

"Noticed that, did you?" It batters away at the boat between us, slowly creating a weak point, a folding point. Scales scrape against the hull. My stomach turns and my fingers clench in fabric that I realize too late is Micah's sleeve. It's the only way to keep them from shaking. "It's getting more aggressive."

I hand Micah my knife and, slowly and carefully—ever so carefully—dredge a small multipurpose sensor-scanner from my coat. I can live without this tool. It has its uses, but we don't have a specific chemical to target. I brought it to be prepared. Sometimes, prepared means serpent food.

I release my white-knuckled grip on Micah's sleeve and fiddle with the settings on the sensor, triggering an extended scanning function that should release slight sonic vibrations. "Hold the boat as still as you can." I pause, search for some manners, which are important even in a situation where a sea snake is trying to decide if you're a toy or a meal. "Please."

Shockingly, he doesn't ask why or argue, he just braces his arms around me again as I reach back and throw the scanner as hard as I can in the opposite direction of Sapphire. The water inside the boat laps loudly against my shins with the effort and a razor-swipe of fins scrapes the hull again. I don't whimper.

Barely.

I imagine the serpent beneath us, enticed by the sudden movement, mouth widening, long trifurcated tongue extended to feel the waves of motion coming from my body. Every breath I take reverberating through its senses. Its fangs scissoring forward, powerful body twisting in the water.

The scanner splashes down in the distance, hitting like a rock, and a jet of water disrupts our vessel as the serpent undulates itself away toward the bait. I glance up and back: the rocky sand beach is within view. We aren't that far. Maybe close enough.

"Move. Now. While it's distracted." I mean to say it urgently with some sense of authority, but the words come out breathy and half-panicked. We crank the engine, throwing caution to the water that pours over the sides of the canoe. Fuckity fuck fuck.

We only need to be faster than the snake. If it gets shallow enough, it can't come at us from below. My heart hammers in my ears, chest tight and wild. It doesn't calm until the soft susurration of sand pushes against the bottom of the boat—if one can even still call it a boat at this point—and I crawl up and over the edge, on to the beach of Sapphire, Micah beside me. The muddy wet sand feels as welcome as the soft wood planks of the deck of the trawler.

"I hope your Abyssal Abductor isn't here," Micah mutters, long fingers curled in the sand. "If he is, he can have me. I'm useless."

I laugh as he flops on his back and stares at the sky, water lapping at his feet. Then I snap my mouth shut and lay beside him, trying as hard as I can to keep a wall between us, to keep from liking him.

Hairline cracks fracture the surface of the wall as fast as I can build it.

CHAPTER 11

Sapphire is every bit as scenic and romantic as I remember. An ideal spot for a tryst, if that was Aymbe's mindset on the date she met her kidnapper. She was a girly girl. She liked pretty things. When she was very young, she'd force us all to have fake cocktail parties where we dressed in our best attire and played music in the living room of my grandparents' house. The cocktails were all water with various dyes, but even then, her heady childish charisma could make you feel drunk. As she got older, she realized that charisma could be used to get things of greater value than colored water. Horrible to think that she used it to ensnare her own killer.

Sapphire may be a great spot for a tryst but it's a less-than-ideal spot to lead an exhausted, irritating, and yet somehow still compelling medic. I'm trying to *avoid* an idyllic tryst. The soft heavy scent of flowers and the driving sound of waves is far too stimulating on the senses.

As though Micah wasn't stimulating enough to my senses.

As soon as we're free of the water, I activate my coms and slip it back into my ear. I assume Micah's is ruined because he didn't plan to be hurled into the sea, so he didn't activate waterproof mode. As I wait for the call to connect, I capture a few photos for Madrigal. She likes a pretty island. Who doesn't?

I also take a sneaky picture of Micah. What? She likes an attractive man, too.

We're close enough to the other island that I'm hoping the coms' local functions still operate, because as scrambled as the ionosphere is, there's no chance the signal will hit a satellite. And there

are satellites orbiting Ginsidik. Hyperpowerful Pierce ones. Probably for the connies to use in case of emergency.

"Cyn Khaw to the crew of the *Calamity*. Micah and I are alive
and unharmed, washed up on the shore of the tall pointy island
to your south."

The response is immediate. "Took you long enough. I'd feel a
lot better about that if I heard my medic. Put Micah on."

As though I hurled myself off the boat in the midst of the storm
because I couldn't pass up the opportunity to murder him. This is
a very suspicious crew. "Micah, they think I killed you. Can you
say something reassuring near my ear?"

"She tried really hard to drown me, but I fended her off, Captain." His breath brushes against my cheek as he speaks. Helpful.
Very helpful.

"If that's the kind of thanks I get, next time I won't heroically
leap from a perfectly safe ship and keep the serpents from eating
your good parts first," I mutter, wringing out my clothes as well as
I'm able.

"So you think my parts are good." The flash of white teeth
transforms his face from what I would classify as "brimming with
character" into "strikingly handsome." I don't like the new classi-
fication. It's dangerous.

"Doesn't sound like he's under duress. Last time I heard him
under duress, he threatened to sew someone's gonads to the side
of their head like earrings." Temper mutters something to Arcadio
and then returns to me. "Do you need backup? I don't fancy repro-
gramming that ancient boat during the night and splitting up will
allow us to cover more ground."

"No need for backup," I say, before I remind myself that the
question was if I *need* backup, not if I want it. Answer's the same,
though. "I don't think the Abductor would normally reuse a location, although everything he's doing with Boreal is a departure
from his pattern. While we know he's capable of extraordinary

violence, the fact that he's never taken on an adult means that two-person teams should be sufficient to handle him on the very slim chance we encounter him unexpectedly. Look for something out of place. Letters carved in the trunk of a tree, an ancient campsite."

I see the expression on Micah's face and clarify for Temper, "Not initials-inside-hearts kind of letters. The 'help I'm kidnapped and in danger' kind. I suppose that would be a little long for a tree trunk. Maybe just 'hel-' and then an extra stabby mark at the end."

Micah raises an eyebrow and speaks loudly enough to be heard over the coms. "An extra stabby mark?"

"Because they got part of the message out and then the Abductor threatened them." Obviously.

Temper snorts. "You've gone ahead and created a whole scenario, haven't you?"

I shrug. That's part of the job. Coming up with scenarios. "The trawlertown just pulled within range of this island chain, so no one from there should have been here recently."

"I've scouted plenty of strange territories." The captain pauses and exchanges quiet remarks with Arcadio before continuing. "We know how to look for something off. Pretty place, though. When the sun came out, the beach was nearly blinding with rainbows. We'll camp here tonight and finish in firstday."

"We'll do the same here." Right. I need to find somewhere for Micah to spend the night that's protected on the off chance I'm wrong and the Abductor really is roaming Sapphire. "I'll contact you tomorrow or immediately upon finding something. You'll do the same?"

"Affirmative." She snickers. "Affirmative. Hah. Imagine if I talked like that."

I share the plan with Micah, who nods and scans the shore. Unlike Opal, Sapphire's beaches are a soft gray. The sand itself is a mixture of white and near-black. The Necklace circles a dead volcano and some of its beaches still hold the memory of lava and ash. Black twisted driftwood creates abstract statues near the tree line.

I study the sand for the familiar pattern of footprints. "No signs a boat pulled up on this beach." As we continue past the driftwood to the emerald-dappled forest, I return to a question that I never asked. "What significance does light- or dark-green pigmentation in tattoos have to you?"

I've only ever seen dark. It's not a great aesthetic. Looks like your veins are molding, which isn't far from the truth.

"Pale is rare. I've only ever seen it in the population of one moon. Only habitable on the dark side, where the native species had adapted bioluminescence. Same principal as the standard green interfacing except it glows in the dark."

I snort. "That would have been handy. A kidnapper who glows would be much easier to track."

He makes a humming sound of agreement. "I don't know what medium-dead green means."

Probably that Tally barely remembers the color. I assume he'd recall a glow.

There isn't a trail because the islands aren't populated, so we wind between black-trunked trees, accompanied by the fluttering tune of the wind as it batters the leaves above us. Jagged black rock splinters up between trees periodically. It doesn't feel like we're gaining elevation until the foliage begins to thin and the rock takes over. It stabs upward in an aggressive jut, an uneven cylinder that dominates the center of the island, surrounded by a deep-blue pool of water. The sapphire color inspired our name for the island. Waterfalls spill from the black rock like massive curtains, in an uneven circle.

"Now that's something." Micah breathes the words, and against my will, I swell with pride, as though I created the island to be admired. He's never yet admired anything I've actually said or done, so I might as well take credit for an island.

"There are caves in the rock behind the waterfalls. About as secure as you can get on this island, although not very comfortable. We can bunk there for the night."

"Does that imply that you'll be sleeping tonight?"

I don't know if he's being critical or worried about his own rest now that he knows I'm a sleep-screamer. Either way, I've deceived him so much out of necessity that I can't bring myself to outright lie again. "I'll keep first watch."

This time he snorts. I take that to mean that he doesn't trust me to properly keep him safe while he slumbers. Which is rude. I've never killed anyone in their sleep.

That I know of.

"About that sleeping thing—" he starts the sentence, and I brace myself for the end. No one else, literally no one, has any concept of how little I sleep, and the lengths that I will go to avoid it. Of how damaged I really am. I know that it's terrible for me—I just can't handle the alternative. Vividly reenacting the worst moments of your life on repeat every single night is intolerable. "Is it always like that?"

In the long list of questions he could have asked, this is one of the most harmless, and I wonder if it's strategy. Easing me into the conversation. "Yes."

Perhaps terseness will dissuade further questions.

"And that's why you don't—"

"More or less." More. The dreams are bad enough, but it's the vulnerability that gets me, in the end. Maybe, someday, I'll find a place to sleep that is so fortified it feels safe, and that night I'll make up years of damaged slumber.

"You do realize that irregular sleep can *cause* nightmares, I assume?"

It's like he can't help himself. He's a medic. No matter what other jobs he's had, even if he was really a gang member in Pierce territory, it's very clear that he is a healer in his heart. He sees what's broken and wants to fix it. Doesn't understand why I'm so resistant. I'm sure he thinks he's helping. My reply comes out in a growl. "I'm aware."

"Are they different every time?" The way he's edging around the question has me more on edge than if he just fucking asked. We begin to circle the central outcropping. I'm looking for the right waterfall. I don't know what he's doing. Maybe admiring the view. Maybe coming up with new questions.

"They aren't dreams. Not properly. They're memories. At least, mostly. My subconscious enjoys embellishment."

Surprisingly, he doesn't ask what the memories are. It's what I expected and I'm disappointed when I don't have the opportunity to snap at him about privacy. The shock, or maybe just the fact that he didn't push for more, makes me offer more information than I normally would. "I've tried everything. Sleeping pills and alcohol make the dreams far worse. Meditation brings them about while I'm awake."

"Therapy?" He grimaces when he says it. Not like he disdains mental health but like he assumes I do.

I tried to get help after I got returned from the infamous run on the *Iceberg*. Would have been a fool not to. The first therapist I spoke to didn't believe I'd survived being spaced and gave me a long lecture about dishonesty. So did the second. I'm sure there are plenty of good doctors out there, but shredding my soul over and over to find the right one isn't tempting. "They didn't believe me."

The tension at the corner of his eyes relaxes. I can't decide if that's sympathy or pity. I don't want either. I'm almost tempted to tell him. To see if he, of all people, will believe what happened on that cold dark ship.

But I don't because I have that Pierce coms in my pocket, and trying to seek connection with a man whom I'm actively planning to betray is low even for me. Maybe I'm just lonely. I should hug the lizard extra hard when I get back to the ship, see if that cuts out this insane desire I have to try to bond with the worst possible people. Person.

Ignoring the urge to rip open my guts and present them on a platter, I approach the slick black rock near the edge of a sheet of water and thrust my hand behind it. My memory had it right. On the off chance that someone else is lurking in the small cave, I withdraw my hand and silently wave Micah closer. He presses himself against the small ledge that edges behind the waterfall and nods. I draw my blaster and somersault through the open mouth of the cave, drenched yet again by the downpour. Yes, a somersault is a strategically bad way to enter. That's why I do it. People are prepared for the smart invasions. They never think someone's going to roll into their lair and pop up with a blaster.

Micah steps around the waterfall, a much less dramatic entrance than my own. The black stone cave is empty. Illumination seeps through the curtain of water, but we're entering second-twilight, so it isn't much. The flashlight on my blaster highlights a small space. Large enough to tell there aren't any lingering human bodies but not enough to detect detail.

"You don't have cave snakes, do you?" Micah holsters his own blaster and moves deeper into the cave. It doesn't go very far into the glossy black rock, about two body lengths, if one possesses a long body. Slightly wider than it is deep. The ceiling of the cave slopes gently up toward the waterfall.

"Don't worry about the cave snakes. They're more afraid of you than you are of them," I tease. There aren't any cave snakes, but talking about them is far preferable to talking about myself. He darts a glance back in my direction that could only be interpreted as panicked until he sees the smile on my face. Then he grabs a handful of water from the fall, splashing it in my direction. The smile turns into a laugh as I continue, "The water is potable, and that ground cover outside makes decent bedding. It's about as good as you can do in the Necklace."

Micah assesses the cave and shrugs. "I've slept in worse."

"While scouting?" I prod, as delicately as I can. It's my turn. Obviously, he has a history before the *Calamity*. He holds the potential for violence. I still don't picture him as the murderer and arsonist that the Pierce Family describes in their bounty. But I could be wrong. I've certainly been wrong before. The fact that I want to strip him out of his ridiculous sleeveless coveralls and see if that sleek muscle extends beyond his arms doesn't mean he's a good person.

In fact, given my general taste in men, it may explicitly mean that he *isn't* one.

Now that we've established that the cave is clear, we leave to gather supplies for the night. This time, I ease around the water instead of bursting through it. It's cold. I've never much liked cold, even before—

Never mind. No one likes cold. No one likes jumping out of ships. They're all things that we bear when necessary. I'm not special—my aversion is just stronger. Micah's answering my question and that's a better direction for my thoughts.

"And before scouting. I've slept worse lots of times." He's ahead of me on the ledge and edges off of it quickly, focused on collecting ground cover. Focusing a little too hard, if I'm honest about it. Like he's trying to hide a reaction.

"Before, huh? I assumed a medic would have a fairly cushy life. Good money in it." Oh shit, unless he was a combat medic. I didn't even think of that option. Nearly every veteran of Family wars I ever met is as fucked up as I am.

"That assumption would be wrong." Still no eye contact. All that I can see is a muscle twitching in his jaw.

His answers are so short, it's infuriating. Is this what talking to me is like? It can't be. I have all that charisma to make up for my laconic nature.

I let him gather his ground cover and retrieve an armful myself. Maybe I can approach this interrogation from a different angle. "I can't place your accent, but it sounds familiar. Something in the Pierce territory?"

"I grew up on the outskirts of Pierce space."

"Pierce space. I hear you can get in a lot of trouble in their way stations."

"I wouldn't know about that." He glances my way out of the corner of his eye as though he understands exactly what I'm doing, and stretches, those long bare arms thrown over his head as he twists one way and then another. My mouth goes dry at the smooth flow of muscle beneath deep-brown skin. My fingers clench around the ground cover. His full lips quirk in a satisfied smile.

Clearly, my interrogation skills are in need of a touch-up. I thought I was good at this. Maybe I never was. When we return to the cave, I linger outside, taking advantage of the last slivers of daylight to look for any signs of the Abductor. When I finally edge around the waterfall, he's built two soft verdant mattresses. I can't decide if it's considerate or presumptuous.

I wish I was the sort of person who could lie down on one. Curl up an arm's length from him and let myself relax. Maybe reach across the space in my sleep and wake up, fingers brushing against his skin, both of us painted in the warmth of the dying light filtered through the falls.

Eventually, Micah reclines on his little bed of foliage, and I crouch near the entrance of the cave, staring out at the water and the darkness, wondering if Aymbe shared this view on one of the last nights of her life. Wondering at what point it went wrong. At what point she went from an adventurous reckless girl looking for love to a victim. If she expected me to come for her, a cadre of constables in tow.

Only five years separated us, but a seventeen-year-old has one foot in adulthood and the other toe still in the fantasies of childhood. I'm sure she never really thought the worst would happen. How could she? So many people gave everything they had to help her. So many people loved her. How could something that terrible happen to someone so loved?

Eventually, the regret is a cracked packet of explosives and I have to move or I'll burst. I slip out from behind the waterfall and pace into the trees, remaining close to the cave so that I'm still keeping watch. I scan the ground, illuminated faintly by light from the small lumpy moon that orbits the Ginsidik at a fast pace. No signs of footsteps besides Micah's and my own. Nothing has been dragged nearby. No marks of a struggle in broken branches or scuffed soil.

The night is silent but for the humming susurration of insects and the ceaseless pound of water crashing down on itself. I want to run. To hit something. That's how I usually keep awake at night. With my stims waterlogged and physical activity restricted, I'm practically crawling in my own skin. I won't fall asleep next to Micah, on an island that just may have a ruthless kidnapper lurking on it, just waiting to jump out at us.

I may like the man, but I don't trust him. Not quite yet.

Not yet? What am I thinking? Not ever. I can't trust him because that would mean I like him, which means I can't turn him in, which means Carmichael Pierce will reveal to everyone just who Cyn Khaw *is* and then criminals from throughout charted space will come after me and mine.

I may have slept recently, but all that means is that my body expects it now. I haven't reached that offish nebulous place where the body doesn't know what it desires. Leaves crack under my feet, filling the air with the bitter scent of crushed greenery. Looking for a sign of the Abductor doesn't cut it and eventually I come to a halt in front of an ancient wide-trunked tree, practically vibrating with the desire for something that I can't even put a name to. Some combination of things that isn't possible.

It's different. It's more. It's just fucking out of reach and always will be.

A minuscule crunch sounds from the ground behind me. Almost overlapping with my own shifting weight, but off enough that it scratches across my already jagged senses. I've been cavalier, assuming the Abyssal Abductor wouldn't retread familiar ground. My hand drops to my hip, palming my blaster. It's half out of the holster when another hand arrests its momentum, pushing the weapon back.

"You're not going to need that." Micah's resonant voice brushes right against my ear. His chest barely skims along my back. Every muscle in my body tenses.

"Maybe I wanted to shoot *you*."

"Could have done that in the cave while I was sleeping. Try again."

"*Were* you sleeping, or were you just playing coy so you could follow me?" I sigh and run my hand through my hair when he releases me and steps away.

"I was bored, not tired. Figured you'd be more interesting if you thought I wasn't watching." He leans back against a tree, nearly disappearing in the darkness but for the dim spark of his banishment tattoo. I want to trace it with my finger.

Or with my tongue.

I gesture at the dark forest around me, at myself. "Yes, fascinating. Clearly this was worth staying up."

"More interesting than the ceiling of a cave. I'm not fussy."

"I'm happy to have entertained you. Now fuck off and let me brood in peace." I walk deeper into the forest, hoping he doesn't follow me.

Wondering what will happen if he does.

Nothing, of course. Nothing will happen because I'd have to be the biggest priap in charted territory to act on any fantasies about the man I'm due to sell out. I've never been the *biggest*.

I might be the second biggest.

He's right behind me, keeping pace. "Is this how you spend your time? Just pace around grumbling to yourself? It's a little self-serving, no? I didn't think ruthless killers were so broody."

I'm tired. I'm lonely. I suddenly want to be back in my office in the Burren, waiting for bad takeout and a game with Madrigal. I want to be somewhere safe and predictable where I can rest on my usual vices. "No one asked you to tag along."

"And miss out on your sunshiny and vivacious company? How could I miss this?"

I spin and stab a finger into his well-muscled chest, suddenly desperate to do anything possible to push him away, because in the still darkness of night I could almost tell him why I'm pacing, why I'm exhausted. I could almost tell him any number of things and none of them would end well for me. Worse for him. "What exactly do you want, Arora? Someone to tell you you're special? I risked my life to save yours today and you returned the favor by accusing me of trying to drown you and then judging me. No one asked you to solve my problems."

"Maybe someone needs to."

My jaw drops. He advances a step and I back up. I didn't mean to do that, but the look in his eyes has me uneasy, because it isn't anger and it isn't irritation. It's something else that I both do and don't want to see, and it sends the blood pounding in my ears.

"Maybe someone needs to watch your back, because from what I've seen, you spend your entire life heedlessly leaping instead of scoping out the territory first. You work your body to exhaustion and then get angry when anyone notices it. You're abrasive as a Mranthian thistle and I bet it's protecting something just as vulnerable inside. You don't trust anyone, and I can't figure out if it's because of what happened to your cousin or something else."

"It's none of your business." I gasp out the protest, and it isn't nearly as convincing sounding as I want it to be.

He steps forward again, and I move backward. Part of me wants to stop and see where it leads—to see if his mouth follows the direction his eyes have chosen and finds my own, and to wonder what it might be like to actually have someone else who cares about my problems—but I have momentum going against me, so he keeps advancing and I keep retreating until suddenly there's a snapping sound, the earth moves on its own, and I'm tilted sideways in the air, wrapped around Micah like we've melded flesh.

I twist and struggle, ropes sawing at my back, my arms, my legs. We swing back and forth over the thick-grassed forest floor. Finally, my brain catches up with my adrenaline. A net. We're wrapped in a net. It's a familiar kind of snare. They even taught us how to make one on the camping trip we took to the islands in school. I try to feel around the edge of the net, but one arm is folded between Micah's body and my own and the other is so tightly encased in the net behind my back that it can't move.

My face is pressed against Micah's neck. His breath is hot against my ear, his lips perilously close to the sensitive skin of my temple. It's a position I may or may not have envisioned a time or two but never like this.

We are—in the least fun definition of the word—fucked.

CHAPTER 12

▪ ▪ ▪ ▪ ▪ ▪ ▪ ▪ ▪ ▪ ▪ ▪ ▪ ▪

Micah's heart thuds in my ear. His chest presses against my body when he sucks in a sharp breath. I almost take one of my own, all wrapped up in him, both exactly where I want to be and the specific place I've been avoiding. When he speaks, I can practically feel the words rise from his chest. "Can you move?"

"I can wriggle my nose and three of my fingers. That's a form of movement."

His sigh floods soft breath through my hair. It's an unearned intimacy, and the enjoyment I'd normally derive from it is reduced. Not gone entirely. I'm still alive, after all. "Same here. We need to get help."

One of his fingers traces a fiery line down my side as he explores his mobility. My shoulder is pressed against his. One of his hands is also trapped between our bodies, alongside my own, knuckles hard against my sternum. I strain for the knife strapped to my thigh. "They're at least an hour away. We don't need help, we need to get *out* of this net."

I try a frantic wriggle to gain some maneuverability, but instead just end up pressed even more securely against his body.

"We're on a team, Cyn. Teams talk to each other. If something goes wrong, they need to know."

He's right, of course. It's only pride that makes me want to keep this little misadventure private. "The activation for the coms on my interface tattoo is near your thumb. I can't reach it, but if you can trigger it, I can warn Temper and Arcadio."

His thumb twists, reaching for the knobby bone of my wrist. On the way, he both scrapes a nipple and activates the music function of my coms by pressing the wrong spot on my forearm. Loud angry beats pump in my ears and I reflexively jump, except I can't jump so instead I just sort of twitch violently against him in the net.

"Sorry," he mutters, maybe assuming all that was because of the nipple.

Finally, he activates the coms, which turns the music off. "Temper. Micah and I just got hit by a snare. We're temporarily incapacitated."

"The fuck?" The captain's voice is sleep-muffled. "Why were you roaming around like wild game in the first place? Don't answer. Any sign of bad guys?"

"Nope. And we just made a whole lot of noise if someone was lurking."

"We're on our way."

"We haven't seen anyone on the island. It's possible the trap is from a previous year. Some group of kids messing around." It's unlikely. For one thing, the net's too nice. This isn't some trawler-town fine twine or twisted seaweed. Also, the trap is secured too high in the tree to be kids fucking around. I do believe that the Abductor may not be present anymore. We haven't seen any sign of habitation.

As I talk with Temper, Micah shifts his weight, the net creaking around us. It moves the tight lines enough that the arm twisted behind my back gains the space to come forward. I have a subdermal blade implanted in my forearm for emergencies, but sawing with it is a Viallanfucker and I'd rather use the actual knife now that I can reach it.

I drop my hand to the sheath on my thigh, which is currently twined around Micah's waist, and slip the knife free before the net can compress around me yet again. He has his own blade out and saws on the opposite end of the net. Our faces are still pressed close enough that I can make out the darker ring around his already dark eyes, glowing in the warm light cast by his banishment tattoo, and the shadows that dimple his shoulders where they emerge from the coveralls.

"Why don't you have sleeves? Normal coveralls have sleeves." One rope splits, and the net sags near my elbow.

"Sleeves get in the way. Drag in wounds. Spread infection. Easier to go without." He's made it through two ropes.

"I assumed you just liked showing off your arms."

I can feel his smile against my forehead. "You wouldn't be the first."

"Some of us have nice arms and don't feel the need to flaunt them."

"They must not be that nice, then." He snaps through two more and I match the momentum. My knee pops out the gap I made. We both wriggle into a slightly more upright posture. Micah's hard thigh rubs a needy cluster of nerves at the apex of my legs, and I bite my tongue to keep from making any embarrassing noises.

"Don't pretend you haven't looked. You've catalogued every part of my body." Sadly, it was because he thought I was a threat, but still, he *has*.

"Not quite every part. Enough to wonder why you insist on dressing like it's winter when we're cooking alive on this planet."

Mostly because the void leaves weird scars. My entire body was frozen. Was stretched by the vacuum. I could afford to fix my face and hands. Most of my forearms. But skin retexturing is expensive. The story of my scars is not a conversation I like to start. I don't like the feeling of children tracing the thin lines cobwebbing my legs because they can't resist the strange texture. I don't like the prickling in the back of my neck because someone is staring at me, trying to figure them out. They're subtle but expansive, like a faint patina of lightning. Eventually, it got easier to just hide my skin.

When last we met, I managed to keep his clinical assessment

very peripheral. The medscan system he used looks for traumas or deep systemic issues. It doesn't register scar tissue. My insides are far less alarming. The scarring in my lungs could just be from a past bout of pneumonia. "I'm afraid people wouldn't be able to control themselves if they were faced with my ephemeral beauty. Better to keep it bottled up."

"Oh really?"

I nod and the movement rubs his chin along my brow. When I look up, he's already looking down, lips a hairsbreadth away. We're teasing, tones glib, but the flash of hunger that plays across his eyes, there and gone again, isn't glib at all.

I open my mouth to reply. His free hand captures the back of my head in the loosened net, fingers spread, cradling me gently as if I was a feral creature. I know I shouldn't be doing this, but I can't remember why. His head lowers just as mine strains up.

As his lips brush mine, every nerve in my body activates. It's the feeling just before lightning in a storm at sea.

Ripe with potential. Whether for devastation or creation is the question. What am I thinking? It's devastation and nothing else. But for the moment, I *want* to be devastated. I want to break down into my component parts and rebuild into someone new. The kind of person who could be with a man like Micah for more than a stolen moment in the dark of a quiet island.

He's patient. Careful. His lips are hot but tender. An interrogation of a new sort that starts soft, but I can feel the barely restrained energy in the body wrapped around my own, in the fingers tangled in my hair. I gasp out a breath and strain up for more, my hand wrapping around the back of his neck and holding him in place.

The storm is building, approaching, and I don't know if I'll be standing once it passes.

The last lines of the net snap beneath us and we plummet to the forest floor, landing wrapped in each other. I pop to my feet faster than I should, every fight-or-flight instinct activated, and grunt when a shock of pain ripples through my shoulder.

"What hurts?" Even that grunt hasn't escaped the medic's attention. The moment is broken. The storm has passed, leaving me electrified and ungrounded.

"It's nothing, I'm fine," I grit through my teeth as I look for an ideal tree trunk to brace against as I pop the joint back into its socket. The last (first) thing I want is Micah's hands on me again. That fortuitous fall to the ground saved me from a huge mistake.

I clasp my elbow and my eyes almost roll back in my head at the throbbing pain that flares to light at the motion. Fuck. I turn my face away and bite the inside of my cheek.

"You're a good liar. Your face doesn't reveal a thing. Smell does, though. Pain releases all sorts of odors. It's sharp. Unpleasant." Micah's hand splays across my upper back as he guides me to the ground. I'd like to say I resist, out of some semblance of pride or even offense at being told I'm emitting all sorts of odors, but I don't. I don't have it in me. Being back here on Ginsidik after so long, seeing the connies, my parents, retreading my cousin's last steps.

It's a lot. Having someone take just one thing off that plate would be nearly miraculous.

My luck, they'd take the plate and leave me trying to hold it all together with my bare hands.

"I wish you'd stop telling me that I smell."

His teeth flash in the moonlight as he smiles, the yellow glow of his banishment tattoo warming his face. "Everything smells. Some things—cancer, landfills, dead fish—smell bad. You're not in that category. You smell like a Family Founder fair at Sunspire Way Station. Like hot fried cake coated in sugar syrup with a slight dash of pepper. Just enough sharp edge to keep it from being cloying."

"I smell like unhealthy food," I repeat his statement.

"You smell delicious. Makes a man wonder if you taste as good."

While I'm distracted by *that*, he braces my shoulder and pops it back into place so smoothly that the agony doesn't even hit me until it's over. I breathe it out and relish the empty looseness that comes after.

When he starts sawing at the remainder of the net above us, I allow it, intuiting what he's trying to achieve. I don't need a sling. I heal fast. Always have. Well, not always. As a child, about ten years old, one of those powerful viruses spread through the trawler, striking only children. A bunch of us were sent off to a Pierce station and they tweaked the normal trawlertown immunity cocktails with something they kept on-station. That's the deal. Pierce fixes children in their territory. One of the rare perks of being in their territory in the first place. They kept me off-trawler for over a year, studying the results, since apparently the disease wasn't in their usual database.

Whatever they did, even though it was just supposed to be immunity, they messed with other things, too. I bounce back from most any injury faster than normal. Four years later, when Aymbe was nine, she was in the exact same situation. They kept her for a year and a half. I don't recall her ever being sick again.

"Now why would you lie about being injured?" He says it as he wraps twine, carefully arranging it to support an arm that will be just fine in about an hour. Shakes his head somewhat despairingly. "Your life is so full of half-truths, I can't tell the ones you tell from the ones you were told. Makes it difficult to trust you, Cyn Khaw."

"You shouldn't trust me," I blurt, guilt and lust and any number of other emotions twisting in my stomach and propelling the words out of my mouth. Just in case you've never captured a bounty, it's generally bad form to *tell* them not to trust you first. "I'm not trustworthy. Aymbe trusted me to rescue her. I'm sure she did. And if she didn't, she probably didn't think it would take me this long to track down her killer. My family trusted me to find her. Nothing good comes from trust."

The forest floor is soft with fallen leaves and filtered moonlight. Micah crouches over me as he fusses with the sling. His eyes find my own and he seems to make a decision. "I'm bad at trusting. It's worked out poorly for me, historically. And yet, somehow, I always seem to run with a crew. Before the *Calamity*, it was a gang in Pierce territory."

My fingers curl around the twine, so close to his own that our skin brushes. I want to hurl myself forward and stop his words with my hands. I don't want to hear about this now, to know if Pierce told me the truth. I want the moonlight on our skin and the soft crash of the waterfall washing through the air. The question comes out of me anyway. "What happened?"

"I was angry when I left my family. I thought my banishment was ridiculous. So I entered unaffiliated space mad and stupid, and I didn't stay there long. I smuggled my way back to Pierce territory, covering my mark of banishment with clothing and eventually an eye patch. It brought me great acclaim in the underworld—an illegal stowaway."

"No one tried to sell you out?" Is my own barometer so off that I'm wrong about him? Could the man who is so carefully tending to my arm also be an arsonist and murderer?

"They did. They didn't succeed. I was part of the Claw, the gang that owns Sunspire Way Station. It was like a family to me. Naima, their leader, accepted me for who I was. She was like a second parent to me. She didn't expect me to limit medical experiments or to do anything but take care of the crew if they got stabbed or shot or anything else that happens during the commission of crimes. I saw an opportunity for a real second chance there. The Claw was small time. Sunspire's a fairly small way station. Can't support a large criminal population. I trusted them like I never trusted my own family."

"I'm guessing this story doesn't have a happy ending."

"It does not." His voice is flat. "We took in a new member—Regan—at my recommendation. He was just a kid—tried to pick my pocket. I thought he had potential. He did. Too much. He escalated our activities, changed what we did so slowly you barely saw what was happening. Soon we were pedaling synth—something I didn't even know until I saw a bag in the street with the Claw sign stamped on the side. Then our own people were getting hooked."

"How did he get power so quickly?" I rest my hand on his own, where it's frozen against the sling. I don't think he even notices it, his eyes focused on something other than me.

"I don't know. I still don't know. Psychopaths can be charismatic. Maybe because he was so young that no one considered him a threat. We didn't realize the danger until it was too late. He betrayed us all and it led to me losing the home I'd just barely found, and the people I'd just started to care for. So when I say I don't trust easily, understand that I mean it from hard-earned experience."

I've never heard him sound so sad. Or say so many words at one time. When the man decides to speak, he really goes for it. I choose to give him something back. It's small, barely a secret, even, but earned. "I heal quickly. My arm would have been fine in an hour or so. Special mods."

His fingers trace so delicately over the sleeve of my coat that I can barely feel their pressure. "But why be in pain for an hour if you don't need to be?"

Why, indeed? Perhaps because some part of me believes I deserve it.

Something catches my focus. Hooray, a change in subject from mutual vulnerability! I scramble to my knees, almost colliding with Micah as he reaches out to steady me, and lurch toward the side of this slight clearing. "There's the trip wire. Bound up in green archlock stalks. We're past the season when archlock grows flexible stems. They've roughened by now. Whoever laid this trap was here a while ago. Perhaps even before Boreal was abducted."

"The Abductor preparing for her, or just happenstance?" He follows the redirection of the subject without protest. An endangered child is much higher priority than our fragile détente—as she should be.

"Could be either. We've never found his prep space before—not when he still had an active kidnapping. Seems off for any normal residents of Ginsidik, though. Either someone's running a drug operation from the island—which is possible, although I haven't seen a crop—or it's the Abductor. We need to dig deeper into the caves. If he did spend time here, that's where he hid out."

At Micah's prodding but without complaint, I update Temper and Arcadio on our status. The captain of the *Calamity* informs me that they're on their way and we should sit tight until they arrive. She takes longer than she needs to in order to tell me about how she and Arcadio had to reprogram the shuttle boat to Sapphire in the dark. I convey that to Micah. He glances in the direction of the waterfalls.

"We could sit tight *in* the caves. While searching them." He angles his head toward our original shelter spot. The fire might even still be burning.

"That would be the safest option. Less exposure." I nod solemnly, and we retrace our steps.

"You ever thank anyone for anything?" Micah's voice comes from close behind me. He moves as bonelessly silent as a sea snake. I thought we were making friends. Now he wants me to thank him?

"I wouldn't have been in the net if you hadn't stalked me out here. I wouldn't have fallen. I wouldn't have needed help without you. You canceled out a debt, you didn't do me a favor." It's the way the universe works. A series of tallies and consequences and scales always trying to balance. "You didn't thank me for hurling myself in the ocean and keeping you from becoming a meaty piece of floss lodged in a serpent's teeth."

"You're right. I didn't. I should remedy that. Thank you, Cyn Khaw, for risking your life to save my own."

I almost trip over my own feet, because of all the responses possible, sincerity never struck me as a possibility. I even cast a sharp glance in his direction to see if he's mocking me, but in the starlight, his face is earnest and steady. Now I have to thank him, too—except it looks petty because I forced the issue and he broke first. My breath catches in my throat as our eyes remain locked and the moment stretches long. The breeze ruffles his hair along his brow. It looks soft.

"I'll thank you. Some day." I rub my shoulder, wishing that it hurt again. "When you know I mean it. When it matters."

We gather our emergency packs, which each contain tiny diode flashlights, and creep in a circle around the large waterfall complex, entering each cave and scanning the soil for disruption, the walls for blood or paint or any other sign. We do not find any signs of potential activity within the caves until we reach the second biggest, almost all the way back to our temporary camp.

A rockslide has taken out the back half. Impossible to know when it happened. Maybe it was disturbed recently, maybe ages ago. I open my mouth and Aymbe's is almost the name I scream. Too late for her. "Boreal!"

No response.

If one or both of them is trapped back there, there's no ransom, no nothing. They'll either die of thirst or hunger or something else alone in the quiet. I reach for the rocks just as Micah points up near the roof, where his flashlight captures a hungry lichen that has spread down the face of the slide. "How long does that take to grow?"

My hands fall on my knees and my breath comes out in a pant.

The energy drains from my body. "It's slow-growing. That would take years. This happened long ago. They aren't here."

Which means we didn't find anything at all. We trudge back to our original cave, to finish the wait for Temper and Arcadio. A dim glow shines through the waterfall, and when we duck under it, one of our flashlights is still on, angled low to the ground.

Might as well finish the search where we started. I angle my flashlight as I brush at the sand on the floor but can't find a pattern in the way it spreads. No footprints. I look for any dropped wrappers or flakes of paper. The detritus that people leave wherever they go. None of it. I'm almost ready to give up when I realize that the light is warped where it strikes the wall.

And there it is. Scrawled on the back wall of the cave, in a tight little crevice that curves slightly away from the mouth. Two words, POISON GREEN, scratched painfully into the stone, the letters jagged and awkwardly formed. A shard of glass is discarded on the ground just beneath it.

I trace my finger over the letters, as though that will tell me anything about their author. It isn't Aymbe's script, at least I don't think so. Her handwriting was more rounded, prone to flourishes, but it's not like a shard of glass is the perfect writing utensil. Perhaps it's Boreal's or some other girl's memory from long ago, finally making itself apparent.

I run my finger over the etched text, dipping into the particularly deep scratch of the letter "I."

"What is 'poison green'?" Micah's solid form moves behind me, his shadow obscuring the message. I want to yell at him to get out of the way. To let her words see the light as long as possible.

I don't. Because that's crazy.

"If we're limiting the reference to Ginsidik, I can only think of one place. Poison Green is near the pole, a large lagoon, nearly fully contained in the mouth of a long-dead volcano, that's become a dumping ground for sewage and refuse. Every season, ships drop waste there. But no sane person would spend time on it."

"How do they control the boundary?" He rubs his hand over his jaw, and the scratch of whisker over skin scrapes at my senses. I want to replace his hand with my own, to trace the fine hard contours of his face.

"Nothing as technical as you imagine. Early on, the space was separated into dumping regions. Each type of item in its own silo. Then a strong winter storm raced through and damaged it enough that when they came back the next year, a wide pool was contaminated, seeping out of the lagoon. They built a seawall. The next year, they built another." I balance back on my heels, hand still lingering on the message on the wall. "Now it's a maze of walls and barges and weighted nets, and the water glows poison green with bioluminescent algae at night. The true name of the place is Stillwater Lagoon, but everyone calls it the Poison Green."

"You don't sound pleased that we have a clue." He finally shifts his weight and the flashlight dances across the letters. I force my hand away and stand to face the medic.

"I'm not. As far as we know, the only trawlertown child taken was Aymbe. I don't think this is her handwriting. Somehow, a victim knew trawlertown slang for a region that no one outside of Ginsidik has ever heard of."

"Are you sure her handwriting would be the same in stone?"

I give a helpless shrug. My shoulder twinges. "No. I haven't seen her handwriting in years. But I taught her to write, back when she was learning. She wasn't picking it up quickly in school—didn't see the purpose in it—and my aunt asked me to help her."

My aunt asked me to do a lot of things to support Aymbe when my cousin didn't feel like doing them. I wasn't smart enough to tell my parents until Mygda asked me to just do Aymbe's homework for her. They put a stop to it. Aymbe threw a tantrum and dropped my mother's favorite earrings in the sea as retaliation. She was twelve, which seems a bit old for that kind of behavior, but Mygda always spoiled Aymbe. She was her baby. The baby of the whole family. "It doesn't seem like hers. Hers slanted forward. This is straight up and down. Her letters were wide. These are narrow."

"If she didn't write it, you think the kidnapper is a local."

"A local doesn't make sense. People don't just leave the trawler-town. It's noticed. If someone scampered off every few years for a long involved kidnapping-ransom ritual, we'd know. Either there is another trawlertown victim that we don't know about, or the Abductor visits enough to pick up local slang."

A disruption to the crash of the waterfall outside and a vicious curse herald Temper and Arcadio's arrival within the volcano. Arcadio looms behind the petite captain like her bodyguard. She shakes out water-speckled hair. "Didn't you say you were staying in one place? Not wandering all over the island? Remind me who scolded me a few missions ago that wandering off was dangerous? We had to follow your tracker."

Something subtle relaxes in Micah's shoulders. The body's reaction to safety. These people are his family. "You know, you could have gone around the waterfall instead of through it."

She sniffs. *Through* is always better than around."

That sounds like everything I know about the captain of the *Calamity*. Arcadio rumbles out a chuckle.

When I show them the message, Arcadio's mouth goes flat and still and his body switches to predatory in an instant. "Boreal carved that. She sends me letters. Through intermediaries so there isn't an electronic trail. She's got a strange way of writing the letter 'g.' Couldn't get the hang of it as a young child and just kept writing it wrong as she got older to be obstinate. We joked that if she was ever in trouble, she'd write me a letter with a proper 'g,' and I'd know to come rescue her."

I study the "g" of "green." Wonky. A strange curl and an awkward tail. I ascribed it to the carving process and bad tools, but

I can see the intention in it now. Turns out, he'll rescue her no matter what type of "g" she writes.

I miss my uncle. I like to think he'd have noticed something like that about my handwriting. Families on the trawlertown are close. My father was an only child, but Aunt Mygda and Uncle Nico were a part of my life since I was born, just as I was part of Aymbe's.

"Something about this seems wrong," Micah interjects, running his finger over the stone. "This isn't soft rock, but she had time to painstakingly carve these words?"

That's what's been getting at me, too. Not just the words themselves, but their medium. "It would have taken hours to carve that. What if it's a misdirection?"

Micah glances back at me, surprise in his eyes. Shocked that I agreed with him?

"This is a clue. It's her writing, I'm sure of it. She's an Escajeda. She's resourceful. No one could manipulate her into doing something she didn't want to do." Arcadio glares at me like *I'm* the Abyssal Abductor. Families and their egos. Of *course* she managed to carve this message undetected with her magical Escajeda powers.

And maybe she did, for all that. What do I know about what talents and training an Escajeda has? Temper told me that Families train their children from an early age in the patterns of kidnapping. Of us all, Arcadio is the expert in his kin.

· · · · ·

There's nothing else to be found on the island. No careful etchings of the kidnapper's name. No little map to the killing field. Boreal has done enough. It's our turn to do our job. The trip back to the trawlertown is uneventful, a new day dawning as we launch, the brilliant bright sun centered in the sky when we find our way back to the sand-roughened decks and ramshackle buildings.

The *Calamity* hunches like a barnacle on one of the floating stern docks, ugly and solid. Caro waits for us, arms crossed and eyes narrowed. I glance around the dock. No connies. No obvious emergencies. Then her eyes go straight to me with the delicate deadly weight of a garrote.

Oh.

I'm the emergency.

I'm not sure which of the many possible things has set her over the edge. A flicker of motion in the shadowed belly of the ship resolves itself into Itzel.

She doesn't look nearly as angry as Caro.

Caro stabs a finger in my direction. "She lied."

Oh no. Which one?

"She isn't who she says she is."

Ah. That lie. I'd almost forgotten about *that* lie.

CHAPTER 13

■ ■ ■ ■ ■ ■ ■ ■ ■ ■ ■ ■ ■ ■ ■ ■

Temper looks at me with an eyebrow up. "This is Cyn Khaw. You remember her. I pointed her out to you a few days ago as she was approaching the ship. You said something under your breath about mass murder. I suggested that beggars can't be choosers." She cocks her head. "You *are* Cyn Khaw, no?"

"Sure am."

"Are you *not* a mass murderer? That would be a nice surprise, I suppose."

"That's not all she is." Caro brandishes a small clear bag containing what looks like my hair. "She's been on the ship before. This is Generosity. From the cult. The cult that wanted to explode a ship full of children." She sniffs. "Her style."

"I'm not saying human traffickers and children don't have *anything* in common, but the list of similarities escapes me at the moment." I go for snarky calm. Arcadio ignores us and heads straight into the ship. Either going to get a larger blaster to shoot me or bored with a conversation that isn't about retrieving his niece. Either way, probably the right call. I wish I could join him. Temper studies me, green eyes unreadable. I shift my weight minutely before I realize I moved and force myself still.

"She lied to us." Caro leads the audience, in case they hadn't reached that conclusion on their own. "Seems important to know why."

"And you collected my genetic material—twice, if you did a comparison—without my consent. Which, if not a lie, is certainly a deceit." I carefully don't look at Micah. I hope he appreciates the discretion.

"Because you were *lying* to us. If you lied about that, what else did you lie about? Are you either of those people or are you some Pierce spy? You certainly look like one." Caro steps forward, still wagging that bag like it makes some sort of point. "We can't trust her. Not with something as important as Boreal's life. Cut her loose, Temper."

Temper turns to Itzel. "What do you think?"

Itzel shrugs. "I could take her or leave her."

Good to know all that time I spent working with the crew on the way here put me on their good side. I wish I left that waste filter clogged with hair and fingernails. Maybe added a few of my own.

"*Leave* her. We don't need her. We have the drones and the scans and eventually something will pop. She hasn't contributed anything of merit yet." Caro's voice is thick with emotion. I don't know why. I don't know why she hates me so much. I've only ever been nice to her. It can't just be the lies, can it? People lie all the time.

Also, I *have* contributed something of merit, she just doesn't know it yet. So there.

"Micah?" Temper asks.

"Micah hates everyone. He's been watching her like he's our security expert. Of course he wants her gone," Caro interjects before he can respond.

I don't think that's the truth. It didn't *feel* like the truth. But who am I to know or to judge? A knot forms in my throat and I square my shoulders, waiting for it.

Micah answers, from close behind me. "I knew, Caro. I knew."

Everything goes quiet. Everything, that is, besides all the sounds from the docks behind us, which includes what appears to be one deeply drunk sailor singing a chanty about the specific perkiness of his brother's wife's breasts. It's an incongruous background for the current conversation. I'd rather be over there. Maybe I could just leave and let them hash this out without me.

Caro freezes, eyes taking on a deep liquid hurt. "You knew? You knew and you didn't say anything? How could you keep secrets for her?"

"To be fair, Micah hardly ever says anything," Temper points out, face still calm.

"How did she manipulate you into silence? Are you *sleeping* with her?" The hurt has transformed to outrage. Not the jealous kind, more like she can't believe he'd be so stupid as to fall for my feminine wiles.

Which is fair. I'm almost complimented that she thinks I'm good enough in bed to earn the loyalty of a man who's flown with her for years.

There's a moment of silence where I assume Micah gives her a look.

"Fine. Sorry. Of course you aren't." She glances at me. "You have better taste than that."

There goes the compliment.

Micah's arm wraps around my waist, part support and part tether. "She's spent her life looking for this madman and she's come closer than anyone else. It's personal for her. I know you have a history with Pierce but that's not her. Cyn is a good person who's spent her life being punished for it, even by her own people. I won't let you do it, too."

The lump in my throat grows so thick I can't even swallow. He defended me. To his crew. It's the last thing I deserve. It would be so embarrassing if I were to burst into tears right now in the middle of this heated moment.

"Why didn't you tell us?" Temper directs the question at me, verdict not yet rendered.

I manage that swallow. Sigh. "Seemed irrelevant to the task at hand. The Children have nothing to do with the Abyssal Abductor, and as far as I knew, I parted on decent terms with your crew. I didn't wrong you. You didn't wrong me."

Micah makes a rumbly sound. "We did more than not wrong you. We rescued you and healed you."

He's an equal opportunity defender, but his arm is still around my waist, warm and solid.

Temper diverts her attention to him, something almost like amusement in her eyes. This whole situation isn't very amusing to me.

"Which made it much harder for me to retrieve Bianca Laitung from the pernicious clutches of said child-killing cult." I wave my hand to forestall the arguments I see brewing in their eyes. "I'll also point out that I wouldn't have been tied up and needing rescue if you hadn't wandered in and offered the Rashahan a medic on a platinum platter. I didn't conk any of you over the head with a heavy object and run away while on board. I asked politely to return, and you decided you knew better than I did. We were never enemies, but we weren't allies either. My mission, my priority, was Bianca."

"She showed dedication to her mission." Micah returns his attention to Caro. The continued support takes all the steel from my spine, turning it unexpectedly mushy. Like I actually trust him, which is preposterous. Trust is a lie. Aymbe trusted her abductor. I trusted my source about the *Iceberg*. *Micah* might be starting to trust me. Lie. Lie. *Lie.* "When we decided to make that volcano blow, she didn't run away, she ran inside to rescue her target. That's the kind of thing we want for Boreal. You know me, I'm the first one to see betrayal in someone. I don't see it in Cyn."

An invisible knife drives directly into my gut. It twists in little circles. Viall. He *does* trust me.

"She *lied.*" She's really not going to let this one go. "What else is she lying about?"

"Over something irrelevant. You know who I actually am. I wanted to save a long discussion of past history, but hey, it's super-fun to have it on the dock of my home. Perhaps we could invite my mother and aunt and you could compare notes about my disappointments." Is it just that she can't get over a lie? That can't be it. We live in the real world and people deceive all the time. Does she really hate anyone who looks like a Pierce that much? I don't know her well enough to hurt her personally. It seems like a rational argument would sway someone like Caro, with a technical mindset. Still, I can be mature when I must. "I apologize for not bringing up our history. I truly deemed it irrelevant."

"Will you decide information on Boreal's abduction is irrelevant, too?" Caro turns and stomps back into the ship, shoulders rigid. "Or maybe you'll share with Micah. And *he* won't tell us, either."

"You withholding anything else?" Temper asks me. Those eyes can be just as cutting as lasers.

I huff out a breath. "Of course I am. I'm withholding most things. Because they aren't relevant. You know everything you need to know. I have no bad intentions toward your ship or your crew or the Escajeda Family."

Lie.

I do have bad intentions toward her crew. Or one specific member of it. The one who just defended me. The one I don't want to betray at all. Who had his lips on mine less than a day ago. The one who's looking at me now with speculation in his eyes. This is such a mess.

The captain sucks some air in through her teeth. "Good enough for me."

Then she follows the others on board. When I move to enter the ship, Itzel briefly steps in front of me, silent as a shadow. The frequent semivacancy in her eyes is gone and the solemn straight gaze she shoots at me is deadly. "If you try to hurt them, I'll kill you and they'll never recover your body."

Well, shit.

"As a special request, if you ever do kill me, leave the body discoverable. Not for my sake. My mother's nightmare is never finding my body. She's had a lot of years to worry about it."

The corner of her mouth crumples, and I decide I don't want to be in that ship right now anyway. I spin by Micah's bunk to pick up Vuur and then head back out to the docks. Micah does not follow me. I tell myself I'm relieved by that. I sit on one of the benches bolted to the dock, enjoying the wind in my hair.

A ripple of vibration shivers up my interface tattoo. Incoming call. Not from the Pierce line, thankfully. It's Madrigal. Within the vicinity of the trawlertown, there are signal relays to boost connections to the relay satellites outside the ionosphere. You can make a connection elsewhere—especially with a fancy unit like the Pierce one still burning a hole in the pocket of my pants. Even if it's a gast coms, I bet it'll connect from nearly anywhere. Those fancy Pierce satellites. I still don't see a way outside our deal. It's not just me. If it was, maybe I could. But it's my family and I've already let them down so many times.

"Wrong number," I answer.

"You're hilarious. You decide to become a comedian?"

"How are you doing?"

"That's a ridiculous question to ask." The sound of bedsheets rustles in the background and a click indicates that she's turned in for the night. "I'm fine. I'm always fine. Bored to tears because no one here has any strategy for games. I tell you, if they had a halfway-sane roommate for me, I might not drive them out. That's how bored I am."

"The trawlertown has an eel and kelp flavor of chips." Vuur burrows through my hair, stinging hot breath dancing on the back of my neck.

"Did you try them?"

"No. Ick. I got you a bag."

"Get another one. We'll eat them together when you get back."

I smile, staring into nothing, fingers curled around the sanded smooth bench. "Maybe I'll have one of yours."

"Cheap. Giving a gift and then taking some of it back. They not paying you to find this Abductor?"

"I'll get two bags."

"Good. But I didn't reach out to talk about chips. Someone was poking around your office yesterday. A constable but not from the Burren."

"Then how did you know it was a connie?" Could it be the Abductor wearing some sort of costume? Playing this game in a new way? Could it be Pierce, getting something to hold over me? If it is, they won't have any luck. The worst thing I've ever done is already public knowledge.

"I know a cop when I see them. They all look alike. Hard jaw, narrow mind. Punchable."

I think about Mo. She got it two-thirds right. I wonder what she'd say if she knew I'd been one briefly? Probably nothing complimentary.

"Did he leave with anything?"

"Not that I could see. Maybe data. Waste of time when they could have just hacked it."

Indeed. I don't think it was Pierce—he already has enough to hold over me. The Abductor doesn't quite make sense either. He's busy at the moment. Speaking of—

I pause to consider what I'm about to say and where I'm about to say it. Step carefully. "This case is a hard one, Madrigal. It's messy. You ever hear anything about Family kidnappings?"

"Good credits in it if you're competent. Good way to get dead if you aren't. Or if you are. Credits, then dead."

"So they really are targets?" Somehow, I thought they were so big they were untouchable.

"Everyone wants to pull a lever, C. If you don't have power, it's an easy way to borrow it. Stupid. But plenty of people don't let stupid get in their way."

"Especially if they were guided by another Family, perhaps?"

"That's an even better way to get dead, but greed blinds one to such things. Someone tried it a generation ago. Kaori Nakatomi wasn't the firstborn. They took the first Nakatomi heir when she was just a girl. Tried to use her to sway her daddy. He was not persuaded."

I grimace.

So Estella may be correct, if someone from Madrigal's background has given it thought and knows of a time when it actually happened. Which leads me to my next question. "You ever hear about a gang called the Claw?"

False innocence coats her tone. "Why would I know anything about a gang?"

"You know about a lot of things." No point pushing our little ruse. "You're quite old."

She snorts. I imagine her pacing the small confines of her room, tracing her fingers over the back of the regal purple chair that looks more like a throne than a resting place. A cabinet in the corner houses all her contraband chips. It's a small domain for a crime boss, meticulously clean and organized. "Piddly gang on a piddly station. Had some turmoil about eleven cycles ago. Change of ownership. They changed a lot of how they did business. The smuggling crew, for instance."

"Can you try to get me more? I ran across a former member. Want to know if he's trustworthy."

"Now how did a lowly regional PI run across a member of the Claw while also being involved in Family kidnappings?" Now her own voice has an edge to it. Pushing me back. Telling me she knows more about me than she usually lets on as well.

"I get involved in a lot of things." I twist the response. "I'm quite reckless."

Which just reminds me of Micah, moonlight in his hair, as he tells me that someone needs to watch my back, since I don't watch my own. "I might be in over my head on this one, Madrigal."

"I've already given you my best advice. Look after your own, stab anyone else in the back if it helps. Stab them twice if it helps more. You'll never regret not trusting someone, but you'll regret trusting foolishly." She hums a breath. The light reverberation of her finger tapping her chin vibrates the coms. "And what I told you before you left. A crew can do more than just one person. You're a smart girl, Cyn. Don't be stupid."

"You get that in a greeting card?"

"Yeah, I picked it up at the shop by the eighth bar on the fifth level. They're getting awfully specific these days."

Vuur lazily rolls down my chest to my lap, sinking a claw or two in to stop its momentum. "Being back here—it reminds me of how often things come down to *have* instead of *want*."

"You're an adult. *Want* is something that hobbyists and spoiled rich kids concern themselves with. Want isn't for people like us." A crunch. Midnight snack. More of those horrible chips that she makes her entire diet.

And she's right. *Want* won't keep my family safe. When it all comes down to it, want is a paltry cousin to need. Enticing as it may be.

"You're right." I lie back on the bench, lifting my feet to rest them on its surface. One arm dangles over the edge, my knuckles trailing on the deck. Vuur paces back and forth on my body, little clawed feet dancing over my guts. It licks the zipper on my coat. "I'm being childish."

"Take care of your own, Cyn. The rest will sort itself out. Just remember that *you* are one of your own."

I've always taken care of myself better than I do anyone else. "I'll talk to you later, Madrigal."

"Send me a picture of a sea serpent. And your parents. And

whoever it is has you tied in knots." She pauses. "And get more of those chips. They sound delicious."

I forgot to send her the serpent video that I captured earlier. I send it, along with the beach on Sapphire, Tally's house, and a slightly blurry shot of Micah in motion. Then I go to be the adult that Madrigal believes me to be and have a conversation with my family.

· · · · ·

It's amazing how quickly I reacclimatize to the sway of the decks under my boots, the cracking clay on my cheeks blocking the bright sunlight, the buoyant gravity that feels like I finally have a weight lifted from my shoulders. Specks of algae and ripples of shellfish mark the edges of the trawler, crawl up the supports of the bridges, and dangle from their high arches.

When I near midship, Etolla appears at the head of a bridge, bony hands clutching the rail and wind blowing her hair. I skitter by her, trying to avoid any additional conversation. When I'm almost across she calls from behind me.

"Six. It's six now."

"It isn't six!" I yell back, cradling Vuur like it can defend me from rogue babies clamoring for adoption. It belches, creating a smoldering hole in my sleeve. I don't know why I don't want to take care of a bunch of little critters. It's so glamorous.

When I cross the bridge closest to my parents' home, I knock a tenacious piece of seaweed off, watching it plop to the water and quickly drift away as the boat speeds ever forward.

My father opens the door, such a welcoming light flashing in his eyes that my stomach cramps with guilt. A lack of affection was never our problem, just a lack of being able to properly communicate. We all want everyone to be happy—we just have a different idea of what that means. I brace my hands on my holster out of pure nervous habit before I realize that's a tad aggressive, but once

I lift them, I forget what people do with their hands during normal social interactions. He solves the problem by folding me in a hug. I stand in his embrace awkwardly, arms slowly rising of their own accord to wrap around his lean back. Vuur clambers down my back, claws digging in, and hides in my pocket.

Clearly it isn't much of a hugger.

I am a blend of my parents. Cygna's features and Parbel's coloring—his Pierce ancestor providing us both with honey-gold hair, tan skin, and brown eyes. There are enough Pierce by-blows on the trawler-town that it isn't a unique aesthetic. I never realized how rare the coloring is until I left home and saw the rest of charted territory.

He captures my hand in his and pulls me inside. My father's hands have always been rough-calloused. He's been a machinist all his life and I know the familiar pattern of abraded flesh like it's an identification. I don't trust the smooth-fingered. They're too far from work.

He has new callouses now. Splayed over his knuckles. I know them because their twins are mirrored on my hands. Splits and abrasions from too long on a heavy bag. Early on, I didn't know how to properly wrap my knuckles. The marks linger. It makes me sad to see them on my father.

Back when I was growing up, when Aymbe was still a child, back before everything that split our two families apart, my parents were musicians in their free time. My mother played the maktang zither in the evening festivals, while people danced on the stern platform of the trawler. My father accompanied her on the low flat foot-drums. Both used to smile so wide you'd think they invented joy. I don't mean to imply they were naive. Or maybe I do. I just know I wasn't any different. The year I joined the connies, when I left school, I was one of the people dancing along, hands in the air and feet beating the same percussive tempo my father drummed— half a beat off, because I've always had shit rhythm.

Aymbe sat in a circle of her peers, grinning that man-eater

smile and picking off the weakest boys in the herd every time she wanted to dance. Back when she was a little child, before the virus that ravaged her and sent her to the Pierce station, she was a terrible dancer. I mean that in the best possible way. She danced free and unencumbered of ego. Meaning, like a lunatic—but a happy one. By the time she was older, it was far more choreographed. She learned to find the beat that I never managed to capture.

My father's blaster is out on the table again. "You didn't used to have a blaster. Where did you even get it?"

I've been in law enforcement or something adjacent my entire life. I know how this story ends. The blaster is unregistered. Not only does my father have a blaster, but he also has an *illegal* blaster that will get him put in one of Mo's sky cells if they catch him with it.

"Your uncle Bobo." He gives me a knowing look.

Bobo isn't my actual uncle. He's a friend of my father's from his childhood. He always had the best sweets on the trawler, and once I joined the connies, I realized that he had a criminal record the size of my arm. All petty crimes, but petty crimes contain multitudes and Bobo tried them all a time or twenty-eight.

My father had a record, too. Much smaller scale and limited to his teen years before he realized that Bobo was a bad investment if what he wanted was an unincarcerated future.

"Bobo had a big forehead," my grandfather pipes up as he walks by on the way to the kitchen. "The ones with the big foreheads are always trouble."

Because their foreheads hide big tricky brains? Because that broad expanse of skin is easily visible to the authorities when they search a crowd? I shake my head. I should not be applying logic to my grandfather's proclamations.

"There's probably a crime already linked to it," I mutter to my father, keeping my voice down. This is my area of expertise after all. Kind of.

He snorts, jaw hardening. "The trawler isn't big. I think I'd know if someone had been blaster-shot. I know what I'm doing."

An argument rises to my lips, but I bite it back. I don't want to hurt him. I never wanted that. I just always manage it some-how—an expert in good intentions gone bad. "Right. Sorry. How have you been?"

"Bella." My mother's voice comes from directly behind me. I leap a little. She loves approaching from behind. Cygna Khaw would have been better off born as an ambush predator. "We weren't expecting you."

"I want to apologize for the other day. I wasn't prepared." Nope . . . that's a mistake. It implies family interactions require preparation. I course-correct before she can pounce on it. "I mean, I didn't handle it well. The Abductor being back here, taking an-other girl, it has me thrown. I didn't mean to be hurtful."

When in doubt, blame a criminal.

"You didn't hurt any of us." She lies blatantly. Maybe that's where I get it.

"What's going on out there?" my grandma calls from her bed-room. "Is that Cyn? Did she bring the medic with the forearms?"

"I used to have quite the forearms in my day," my grandfather calls up the stairs at her. "Strong as a serpent at the nets. The girls were lining up in droves. The smithy was the hottest place on the ship!"

Grandma guffaws, then pauses. "I wonder how many a drove is. Maybe a trove, like treasure."

"Did you say 'grove'? I'm not talking about trees."

"He's not here!" I interrupt the tangent before it can really get going. "It's just me."

A huff from Grandma's bedroom. "Don't see the point if you aren't bringing him. Babies don't make themselves, you know."

I really wish people would stop talking about babies. And the making thereof.

"I don't think she's here to talk about the medic who she claims is not her partner but watches her like he is." My mother gives me side-eye. "I'm not sure what she is here to discuss since she's done her best to avoid us for years. Even when we do speak, we only get information on her houseplants."

"I enjoy the broadleaf updates!" my father pipes up in my defense. "Those can be so hard to keep alive."

In truth, I don't actually have a broadleaf. At least not a live one. I brought it up one day when I wanted to end the conversation, thinking they'd find it boring, and now my father never misses an opportunity to ask how my plant is.

I push forward with the conversation. As determined to force a result I see as morally correct as I was when I tattled on the connies. Probably to as successful results. "I was rude. And I feel badly about it. Aymbe's kidnapping damaged something in us. Maybe in this whole fu—um—this whole place. I don't know how to say the right thing anymore. So when I do know the right thing, I have to say it. I'm sorry."

They all look at me like I'm being deeply weird. Because I'm being deeply weird. Earnestness doesn't come naturally to my family. I rub my hand over my forehead, little flecks of sun-reflecting clay cracking off on their impeccably maintained floor.

"Save that maudlin stuff for your medic," my grandma calls from her room.

He wouldn't appreciate it any more than they do.

I gently nudge the clay flakes under the chair with my foot. "All right. Thanks. Now that that's cleared up, I need to go back to the ship. I'll let you know if—when—we find him."

My mother nods sharply. My father fidgets with a blaster part. He breaks first. "You don't talk about your life much, on that moon where you've set up shop. Are you happy there?"

"I make a good living." Which isn't the same thing, and from the look in his eye, he knows it.

"Do you have a community?" My mother gets to the part that's more important to her.

"I have a friend." I wonder if Madrigal would take offense to the title. I dredge Vuur out from the pocket where it's been riding. "I have a lizard."

Her look tells me that isn't the same thing. My dad extends a finger. Vuur sniffs it and then rubs its jaw against his nail. I try again. "I have enough."

Clearly that was the wrong thing to say, because they both look crushed. "You could have had your family. You could have had a community. A partner and children of your own. A real life where your skin sees sun."

And there's the crux of it all. I chose the Burren over them. I chose slimy noodles and poverty and crime in exchange for the illusion of independence. It isn't that simple, of course, but it is to them. I used to like children, I realize. Used to spend time in the nurseries after school, keeping an eye on the new walkers. When I got older, I taught swimming lessons.

When you have an obsession, like I have the Abductor, it eats away at things like that. I haven't dated in years. I haven't thought about children. They don't fit in my life. I just do what I can to save the ones in over their head.

I haven't thought much about my family, either. In my memory, they've been frozen in time. Not from when I left, but earlier. From my childhood before everything went wrong. Maybe in not telling them who I really am, I lost the opportunity to know who they've become.

My parents both see me to the door. Together. Like I'm a valued guest, not like I'm family.

CHAPTER 14

When I return to the ship, I make a direct line to the bag I've transferred to Micah's bunk, where my stims are stored. It's been a long day and there isn't time for my kind of sleep before we go. A large hand wraps around my own as I pull the packets out of the bag, holding me in place. The man moves quietly. His body braces me against the bunk. It could feel like a trap, but instead it could almost be mistaken for support.

"Those things will kill you." That ridiculous voice scrapes over my ears. I ignore the temptation to melt back into the long strong line of his body.

"Thank you so much for your advice. Clearly, the smartest approach is to change as much as possible while we're on the hunt for a kidnapper who has a girl in his clutches. I wonder, will Boreal's mother thank you for ensuring I maintain a healthy diet?" I'll be a mess if I stop the stims. It won't help anyone.

"Handy excuse. I bet you always have one. Always have a crisis that keeps you from looking after yourself."

Of all the gall. How dare he completely accurately sum up the situation? "I'm not your responsibility."

"Clearly, you need to be someone's."

My back goes steel-bar straight so quickly that I feel a vertebra pop. "Excuse me?" I spin on him, stims still clutched in my fist, my fist still clutched in his, almost like we're dancing. I let it go on the island because it sounded more like he thought I needed backup. This is not that. "Did you actually just say that? What kind of troglodyte are you? My health is none of your business unless I'm bleeding out on your exam table. You might be my medic, but you aren't my doctor."

I don't want him to look at me like I'm a patient.

He raises one dark brow. "Elucidate."

"You're responsible for triage. Not my overall health. You aren't responsible for *me*."

"Thank any deity who's listening for that. It would be a full-time job. I don't want to be your doctor."

"Could have fooled me."

He narrows the minuscule space between us slowly, like he's afraid of spooking a nervous animal, which isn't half wrong. It isn't any part wrong. He hasn't released my hand yet, but his fingers gentle around it.

"I'm done dancing around this. I know who you are, Cyn Khaw, and if I'm your doctor, I don't get to be anything else. I very much want to be something else." That fucking *voice*. I can't handle it sometimes. Deep and dark and full of near-tactile promises.

"What do you want to be?" When did my own voice get so breathy? My palm goes sweaty against the stim packet. My legs go loose. My heart pounds like it wants to leap into my mouth. What if I kiss him again? What if he kisses me? No wants, I remind myself. Time to change the subject. Time to change it *fast*. I clear my throat. "You didn't tell the crew you knew who I was all along."

"I told Temper the moment I discovered you." He shrugs when my eyebrows shoot up. "Clearly, she didn't tell the others. She's my captain. You were a wild card. I've learned before that trusting blindly goes poorly."

I take a step to the side, hand dropping out of his, jaw hardening. I have no right to feel betrayed by that, but I do. Thankfully, it kills whatever pressure was building earlier. I tap the stim packets against my palm. "Perhaps you should direct your attention to the rest of your crew's health. They're here for the long haul, after all. Leave me what crutches I have left."

Something flickers across his eyes, like he realizes he's played his hand poorly. "You're far more interesting than the rest of the crew. And far more reckless."

So he's just bored? That's all this is? I mentally shake my head. Why should I care what's motivating his strange interest in me? It's too much. I can't handle one more thing. One more *want*. I brush him aside and leave the bunk.

My stomach churns with unhappiness. Palms still sweaty, I portion out a dose of stim into my water in the mess. When I knock it back, it tastes sour. Temper enters the mess behind me, refilling a canteen. "You're causing a lot of uproar."

"You already knew." The slight shaking in my hands evens out.

She shrugs. "Sure. I was honestly relieved to learn your secret identity because it means you weren't as criminally stupid as I thought you were back on Herschel. So eager to return to that wackadoo."

"Bianca didn't know what she was involved in. You probably know the type. Ties her future to the closest man and makes bad choices based on proximity. It got her banished, and then it got her in the cult. Her parents couldn't do anything about the one, but they could about the other. She's basically a good person. Also a dumb one. Dumb didn't merit Rashahan's treatment."

"Arcadio and I have a debate. Maybe you can settle it. You ever see a lizard on that planet?" She grins conspiratorially. "Or do you think that was people meat Rashahan served?"

"Never saw a full lizard. Saw a tail once, poking out from around a corner."

"Not the whole lizard?" She nods sagely. "Probably a decoy. People get twitchy when they think they're cannibalizing their fellow cultists."

"People don't think they're cultists at all." Not sure why I feel compelled to point it out. Maybe defensiveness of poor Bianca. She just wanted a new home. I drain the rest of my glass and set

it in the decontaminator. "They lost a community, and they want
another. Not justifying exploding a ship full of kids or anything,
but someone like Rashahan preys on their vulnerabilities. It's a
problem caused by the Families and their one-size-fits-all punish-
ments."

"Fuck, you're serious. You and Caro would probably get along
if it wasn't for the whole 'lying and spacing a ship full of people'
thing. For someone who's a former biohacker, she sure likes being
judgmental." She winks at me and puts her finger against her lips.
I raise my eyebrows. Biohacking isn't technically illegal, but it's
outside the bounds of the medical establishment. I don't know
many people who have a hand in it outside the Pierce Family—I'm
probably evidence of that hand. Maybe that's why Caro dislikes
me so much. Some bad experience with them.

I sit at the table, rubbing my temples. A dull ache has started to
rise in my head. While I was out, they've been prepping for our
trip to Poison Green. "We should target arrival at Poison Green
during the night. It's a big space. Between the moons and the bioluminescence of the water, it'll be light enough to see, but still
sheltered."

"Do we limit our search to the land, or is it possible to stand on
the refuse?" The captain takes a slug of water from her canteen.

I pull up my datapad and project a map to the holo-table in the
corner. Poison Green appears above it, outlined in flecks of light.
It's beautiful, albeit toxic. A low wide crescent of mountain with
a wide lagoon within. The wall over the mouth is first steel, then
floating, then net. Plates of steel go all the way to the seafloor, but
over time, they crack and buckle, and squiggles of refuse leak out
into the sea.

Within the lagoon, massive barges hold city blocks of trash.
They float, unconstrained, like a pond coated with the broad
leaves of the illium plant. Some of the barges contain toxic waste,
some rust-damaged building materials, and others a kaleidoscope

of small trash. It's the size of a town, maybe bigger than the trawl-ertown itself, and nearly impossible to properly map, because the layout of the lagoon is always changing. The water glows blue-green, which is not visible in the poor-quality holo.

"It's possible to stand on the refuse, but dangerous. If I, person-ally, was a kidnapper, I'd never set foot on the barges. Because I don't really want to grow a third limb or lose all my hair, which is what will probably happen if one spends too much time out there. If I was a kidnapper who cared more about staying invisi-ble and less about my health? I'd be on the barges in an instant. It's hard to find someone in all that trash. Especially if you're squeamish."

"We aren't squeamish." Itzel. She's crept into the mess as we were speaking. She's wearing a pair of fingerless gloves and her hood is up, dark eyes gleaming in the shadows. She pokes a finger at the holo-map. "Are there caves in the caldera?"

"Good question." I zoom in on the surface of the land. It re-solves into tall narrow hexagonal pillars, honeycombed together into a structure. "It's not land, per se. The caldera is made of black basalt columns. They fit together perfectly. It's not the type of structure to naturally form caves."

Itzel leans forward, nose almost touching the holo. "Fascinat-ing. I've never seen anything like that in person. They look almost like stepping stones. Do you know how they formed?"

"Not well. I'm no geologist. I think it's not unlike how mud dries into hexagonal shapes, except the cracks propagate down-ward and you end up with columns."

Itzel shoots a glance at Temper. "I'm taking my sample kit. It won't get in the way."

"I wouldn't dream of telling you no."

Micah enters the mess from the cabin area, wiping his hands. "That would be a first."

"I hardly ever say no!" the captain protests.

"Maybe not to Arcadio. To the rest of us?" The medic walks by me and leans against the holo-table, studying the layout. I do not study his tight behind in those coveralls.

Much.

He glances back in my direction and catches me not-studying him. A wash of heat floods my cheeks. I may be sending mixed messages.

"She says no to me all the time. When are we leaving?" Arcadio strides into the room, already wearing sleek expensive body armor and a killer's face. His armor looks brand-new.

"It's not close to the trawlertown." I zoom the map out to show the arc of the planet. A small flashing dot indicates our location, and an "X" marks Poison Green. "If we take the *Calamity*, we'll have to land on the caldera and that will attract attention. It might make the Abductor do something hasty. We don't want him to know we're approaching. The fastest ship in the trawlertown will get there in about one solar day but the average ship will take far longer than that."

"We won't be taking one of those ships again." Temper's voice is clipped. Micah chuckles. Caro enters the room with a sour face and crossed arms, which she somehow points conspicuously in my direction.

I cock my head in question at Micah's laughter.

"Captain gets seasick," he clarifies. "Unhealthy to arrive there all dehydrated and drenched in vomit."

I wince. She did look green on our way to the Necklace.

"I thought I'd outgrown it," the captain sniffs.

"That's not a thing a person outgrows," the medic rebuts.

"Either way, we don't need to rent a ship. We'll do a flyover in the *Calamity* and parachute to land. There's a lot of territory to cover, so we'll split into two teams. Itzel, Micah, and Cyn, cover the west side. Arcadio and I will cover the east. Caro stays with the ship—close but not too close—in case we need remote firepower.

No coms. Tap twice if you find something and we'll track you. We don't find anything on land, we move to the barges."

"The atmosphere fried my Family's tech, but we should be able to track her by the composition of Boreal's chip. It contains traces of korsnik." Arcadio wipes out my map and a chemical compound appears on the holo. Temper walks over to him and places a hand on his shoulder, squeezing gently. His head tilts toward her as though she possesses gravity sensed only by him.

Caro takes over. "Korsnik is a rare element mined deep in Escajeda territory. We scouted a planet for it not that long ago. I programmed a detector, but it requires close proximity. About the diameter of the ship. That's too close to scan the planet, but with a tight space like this it should be effective. When you all leave the *Calamity*, the drone swarm will leave with you and map the territory for korsnik."

It really is like a scouting mission. They're well organized. Well planned. It's strange not making a plan of my own. Also, nice. I never have backup. It's comforting. I'm not used to being comforted.

I could *get* used to it.

But I won't. Because in seven days, I'm going to betray Micah to save my family, and then, no one will ever work with me again.

CHAPTER 15

■ ■ ■ ■ ■ ■ ■ ■ ■ ■ ■ ■ ■ ■ ■ ■

There's one key issue with our plan that I'm in denial about right up until I'm poised in the cargo hold and Temper tosses me a parachute. I have to jump out of the ship—directly from the air lock. I nearly died to stay inside a ship once before. The thought of stepping out an air lock into open air is one of my worst nightmares. Second only to being in the void when it happens.

I thought I could push my way through it on moxie and will, ignoring the way my stomach churns and my vision tries to tunnel. I had planned to take enough stims to provide artificial moxie, but with Micah watching me like a sniper, I haven't taken as many as I usually would and now I'm clammy and messy. My nerveless fingers fail to catch the chute and it crashes to the floor at my feet with a clang so loud that everyone turns and stares. My hands are shaking. They're shaking so hard it's like the void has already wrapped itself around me. I wipe them off on my pants. Do it again. The breath sticks in my throat. I'm hot. Or maybe cold. I awkwardly place my body in something like a casual position.

Maybe no one notices. Sure, no one notices the crazy lady in the middle of the hold. My armor is strangling me. It's tight at the neck and the chest and everywhere and I can't breathe.

There isn't enough air up here.

There's no air.

Two big hands bracket my cheeks and Micah stares into my face. Reading something into it. "You're having a panic attack."

"No shit," I gasp. Shadows dance at the edge of my vision. My heart thunders in my ears. He smells good. Like spice and the cleaning solvent in the ship's clothing decontamination system.

"Close your eyes."

I do it. Air remains elusive. My breath escapes in short pants. An icy deluge swamps the back of my neck and I yelp, eyes snapping open. He drops a canteen by my side. Everyone else is carefully congregating on the other side of the hold, not looking at me.

"What the fuck, Arora?"

"Close your eyes." For once, his voice doesn't sound like sex. It's low. Calm. Soothing. Safe. "Focus on the feeling of the cool water on your neck. Focus on breathing. That's all you have to do. Just breathe."

I suck in one long breath. Another. The relentless din of my heart slows and calms. Water trickles down my back. I shiver. Breathe some more. When I open my eyes, he's still there, hands on my face, eyes locked with my own. I realize that my own hands are clutching his waist, fingertips digging in like I'm trying to burrow to his center.

A warm small weight collides with my back and I almost shriek and wave my arms until I realize that it's Vuur, climbing up to its habitual roost on my shoulder. Its small scaly head brushes under my chin.

Something about its slight mass steadies me. "I thought I locked you in the room for your own safety."

"I retrieved it." Itzel steps away. "You seem to do better when you have something to protect."

I utterly lost my shit. I can't do this anymore. I can't keep living like this. My breath starts to shorten again, and of my own volition, I close my eyes. Focus on the water.

"I'm sorry." I whisper the words under my breath. "I'm fine. We have to go. I'll be fine once we're on the ground."

I will. Even once we fall. It's the leaving the ship that's the problem.

"We're talking about this. Later." A muscle twitches in Micah's jaw.

"Later," I agree. Force myself to unlock my fingers from his armor. I step back.

Something lights in his eyes. "You trusted me."

A completely different kind of panic shakes its way through my body. I didn't. I won't. I *can't.*

Micah shakes his head and gives me that same speculative look. Vuur takes the opportunity to collect more head scratches from him. "Red-flag woman."

It surprises me into a weak smile. "Don't forget it."

"How could I?"

Feeling shaky and cold and refusing to look at the hatch, I scoop the chute from the floor and shrug into it, hands buckling and tightening straps on autopilot because if I think about it, I'll go right back into the void. "Everyone can go back to being normal. I'm fine."

"Was there a problem?" Temper's voice is bright and clearly full of lies. It's considerate of her. "We needed to look at the weapons. Didn't see anything."

Itzel nods. Caro is flying, so, thankfully, she missed the entire escapade. Arcadio glares at me like he's imagining me falling to pieces when it comes time to rescue his niece.

Fair. I would be, too.

"I have an issue jumping out of ships. Old history. No particular traumas with shooting kidnappers and rescuing children. I'll be reliable planetside." He won't believe me, but I need him to know that I prioritize his niece and her rescue.

How often do you leap out of a perfectly good spaceship? It isn't exactly naive of me to consider that it wouldn't come up in the course of doing business. You walk out plenty, but you don't jump and fall and fly. I glance over to find Micah still watching me.

I told him I would thank him at some point. When it really mattered. But not yet. Now is too soon for "thank you." Still seems like a debt more than an offering, so I avoid the magic words. I can't thank someone I still might betray. "I appreciate it."

He shrugs like he doesn't know what to do with that, maybe a tinge of disappointment colors his eyes, and he looks away. I slide my helmet on, completing the digital link with my armor.

Temper and Arcadio make their jump without drama. As it turns out, the open hatch and rushing wind is sufficiently different that I'm able to line up and prepare for my own. Itzel and Micah bracket me. I carefully tuck Vuur into one of the pockets of my coat, which may be silly as it, of all of us, possesses wings.

I don't panic again, and when I jump, the wind snatches me from the open cargo doors. It roars by my ears, sharp and bracing and real. Not the cold emptiness of the void—the body armor slightly insulates against it. The warm humid spice of my childhood. I let it buffet me into calm, and when the dark earth rushes at me so quickly it feels like I'm going to crash, I pull the stealth chute. It deploys, jerking me back and up as the wind catches and holds me.

I am not thrown to the empty vortex of space. I am not gasping my last breath. I am not alone and terrified. I am gently floating over a dancing gleaming sea, the waves of toxic algae flaring and fading as they batter against the shore and the barges and the trash. I am above the glowing Poison Green. And although I cannot see Itzel and Micah, I am not alone.

It's enough to fully set the blind panic behind me. By the time I carefully land on one coal-black basalt column, just large enough to hold me like a pillar, I am myself again. The night vision of my faceplate isn't sensitive enough to be washed out by the glow of the algae against the shore.

This is a place of folklore, which is funny considering the relative newness of Poison Green. Something about the sharp black columns and the glow of the sea, the inherent danger, breeds myths. They say the fox-fire glow lures sailors within the lagoon, where they either melt into the waste, run aground on the shore, or become part of the glow, toxic and contorted and beautiful. People disappear around the Green all the time. The sea has always had its sirens and this inhospitable shoal is a modern lure.

I roll my chute over my arm and shove it into the pack at my back, careful of the lines that drag behind it. As I work, Vuur clambers halfway out of the pocket and starts gnawing on a nearby button. When I'm done, Itzel has found me, and the two of us together find Micah, down the basalt staircase near the glowing blue-green water.

"You had a place as glorious as this, and you used it to house your waste?" Itzel's forlorn murmur barely reaches my ears. She crouches on the ground, hand splayed on a black column not that much larger than her two feet pushed together.

"It wasn't as glorious before the waste." This is certainly going to decrease my popularity, but I can't help trying to defend my home. "The algae came later. Once we gave it food. Waste has to go somewhere and launching it into space is a massive waste of natural resources."

"And this isn't?" She sketches a shape into the slightly convex top of the column with her fingertip.

I can't argue that. It is, but we still need to live somewhere, somehow. The trawler must keep moving. If it doesn't, space stations lose energy and thousands die. Or farm domes lose energy and millions, if not billions, die. Algae is used for regenerative energy, which means it's used for things that need a lot of consistent power. Like crop domes. Like air systems.

The caldera of basalt columns is shaped like a crescent moon, tall and thick in the center and narrowing and approaching the sea at its points. The collection of drones that Caro released are invisible above, but no signals of life have been sent to our helmets. The glow of the bay attracts my attention.

That's where they'll be. Because it's the most horrible place to go. The place where a child can't escape, because what hope is there, floating on a barge of refuse in the midst of a toxic sea? That's the way the Abductor thinks. He's always one step ahead.

But that doesn't mean we should ignore the arc of columns. Itzel, Micah, and I spread out so that we're in a line but barely visible to each other and follow the formation of the land, scanning the columns for anything out of place. It's a pretty night. If a child's safety wasn't on the line, this might even be pleasant. The glow of the algae rises and falls in the surf, dancing across the stone. Vuur makes a low whirring sound, small golden eyes locked on the moon. Probably it looks like a large sky-lodged chip of silver.

About a third of the way to the center, a light flashes on the corner of my face shield: Itzel activating the signal to attract our attention. I retrieve my blaster—keeping it out while searching uneven terrain is a great way to accidentally shoot yourself in the foot— and approach. Micah, who was on the far edge, follows. When we reach her, I'm not sure why she signaled. The line of the columns is unbroken. No figures or forms. No sounds.

"What is it?" I hiss into the coms.

Itzel points one finger at the column directly in front of her. It's nearly wide enough to support the three of us standing on it at the same time. "This one is hollow."

Well . . . shit. We all feel around the edge of the column until Micah's finger hits a slight depression, flipping the edge up on invisible hinges. A narrow ladder leads down into a glowing-bright space below. Not glowing with algae. Glowing with bright warm light.

I lever myself onto the ladder before the others can stop me. If the Abductor is below, our element of surprise is already spoiled. All we have left is speed. I slide down the edge of the ladder, feet and hands to the side rails to slightly control my descent. Vuur launches from my shoulder, awkwardly fluttering down. Micah swears through the coms and leaps after me.

When I hit the bottom, I roll to the side, blaster elevated, and freeze.

Flowers. It's a cave full of flowers.

Why the fuck is someone growing flowers in the middle of a toxic dump?

Micah swears again when he hits the ground. "Itzel, get down here and tell me I'm not seeing what I think I'm seeing."

But she's already here, landing as quietly as if she'd taken a gentle step rather than dropped several body lengths. "I can't do that. You're seeing exactly what you think you're seeing. Plankat nibarat."

I still don't know what they're talking about. I scan the chamber carefully. It's expansive. Maybe a quarter of the size of the trawler-town. Grow lights line the ceiling and soft soil has been filled in below our feet. A series of irrigators spreads under the long stalks. The flowers are blue with brilliant yellow-and-white centers. Each bloom is the size of one of my hands. A search reveals that no people are present at all. It's probably operated using primitive AI.

A large machine covers one entire wall of the room, a biolu-minescent glow coming from within several plas-glass cylinders housed within its frame. I'm no scientist, but someone's processing the glowing algae.

"Fuck. Not again." Micah plucks one flower from the stalk and twirls it between his fingers.

"What's plankton nibari?" Do I have to pull it out of them?

"Plankat nibarat. The only completely banned crop that I know of. We've been hitting grow ops in this region of space for the past few standard years." Micah stores the sample in a pouch at his waist. Vuur makes a fluttering leap for the lights above but can't quite get itself airborne. It glides down and gnaws on the sprinklers instead.

"Why is it banned?"

Itzel collects soil and water, scooping up Vuur while she's at it.

It settles on her shoulder contentedly. When I first came aboard, it was skittish of the others. At some point in the past few days, it seems to have bonded with them even more than I have. Even Itzel, who first called it a monstrosity. "When we first started working at optimizing humans with mods and genetic hacking, the one thing that eluded both scientists and doctors was a method to boost intelligence. Changing the brain triggers too many other changes. Plankat came close. It made people brilliant. It also made them violent, paranoid, and unempathetic. Which is a bad combination. People died and the plant was banned because it was deemed too destructive to even experiment with."

"What does this have to do with Boreal?"

They turn equally perplexed gazes my way. Itzel spreads her hands in a shrug. "I can't think of how it could. Refining plankat is a delicate and complicated process. None of that equipment is here. They're doing something to the algae, not the plankat. I can't see how a kidnapper would benefit from it. None of the children have been changed when they returned home, have they?"

"I think I would have heard about them all coming home as violent killers."

"Could be we just encountered someone else's illegal grow op. It's a good spot. You said people keep away. The two things could be unrelated." Micah scoops the lizard from Itzel's shoulder and places it on his own.

"And we need to get back to our search before the sun rises," I finish Micah's thought. When we're confident this isn't the Abductor's hidey-hole, we climb the ladder back out. Vuur transitions back to me.

We patrol the rest of the basalt land, with no joy. One large flat barge nudges close enough to the crescent that we can leap to it, if we are careful. We do. Itzel lands as light as a drop of rain, Micah lands just as completely but heavier. My foot skids out from under me but I catch myself and step forward onto the slick deck, sidestepping a fetid mass of food. That's good—I didn't completely embarrass myself in the stealthiness competition. Vuur cackles a little chirp that sounds like its having fun.

There isn't supposed to be food here. We recycle food or use it as bait. Some ship or resort or someone else has missed that directive and the whole barge reeks of decay. I poke at it with a gloved finger. The side of a bag splits open and a gob of what appears to be zombified serpent pasta oozes out. Fairly fresh, in the scheme of things. Maybe someone visiting their farm. Maybe something else. I step back, wiping my finger on my armor pants. The edge of this barge is near another and we leap from one deck to another, approaching the center of the bay. The barges rock gently as we go from one to the next.

With each barge we cover, I mark the vessel on the map projected in my helmet. On the opposite side of the lagoon, other ships glow to life in the map as Temper and Arcadio clear them. The sky above begins to glow with the first signs of early dawn, violet instead of black.

We reach a gap between ships. Our barge has floated away from the others and only the glowing sea is visible on each side, an abandoned tugboat in the center of a small isolated pool. Micah and Itzel flank me as we stand on the edge of the barge, waterlogged wooden pallets moldering behind us. We take turns plotting paths to the tugboat, hopping from one abandoned vessel to the next. I'm debating a particularly unappetizing small rowboat that may or may not be riddled with holes when a light flashes within the tugboat's cabin. There and gone before I even fully register it.

The breath catches in my throat. I mark the tug with a vibrant red on our projected helmet image and tap my coms twice. Someone is there. A drone sweeps by me, close enough to ruffle my hair, and flies over the barge. The red light flashes.

Korsnik has been detected.

I map a path of likely ingress for Itzel and Micah. While they take the safe route, I'm going to dive in. The Abductor is no fool. Odds are high that he lays traps. But the layout of the lagoon is so ever-changing that proximity is not guaranteed. There's only one way to ensure that I make it there undetected. Traps likely won't be set up for aquatic approach, because only the borderline suicidal would ever enter this water.

Lucky me.

I waterproof my coms and weapons, point emphatically along the path I outlined, hand Vuur off to Itzel, and dive into the glowing sea. I slice through the water like a knife, algae curling and billowing away from me in plumes and coils. It's warm in the shallow lagoon, even in the early morning, and the light coming from the algae outlines particles of floating trash. I keep my head under the water, trusting in my lung capacity even after this long off-world.

A splash comes from behind me. The idiot. I can make the swim without coming up for breath. He can't. There was a reason I outlined a path for them to follow. Too late now. Thankfully, Micah strokes through the water with far more competence than he showed when he fell from the deck during the storm. Itzel, at least, stays dry.

I reach the hull of the tugboat ahead of Micah and do a quick lap around the ship. Two bombs, one at starboard and the other at port. The explosives are contained in clear plas-glass boxes. Thin wires extend up toward the rail. Triggers. If he senses anyone nearby, he'll scuttle the ship and destroy any evidence. They aren't big enough to kill everyone on board, just to disrupt everything. He's planned for this. He's spent time here. Adrenaline thrums through my body like a chord pulled tight. My focus narrows. This is it.

Today I will face Aymbe's killer. Today I will save the final girl, before she has to be ransomed, so she doesn't have to wait out the time in fear. Today I will end my hunt.

Tomorrow—

I don't know what comes tomorrow.

I peel back the rubber stopper around the wire entry point to the boxes, allowing the water to flow in and flood the explosive. Most bombs are triggered by sparks. They don't travel well in water. He may have some sort of sensor that will let him know if a wire is cut. Boxes in water can get wet—hopefully there's no alert from my tampering.

Our coms are silent. I point at the explosives and then at the damaged rubber stoppers. The deck rocks above us, and the creaking thump of a footstep tickles every nerve ending on my spine. The tugboat is not a small vessel. In fact, it's probably around the size of the *Calamity*. I point Micah at the midstarboard ladder and I take the midport ladder. Ideally, we'd be in teams of two, but Temper and Arcadio have yet to arrive, and we can't wait. Not with the sun inching ever closer to the horizon and the sky growing ever brighter. We won't be invisible much longer.

I pull myself up the ladder, slipping onto the deck with my blaster out and the intensity turned up. The deck is clear. A narrow walkway wraps toward the stern around the helm. The living quarters are down below. I crane my neck to look through the window into the helm. It's empty. Dust-free. With careful steps, feet braced in case I need to fire, I creep back to the ladder that descends belowdecks. I pause in front of the ladder. Footsteps below. Not close.

I swallow, hand clenching around the blaster, and take one step down the ladder. It's almost like a staircase, so I can descend without my hands if careful. Careful is all I want to be, so I step as quietly as possible. I nearly run into someone in the darkness, my finger tightening around the trigger, until I realize that it's Micah, descending the starboard ladder. We move toward the back of the boat, where the primary sleeping cabin should be. I face the cabin, he faces the hall behind us, his shoulder pressed against mine in the tight space. The back of the boat is the steadiest, so that's where captains invariably sleep.

My hope is that's where they keep prisoners, too. It's not like tugboats usually come equipped with a brig. Another footstep comes from the fore of the ship. Micah's shoulder stiffens against my own, but we continue our progress toward the aft. Water creaks against the hull. It would be soothing if my heart wasn't lodged in my throat. The door to the back cabin is closed, a key sticking out of the lock.

Confident Abductor. Or we just broke into someone's lovely trash-viewed vacation property. I turn the key and slip into the room, immediately ducking as something heavy flies by my head. I reach out and grab the arm of my attacker, pushing her backward, my hand flashing out to cover her mouth. Micah follows me into the room, shutting the door behind us. Wide dark eyes stare at me under disheveled brown hair.

Boreal Escajeda has her mother's features: sculpted perfection. She appears unharmed and in one piece. I'm able to keep myself from being brained, but what appears to be a piece of the bed frame drops from her fingers as I halt its momentum toward my head. I lunge for it, but it thuds to the floor with a heavy thwack.

A creak comes from outside. We all spin to face the door.

I lift my face shield, glancing back at Boreal. "Your mother sent us. Your uncle is close. We're trying to get you out of here."

Hoping that's enough to keep her from trying to kill me even more, I spin with my back to her and point my blaster at the doors. Micah takes the other side, bracketing the doorway. Footsteps approach. Not as heavy as I expected. In my mind, the Abyssal Abductor is a monster of a man. Massive and terrifying and unyielding as a sea snake. Tally said he was tall but he never said he was large.

"Get behind the bed," Micah directs Boreal.

Not that there's much for her to hide behind. The bed frame is present, although partially broken in her attempt to create a weapon. Resourceful kid. Boreal pauses, clearly debates questioning us, but then retreats behind the bed.

Footsteps approach the door. Pause outside when they see the key is missing. Where is Itzel? Where are Temper and Arcadio? I steady my blaster, sight down the top. Steady my breath and my intentions.

Boreal ducks low. Smart girl.

The door swings open slowly and the Abyssal Abductor steps inside. Her brilliant Pierce-gold eyes catch mine and a slow smile creeps over her face.

"Shoot her!" Boreal screams.

I freeze. Aymbe grins at me from the doorway like no time at all has passed, that man-eater grin she practiced in the mirror every night when I babysat her. Her body is whole and healthy. Her eyes are hollow.

"Bella! It's so good to see you at last."

CHAPTER 16

Something cylindrical and metal drops from Aymbe's hand and she smirks before ducking back into the hall. Boreal screams. I flinch, waiting to explode, until smoke billows from the dropped grenade and I shove Micah back. "Get Boreal off the boat!"

"I'm not leaving with him!" the little girl screams behind me. This seems a misplaced application of caution.

Without fully thinking about it, I hurdle the smoke and blindly follow my shockingly alive cousin deeper into the ship. How is she here? How is she anywhere? She was taken. She was killed. We found her jacket, her buoy. Her blood. Did he somehow mod himself to look like one of his victims? But no, this Aymbe was her size. Her build. Her same wide bright smile.

It's her. Somehow.

I can't think of a *why* that ends happy.

She's on his boat with his victim. And, ostensibly, no him.

The ship is still and quiet before me. Darkness stretches the full length of the vessel, and all doors are closed. When she was young, Aymbe and I played hide-and-seek in the trawlertown. Our five-year age difference didn't seem like much back then. I always went high, lurking at the junction of a gantry or a conical rooftop. She went low. The engine room or the net storage space. Somewhere smothering and dark. I bolt down the hall, ripping open doorways and clearing the rooms as quickly as I can. There aren't many. Besides the bedroom, there's a small galley along the hall and a second bedroom across from it, covered in strewn clothes. Connected to the bedroom is a tiny bathroom with a dingy frame around a porthole letting in the morning light. Cosmetics clutter the meager counter space.

The closet is empty. Probably because the clothes are scattered everywhere else.

She might be a ghost, but she's still a slob.

That room cleared, I move on toward the front of the boat. One ladder leads down to the engine room and another leads up to the deck. I take a breath and leap down the ladder, just like I did in the field of plankton flowers, ducking low as a thick length of chain slams into the ladder where I should be standing. I capture the chain, coiling it around my wrist and yanking it toward me. Aymbe stumbles out from behind a beam, chain pulling at one of her hands, a nasty blade in her other hand. She slashes it at me.

She's not the first to take a swipe at me and she probably won't be the last. She *is* the first family member. Verbal swipes, sure. Physical, no. Maybe she's still the victim here. Somehow twisted by the real kidnapper. Afraid of him. Afraid of everything. I can't just shoot her, and I don't have a chance to adjust my blaster's intensity. I step to the side, chain still in my grip, and loop it around her knife wrist, snapping the chain back toward the ladder until her hands slam into it, knife dropping from her grip.

She kicks me in the knee. A vicious strike with her heel that knocks my joint back. "Ow! Jerk!" I yell, as though we're still kids wrestling as opposed to whatever the fuck this actually is. Without the armor, I'd be in trouble. The force of her blow drives me back enough that I lose my grip on the chain as she shakes herself free. Light from above stabs down into the engine room in a smoky shaft, illuminating her pale blond hair. We're both of us Pierce by-blows. It used to make me feel like I had a sister. I don't know what the fuck I feel now.

Pain. I feel that, as the fucker punches me directly in the boob. Clearly, even if she is afraid, she's not hesitating to be vicious.

"You aren't supposed to be here yet, Bella," Aymbe hisses. "No one is supposed to be here."

And here I thought she was happy to see me. She leaps for the ladder, but I catch her ankle, pulling her back down. Her chin snaps on one of the steps.

The look she gives me is complete deranged fury. "I'm done playing now."

She whips a blaster out from a hidden slit in her designer tunic top. How does a woman who's been missing for years have better clothes than I do? I don't have time to dodge. I don't have time to do anything but stare down the barrel of the blaster and try to figure out exactly how I've been so wrong for so long.

Also revisit my various life regrets, but there are too many to dwell on, so I decide to skip that endeavor. I lift my hands, palms up, doing my best to look like her cousin instead of her enemy. She doesn't seem persuaded. Her hand tightens on the blaster. I've never been the type to go out in the middle of a surrender, so I make the lunatic decision to lunge directly at her. Just as I shift my weight, a furious shriek reverberates from above.

"Sow! You made me miss the end-of-term dance! I am going to *eviscerate* you." Apparently Boreal hasn't been safely evacuated yet. She is the daughter of her mother, after all. She was born to hold a grudge.

Aymbe's eyes dart above at just the moment that I dive for her midsection, driving my shoulder into her stomach as I shove her blaster wide.

Wrestling Aymbe isn't the same as it used to be. When she was ten and I was fifteen, I had to be careful not to hurt her. Now we're both adults and she's clearly not worried about hurting me at all. She smacks a hand into the side of my helmet, which doesn't do a thing to injure me but does nearly deafen me.

I snap my head forward, ramming the edge of the helmet into her face.

"Viallanfucker!" She twists away from me, fingers tight around her bleeding nose. She manages to regain the blaster and fires, the shot lancing over my arm. I crawl forward, trying to regain the upper hand. Thudding footsteps come from above. Micah really isn't rushing at that whole rescue-Boreal thing.

"I hate you!" the kidnappee in question screams as she hucks the still-pumping smoke bomb directly on my head. "You think you have any power over me? You think my mother would ever pay you? You're beneath us!"

"Please stop helping!" I scream up at the hatch, momentarily blinded by the smoke and the concussion. Probably not an actual concussion.

A short pause. "Oh. Sorry."

I can't see a fucking thing. No one has shot me yet, but also no one is within reach. Where did she go?

When the smoke finally clears, I find the engine room empty, Aymbe escaped to the deck via another exit. I emerge from the engine room the same way I entered it and follow Micah and Boreal to the deck. Aymbe is already gone.

The sky above is pale lavender, the sun close to cresting the horizon. The water still glows dimly, blue-green and virulent. I turn to face Boreal with a raised eyebrow.

"What was that?"

"She thought she could kidnap me." She seems angrier than she is scared. Then again, if she's anything like me, she'd chew her own arm off before she'd ever admit to being scared. Boreal is only twelve, which is an age where you believe you can pass for an adult if you just put on the right act. Hers isn't as polished as her mother's yet. She has the beauty and the high-handedness. But her chin quivers and her arms wrap around herself like she's trying to give herself a hug.

I don't crouch down to her diminutive height. That would be offensive. She clearly wants to be treated like a woman. I take a flying guess at what she wants to hear. "Your mother knew you would be able to handle yourself. She told me how proud she was of your adaptability and endurance."

The quiver in her chin steadies. "She said that?"

"Of course. She never would have risked a rescue if she didn't believe you could handle yourself."

It's probably even the truth. The baby Escajeda raises her head, nose high. "That sow told me I was going to make her rich. That she'd have a hook in my mother that she'd never remove."

"You showed her." Micah pats her on the shoulder. "But maybe now you'd like to get off your ass and escape?"

Her jaw clenches and her knobby arms cross. "I'm still not going anywhere with you. Where is my uncle?"

As I gaze out the porthole, I see a familiar shock of long blond hair ducking behind a crumple of rusted metal in a ship to the west.

Aymbe. I could still catch her.

"You're safe now," I mutter to Boreal, following Aymbe's retreating form with my gaze, conducting mental math of risk and reward. I get paid for Boreal. I get my *life* back if I get Aymbe, too. A life I've never had the chance to live.

Boreal snorts. "*She* told me that a lot."

"Well, she's a liar and so am I. Difference is, I didn't kidnap you." I keep my eyes trained on the ship. Aymbe's about to leave my field of view. I can't just let her escape. "Micah, keep an eye on Boreal."

I race after my cousin, helpless as if there's a string tied to me.

"Don't do this, Cyn!" Micah roars behind me, caught between protecting the innocent and providing backup. It's really no kind of decision at all. I know what he'll do. I wouldn't be following Aymbe if I didn't trust him to keep Boreal safe.

My blaster's still loose in my hand. I don't know if I need to use it—if I *can* use it. My history is rewriting itself over and over until it's illegible, and all I can think is that, somehow, my cousin is alive. She survived whatever left her clothing bloody and torn.

I leap to the closest barge. Stick the landing. Run across its dew-slick deck and use a long pole to vault to the next barge. Then the next one, until finally I've reached the one Aymbe was on. I tear around the crushed metal lump and stop short, feet skidding, as I find myself face-to-face with a ghost.

And her blaster, which is pointed right between my eyes. Face shields are the weak part of a helmet. They have to let in visible light so you can see, which means that they let in visible-light-spectrum blaster shots, albeit attenuated.

"Took you long enough." The corner of her mouth quirks in a satisfied smile.

To catch up? No.

To catch *on*. Because I do, at last. All the denial I've been erecting into a clumsy barrier blown down like a damaged seawall in a storm.

"You wanted me to catch you?" I blurt, as though that's the most relevant thing.

"Why would I want that?" She tries that smile again. The one that melted hearts all over the trawler.

"That never worked on me, Aymbe. I knew you practiced it in the mirror every night. Smiles don't work if they aren't real."

"Of course they do," she scoffs, smile dropping but the blaster unwavering. "They work better. And yes, I wanted you to catch me. It was taking you *forever*. I just didn't want you to catch me *now*. Our game was supposed to go on longer."

"Forever to realize that the most notorious kidnapper in the system was actually one of his victims? Who was murdered by him? It's hardly intuitive." I step carefully to the side, where a bag of sand has split on the deck, providing a less slick surface in case I have the opportunity to launch myself at her.

"I wasn't murdered by him," she snaps, glaring. "He *couldn't* kill me. He tried his best, but it wasn't good enough. He didn't have what it took to kill me. He hooked me to a weight and dropped me in the sea and I still didn't die. I tore that hook out and climbed the buoy line from the depths. Pathetic. What kind of killer lets the sea do their work for them?"

She leans against the shattered steel as though waiting for my applause. When none is forthcoming, she continues, "I killed him, of course. It was what he deserved. Poor fool never saw it coming. Looked at me like I was one of those gasts the clouds form on the cliffs in the fall. He was so scared. That was the first time I realized how it felt for someone to be afraid of me. He was dawdling around, probably enjoying the afterglow. Disgusting." She pauses, gives me that beaming smile again. "But you would know, wouldn't you? You know exactly how good it feels. His body count didn't come close to meeting yours. That's when I started leaving clues for you. When I realized that we're the same, Bella. The two most infamous villains in Pierce territory."

Something cracks in my chest. Aymbe is the Abyssal Abductor. The new one, at least. The *more* murderous one, if the statistics are judged. The nightmare in my closet—at least, one of them. The person who caused me to board the *Iceberg* because I thought I had a chance to rescue her.

"Why?" It's all I can think of to say. "You could have come home."

"Why?" She cocks a brow, lips twisting but blaster steady. "What did I have to go home to? To just be some girl on a trawler? I was better than that. Powerful. Superhuman. Superior. I was reborn to something new."

"Your father died!" I blurt, as though I could break through to her somehow. "He died trying to save you. Your mother was destroyed by losing both of you."

"Why would I go home to that mess?" It's like she's bewildered about why a person would go home to her grieving mother. "Sounds awful. I was free. I had a ship. And I had a new job. You'd be amazed how easy it is to get a kid to wander off with you. I was much better at targeting good ransoms than the old Abductor. I was superior to him in every way."

"You didn't just ransom them. You killed them if their family couldn't pay. I know the truth, don't try to pretend this was purely about making money."

"They all had the same chance I did, of trying to get away on their own." Her blaster's moving a little wildly now. "None of them were good enough. They didn't fight like I fought. They didn't even try! The one you just swept in and rescued—she cried for her mother."

Yikes. None of us ever imagined she might have realized she could be a better villain than the man who took her.

That she thinks I'm just like her.

"We are not the same." I spit it out, blaster wavering at my side, waiting for my opportunity to sweep it up and shoot. "I did what I did in self-defense, after they fucking spaced me. It haunts me to this day. I can't fucking sleep without hearing the bodies hit the walls of the ship."

"My first kill was self-defense, too! It makes you feel so powerful, doesn't it? To kill your captors. To make them feel weak. Makes you embarrassed that you were taken in the first place."

A million moments from our childhood make sense. That practiced smile. The way she manipulated all the boys. The way she manipulated everyone. Fuck . . . I owe Enderson Tally an apology. I bet he was on to her emptiness, and she accused him to discredit him. "*Viall*, Aymbe, you're hollow as a shell, aren't you? You always were."

"I don't know what you mean." Wide eyes.

"Drop the act. I might not have seen through you then, but I do now. This will kill your mother."

"Only if she finds out. Maybe not even then." She shrugs and shifts her weight. The first rays of the harsh blue sun crest the horizon and reflect from the twist of steel by her head, drowning us in reflected glitter. It looks like a dance floor, not a toxic spill in the middle of an ocean. "You won this round. Points to you. Although it was awfully on the nose, me going home. I really had to spell it out. Next time, it will be more challenging."

"This isn't a game, Aymbe. These are real people. Real little kids like you were when he took you. There's something wrong with you if you can't see that."

There's everything wrong.

"They aren't anything like me. We've been over this. *I* escaped. *I* defeated him. I'm *better* than they are." Her lip curls back into a sneer but her eyes have a speculative gaze. "You could join me, you know. We could pick kids who fit your exacting requirements. What about the children of those traffickers? I bet they never had a struggle in their lives. We'd be making charted space a better place."

Wave after wave of disgust and horror crash into me. I could handle this if it was a stranger. I'd have the distance necessary to manipulate them. I feel like I've been shot in the gut.

Actually, no, I don't. I've been shot in the gut. That was better than this.

I have to be smarter. The way I see it, I can either convince her to turn herself in (seems unlikely at this juncture), shoot her right now and end it all (her blaster is better aimed than my own), or pretend to go along with it. Pretend that I'm every bit the hollow shell that she thinks me. Then, when she turns her back, I can stun her and drag her from this barge.

"A better place?" I say it as though it never occurred to me before. Because it didn't. I'm not a crazy person. I'm not sure she is either. She's something else . . . something sane enough to commit this kind of crime but twisted enough to think it's a good idea.

"Of course. It's been so long. I'm lonely. It would be a great diversion to have a partner, Bella. And who would ever suspect

Cyn Khaw, the great huntress of the Abyssal Abductor, of being the Abductor's sidekick?"

"Partner," I say, because it's the sort of thing I'd say. "I'm older than you are. I'm not a sidekick."

That smile goes wider, and I'd almost think it was real if I didn't know better. A trail of fear skitters down my back, cold and bracing as the water Micah poured earlier. Fuck. Fuckity fuck fuck. I carefully holster my blaster, taking the risk that, if I stay interesting, she won't be motivated to shoot me. "We should catch up somewhere less likely to get us caught. What about the Necklace? We could go to Opal."

"You and your stupid Opal. Sapphire has the caves. Ever so much more valuable than pretty beaches. Although you know that already, don't you? You wouldn't be in Poison Green if you hadn't found the message I allowed Boreal to leave you."

Poison Green. Of course. Only locals call it that. Am I a fool for not considering the most least-obvious culprit?

Maybe. I thought I was so jaded that nothing could surprise me. Micah called it, something was wrong with that message.

"You're always one step behind me, Bella, that's why you're the sidekick."

I work my jaw. "Where would you feel safe, then? We can pick a new victim."

All I need is her back turned. Just one moment where she isn't on her guard, blaster pointed right between my eyes.

"Not victim. Target," she gently corrects me, something like anticipation in her eyes. She always was a know-it-all.

"How did you know about Boreal?" Maybe she'll share some of what she knows.

"All that money funneled to a moon for a nameless little girl? A Familyless girl with a massive security force encamped nearby and periodic visits from a woman who looks enough like her to be her clone? Anyone paying attention could have figured it out." She creeps forward, bright smile still pasted on. Blaster leveling at my face yet again. "My friends always pay attention. So do I. Clearly there were credits to be had."

A lizard hurls itself over my shoulder, wrapping its small wings right over my cousin's face. I scream, terrified that she's going to injure Vuur, but she fires a wild blast just as a bolt of light hits her in the hip. A body smashes into me, sending us both tumbling over the field of refuse. A splash sounds. Running feet.

I thrash against the bags of trash and the unyielding body above me. One of the scattered sun-glimmers finds its way directly into my eyes. I duck my head to the side and realize that Micah is poised above me, arms braced by my head, legs pressed into my own.

"Get up, Micah." The clipped voice from behind him is so cold and hollow I barely recognize it as Itzel's.

"Not when you sound like that." He settles in for the long haul, more of his weight draping over me. It's not unpleasant but it would take a lot more than that to get me going at this moment. I could maybe handle the trash and the witnesses—it's the existential typhoon brought up by my cousin's reappearance that's the real mood-killer.

"They're working together. You heard her. She wants to find a victim with her *cousin*." Itzel's blaster is unwavering.

I did not predict this complication when I decided to lead Aymbe on. "Where is Vuur? If you hurt it . . ."

"Your lizard is fine, although clearly protective. Vicious thing." There's a strain of approval in Itzel's voice.

"That was so cosmic!" Boreal squeals. "You have a flying lizard! You shot her. You guys are the best."

Which leads me to the next moment of concern. "Where is Aymbe?"

"She fell off the boat. She's floating face down. Either drowned or dead from the shot."

I start struggling against Micah in truth. Something I glossed over earlier shoots to the forefront of my mind. "No, she isn't. She *doesn't* drown. Get to her, get to her now."

The both of us were deprived of air and ideal pressure conditions for far longer than a human body is meant to weather. Far longer than the standard mods would tolerate. I thought it was just me. I thought I was the only freak who could survive.

I'm not.

What did the Pierce Family do to us when they cured us? This isn't the standard immunity cocktail. This is something else. Something . . . experimental. It's the only explanation for why two ostensibly normal girls from a trawlertown would survive such extreme traumas. They did something to me, and years later, they did an upgraded version on her. With testing so traumatic that I still don't remember it to this day.

They changed us, and one of us came back broken. She was so young I didn't notice the alteration, but now, now that I have the new perspective, I can see every little manipulation. Everything she did to seem sweet and helpless as she smiled that predatory grin she practiced in the mirror. As she learned to hide what she'd become.

"You don't understand." I shove at Micah and almost shift him off of me. "She won't drown. She maybe can't. *He* tried to drown her. It didn't take."

"Don't let her move." Itzel's footsteps retreat to the edge of the barge.

I shove at Micah again. He doesn't move except to give me a visual scan. "You're bleeding. You'll make it worse."

I'm not—I am. A hot trickle of pain laves the lower edge of my ribs. "She shot me."

It shouldn't surprise me. It does.

Itzel swears. "The Abductor is gone. We'll have to question her collaborator."

"I'm not her collaborator!" I protest, cheek pressed into a very pungent sack of something. Eggs, maybe?

"She's telling the truth, Itzel. I don't generally shield the bodies of serial killers." Micah glances over his shoulder. Seems to deem it safe enough to stand. He reaches down and hauls me to my feet. My side screeches in pain. "Every fucking time there's danger and someone's at risk, she runs headlong at the danger. She did it in the volcano, she did it on the boat on our way to the island, and she did it here when the Abductor revealed herself. She's even worse than Temper, because for some reason, Cyn also thinks she's a soulless hard-ass. If I've ever met someone desperately in need of decent backup, it's Khaw. She was trying to lull the other one into a sense of comfort. And she was probably going to get herself dead in the attempt."

"This could be part of a long con," Itzel argues, apparently assuming I'm far more dedicated to the cause of deceit than normal.

Micah grumbles out a breath and offers the next statement like a gratuity he feels may be unearned. "Everyone's scent fluctuates when they lie. Hormones, nerves, sweat. All tiny things that change biologically. She isn't lying."

Every lie I've ever told in his presence flashes through my memory, but I decide to ignore that crisis in favor of the present one. I've never explicitly told him I'm *not* planning to turn him in for a bounty.

"Where did you get that lizard? It's so cunning. Ow, it bit me!" Boreal continues her extolling of Vuur's virtues. That's good. The brave little lizard may have just saved my life. She lifts it in both hands. "Oh, it just licked my finger. That's like a lizard kiss, right? I just got a lizard kiss."

"You expect me to believe that she didn't know her own cousin was the Abyssal Abductor?"

"Not the original one." I piece together what I've deduced

combined with what she told me. "There was an original one. He took the first few kids, the older ones. Took Aymbe, too. She survived after we failed to make the ransom drop and killed him before he could kill her." I shake my head, bewildered, still not fully understanding how she could twist so thoroughly. "And then, I guess, decided to take up his mantle because it seemed like easy credits and a trip off-planet. Probably even stole his fucking ship. She's the newer, more ambitious Abductor. The one who takes rich kids. While I was hunting her, thinking I was hunting her killer, she was taunting me."

What do I tell her mother? "Good news, your daughter's alive! Bad news, she's absolutely fucking crazy!"

Will she believe me? I barely believe me.

. . . . .

Caro drops a small lift from the ship to the rock below, the engines buffeting us against the basalt pillars. The plan is for Temper and Arcadio to take Boreal straight home while the rest of us investigate the grow op and try to track Aymbe. With Aymbe on the loose, no one wants to risk Boreal on-ground longer than is necessary. Boreal's still doing a good job of playing tough, but her fingers are clutched around Arcadio's hand like she's trying to strangle it. Vuur makes a whirring upset noise and rubs its face against my jaw.

I can't keep bringing it into danger. This is no kind of life for the little guy. It almost got shot for me today.

I gently detach it from my shoulder and approach Boreal. I extend Vuur and she instinctively reaches for him, squealing a sharp breath when it races up her arm and curls its tail around the back of her neck. It looks good there.

"I need you to take care of Vuur, just like you took care of yourself on the ship," I tell her. It's harder than I thought it would be. I care about the small lizard. I wouldn't be doing this if I didn't. "It loves brass. It hates nickel. It needs iron. It will eat all your jewelry, but it will love you unconditionally."

It takes this opportunity to lick the small metal hoop high on the rim of her ear. Boreal bites her lip and grabs my hand. "Thank you."

She's thanking me for more than Vuur. "You would have made it out on your own. I have every faith in you."

I have *some* faith in her. But right now, she needs confidence more than she needs truth.

I kiss the top of the lizard's head. Whisper for it to be good. It burps a spark that tickles the edge of my nose. Then I step back with Micah and Itzel as they board the lift and leave.

"That was a kind thing you just did." Micah keeps his gaze on the departing ship, hands clasped behind his back.

I swallow the lump that's formed in my throat. "The lizard isn't meant for a life like this. She can take care of it."

He hums a noncommittal sound. "Then it was a kind thing two ways."

We search the plankton flower cave until midday but don't find any evidence of who erected it. Nor do we find a link to Aymbe. It's professional, which means there's no calling cards left lying around.

"If it's so dangerous, should we destroy it?" I ask the others.

Itzel shakes her head and caches a few cameras. "Not until we know more about who's growing."

We end up back in the tugboat after detaching the bombs. There's no sign of Aymbe.

I don't know how long she can hold her breath under water. My situation is different from hers and I haven't fully tested my capabilities. Maybe I should have, but mostly I've done my best to forget. I assumed it was a fluke. I didn't connect it with the Pierces, because as far as I knew, I was alone in the ability to survive. If Aymbe swam up from a trench, impervious to water and pressure, it's more than just a few minutes.

Maybe her mods are more powerful than mine. They had years to make improvements, after all.

I should have tried harder to follow her, but it was too late. No bubbles on the water, no trail. No handy tracking chip. No trail from a speedboat, tracking her route from Poison Green. And she does have another vessel. No way would the Abductor be relying on this junker of a boat to get around.

I know who it is now. I know who *she* is. I never had that advantage before. I may not know what's happened in the last ten years, but I know what happened in her life before that. I can find her, eventually. Hopefully before she takes another.

We have to get to the trawlertown. I wad up a shirt from Aymbe's bed and press it against the wound in my side before I descend to the engine room.

I know enough about engines from my own ship to assess the state of the tugboat. It'll run. If I put in a little work, it will run faster. I do the bare minimum to get us in motion. As I work, the other two clear the rest of the ship for any traps.

I'm relieved to be alone. Breakdowns are so embarrassing in public. My hands shake around a wrench until I'm forced to put it down. I crouch, palms gripping my legs, and breathe out a fluttery breath. She's alive. I threw away my life—my family—with both hands to avenge her and she's alive.

And *awful.*

She felt her own power for the first time and chose to seek more of it. I felt mine and it terrified me. She killed innocents. She tormented families when she, of all people, should know better. Can the blame be put on Pierce's meddling?

If so, what does that say about me? Am I, also, what they made me? Little spots dance in front of my eyes.

This is going to shatter Mygda. How do I tell her? How do I tell my family that I'm hunting my own cousin? I lock my fingers harder on my legs. A wash of heat floods my skin. Breathe in. Breathe out.

I see Micah's face before the jump, cradling my head in his hands, gaze boring into me. The cool trickle of water down my neck. I breathe my way through the tightening of my chest, the quivery feeling in my body.

I can't keep living like this. I need to make a change.

A different change, that is. Today was a pretty big change already. Next time I should really specify a *good* change.

When I'm back to feeling like a person, and the tugboat engine is back to acting like an engine, I go up to the helm. We creep out of the lagoon, pausing for me to activate the locks that release us to the sea. I'm at the wheel when Micah and Itzel enter the space.

She doesn't apologize for almost shooting me.

"Time for you to get patched up." Micah puts a first-aid kit on the counter.

I nod and Itzel takes my place at the wheel. I remove my coat and Micah carefully peels my shirt up and away from the wound, only exposing the bloody flesh necessary to do his work. After this long, the blood has dried and partially scabbed, making it painful enough that my thoughts don't drift in other directions.

Much.

I'm still human after all. When I imagined Micah undressing me—yes, of course I've imagined it—it wasn't precisely in these conditions and Itzel wasn't perched next to us, watching like a guard in case I decide I want to attack her crew member just because my cousin made it look fun.

Also, it didn't hurt quite so much. A little, maybe, in that way of pressing urgency.

Anyway, it's not like that. The only anticipation is about how soon I can get patched up and back to hunting Aymbe. Micah continues to poke at me gently, like he expects my guts to pop out of the wound in my side and say hello.

"It's not that deep," I mutter. It isn't. A scrape right along the lowest rib but not even deep enough to show cartilage.

"That's not what I'm assessing. My travel med kit is good for triage but not great for long-term care. I'm not sure if I can keep this from scarring."

I laugh before I can stop myself. When they both look at me like I've completely lost my mind, I decide that the time for truth, of one variety or another, has finally come. I tug my blood-crusty shirt over my head, leaving myself in my compression bra and pants.

And scar tissue. A plethora of that. The void leaves its calling card. In my case, a tracery of cobweb-fine threads cover the surface of my skin in a chart. They're subtle, almost like a pale tattoo, but they're everywhere. As far as I know, no one alive has scars like this because the things that leave scars like this don't leave people alive.

"I'm not overly concerned about scars," I clarify, as both of them stare at me with slack jaws.

I even surprised Itzel, whom I was beginning to think was part android. Only part, though. Amazing how she mode-switches from scattered scientist to efficient killing machine.

"What the fuck did that to you?" Micah reaches a hand toward my upper arm and then pauses, glancing at me for permission. I allow it. I also thought that, if he finally got me without clothes, he'd be more awed than appalled. I'm really disappointing my own expectations today.

"Nothing at all," I say, which is the honest truth.

CHAPTER 17

■ ■ ■ ■ ■ ■ ■ ■ ■ ■ ■ ■ ■ ■ ■ ■

Of course they don't accept that answer. I don't expect them to. It's time for honesty, after all. Long past time for it. The thought lifts a weight I didn't even know was on my shoulders. And when I take in their curious-but-trying-not-to-be faces, it all comes out. "When I was ten, and then later when Aymbe was nine, viral waves went through the trawlertown, striking primarily children. The Pierce Family has a program where children within its territory can be sent to one of the five Pierce medical centers and assessed for health. We both were sent off-planet and treated."

"Most Families have a program like that. It's bad press to allow your vassal children to die." Micah finishes tracing one of the scars on my arm and returns to patching up my side. I'm shockingly relieved that he didn't flinch away in disgust. Others have. There's a reason I haven't been intimate in ages.

Well . . . a few reasons. My personality and singularity of focus might have something to do with it, too.

"They held any children they took for follow-up exams to en-sure we were in good health. Most of us survived. Not all. As you likely heard Aymbe say, her kidnapper dropped her to the bottom of a trench when we failed to pay. She *swam* all the way back up. No standard mods for vassal children are *that* good. That's not just oxygen, it's pressure, too. Temperature. Humans aren't supposed to survive in those conditions, and she did, against all odds."

"If you believe her. She could be lying." Itzel taps the wheel, a tiny course adjustment.

"I believe her because a similar thing happened to me." Perhaps they'll let me leave it at that. No, of course not. How could they? *I* wouldn't let me leave it at that. Micah's fingers stroke slowly and soothingly over my side, tracing little lines of pain and fire. "You've both heard of what happened to the traffickers aboard the *Iceberg*. If you didn't know before, I'm sure Caro told you. What you don't know is, prior to the whole venting-the-ship-to-the-void thing, they spaced me." I trace a hand over my scarred skin. "A person can survive maybe a standard minute in space. And that survival would come with pretty severe damage. I was there much longer. That's what caused this. After about ten seconds, the water in your body starts boiling. It causes extreme swelling. Some makes its way to your skin's surface and freezes. Usually freezing isn't an issue in space. At least, not the main one. There's no conduction or convection, only radiation. You'd freeze slowly if you live long enough. Usually, people don't. There's no possible way I could survive unless Pierce did something extra to me. Unless they muddled with something that was never listed in my files."

My voice sounds dispassionately clinical. I don't say anything more. I don't tell them how the mere thought of that cold emptiness sends me screaming awake any time I try to sleep. I don't say how I can still feel the ice cracking on my face. How looking through that open hatch, into the black, froze me inside as well as out. This moment isn't about me. It's about Aymbe and what they did to her.

Micah squeezes something sharp and stinging over the long graze in my side, pinching the edges of my skin together with his fingers until it fuses into an angry red line. Then, ever considerate, he carefully wipes the blood away with a piece of gauze, fingers steady and slow. Gentle.

I also never figured that his fingers on my naked skin would be gentle, so I'm reevaluating all my expectations.

Itzel glances at her crew member. Her fingers are twisting into some sort of shape that I don't even recognize, like it's a stress reaction. "It's not just Nakatomi. At least Pierce, too."

"What isn't just Nakatomi?" I'm behind the curve. I was expecting questions. Doubts. Micah asking why my lungs didn't collapse when they absolutely should have. Not that I have answers for any of those questions, but I expect them.

"You probably heard about what happened on Herschel Two—besides the part you were there for. Most people have. It's why Nakatomi is currently being disbanded and why they're out of the Five. They were trying to power-grab and partnered with Frederick Reed, who managed to snake his way out of blame." Micah finishes with my side and stands back and away, gaze leaving my wound and returning to my face. "Clearly, they aren't the only Family in the Five who are reaching beyond their current means for more."

Well, of course they aren't. I push off the table to my feet. "People don't get to high-power positions and then just decide they have enough. Why be part of the Five if you could be the One?"

Itzel shakes her head like she doesn't understand that kind of thinking. Her full lips purse. "But medical experimentation on children? Just for better mods for a slight advantage? The risk of failure is so high. So is the risk of being caught."

"Not if you think it can never happen to you. They've been untouchable for years. On the rise. Why would they expect consequences?" In my experience, no one ever expects consequences for their actions. Bounty hunting can be shockingly easy because the bounties all assume that they're special and nothing bad will ever happen to them. It's nice to disrupt expectations as much as possible. "I'm sure everyone in the Five has some grossly illegal scheme in place to seize more power. Why would anyone stop experimenting with something that could completely change their place in the power structure?"

The biologist sighs, leaning a hip against the instrument panel. "You and Caro have more in common than either of you think. So cynical. I hate it. Things were easier at the monastery. You prayed when you prayed. You slept when you slept. You killed when you killed."

Sounds nice.

Wait.

Suddenly the tattoos that line her hands and wrists make sense and I realize how close I came to death earlier today. "You're an acolyte of the Dark Mother of the Void."

She flashes me a carefree grin that's somehow both sexy and horrifying. "Former. I've retired."

I didn't know that was an option. I also don't know how a Voidian acolyte finds herself on a scouting crew in the middle of nowhere. In an effort to appear more worldly, I nod as though I understand.

Between Caro, who is suspicious enough to run DNA tests on strangers and apparently experienced in biohacking, and her own pocket assassin, Temper certainly has put together a crew that would be as equipped for regime toppling as it would be for scouting.

Or crimes. It would also be very equipped for that.

. . . . .

The stars above spread like confetti tossed in zero-g. Which, I suppose, is basically what they are. Ribbons of aurora light in red, purple, blue, and green thread the space between the stars and dark, a light show spurred by solar radiation hitting the active ionosphere. It's beautiful but inconvenient, because without the extra oomph of the trawlertown relay systems pushing through the ionosphere to the satellites, our coms don't work much farther than the rails of the tugboat. Meaning I can't warn a fucking person until I get back to the trawler. I lean against the rail as the boat makes its slow progress to intercept the trawlertown.

Now that our destination is set, we travel on autopilot. Itzel and Micah have long since retreated belowdecks to sleep. I showered off Poison Green, but my nerves are sparking under my skin. The wind ruffles my hair, and the familiar salt-soft scent of the sea permeates my senses.

I miss Vurr. I only traveled with the lizard a short time, but it burrowed under my skin.

Pressure builds beneath my eyes, the struggle to keep them open increasing by the moment. My head feels like I stuffed the parachute in there instead of in the pack, slow and muzzled. It's heavy, so heavy. My mind is awake, but my body is exhausted. I pinch the skin of my wrist and the pain stabs me awake.

"That's why you don't sleep." Micah's words are startling enough that I jump slightly, yelping a little squeak as my fingers curl around the rail for support. How embarrassing.

"What?" I ask, intelligently.

"And why you didn't want to jump from the ship earlier."

"Didn't want" is a kind way of putting it. I consider a million defensive deflections and settle for the truth. I'm tired. The night stretches before me, and shadows already crowd at the corner of my eyes. "It leaves its mark on more than the skin."

"There's more, isn't there?"

"There's always more." I slouch against the railing, and he strides from the shadows to lean next to me, shoulder brushing my own as he carefully looks out at the water instead of at me. I have no such compunctions and study the way the starlight makes his skin glow, the way the wind plays with the waves in his hair. The strong arch of cheekbones and the stubborn jut of his chin. The dim Pierce-yellow glow of his banishment tattoo. "No matter how many words I used, there would be more. I told you the bones of it, though."

He traces the line of my knuckles where they clench around the rail. Strokes back to my wrist. "Bones are important. They aren't the whole picture."

It was stupid to use an anatomical metaphor with a doctor.

But I am stupid. Stupid-tired, stupid-naive to never once consider Aymbe could be a killer, stupid-trapped in this deal with the Pierce Family because I can't possibly betray Micah now, not when I know him—not when I've seen who he really is. When he's defended me. He can't help but take care of others. But I'm going to need something else to hold over Pierce to keep my family safe. Some distraction. I reach down to the smooth coms shape in my pocket. My fingers brush nothing at all.

It's gone.

I scrabble in the pocket. The other side. Still gone. Well, fuck. That's not good. How did I somehow lose a priceless tether to a man who wants to use me just slightly more than he wants to punish me? Probably one of the many times in the past day that I was tackled. Another item for the stupid list. I'm so screwed.

And so, with all that stupid on the table, with the possibility of betrayal off of it, I decide to do something I've never done before.

I decide to tell all of the truth. I tell him about showing up desperate to save Aymbe, only to find that my cousin was never there at all—bad information from a bad source. Getting to the ship too late to rescue slaves already sold to market. About them taking off ahead of schedule while I was still sneaking around the vessel, trapping me. About holing up in a wall panel because I couldn't escape. About falling asleep and only waking up when they yanked me out. About the long-short journey to the air lock, dragged on a rough metal floor with jeers and kicks and laughter to speed my way. I don't know why they never tried to sell me, what made me waste instead of commerce. Not that I wanted to be commerce—it's a strange thing to be hung up on.

I look out over the water, carefully avoiding eye contact as I share what it felt like when that air-lock hatch closed. The blind fucking panic and fear and the stupid desire to *live* that overwhelmed everything else. I tell him about what it's like to be in space. The cold taking root in my mind. The nothing at all. The feeling of surety in my fate and wondering why it hadn't reached me yet.

Now his hands are the ones clenched around the rail, each knuckle a blade against his skin. If humans emitted an energy field, his would feel like lightning. I almost imagine I can sense it.

And then, because I've told him about the fear, I tell him about the violence. The horrible journey to the helm. The sound of bodies as they jetted their way to space, meaty thumps against the bulkheads, ceilings, and floors of the ship. About passing out in the helm and waking up days or hours or moments later, feeling weak but, besides that, good as new.

"You heal fast." He repeats what I assured him days ago, and I nod.

And then, because this whole story has been pretty explicit in its negative light, I add in that I did track down all those trafficked people and rescued them afterward. I never became famous for that. It's less lurid. Doesn't sell subscriptions.

I wait, in the starlight, for him to make the same assumptions Aymbe did. Caro, too. That he's traveling with a mass murderer. Someone more dangerous than the woman we just encountered.

Or maybe worse, that he's traveling with a dupe. A bounty hunter who was so green at the time that she let herself be caught and spaced. So naive that she risked it all to rescue a woman who wasn't even in any danger. Someone who was stupid enough to trust a source just because she wanted them to seem trustworthy.

He doesn't say anything, but those fingers return to tracing my wrist with a slow steady glide. It's like he's turning my volume up and then down, ratcheting my nerve endings until impatience finally overwhelms nerves and I turn to look at him and demand he say *something*.

His face is right there, a breath away, and he's studying me with an expression that's so complicated I can't suss it exactly except it doesn't contain fear or disgust or any of the things I was worried about. It's like I'm a book written in a language that he doesn't quite understand. The hand that was at my wrist slowly, achingly, moves up my arm, avoiding my interface tattoos, slithering a trail of sparks along my nerve endings even though it's tracing my sleeve, not touching my skin anymore. There's something about the slow deliberation of the gesture. The surety.

This is different than the last time we were this close. We've spilled honesty between us. It's terrifying.

I can't read his eyes in the dark. In the meager light cast from the aurora above and the banishment tattoo on his face, I think they're asking me a question. Having just flayed myself bare, I can't handle one more moment of vulnerability, and rather than answer, I angle my body toward his own, hoping that the physical gesture allows the grace of claiming this was all just a mistake if I'm interpreting this moment wrong. His hand curves up and over my shoulder blade, the slope of my neck, and finally coils in the back of my hair, messy snarls where it came undone in the chase and the water.

He's giving me time to retreat. I'm not in the mood to retreat. All of my decisions have been based in fear. Every single one. I've been afraid of disappointing my family, of being trapped, of not finding Aymbe's killer—big whoopsie there—of not surviving, of going back to that air lock one day, vulnerable and exposed and alone. Of letting someone or everyone down again. So afraid that I don't let anyone anywhere near me, because something just might go wrong. It's already mostly all gone wrong, so the self-protectiveness feels a bit stale.

I'm tired of fear. I'm so fucking tired of it.

So I step closer, devouring that last tiny distance between us until we're chest to chest and I have to look up into his eyes instead of over at them. My heart thuds in my chest, so loud that he almost certainly can hear it. The rail presses hard against my hip. He goes predator-still. The kind of motionlessness right before a pounce. Except I beat him to it. I close that last imperceptible distance between us, pressing my lips against his in a brush that's almost chaste considering how I'm feeling.

It's a request for permission, really. I don't think I've read this wrong, but after everything with Aymbe, I'm not exactly trusting my judgment. I'm not sure I can handle him flinching back in revulsion. He doesn't, thank Viall. Instead, his thumb traces my jaw, angling it until we're in perfect alignment, and then he takes over completely.

If my kiss was a gentle request, his is a wholehearted acceptance. His mouth slants over mine, hot and hungry and encompassing, heady as going without oxygen only not nearly as frightening. My head suddenly goes fuzzy for a reason entirely different than exhaustion. The world goes carefully completely blank until all I can feel is his body pressed against my own, the way his muscles roll under my fingers, the way my breasts smush against his chest. The way his lips seem to know everything I want just a second before I think of it.

I gasp in a breath, and he takes advantage of the moment to slip his tongue between my lips, taking sips of my mouth until I rub my own against it, warring between ourselves. He draws back and nips my lower lip. I take offense to the withdrawal and follow, nibbling his own lip. He makes a sound that's half growl, half grumble and suddenly the hand that was on the rail curls around my waist, hauling me against him until we're pressed so close that there's no telling where I end and he begins. His other hand tightens in my hair, tilting my head just right until I'm fully encompassed. Wrapped up in him. Breathing him.

My own hands stretch under his arms, curled up over his back, fingertips digging into those strong shoulders, like if I just hold hard enough, he'll never stop what he's doing. I nuzzle my way up the thick column of his neck to the small hollow at its peak, pausing to delicately lick the smooth dark arc of his ear. There's a hint of some other scent there. The flowers from the cave, I realize, and in that moment, a realization crashes down. The shock of the thought is enough to fully wake me up.

"What's wrong now?" he grumbles, drawing back the moment I stop. Well, his head draws back. He's still holding me so close it's like we're welded together.

I don't mind.

"What if they did something with that plankton nibari?"

"Plankat nibarat," he absently corrects, ducking to kiss a hot line along my jaw.

I capture his coveralls and yank him away from me. It doesn't actually move him, but it stops his lips a hairsbreadth from my own. His eyes pinch shut like he's in great pain.

"I feel like this is going to be a distraction for you."

"What if Pierce gave it to her? What if they made her into . . . this? Not just the extra experimentation with her body. What if they tried to tweak her brain and they broke it instead?"

What if they did it to me, too?

"They didn't use it on you." His fingers dance along my scalp, a massage that sends shivers through my body.

"I didn't say that." Did I?

"Didn't have to. You aren't a psychopath. You spend too much time considering what other people think. You obsess about whether or not you've done the right thing." He presses a scalding kiss under my jawbone, and I momentarily lose my train of thought. "It's not that I'm not intrigued by this line of conversation, but I feel like if we pause, you'll get skittish again. I just got my arms around you. Medical research from a decade ago will still be here in an hour."

"An hour?" How did my voice get so breathy? It's supposed to be firm with conviction.

"Two hours?"

"Um." Now he's licking a velvet-smooth path from where he kissed all the way to my ear.

"What if *they're* the ones growing it? Ginsidik is a Pierce planet. Protected by a hyperactive ionosphere so busy that if someone finds the crop, they can't coms out the location immediately. They have to go to the trawler. The Pierce Family could be hunting us down even now," I gasp out, lacking the fortitude to actually pull away. Also, the Pierce Family will be hunting me soon no matter what.

Unless I find a way to discredit them. *Viall.* I could *use* this. If I can prove it's theirs. I can get out of this with Micah and my family and my identity intact.

He pauses, mouth directly over my ear. "You want me to think about the Pierce Family right now?"

It shouldn't be sexy. It absolutely should not. But his voice is like being draped in expensive fabric, and as it whispers into my ear, it's hard to pay attention to the words when the tone says, "I want you naked and screaming in the next minute."

I want that, too. But I'm momentarily blinded by the possibilities and the fact that I may actually make it out of this alive. With *everyone* alive.

I can save Micah. I can save my family. I can save Myllie and all those trawler kids I saw racing around the decks.

I lean forward and gently bite his lower lip, pulling it slightly before I release it. "Not tonight."

I have to be sure. I have to have a brain capable of focusing on the moment. On Micah. He deserves that. I deserve that. We have time before we get back to the trawler. A day and a half.

"Hot and cold." He sighs, a rueful smile twisting those lips. "So many red flags."

"Is it bothering you enough to stop?"

He releases me, carefully moves away, and the cool breeze slaps me in the face. The glow of his banishment tattoo is stark in the darkness. "Something you should know, Cyn. The only thing that's going to get me to stop is you saying no. Not scolding or timing. Not anything else you're coming up with in that devious mind of yours."

He thinks I have a devious mind. I should be offended, but instead, a smile curls at the corners of my mouth and I take a careful step away, because my only other option is hurling myself back in his arms.

I retreat belowdecks to the bathroom and take another real-water shower. It's cold. Somehow, though, when I get out, squeaky clean and polished, I'm still as overheated as I was on the deck of the boat. But my mind, it's racing down dark and torturous paths, trying to focus on next steps.

CHAPTER 18

When firstday dawns, I'm much cleaner, even more exhausted, and hornier than a sea serpent after a typhoon. That's when they migrate toward their mating territory. Don't ask me why. I don't make the rules.

I also don't have any more answers about plankat nibarat and its possible use and am deeply regretting my decision to postpone last night's activities.

I root around in Aymbe's scattered clothes and find a pair of formfitting black pants that fit and a pretty stretchy shirt with short tight sleeves. I rarely wear short sleeves, but Itzel and Micah have already seen my scars. No point roasting in the sun.

I strap my blaster on my thigh and run a comb through my hair. When that produces a terrifying and near-vertical frizz, I resort to the usual three tight braids that hug close to my scalp. When the strands are free, it's too easy to imagine Micah's fingers tangled in them as they were last night.

Itzel meets me at the helm and presses a glass of something hot into my hands. I take an eager gulp before I realize it's some sort of warmed juice that won't do a fucking thing to wake me up. Might give me cavities, though. So there's that. I don't spit it out. Juice is healthy. It's important to have something healthy every once in a while.

"You look like shit." She says it brightly enough that if I wasn't paying attention, I might think it was a compliment.

"That's good. It's easier to look how I feel. That way expectations are lower." The newly mended wound in my side still smarts. Micah spread some sort of numbing ointment over it yesterday, but it's worn off overnight, leaving me with small pain-tingles dancing over my ribs.

Itzel nods like I've espoused great wisdom. "The Dark Mother of the Void doesn't care what we look like. Only what we do in her name."

And just like that, back to being creepy.

"I don't do anything in her name."

She gives me a narrow gaze, like I couldn't be more mistaken, but luckily, Micah comes in and disrupts our moment and she doesn't share. Instead, I check the charts and see, with some relief, that we're still on our intersection course. "We'll hit the trawler-town in three solar cycles. Have you had any luck with your coms?"

Itzel taps her finger against her ear. "No. I did see the most fascinating floating plant with ten-pointed leaves."

Sure, that's the same.

"No joy with the coms for me, either." Micah's eye contact is intense. Like he's asking me why I didn't join him after our tryst on the deck and my shower. I'm asking myself the same thing. Between my suspicions about plankat experimentation, the mess I'm in about Aymbe still being alive and being a kidnapper/killer, a sudden horribly vulnerable feeling after literally exposing nearly all of my deep dark secrets, and that one final secret about Pierce's bounty, I'm back to running scared.

I can admit it to myself.

"We need to talk." His voice has enough weight behind it that I'm concerned about the contents of the conversation.

Looking for a distraction, I stare out the windows of the helm. "Boat."

They both stare at me like I'm crazy, so I point over Itzel's shoulder. "Boat. Approaching. Quickly. There aren't many reasons for someone to be on open water out here. I'd make odds they're pirates."

Or they're whoever is farming the plankat.

Or *both*.

I shake out my wrists and unsnap the safety tab on my holster. "The smoke trail we're leaving makes us stand out. They'll take who they can get. There's plenty to salvage on a tugboat, even if it's just engine parts. Or if they farmed that flower, they could be coming to kill us before we can inform anyone."

"How do they attack?" Itzel asks, approaching the rail. The boat is nearly upon us and churning water surrounds both of our vessels.

I have no idea how they attack. I've never been attacked by pirates. I've heard rumors but they're basically mythology.

Five grappling hooks snare the rails of our tugboat from below.

I guess *that's* how they attack. In advance of the boat, which is probably a decoy. Maybe brought to the ship by one of the trawler-town custom serpent-shaped solo subs underwater.

I wrestle my blaster from its holster and run to the rail just in time to greet the first cresting pirate with a face full of light. Co-herent high-intensity light. He collapses back, splashing down below. Micah's already dispatched another and Itzel a third, but while we were acting, at least ten more hooks hit the rails and two of the pirates have already made their way to the deck.

They look about how you'd expect pirates to look. Bad teeth, bad hair, sun-damaged skin. Metallic gills embedded in their necks, locked in the closed position now that they're in the air. They also smell about how you'd expect pirates to smell even after coming out of the water. They've all been banished, which should mean that even being on Ginsidik is a death sentence if they're caught, but being pirates, perhaps that isn't a concern. The glow of a Pierce banishment shines on each of their faces.

One slashes at me with an actual sword. I don't know what kind it is. I didn't think people used swords for anything besides inter-Family honor killings for centuries. He flicks some sort of switch, and the fucking thing starts to vibrate. I saw something like that once on a knife that was made to really efficiently cut cheese at a restaurant I couldn't afford.

By "I saw," I mean, through a window, from the outside.

I lean back, raising my blaster, the blade whipping so close to my neck that I can feel its passage in the air, the song of the blade, and suddenly, Micah is between us, blocking my shot as his hand grabs the sword-wrist and his other stabs something efficiently into the pirate's side. The smelly man drops to his knees on the deck, mouth open. Blood dribbles out. It dribbles out one improperly shut gill, too.

There are two reasons to bleed from your mouth. You bite your tongue, or you're severely fucked up inside.

I think he's severely fucked up inside.

"I had him!" I protest. No one likes to feel like deadweight.

The medic raises an eyebrow dubiously and approaches the rail.

Itzel dispatches her pirate with spare efficiency, a blood trail spilling from his throat, just in time for the next five to make it to the deck. In the crush, there are too many bodies to use our blasters effectively. One pirate shoves me from behind and I almost go over the opposite rail. The water rushes at me but I catch myself and kick back as hard as I can, connecting with his jaw and buying myself enough space to turn and fire three pulses directly into his heart. Another pulse blast scorches into the rail beside me, and I hurl myself to the deck, rolling toward the center of the boat as I do, because it's always better to present a moving target.

As I roll, I catalogue the fight. Three of the pirates are armed with blasters, but they're encountering the same issue we are— they can't use them without risk of hitting one of their own. Micah moves like oiled lightning: fast, deadly, and smooth as water. He dispatches or immobilizes foes with ruthless precision. He moves in sharp abrupt angular strokes, vectoring across the deck. I'd expected that, as a medic, he might have some compunctions about physical violence. Clearly, I expected wrong.

Those lovely glistening muscles aren't just for show.

There's a chance I think about his muscles too much.

Itzel seems to teleport, darting around the deck with such ruthless abandon that you'd think she ordered up some pirates because she was bored. She's like a deadly storm, a knife in each hand and a serenely calm expression on her blood-spattered face. Where Micah fights in straight lines, she fights in arcs, swirls of circular motion. Every so often, when they come close to each other, their styles meld and merge. They must train together.

A foot stomping down near my shoulder reminds me that it's my job to keep fighting and not pause to admire my allies. They're much more admirable than I am. I learned how to fight by soaking up every bit of opportunity and every lesson that was even half-heartedly taught me. Means I don't have much of a style beyond "stay alive by any means necessary." The pirate above me aims a kick at my head, but I manage to bring up my blaster in time to fire at a raggedly bearded face. I graze it. Which is disgusting. He stumbles back and I kick his knee. He collides with Itzel and immediately is no longer a problem as she slides one of those blades into his side. More hooks hit the rail and I fire at the lines connected to the hooks, snapping them off into the water and blowing a series of little scorch marks through the rails.

A blaster shot skims close to my leg and I yelp, abandoning the defense and returning to offense, trying to keep distance and shooting at anyone who isn't shaped like Itzel or Micah.

For a little while.

My fucking blaster runs out of juice. It's only got the most expensive and high-capacity battery on the market, but I haven't charged it in a while. I thought I was hunting *one* kidnapper. You don't need that many shots for one person. Certainly not the hundred or so that I've already expended today.

Shut up. A hundred isn't a lot. Aim doesn't matter when you have an endless battery.

Yes, it wasn't actually endless, I'm aware.

An arm lashes out from behind me and grabs my shoulder with crushing force, pinching muscles and bone and nerves together. I grunt out a breath and kick back with my heel, connecting to something but clearly not something critical because I'm spun to face a large toothless pirate woman—good for them, being all progressive and gender-inclusive—who punches me directly in the eye.

"Fuck you!" I blurt and blaster-whip her in the side of her head, because I'm currently without a useful weapon and it seems like a good idea to repurpose. I follow up the blow with one to the neck. The thing about not having a specific school of training is that I go for the soft squishy bits that *hurt* more than I go for complicated locks or strike patterns. Her hands fly up involuntarily. Take that, pirate woman.

After an exchange of jabs, hooks, and crosses—never uppercuts; I'm shit at uppercuts—I get her to the rail. It's little effort at all to hook her feet with my ankle and tumble her over the edge.

When I turn, I immediately yelp, because a bald dirt-smudged pirate man is right behind me, knife raised to stab, a horrible look in his face.

Horrible because of the knife that was just yanked out of his neck, I assume. He falls, revealing Micah, carefully wiping the blade on his pants, his facial expression somewhere between "I am cranky about the breakfast options" and "wouldn't mind going back to bed."

My facial expression, I assume, is somewhere between "Dear *Viall*, is there blood in my eyeball?" and "I am about to throw up in the next few seconds."

Luckily, there isn't, and I don't—yet.

Itzel dances between the last two pirates, death in motion, and soon both are on the deck.

The poor deck. It's going to be red now. Unless they have a special blood-resistant varnish on tugboats. Maybe they do. I don't know how tugboats are finished.

The boat rocks beneath my feet, smooth and rhythmic. In the sudden post-battle silence, the sound of dripping blood is apparent. My hands are shaking. A chill slithers down my neck, the hot-sweat kind of chill you get when you're ill. There's a lot of blood.

Whoever is presently captaining the pirate vessel seems to think better of their plan, and it slowly turns away, abandoning the tugboat of death for a better target. I can't quite make out the person at the helm. He doesn't look like the other pirates. Clean. Tidy. With the cracking mud of trawlertown on his face and a constabulary uniform. Well, fuck. I notice the actions of the vessel because I'm vomiting over the edge of the boat. I didn't manage that not-throwing up thing for long.

All that warm nutritious fruit juice gone to waste.

Micah strides across the deck to my side while Itzel efficiently shoves bodies between the slats under the rails. Each dead plop in the water reminds me of bodies rattling around the walls of the ship. I heave again.

"Are you injured?" Micah asks, hand clamped against a wound on his hip.

"I'm disgusted." It shouldn't need to be said. I've killed people before. Too many. Not like this, though. Not when my boots squish in their blood. Micah's a medic. His stomach is steel in the way that few achieve. Not just in observing gore, which would be expected, but in meting it out.

Trusting that there's nothing left in my stomach, I wipe my mouth with the back of my hand and straighten. Tiny flecks of water pepper my face when the wind, waves, and boat collide. It's grounding. I take a deep breath. That feels so good that I take another. "Not disgusted by you guys. Just by this. This . . . *waste.*

How can you be so normal after that? How do you reconcile kill-ing if you've been trained as a healer?"

Maybe I'm just a wimp.

His shoulder bumps against mine. "I don't fight in wars. I'm not a merc. I don't kill for fun or profit. I kill to defend. When it's necessary. Unfortunately, in my life, it's been necessary more than I'd like it to be."

And there it is. It's how I feel, too, although in my case, defend-ing others is more frequently defending myself. It haunts me, but not as much as being dead would. "Sometimes it seems like there's no way to live if you aren't a killer. Maybe off the chart. Some-where that doesn't have any of this mess."

There's a tiny fleck of blood on the edge of Micah's jaw. I reach out to wipe it away. He freezes. Just as my thumb makes contact with his skin, his legs go out from under him and he drops to one knee, the first time I've ever seen him ungainly.

I grab his shoulder and perform a quick scan. Blood soaks the black fabric of his coverall pants. "Shit, Micah."

His eyes flutter. Itzel appears at his side like he teleported her from the stern deck. "What is it, what happened?"

I grab the fabric at his hip and rip it. A long deep slash mars his skin. I rip my stretchy shirt off and hold it over the wound, redi-recting my attention to him. "What the fuck were you thinking? You thought you could just hold your skin closed while we had a conversation?"

"I thought you were hurt," he mutters. That absolute idiot. I could hug him if I didn't want to slap him so hard.

"Well, I'm not and you are." I glance up at Itzel, who looks like she's considering stabbing me herself to get me out of the way. People like Itzel, no matter her training, are action-oriented. They need tasks. Distractions. "He left the first-aid kit in the helm. Can you get it for me?"

She gives a quick quirk of the lips, like it's a reflex, and jogs to the helm. I press down on the shirt, quickly soaking with blood. "And you, medic, are going to stay awake long enough to tell me what to use to patch you up. Otherwise, I'm going to guess, and you'll probably end up with rhinestones embellishing your scar tissue."

"Promises, promises." His voice grows faint.

I squeeze a bit harder, wincing with him when I cause enough pain to make his eyes flash open. "Stay with me, Arora."

Itzel skids to my side on her knees, kit already open, and I pull out the same caulking gun–style tool that Micah used on me last night. His bloody hand wraps around my own, arresting its momentum.

"Wait a minute on that. You might want to disinfect the wound first. Unless you're trying to kill me with infection."

Of course. I know that. I was so driven by the desire to stop the bleeding that I wasn't thinking. Probably because I'm so exhausted that it feels like I have weights on my eyelids and a little traumatized by all the pirates. Like a *normal* person would be. The adrenaline of the fight is crashing, leaving me shaky and half-numb. "Just making sure you were paying attention. You passed my test."

I reach into the kit with my other hand and retrieve a tube of disinfectant, labeled with a brilliant red cap. I pull the cap off with my teeth and squirt it liberally on and around the wound, my hands, and the equipment. The sharp spike of alcohol permeates the air. Micah grunts under his breath, so I suppose it hurts. I will my hands to stop shaking and pinch together the angry red skin before applying the gun of skin glue to his hip. It closes as easily as the wound on my ribs.

Like he did yesterday, I swab away the blood carefully as Itzel puts the kit back together. She scans the horizon. "Ship's making good time away from us."

"We probably killed most of their crew." And by "we" I mean Itzel and Micah. I killed maybe three members of the crew. *Maybe.* Probably fewer.

She studies me with a somber expression. I notice that her hands shake as much as mine do. She grasps the strap of the first-aid kit to still them. "You did well. You had our backs."

"Are you okay? Uninjured?"

She gives a tight nod. Looks around like she's waiting for someone else to offer her an out from this conversation. I inject hemorejuvenation compound into Micah's arm. The body would take a month to replace the blood cells Micah lost. Hemorejuvenation, recently developed by the Chandra Family, speeds the process. By secondday, he should be back to full strength.

"Are you sure?" She's an assassin—she can't be upset by all the killing, can she? What do I know? I'm a mass murderer and I was just hurling breakfast over the side of the boat. If she is upset, being surrounded by the bodies of those she just ended is probably not beneficial. "Can you get him below to a bed? I'll take care of cleanup."

"I can get myself to a bed," Micah protests, but his words are slurred together so it sounds more like "Ahcn m'self t'bed."

I look over his body to Itzel, eyebrows raised. She gives me a knowing expression of her own. "I can."

"Good."

I help drape one of his arms over her shoulder, and as she moves him toward the ladder, I pick up the broad-based mop hooked on the side of the helm and drop a bucket over the edge of the boat, retrieving some seawater to dilute all the blood.

By the time Itzel returns to the deck, the bodies are gone and I've eliminated most of the obvious blood pools. She silently removes the last of the spatters from the rail and the side of the helm. When she's done, she stands in the prow, fingers twisting in almost arcane symbols as she murmurs words to herself.

I don't look away in time and she catches me watching her. She glances down at her own hands, smoothing her fingers out. "I speak for the dead, to ease their path to the Dark Mother. Perhaps she will carry them in her hands rather than grind them beneath her feet."

I make a mental note to read up on the Dark Mother of the Void's views on mass murderers. Being carried sounds better than being ground under a goddess's feet. "I'll never get used to it."

"To what?" She cocks her head at me.

"Killing. I know it's naive, with my reputation. But I hate it every time. I don't do"—I wave my hands all around, encompassing our current situation—"*this*. I lurk somewhere and stun a perp from behind, carefully restrain them, and drag them to the authorities. Sometimes someone gets hurt, but usually, everyone lives."

She's silent for so long that I fear I've misjudged things. "At the monastery, they said I was built for it. Killing, that is. That they'd never seen someone take to it so naturally. Like I had other senses than normal people."

Now that she's started, I hope she keeps going, because I don't have much to add. No one's ever praised my murder skills.

Except Aymbe.

"They were right. When I'm doing it, it feels natural as breathing. As dancing. I love dancing. I feel like light out of a blaster. Directed and free. It's after that's the problem. When I see what I've done. When I think about how they had parents and maybe kids. If they have a pet who won't be fed now that they're not coming home. If they had a comfort toy as a child and if it was shaped like a cloud or a ship or an animal. I can't turn it off."

I squint into the sun, like it will wash away my need to rest. She's given me a truth. I might as well trade one in return. "I don't sleep because when I do, I relive what happened on the *Iceberg*. Not just what they did to me, but what I did to them. It's both. Doesn't matter that they tried to kill me first."

She looks past me at the waves. "I don't dream at all. Special meditations they teach at the monastery. Can't have an assassin feeling too many regrets, even in their subconscious."

"You could stop meditating now. If you aren't assassinating people anymore." Dreamless meditations? Sign me up. "Could you
teach me?"

"It took me fifteen years of intense practice to master it. At this
point, it's too late to get them back."

There goes that thought. I don't have fifteen years. With the
lifestyle I've led the past few weeks, I may not have fifteen days.
Pierce certainly doesn't want me to.

"Besides, dreaming is important. You don't want to lose it. If
you don't dream, it takes time to figure out what to live for."

Clearly, we aren't thinking of the same kind of dreams. "What
do you live for, then, if you don't dream?"

She smiles, but it isn't exactly a happy expression. More like she
wants it to be happy but hasn't figured out how yet. Gestures down
toward the cabins. "My family. The new wonders of the worlds.
The darkness at the edge of the chart where the Mother sleeps. A
roll around a space-station bedroom—or public restroom, or cargo
hold—with a willing partner. There are plenty of things to enjoy
in the present without dreaming of the future."

I'm not sure what I live for. Trying to repay our debts. Trying
not to disappoint my family—again, I mean. The thought I'll catch
Aymbe's killer, which is certainly twisted and overcomplicated now.
It isn't exactly a rosy forecast. "Is that why you left the monastery?"

She throws a flake of something in the water. "I would never
have left. I had a purpose there. I was making charted territory
better, even if it hurt every time I did it. Getting rid of people who
were truly appalling. They kicked me out."

Ah. For her own good, probably. It's rare that we agree with
others about what is for our own good. I certainly never have. "Are
you going to be all right after—" I gesture around the deck.

The corner of her mouth curls up. "I'll be fine. I'll stay up here
and keep watch through firstnight and be refreshed by secondday."

"While you're doing that, I'll check on our patient."

She nods, not taking her eyes from the water.

I think Micah's asleep when I enter the dimly lit cabin, fresh from another shower and clothing change, cracking the door as silently as I can and approaching the bed. It's only when his large hand snakes out and clasps my wrist that I realize my mistake. "You're supposed to be resting."

"How the tables have turned." There's wry laughter in his voice. A sliver of light slashes across his cheekbones, highlighting their angles. "So are you."

"Clearly, you're feeling fine." I start to disengage but freeze when his fingers tighten.

"Stay."

I look around the room. Small, dark, still cluttered no matter how much I straightened it up when looking for clothing. "There's nowhere for me to sit."

His dark brows perform a half waggle over sleepy eyes. "I could think of a place or two."

"You don't have the energy to open your eyes. You couldn't handle it."

His expression says that he's in the mood to argue that point, but then it relaxes. "It's a big bed. Just rest with me. For a moment."

It's dark and warm and I'm tired, so tired. What would it hurt to sit down for a second? I ease onto the edge of the bed, reclining on the surprisingly soft mattress. Beside me, in the dark, he huffs out a pleased breath, his hand dropping from my own to rest against my stomach. His thumb drags slowly over the sliver of skin exposed between my pants and my shirt, and a tiny shiver traces its way down my spine. The mattress dips in the center, rolling me back until I'm cradled by the warm weight of his body.

It feels safe here, with Itzel keeping watch above and Micah's hand on my skin. My eyes drift shut, and darkness surrounds me.

CHAPTER 19

. . . .

The hatch slides open and the void encompasses me in nothingness.
My skin stretches. The kind of cold that quickly becomes nothing
at all soaks my skin. My muscles. My bones. Makes a home in my
body. Slows time. Rimes my eyes. Sneaks within my mouth and
freezes my tongue in place. My blood is a sluggish stream, too thin,
like antifreeze. It lasts a lifetime.

It lasts an instant.

Forever.

It will always be there, scarring me straight to my core.

The pressure tries to crush my insides to pieces.

"Cyn. Cyn!"

The voice doesn't belong. It's warm. It's alive. I come to my
senses gasping, so wrapped around Micah that I'm like one of those
deep-water cephalopods we only ever see when they float to the
surface after death. My fingers are clenched against his chest, his
shoulder. One of his arms is strong at my back, cradling me against
his body. The other hand smooths the hair back from my face as he
looks down at me, a worried line tracing between his eyes.

I'm in bed with him. Why am I in bed with him? Firstday rico-
chets around my mind. The fight. He was injured. He's supposed
to be mending and instead I'm coiling around him like I want to
crush his bones. I try to push myself up and away, only pausing
when the arm around my back doesn't let me move.

"Sorry." I try to shake away the cold of the void, but the only
thing that does it is the heat of his skin.

His skin. I blink. At some point, he visited the shower and

returned to the bed wearing a low-slung pair of pants and nothing else. My fingers tighten again of their own accord, dimpling smooth dark skin that's still slightly damp. He smells like clean sharp soap and sunlight.

"Don't be sorry." That voice rumbles through me. Low and molten, and some inner part of me that was clenched tighter than a fist melts. The banishment tattoo glowing under his eye highlights the strong angles of his face. I want to lick it.

"You're supposed to be resting. Healing."

"I'm rested. I'm healed."

I shake my head, still trying to push away with my arms—which is a mean feat considering that my hands are refusing to let go. "*Viall*, your hip. I'm *lying* on it."

Those full lips curl into a smile. "I noticed. I also noticed that you reached for me in your sleep."

Is it possible to disappear from mortification? I give it my best shot. Try to offer an explanation, because he's certainly due one after I practically mauled him in his sickbed. "You're warm."

His smile grows even bigger. A dark shadow of beard shades his jaw. "You have no idea."

His hand traces up my back excruciatingly slowly, a trail of fire licking up my spine in its wake. As it traces the back of my neck and into my hair, I make my decision. I'm done lying to myself. The Pierce coms is gone, and I've already decided I'm not going to betray him. I'll figure out another way to ensure my family's safety. Maybe convince them to leave with me when I go. I want him. I've wanted him since I last set foot on board the *Calamity*, and everything I've learned subsequently has done nothing to change that.

I melt back down on him, boneless as a cat in the sun, soaking in that heat, the slow motion of his hands on my skin slipping under the hem of my shirt and smoothing up my back. I lean down until my lips are a breath away from his. "Heat me up, Micah. Set me on fire if you can."

The world spins and I find myself on my back, Micah poised above me, one broad thigh pressed between my legs, his groin against my own, his arms braced on elbows to keep most of his weight off of me. I trace the contours of his chest, dragging my fingers through the light dusting of black hair that fans his pecs. The slide of skin on skin is almost hypnotic, heat seeping into every pore of my body. I want to purr.

He settles tighter against me, lowering his mouth to mine, showing off just how easy it is to set me afire, because I go up in flames, lust combusting through me like a forest fire, like a star. I'm burned up and reformed into something new. I'm not even fully aware what my hands are doing anymore, clutching arms and shoulders and hair, tracing his jaw, digging into his waist. My hips roll, a solar flare setting off in my core as I heedlessly rub against him. He maintains a smooth, almost languid rhythm that seems to be created just to drive me insane.

I fiercely kiss him back, desperate for more, for the feeling of being safe in someone's arms, of being warm. I break away from his mouth and kiss a line down his jaw, the strong tendons in his neck, the breadth of his shoulder, one of my legs wrapping around his thigh. I'm wearing too many clothes. Apparently Micah agrees with me, because his hands slip up from my hips, dragging the shirt over my head and somehow taking my compression bra with it. When he settles back against me, my breasts press against planes of hard muscle.

Not to be outdone in the undressing game, I tuck my fingers below the waistline of those low-slung pants, tracing the round curve of his ass. Proof that he's as far gone as I am presses insistently against me, or maybe I'm pressing insistently against it. I tug on his pants.

He responds by moving his hips out of reach, kissing a line down my sternum, licking a spiral around my left breast, ending with a flick of his tongue against my nipple, the sudden sensation enough to make my hips twitch again. I trace my fingers through his hair, marveling in its thick softness.

"More. Do more of that," I command.

"Are you sure?" He flicks his tongue out again, eyes heavy-lidded, and I quiver. "But you have this whole other side that's been ignored."

"That's an excellent point," I gasp, fingers tightening in his hair. "Equality is important. Do the other one. Do it now."

"You're very demanding in bed. I don't know why I'm surprised. You're very demanding in everything."

"Too much talking, not enough licking."

Thank Viall, he complies. It's every bit as good on the right side as on the left. Too soon, he continues his downward path, stubble scraping at my skin in a way that electrifies every nerve ending. When he reaches my waist, his tongue traces the line of the pants, dips below at the hollow near my hip. Before I know what's happening, he's got the button undone and he's slowly tugging them down, dark eyes locked with mine, cataloguing my expression, looking for hesitation or uncertainty or anything else. I'm an open book, flayed raw and exposed, and I don't know exactly what is in my gaze, but it appears to be "hurry up," because he does, finally, dragging my pants and underwear down and tossing them across the room before settling back between my thighs.

I have a moment for hesitation. To enjoy oral sex, one must have the ability to relax into it. Relaxation is not a strong suit of mine. I should probably warn him off because it can be a fruitless endeavor and disheartening to a man. My hand on his shoulder freezes him. "You might not want to waste your time."

"Because you won't enjoy me tasting you?"

"I can't come this way." My voice hitches up slightly at the end, like it's a question instead of a statement of fact.

He licks a lazy line up the inside of my thigh, pausing right at the apex. "Sometimes it's about the journey, not the arrival."

That talented tongue flicks right against my center, and I completely rethink my reticence. "Good point." The words sound choked. I might as well let him try.

He continues to prove that point, alternating with delicate light licks and long rough drags of his tongue. One big hand brackets my hip, holding me in place, while the other one delves below, stroking between my folds before a finger works its way into me, slow and smooth and curling at just the right spot. I make a sort of gagging noise in the back of my throat.

It's deeply sexy, I'm sure.

I don't even care, because something is rumbling within me. Something powerful and wholly unexpected.

I prop my feet against his broad back and allow my eyes to roll back in my head, lost to the sensation. As journeys go, this one is pretty sensational. Resonance builds in my body, first a hum and eventually, as his mouth and hands continue their work, a deep clenching vibration that finally unleashes itself on me like I've been struck by lightning. Wave after wave of that wonderful electrifying charge sweeps through me until I'm boneless and limp and Micah crawls his way up my body, nuzzling the curve of my waist, the underside of my breast, the edge of my jaw. The expression on his face could only be described as smug.

"Can't come that way, huh?"

"Hrngh."

His chuckle is as smooth as chocolate and *I'm* the one who melted. So that's what everyone's talking about when they say how good that is. Huh. Consider me a convert to the church of Micah's tongue. He starts to pull away and I manage to find the muscle control to capture his wrist. "We aren't done yet."

"I have no intention of being done." He rearranges us so that I'm spooned against him, head resting on one broad bicep, the other arm wrapped around my waist, one leg between mine. I press back into him, reveling in the hard strong line of his chest against my spine, the power of his legs. All that glorious heat at my back.

I could almost go back to sleep, except I'm needy for more sensation. I roll my hips back into his groin, angle my head on his arm so that he can bend down for another one of those drugging kisses. His free hand, the one I'm not pinning in place with my head, traces up my torso, thumbs scraping over my nipples, fingers pressing in as they drag down the center of my chest.

I reach behind me, find the hot iron rod of him through the fabric of his pants, trace its shape with such care that it feels like I have it memorized by touch. It twitches, and I wrap my fingers around as much as I am able, dragging my thumb over the tip. Now it's him who's rolling his hips rhythmically against me. A slow bump and grind. Between my free hand and his own, we get his pants shoved down, and I trace my fingers over the velvety texture of him before he captures my hand and brings it forward, lifting my top leg and draping it over his own as he rubs himself back and forth against me from behind.

I feel like I could come from this alone. I throw my head back against his shoulder and he nuzzles against my cheek before taking my mouth just as he starts to push his way within me. My body bends like a bow, pinned at two points, overwhelmed by sensation as his hand strokes over my chest, fingers rolling my nipples. He's moving achingly slowly until I snap my hips back, impatient, and take him in one smooth hot glide.

I can't stop the throaty moan that escapes just as he rumbles a growl, and his fingers tighten at my hip while he withdraws and then eases his way back in. Slow. Patient. Like he has all the time in the world. Like he's memorizing every sensation in every instant. I close my eyes and kiss him, a slow trickle of sweat tickling my back where it presses against him. His fingers drift down until they trace over my core, reigniting all the nerve endings that just managed to catch their breath. With his hand on one side and his body against the other, I'm pinned in place, squirming as that same electrifying sensation plucks each nerve ending like a string, building to a crescendo. All I smell is him, clean and fresh and musky. All I feel is his skin. All I need is more of this, forever, and nothing else.

My blood pounds in my ears. My limbs shake. I fall apart cradled against him, wrapped up in his heat and his body.

As I quiver in his arms, he finally accelerates, driving into me from behind with long strong glides, fingers still keeping their maddening rhythm and suddenly, out of the blue, I roll back over the edge, plunging into another orgasm like I'm falling into a warm lagoon. He gives one last hard thrust, seating himself fully within me and the sound that rumbles out of him should be recorded and played at fertility clinics, because it's guaranteed to drop eggs all over charted space.

Not mine. Mine are controlled by nanos. Take that, Etolla.

He wraps around me like a blanket and presses a kiss against my temple, fingers tracing patterns in my sweat-slicked skin. I'm utterly boneless. Sated and soothed and like someone's turned down the static in my brain until it's barely audible.

"Fuck me, Micah. That was . . . something."

He squeezes his arm around me in a hug. "I did and it was. It'll always be something with us, Red."

"Red?" I mumble, sleepily.

"Because of your flags." I can hear the smile in his voice.

I'm still thinking about laughing when I fall asleep yet again.

. . . . .

I wake slowly, blearily. I'm warm. Hot, almost. A long scalding heat source brackets my back. Micah, burning away all the cold. I carefully stretch against him, luxuriating in the feeling of actual relaxation.

My mind finally catches up with my circumstances. I slept. Actual sleep with no dreams to speak of. Sleep like I haven't had for years. Sleep like I've *needed* for years. I could cry, it feels so good to wake in safety and comfort. It's dark out, but the sky through the porthole is tinged with the first flush of light, so I can't have slept for long. The fact that I slept at all is something like magic. Micah murmurs something and pulls me closer. I roll my cheek against his shoulder, wriggle around until we're facing each other. He tightens his arms around me, pulling me into him as he rests his chin on the top of my head. I consider trying to go back to sleep, just to make the moment last longer.

"You slept," Micah rumbles the obvious.

A smile overtakes my face. "I did. I suppose you're going to take credit for that."

There's a joke in there about the medic doling out some medicine that I'm too lazily sated to try for.

"Empirical evidence suggests that I'm responsible."

I poke him in the tight band of muscle that wraps his waist. "I suppose we can try again and see."

His laughter reverberates in my ear. "Right now?"

I think I might pass out if we tried again right now.

Then again . . .

"When I said we need to talk, I was serious." He keeps his grip around me, halting the instinctive flinch away. "About plankat nibarat and your Poison Green."

That's not what I expected. "What about it?"

"You were worried about its side effects. That it makes people smarter but also psychologically damages them. Well, I think I figured out why they're farming in Poison Green."

"What? When?" I blink.

A slow laugh rumbles through him. "Night before the last one, when I was all revved up with nothing better to do with myself than study samples we collected after the rescue—and you were taking a shower that lasted forever."

Ah. That night. I was mostly pacing and being horny.

"The bioluminescent algae have properties similar to Elanjal, a drug used to treat patients with violent personality disorders. I won't know until we get to a lab instead of just using Itzel's kit, but it could be the trash-eating algae is exactly what they need to use plankat without the consequences."

"Shit." Right under our noses this whole time.

"Shit, indeed," he agrees.

Another thought occurs to me. "She said she thought she'd be protected. Aymbe. Down in the hold. She didn't expect us to find her yet. She was working with someone. Maybe the farmers."

He makes a low humming sound of agreement. "Makes her more dangerous."

"If you two are done in there, we're approaching the trawler-town," Itzel hollers through the doorway, and I startle into a sitting position, Micah's arm still draping my waist.

We aren't supposed to be approaching the trawlertown for a whole solar day. It takes a moment to register. I slept through a night, second day, and a whole other night. No wonder I feel rejuvenated.

Also, orgasms. Those do a great job at the rejuvenation, too.

Micah stretches onto his back and folds his hands behind his head, a triumphant smirk on his face, like he's going to ask me to post a recommendation of his sexual prowess to the ether. His mark of banishment flashes just under his eye, a mischievous spark. Sprawled on the bed like this is the first time I've been able to appreciate him in all his naked glory.

There's a lot of naked glory. A broad chest tapers to narrow hips, lean but muscular thighs, and shapely calves. All of it covered with dark-brown skin that's flecked with so many interesting scars that I want to dive back into the bed and explore each one. Even in repose, his shaft is large enough to be impressive. Growing larger as I watch it.

I yank my eyes away. We don't have time. He reaches out a hand to snag my waist again, a mischievous gleam in his eyes. "We could be fast, Red."

"I don't believe that for an instant." I lean down and plant a kiss on his lips anyway, slow and sweet and deep, before getting to my feet and grabbing a change of clothes.

After another shower, I climb to the deck just in time to see the trawlertown come into sight on the horizon.

CHAPTER 20

If this is what people normally feel like after a full night of sleep, sign me up. My muscles are both slightly overused and languidly rejuvenated. My mind is the same. I spring from the tugboat to the dock, blaster holstered on my hip even though it's still completely out of charge. The tugboat was too old to have appropriate adapters for charging.

"I'm going to the dockmaster to meet Caro and check out our supplies." Itzel follows me, barely rocking the dock, and immediately heads to the closest barge and the just-better-than-ramshackle building that sits at its edge. Apparently, just before we got to the trawler, Itzel got in contact with Caro on their ship's coms. While Temper and Arcadio continued to Estella with Boreal, Caro stayed at the trawlertown to wrap up the crew's payments and practice her moral superiority.

I wouldn't have minded if she *hadn't* stayed. Things have been going well with Itzel and Micah. I don't need to add their distrustful crew member to the mix. As soon as Caro got in contact with Itzel, she notified the connies and sent a message to my family's stream.

I swallow, looking toward the tangle of streets that extends in front of me. "We need to discuss how we take this public. Pierce has been experimenting on children, there has to be a way we can exploit that—even without proof of the plankat nibarat."

And that has to be enough to keep Micah from their crosshairs. "I should probably also have a very awkward conversation with my family."

"You didn't call them on the coms?" Micah's presence is a familiar brush of heat against my skin.

"The signal from the tug was bad earlier. Couldn't connect because of the ionic storm above us. You didn't even know Caro was here until right before we docked." And I welcomed that delay. I have no idea how to broach this conversation. I push my hair back. I didn't have time to rebraid it, so the wind is blowing it in my face.

Micah offers to come with me, and I accept because it will be useful to have a witness. They won't want to believe me. Who would? I don't want to believe me, and I was there. Also, it feels good to have him at my back.

We make our way over delicately scalloped bridges, gently sloped streets, and around tight corners. Along the way, we run into Etolla, who appears to be spending her days roaming the streets and looking for me. She eyes Micah. Glances to me. I shake my head sharply. I don't like where this is going at all.

She looks back at Micah. Holds up seven fingers.

Seven? Not unless they all come out in one go like my uterus is a waterslide.

"Why is that woman sending you secret messages?" Micah glances between us.

"She told me I'm going to shoot out babies like blasters shoot out light." I'm trying to give him pause.

He does not take the pause. Instead, he raises his eyebrows and flashes ten fingers at Etolla. She breaks into a huge smile and nods enthusiastically at me. I regret every decision I've made in the last day.

No, I don't. But I might. After ten babies.

When we stop in front of a familiar green-painted house with a yellow door, I puff out a breath. Fortify myself for what comes next. The door swings open under my knocking fist and a chill of unease is born in my spine. My mother hasn't left their door unlocked since before Aymbe was taken. Since before the entire trawler changed from a place where people as well as doors were open into a place with locks and shutters.

Metaphoric shutters. They had the physical ones already. My palms immediately grow sweaty, and my heart fills my throat. Hand on my useless blaster, I shoulder my way into the house, Micah at my back.

Unlike the last time we were here, my father's blaster parts are put away. The kitchen is spotless as usual. Holos of the whole family together when I was just barely an adult, on a rented pleasure boat, play in a loop over the fireplace on the far wall. Aymbe is there, apparent at the end of our little family line, the youngest, my arm thrown over her shoulders, her man-eater grin in place even though there were no men present to eat.

The small undercounter dishwasher blinks green-lighted confirmation that the sanitization cycle is over. Everything is perfectly set to order—except everyone is missing. They could be out doing errands or enjoying a walk by the sea, but their absence combined with the unlocked door triggers alarm bells. A small scuff mars the polished wood of the floor. I reach down and scrape at it with my fingernail while I look at the floor from a new angle.

A speck of blood is almost invisible under a cabinet. The chill grows to an icy spike.

"Is anyone home?" I yell, hand on my blaster.

A thud comes from my aunt's room. Muffled noises. I'm through the door before it occurs to me to find a weapon, which, as it turns out, is for the best, because Aymbe isn't waiting with hostages, she's *left* some of the hostages. My grandmother and grandfather, hands restrained with unyielding plastic ties and tight gags cutting into the corner of their mouths.

I remove the gags while Micah cuts them free. My grandmother is dazed, eyes wide and mouth drooping at the edges. My grandfather isn't faring much better, but he clears his throat.

"Aymbe." His throat sticks and he clears it again. "Aymbe did this."

I nod. A stupid gesture that's as ineffectual as it is meaningless. "We ran into her in Poison Green. She's—not herself anymore."

"Not herself!" My grandmother's voice shakes in outrage that's just barely masking a bone-bruised sadness. "She tied us up at blasterpoint and then kidnapped her own mother. And your parents. She said she'd shoot us. Our Aymbe, back from the dead, and she threatened to kill us."

That actually sounds exactly like "herself" as I've come to know her the past few days. I also don't have time to get into the whole situation. "Did she say where she was taking them?"

She hands me a note. A ransom note. The same wording as the one that was left for Aymbe herself, except she's demanding more for the return of three people. Credits that I don't have. I'm not the sort of woman who has a healthy savings account. I'm the sort of woman who eats gut-busting noodles because they're cheap and easy. Who lives in a dive decorated by the art of the very woman who just kidnapped the rest of our family.

She's giving me three days to dredge it up. Usually, she offers a month. She's signed it with a little happy face in the loop of the "y" in her name.

What a fucking monster.

And I'm a fucking fool. How did I not see that she wouldn't be licking her wounds somewhere with her mysterious ally? Of *course* she's back at her old games. I was so stunned by her identity I didn't even consider that she'd go after our family. She ignored them for years. I should have realized that some deeper game was being played.

They don't know anything else. Aymbe's getting desperate and messy but she isn't *that* messy yet. Micah checks both of my grandparents for injuries, but beyond the superficial, they seem fine. We drop them off at the local clinic just to be sure, and as I step out the door, it all crashes on my shoulders. I stop, suddenly incapable of forward momentum.

"She has them."

"She does." Micah isn't the type for sweet nothings. No false reassurances that they'll be fine, that Aymbe would never hurt her family.

We both know better than that.

"I thought she'd hide. Take a new victim that would net her a lot of credits in a few months. But I didn't think like *Aymbe*. I thought like myself. She was weakened. Shot. Even with our healing, she wasn't in shape to get a normal target. She needed someone she could take by surprise. Someone who'd walk right into her snare of their own accord." She also needed someone who would make me completely irrational and likely to make a stupid mistake. Check. And check. This game of hers. This stupid fucking game that only one of us is actually playing. What's her goal? Does she even have one, or is the game itself the entire plan?

Where would she take them? Back to the Necklace? Poison Green? One of a thousand other tiny islands that freckle the sea? I think some part of her still wants me to catch her, but she doesn't want it to be easy. She won't return to places she took other victims. Any spaceship leaving the trawlertown has to file a flight plan. She won't risk that traceability. It means that she docked her personal vessel somewhere other than the trawlertown. She needs easy access.

Fuck the payoff. That was where we made the mistake in the first place. I'm going to catch the brat, not pay her.

"We have to go back to the docks." I shove open the door and leave the house at a run. I pant an explanation as I race over bridges and unevenly planked streets. Water pools in the cracks between walkway and buildings. "Her spaceship must be hidden nearby— but not on the trawler. My guess is her ship is somewhere in the Necklace. It's the only place close enough for her to feel separate but safe. The only place where she can hunker down and set traps. If she rented a boat, that's traceable, too. They tag all their vessels.

They didn't used to. She might not know about it. I only do because I saw the tag IDs when we were in the station."

Itzel's sitting outside the dockmaster's house, poised on my
weapons trunk with one knee tucked up under her chin and one
leg dangling. Caro's back is to me, her arms crossed over her chest
as she says something to the biologist. I don't bother to greet them,
just race by the engineer to the door, wrenching it open with
enough force that the receptionist startles and yelps when I burst
in. Itzel and Caro follow us into the office.

"You either took docking pay or rented a ship to a woman in
the last few solar days. She'd be a stranger," I blurt at the startled
receptionist sitting behind a ramshackle desk. I never thought to
ask about a woman when I questioned people about the Abductor.
It would have opened up so many avenues, but we knew that the
Abyssal Abductor used to be a man. Even if we'd had Tally's statement earlier, we would have chased a long-dead man. I may owe
him *two* apologies.

The receptionist blinks, like he suspects that he's ingested some
sort of illegal drugs and we're hallucinations. I glance at the name
tag on his chest and flash my bounty-hunting holo-credentials
from my interface tattoo to his own. "Hadrion. Great name. We
have reason to believe that woman is working in concert with the
Abyssal Abductor, who has recently taken another victim. She just
walked off this trawler with my parents. You know them, probably,
Cygna and Parbel Khaw. Also my aunt, Mygda."

"Records are private," he sputters, clutching his datapad like I'm
going to snatch it out of his hands.

So I snatch it out of his hands. More sputtering. He comes out
from behind his desk as my fingers fly across the screen. I dance
backward and Micah intercepts him before I have to awkwardly
kick at him. There it is. Yesterday. I was sleeping comfortably for
the first time in years and Aymbe was docking a high-speed boat
under the pseudonym Mygda Cybel.

Of course she mashed together our family's names into a pseudonym just to rub my nose in how far behind I am. So Aymbe. What a bitch.

"Did you keep the drones here or are they with the *Calamity?*" I ask Caro. If she says one snappish thing to me instead of helping, I might take off her head right here on the dock.

"We have a whole swarm, as well as one of the atmospheric-mapping drones." She doesn't even have an edge in her tone, which shows either that I misjudged her or that she's much smarter than I previously thought. Hadrion tries another feeble attempt to get around Micah and is blocked yet again.

Perfect. "Aymbe's bought a fancy tsunami-class speedboat, falsely tagged with credentials from another vessel. She never could resist the best. At some point when my family's lives aren't in danger, we'll need to investigate how she's getting the kind of funding that purchases a tsunami-class. There are maybe ten of them on the entire planet."

Caro peers over my shoulder, studying the schematics. "Their exhaust is unique. Even if she's got it safely stowed away, I should be able to trace a relative path based on airborne particulates and wind patterns. Then the swarm can pinpoint an exact location."

A shudder of relief shakes my body. There's a plan. We can find them. "Given our current position, my guess is she went back to the Necklace, because it's the easiest landmass to access."

And it has innumerable hiding places. I transfer schematics on tsunami-class boats through my interface tattoo to everyone else's as I look through Hadrion's datapad for available rentals. Nothing that appealing. Nothing that will keep up with a tsunami-class. Except—

"I have an idea." I toss the datapad to Hadrion and turn to the door. He fumbles with it but manages to capture it before it breaks on the floor.

"It always goes poorly when someone says they have an idea and doesn't just say what the idea is." Caro holds the door for Itzel.

"It can't be as bad as Temper's usual ideas." Itzel pats her on the shoulder as she passes.

"We're stealing a connie boat."

"Fuck," Micah and Caro say almost in unison, and Itzel just shakes her head before Micah continues, "Bad ideas must be contagious."

"If I ask them, they'll ignore me. You saw how Mo reacted to my return. It'll become an opportunity for him to posture, and we don't have time for that. He even knew that Tally had seen her with someone and he didn't bother to tell us at the time. That's how closed-lipped the priap is. He cannot handle someone getting one over on him. If we steal one of their high-class pursuit ships, we'll travel quickly and guarantee a constabulary presence when we need to capture Aymbe, because they'll be trying to retrieve their ship."

"How good are these ships? If she has a tsunami-class, how can you guarantee that they can keep up?" Caro hoists a giant pack from the pile on the dock and sets it on her shoulders.

"There's a reason I know how many there are on the planet. Two are in the constabulary docks of the trawlertown, purchased because if they have to police the seas, they need to catch anything sailing on them."

The one good thing I managed to do while on the force. Caro whistles a low tone. "Never mind how your cousin affords such things, how does a small trawler constabulary force?"

I huff out a sigh as I grab a bin and heave it onto a nearby hover pad, not even sure where we're going but knowing it needs to be away from the docks. "You missed the discussion in the tugboat on the way in. Suffice it to say this trawlertown has a closer-than-usual relationship with the Pierce Family. Assume that Mo is up to his eyebrows in any type of activity that could benefit the Pierce Family. Also assume he's compensated well for the service."

"If you think I'm going to let that go without more questions—" Caro starts to argue, but Itzel interrupts her.

"Pierce experimented on children, Caro. She was one of them. So was her cousin. Maybe plankat was involved. I'll tell you more later, but right now we have more pressing interests."

The engineer abruptly shuts up, a sick look on her face. More than the revelation merits. While experimenting on children is certainly horrible, it's clear that Caro was already prepared to believe anything bad about Pierce. Why is *this*, in particular, so shocking to her? "We can base in my parents' house. My grandparents are going to be kept in the clinic overnight—more for their sense of security than due to their physical state. The instant I figure out how to sneak onto the connie docks and take that boat, I'm leaving."

"Oh, *you're* leaving?" Micah's voice is mild. "No backup, just sailing out into the abyss?"

"It isn't your problem, I understand. They aren't your family. It isn't your bounty." And I don't want them near the danger, honestly. Micah has already risked himself too much for someone who, until recently, planned to betray him.

"Apparently a good night's sleep makes you even more suicidal than exhaustion does. You don't have to go alone, and it's insulting to us to assume that we'd let you."

My mouth's already open to argue when I snap it back shut. He's right. And even if he's wrong, I need them. I nod.

The familiar green building rises in front of me so quickly that I almost ram the hover pad into it, I'm so intent on fermenting in my own thoughts. A quick course correction pushes the floating crates of goods directly through the front door. It hovers in the living room, dwarfing the space. It seems wrong to see my weapons trunk in the place where I was raised, in the home of the most peaceful people I ever knew.

I remember my father's blaster. Maybe not so peaceful now. Maybe they have a whole armory in my old attic bedroom. Maybe I should stop making assumptions and focus on the task at hand.

While the others come inside with their own burdens, I push the crate to the far wall, between two armchairs, and sink into one, elbows braced on my knees. "The connie dock is next to the station, only accessible from within. The current on the outside of the trawler has a strong undertow. You can't just dive off the side and swim into the dock without getting pulled under the ship or tangled in the nets."

"Can it be breached from the exit point, via sea?" Micah pulls a heavy pack from his shoulder and tosses it on top of a hover pad that's floating in the kitchen. Itzel and Caro peer around the living area with prurient curiosity.

I shake my head. "The exit point is gated, and the gate only opens when it detects the signal from one of the ships."

"We could blow a hole in the gate." Caro shrugs a lazy shoulder.

"Tempting. The goal is to *not* get arrested for real, though, so I'd like to limit the property damage."

"So we go through the prison. Not so hard. How many constables work in a shift?" Itzel hops atop the crate that she and Caro pushed, barely disrupting its hover mechanism.

"Around ten work in each shift, but six out of ten are on patrol and four man the station. One of the four will probably be on guard near the sky cells on the roof. That leaves three we need to get past."

Micah smiles when I say "we." It's good that it takes that little to keep him happy, because I don't have much more to offer. I wish I could call Madrigal. I record a message for her anyway. Someone on the outside should know what's happening. I trigger the coms to send the recording when the message can go through the ionosphere to the relay satellite in orbit. I also send her a picture I covertly took of Micah on the deck of the tugboat. Because someone on the outside should also know how good his arms look under starlight.

· · · · ·

We move on the station at midnight, several standard hours after the shift change, when they're inclined to be lazy. It drove me crazy to wait this long, but it gave us time to recharge our blasters, sort our body armor, and prepare what we needed. A feeling of dread shrouds me, like we're walking into something we don't fully understand. I'm glad Vuur is safe in Boreal's care.

We had hours to come up with a plan, but the best we could manage with so many variables in the air is: distraction, surprise, escape.

It's slightly more complicated than that. Caro has offered a distraction, twelve emergency calls coming from disparate parts of the town to reduce the number of connies manning the station. The problem is, I expect there to be six connies already patrolling and four in the station, but eight leave the station, meaning they have either redistributed their patrols or increased their head count. Maybe we should have planned for more emergency calls.

Too late for that. We crouch behind the shuttered eel-vendor's booth across a narrow canal from the connie station, just a sprint over a bridge, across a walkway, and through the front door. Once we're inside, it's maze-twist through the desk area.

"Lights out in three . . . two . . ." Caro begins the countdown. Most of the planned parts of this little escapade are Caro-dependent. She's shutting down the grid around the station just long enough to be a distraction. When she's not being a pain in my ass, she's shockingly useful at crimes. I'm in my spare armor, which is the lightweight stuff that doesn't block as much but also doesn't kill you from heatstroke. Because my other armor reeks of garbage.

"One."

Nothing happens.

We wait a bit. Still nothing. "We meant the lights in the connie station."

"I *know*," the engineer growls, fingers dancing in the air as her interface tattoos and augmented visor project something I can't see. "What exactly are you contributing to this rescue besides the crisis itself?"

"She gave schematics of the station," Itzel offers.

"She found Arcadio's niece. Seems you all forgot that little contribution to the mission." Micah's warm hand curls over my shoulder, squeezing gently.

"That was the last mission. This is a new one. Keep up." Caro stabs a finger aggressively into something in empty space and then does it twice more.

The lights across the street go out.

"Thank you," I offer her, because I can be gracious when the situation calls for it. Keeping low, I run for the bridge, avoid stubbing my toe on anything, and cross the open deck before shouldering my way into the station, finally recharged blaster drawn but carefully dialed to stun mode.

A clatter comes from my left as someone stumbles in the dark, but I'm already past them, darting down an aisle until my night vision tells me that I'm about to collide with a connie just stumbling up from his desk. It's Mo.

Of course it's Mo. It couldn't be Stewie, the janitor. I try to dodge to the side, but Mo takes up a lot of space. My hip collides with him, and he reaches out. I wriggle out of his grasp but hit a chair. It rolls away, rattling against the floor. I bite my lip to contain the curse that tries to escape and regain my balance just in time for Mo's flailing hand to smack me in the helmet. I clutch my hands to where my ears are, as though that will do anything, and allow my momentum to carry me past. All that matters is the door. Micah, Caro, and Itzel take other paths through the lower level, but the only officer on the floor appears to be Mo. I collide with the door shoulder-first, and it doesn't budge. Usually, they don't leave it locked on the dock side. Or, at least, they didn't ten years ago.

My fingers flash over the control panel, trying the code from way back when I was on the force.

It creaks open. Yikes. That's not great for their security.

I'm just wrestling it open when I hear Mo's officious voice telling us to stop in the name of constabulary law.

A blinding flash of light comes from his blaster, but it's wide and strikes the wall beside the door as I race through and set foot on the floating dock, the others behind me. I steady Micah, who was unprepared for the force of the moving water under the dock, which bounces and tilts as the trawler slides through the sea.

"Fuck," Caro yells, and there's a half splash and a scuffle of sound.

I glance over my shoulder. Itzel's caught the engineer with one leg in the water and yanks her back to the tilting dock. Caro's still waving her arms in front of her like she's actively using her augmented projection system instead of running for her life. There isn't time to see if everyone is all right, because Mo will be after us in a moment if we don't get to the ship.

Both tsunami-class boats bracket the end of the docks, sleek, black, and deadly. They're shaped like knife blades. As they accelerate, the boat will practically fly, only the razor-sharp foil remaining in the water. I vault over the rail to the deck of the boat, aiming for the small helm. The magnetic lines that connect the boat to the dock are easily disengaged after I hear the three thumps that indicate everyone else is on board.

The door of the connie station explodes outward in pieces. Mo stands in the frame with the biggest fucking blaster I've ever seen with the exception of the one that was actively operating inside a volcano.

"Why did he shoot the door?" I yell as I activate switches and flip on the engine, trying to aim the ship away from the rapidly approaching dock behind us now that we're no longer tied to our berth.

"I remote-locked it behind us." Caro's practically flat in the prow of the boat, which is both a good place to be and a good position to be in.

"I could kiss you." I finally manage to pull the ship away from the docks smoothly, threading the space between the dock ends and racing toward the exit gate as Mo thunders down the dock, blaster raised like he's willing to explode his own ship rather than let us escape with it, flanked by other connies.

The gate starts to slide open. Slowly. Mo shoots again. I try to shift the wake of the boat to shake the docks. The churn collides directly with the dock as he stops to aim, sending him face-first into the sea, quickly flowing away as the ship moves forward.

"I've got the gate code." Caro throws a hand toward the gate, her interface tattoo expelling the signal through the air toward the control box. It slips open easy, as if we were a legit vessel. Once we're clear of the station, I open it up, accelerating as fast as the ship will take me. As the ship gains speed, I wave the message from the interface tattoo on my wrist through to the station.

It should explain why the ship was stolen. In words that are simple enough for even Mo and his connies to understand. If they bother to read it. My hope is that, combined with everything else, it'll keep us out of sky cells. Technically, a bounty hunter's license allows me to commandeer vehicles, but I don't think it's supposed to apply to constabulary vehicles.

The boat hums beneath me, a thunderous growl that spikes to a whine as the whole vessel rises into the air, screaming forward into the night toward the distant island chain that may hide Aymbe and the rest of our family.

CHAPTER 21

■ ■ ■ ■ ■ ■ ■ ■ ■ ■ ■ ■ ■ ■ ■ ■

"Airborne particulates from the exhaust signature indicate you were right in your hunch as to Aymbe's destination." Caro's armored head pops up from belowdecks, just high enough to address me face-to-face, which is technically unnecessary, because we're all commed, but a nice gesture. "I can't trace it precisely yet, but data indicates that she's on one of the three most distal islands in the chain."

Ruby, Etamarine, or Iron. Ruby is the closest to us, so named by me and Aymbe because of the flowers that bloom in the high summer months. Etamarine is next, named for the brilliant blue water that surrounds it, caused by the long shallow run-up to the beach. Also for its history as an actual etamarine-mining location before the stone was picked clean. It's eliminated as an option because there's no way a ship with a rudder like the tsunami-class would be able to make it to the island at anything but suicidal speed—and it couldn't leave at all, because boats all start slow, which means the deep rudder would be fully submerged.

Iron is last, so named because there isn't a thing living on it. The island is all smooth weathered rock. Good place to hide because it's got caves like Sapphire's, but I never spent much time exploring it because it's both slippery and boring. Which Aymbe knows. It's also surrounded by sharp outcroppings that can wreak havoc on a ship that doesn't know exactly the right way to approach.

"Focus your surveillance on the most distant of the three," I suggest. "It's the biggest pain in the ass, which means she'll probably go there."

"Your family seems superhealthy," she mutters, as she and Itzel retreat beneath the deck.

"My family is fantastic with one spectacular exception." Well . . . my parents and grandparents are fantastic. Aunt Mygda could have been, maybe, if things had been different. I course-correct slightly to pinpoint Iron. The wind pushes on my helmet and the moon washes the waves with a silver glow. Any other day, I'd be enjoying every minute of piloting the fastest water vessel on Ginsidik. I'd take off my helmet and let the wind run its fingers through my hair. Let it burn my cheeks.

I've seen exactly how cruel Aymbe is capable of being. The original Abductor isn't the only one who killed after ransoms weren't paid. She did, too. She plays games. She always did. And it's entirely, completely, my fault because I didn't catch her at any point over the past few years. I should have seen it. She changed completely after her time with Pierce, but she was so young and we were so happy to have her back. Everyone's a brat as a preteen. It seemed like a normal evolution, not a mutation.

An arm bands around my waist from behind and a strong frame braces me. I don't jump or kick or any of the things I'd normally do because, somehow, my body already recognizes Micah's presence. Instead, I melt into him, allowing the hard line of his body to support my own.

"Stop beating yourself up. Normal, rational people don't do what she does. You're one of her targets just as much as anyone else is. She's played the slow game with you, but that doesn't mean you won't win."

"Do I smell crazy?" I tilt my head back.

"You smell delicious. Good enough to eat. And maybe not exactly sane. Sane people don't spend their lives hunting their kin's killers. Sane people move on. They forget. You aren't that type."

Fair. "I spent my whole life trying to avenge her without realizing *she* was the villain. I'm a fool. It was bad enough that I failed to catch the Abyssal Abductor. It's magnitudes worse that I *knew* her all along." I lean on his shoulder, enjoying the support more than I should, although I'm starting to forget why I shouldn't enjoy it.

His chest moves in a sigh. "Remember what I told you about my time on Sunspire Way Station? With the Claw and Regan the untrustworthy?"

It shocks a chuckle out of me. "That sounds like one of the Family titles they give when a head steps down and takes an emeritus position. Ayo the Benefactor or Raylan the Conqueror. The ignoble version of that."

"You aren't so far off. Except he was on his way in rather than out. At the time, I worked hand in hand with Naima, the leader of the Claw. We knew he'd gotten out of control. I still liked the kid, I just thought the power had gone to his head. I was wrong. Regan killed a station guarda who was investigating us. Left the body in the central plaza with a claw etched on the skin of his chest. I was across the station treating someone with a synth overdose. Nasty drug. A little bit combats claustrophobia—makes it popular in a way station. Just a bit more makes you feel like you're flying. More than that makes you *try* to fly. People jump from balconies. Try to open air locks. Anyway, I was wrestling the overdoser from the edge of a walkway, trying to get a needle into her, when I saw the smoke."

Smoke on a way station is a big fuckup. They take that shit more seriously than any other crime. It's next to impossible to find a flame source simply because fire kills in any number of ways: exploding oxygen tanks, smoke inhalation, temperature deregulation. Murder isn't as serious a crime as arson.

"When I got back, I found the Claw flophouse in flames, the fire brigade pulling bodies out. Naima was the first. I could barely recognize her." He shakes his head, the movement gently bumping the back of my helmet. "She was like a second mother to me. She took a chance on me when no one else did. Regan knew we were going to stop him. Someone warned him. He set the fire and framed me for it."

Some tiny bit of tension I didn't even know I was holding leaks out. I should have known Pierce would spin the truth. No wonder Micah didn't trust me. I showed up in his life, with his new family, spouting more lies. Lies that he could detect immediately. But now is probably not the time for that particular conversation. "I'm sorry she died."

He's silent for a moment. "I am, too. She was a good woman. She took in people like me who were lost. Yes, she was a criminal, but Pierce laws are laughable. Why should you have to smuggle painkillers to medical clinics? Why should you have to smuggle non-rotten fruit? People were getting fucking scurvy before she took over the black market."

"What happened to Regan?"

"That fucker came to her funeral. I tried to kill him. Just missed. That was when I realized he'd been working for the Pierce Family all along, because suddenly they had a warrant out for me—naming all of his crimes. Except attempted murder. That one I'll own." He shakes his head again, arms tightening until they're just shy of painful. "I only barely got off the station. Ven—he was the old captain before Temper—did most of our smuggling. He happened to be there at the time and got me away. He was a priap and a bad captain, but I owe him my life."

I check the surrounding area for hazards and flip on autopilot so I can turn in the circle of his arms. I reach up and lift his visor. The glowing mark of banishment flashes below his eye. I kiss it gently. He trusted me. People never trust me with themselves. "What happened to Regan?"

"I never knew. Probably still there, successfully murdering anyone who gets in his way, because the Pierces support enough crime to keep their people afraid." He rests his helmet's brim against my own, lips tantalizingly close. "All that to say, I understand what it's like to trust someone enough that you're blind to them. And I know how much it fucks up your judgment later."

"Want me to space him? It's like my signature move." It doesn't even hurt so much to say it.

"You don't need a warrant in your name, too."

I stretch to my toes and press a kiss against his lips.

The both of us have been bitten so sharply by trusting others it's amazing there's still any faith left to offer. Just moments ago, I would have sworn that my well was dry. Maybe he thought the same thing of his own. So I give him the biggest gift I can. Because he has proven himself worth it every day I've known him, even when he was suspicious of my motives, and I was suspicious of his. "I trust you, Micah. You're worthy of trust."

"You are, too, Cyn. You've been through some of the worst things a person can and came out kicking. I trust you at my back, front, or anywhere else."

I resist making a joke about how we had each other back, front, and anywhere else in the tugboat. It would ruin a lovely interaction. He kisses me, and despite the cyclone of emotions pummeling me, I manage to find a sliver of peace.

. . . . .

It's just a moment. Before long, the Necklace is in sight, visible in the cool violet light of the dawn. Iron is a small sullen lump at the end—a clasp rather than a jewel. While I was piloting, Caro and Itzel took an inventory of the items belowdecks. There's a standard emergency kit. Some flares. Rescue vests and fresh water. Nothing particularly useful for our purposes until you get to the cubby at the front, which houses a small flotilla of personal submersibles.

The small units are barely more than an engine and handles, intended to drag a person through the water. They're probably newer versions of the devices the pirates used to approach our ship beneath the surface. A handful of oxygen filtered regulators clutter a bin nearby.

"We can't approach Iron on the boat." I poke at the regulators. Vaguely clean looking. "She'll be looking for us."

Caro curses from the other side of the room, staring into space as she twists her hands in the air. "Fuck."

I glance from Micah to Itzel.

"She found a shield on the south side of the island and can't hack it." Itzel straps what appears to be an armory's worth of weapons to her body. "It's so good she didn't even notice it the first time she scanned the islands."

"I *can* hack it," Caro snarls. "I just *haven't* yet."

"You think it's Aymbe's ship?"

"Maybe. It's a fucking big ship if it is. There is invisibility shielding in the area and a signal-dampening shield around it that just reads as a dead zone. If it's your cousin, she's got a benefactor out there. No normal person can afford tech like that."

"Don't *you* have invisibility shielding?" Micah asks Caro, as he loads his own weapons in holsters.

"Yes. The size of a large bedsheet. Not the size of a spaceship. Not a spaceship. Maybe a spacecarrier. Mine only fools the eye. And I got mine because I did a favor for . . . well . . . someone who was gracious."

Micah raises an eyebrow.

"What kind of favor? What kind of graciousness?" Itzel thumbs the intensity up on her blasters.

"Get your mind out of the gutter. Some people have real needs."

"Yeah, they do."

"Back to the subject," I interrupt the two women. "Are you going to be able to hack it in the next few standard minutes? Because if not, we're just going to have to avoid the area. If we take the submersibles, we can come ashore anywhere with relatively calm waters."

Caro shrugs her shoulders and keeps tapping at the air.

"What's the plan for when we get on the land?" Micah approaches me carefully, as though he's noticed that my nerves have sharpened with proximity to the island.

The Abductor—Aymbe—believes that we are the same. Believes that whatever thing is broken, deep inside her, is matched by a similar fracture in me—evidenced by my actions on the *Iceberg*. That, at least, is something I can use.

Which means my only chance to take her by surprise is to let her think that I'm just as fucked up as she is. To applaud her mastery of crime as though my highest priority isn't to wrest my family from her hands. She was skeptical before, but the taunting and baiting was all done for a reason. She thinks I'm like her—that I just need a little push in the right direction.

"I need to approach her on my own. It's the only way to possibly catch her by surprise."

"You aren't suggesting that we hang around the boat waiting for you to be horribly murdered, are you?" Micah crosses his arms, leaning back on the frame of the hatch that leads below, staring down at me from his position on the ladder.

"Did I say that?" I grab one of the submersibles and a regulator. Realize I'm being a brat. Breathe out a slow controlled stream of air. "Sorry. I'm suggesting that I approach her alone, while you three either guard the perimeter or hold down the ship. I don't know everyone's areas of expertise, so I can't assign you roles."

Lie. I know their areas of expertise, but if I tell Caro what to do, she'll disagree just to be obstinate. If I tell Micah what to do, the noble idiot will probably decide to ignore me and be a hero. I have no clue what Itzel will do, but probably nothing I predict. Temper is their captain. I'm not. This is not the time to experiment with leadership.

Micah shoots me a look, and I can tell that he detected that particular deception but isn't going to make a big deal out of it.

"I need to convince her I want to join her. Catch her by surprise. She won't believe it if you're all along for the ride."

"How about you approach her with me—and then pretend to turn on me? She wanted you to be like her. Betraying one of your own would fit the presumption." Micah uncrosses his arms and braces them on each side of the hatch. Technically, he's blocking my path up. Not technically, he's displaying those exceptionally yummy arms to full backlit effect, and I don't have a problem with it.

Also, it's a fantastic idea that I want to resist because it puts too much trust in me not to fuck it up. But I can't resist it because this *matters*.

"We'll lag. Keep an eye on the ship and ears to the coms," Itzel says, as Caro yet again stabs the air angrily, muttering under her breath at the apparently unhackable invisibility shroud.

"Don't approach the south side. We can't predict the variables if we can't see the space." The engineer's voice is a touch too loud. I guess Caro actually is listening, despite her distraction.

"When we reach the shore, Micah and I will take lead, you two will lag and try to figure out what's being hidden. I'll pretend to be her biggest fan—tickled fucking pink to bring my own hostage to the party."

"She tried to shoot you the last time," Itzel points out, grabbing a submersible of her own. "What if she doesn't believe you?"

"Aymbe *wants* to believe me. She wants someone to admire her, always did, and oddly, the fact that I've spent my life hunting her fits her delusion. As long as I play the part well, and Micah pretends to be shocked at my sudden betrayal, she'll believe I'm exactly like her, because she doesn't have the imagination to truly understand what really motivates people who aren't deranged lunatics." I roll my shoulders, bracing myself for what is to come as I hand Micah his own submersible and filter. "She was like that after her time on the Pierce ship, although I didn't realize it. She always believed someone had an angle. Whenever anyone said they loved her, she thought they wanted something. I remember my grandfather offering her a treat from a vendor over by the water's edge and she studied it like it was poison and then threw it over the edge."

Which is a fucking sad way to live. Take treats when you can, I always say.

CHAPTER 22

We make it through the shoal without getting crunched to bloody bits against the rocks.

Iron is an imposing island—rarely visited because, well, it's shitty and ugly. Literally shitty because some form of migrating lizard uses it as a nesting ground in this hemisphere's late winter, coating rock surfaces with feces and food scraps. The slick dull-gray rock slopes unevenly and gradually, like a handful of shards were dropped into the ocean. Little rivulets of seawater channel toward the distant center of the island, winding their way through sharp stone monoliths.

"Shocking to think this wasn't the first island to come to mind earlier when you were predicting where your cousin would go for a romantic tryst." Micah sidesteps a particularly large—and possibly calcified—pile of seabird excrement.

I shrug. "I had to consider Aymbe's preferences. I, of course, would have chosen the cold pointy island covered in shit."

He nods like that fits his expectations. Probably does. His fingers briefly thread through mine. I squeeze them.

I let the silence stretch as we move slowly around one rock face and turn toward another. Then I can't handle it anymore because silence gives my brain time to paint vivid pictures of what we might find.

"My family—" I'm so bad at this feelings thing. But he needs to know my priorities. "I left them. I ran away because all I could see was their expectations to put all their hopes for Aymbe on to me.

I should have tried to work through it instead of running away. If it gets bad, I need you to promise that they're your first priority."

"That sounds like you're planning on doing something deeply stupid and you want me to agree to back it."

"It's not stupid to—"

He interrupts me. "And if you think I'm going to just leave you when—"

Something glints in the corner of my eye, and I throw myself bodily in front of Micah to stop his forward motion, hands flat against his chest. He bumps into me but hooks a hand behind my back to stabilize us. His brows lift in query as he looks down at me. "Distracting me with your feminine wiles won't work."

"If this was a wiles moment, my hands would be a lot lower than your chest." I step back and point to the cobweb-thin wire stretched across the trail just in front of us. As he leans down to study the trip wire, I scan the cliffs. "There it is. That pile of rock up there. I thought there wouldn't be traps because a stone island is hard to manipulate that way. I didn't consider rockslides."

"Your cousin is a fan of the primitive traps, isn't she?" Micah carefully steps over the wire, and I follow after sketching a quick arrow pointing at the trip wire on a rock face with one of Caro's charcoal markers. "The net was a lot more fun."

It sure was.

We continue up the switchback trail between monoliths, slowly gaining elevation. Two more rockslides avoided, and two more arrows mark our path closer to the center of the island, where a collection of fractured stone that looks similar to a partially crushed glass barometer ball towers above the rest of the rock.

Micah seems to agree that this is the most likely place for Aymbe to be hiding and goes low and still as soon as I do. We both creep closer to the structure.

"When I imagined you catching me, I didn't think you'd be crawling." Aymbe's loud amused voice comes from the side of the rock structure. She's sitting against the stone, leaning back like she came out to enjoy the sunrise, dressed in camouflage that matches the rocky terrain perfectly.

I straighten. This is salvageable. When I speak, my voice is bright. "I suppose this is why I have to be the sidekick."

She flashes that glowing smile, directing it at Micah this time. "And you brought a toy."

"Not for you. My toy." I band a hand around Micah's wrist in a clear claim-staking. Maybe I also just want to hold him.

"Your what?" Micah pulls his hand away, playing his part. I hadn't realized how much his voice has softened when he speaks to me compared to when I came aboard the ship. His sudden return to cranky irritation is vividly believable. "What are you talking about?"

I pull my blaster, pointing it at him. From her angle, Aymbe can't see that the intensity is thumbed down to the training setting, so low that it wouldn't do much more than shock him even if I'm forced to pull the trigger. "Do be a pet and go to the cave."

"I believe the correct term is a 'henge.'" Aymbe pops to her feet, dusting off her hands. She approaches us as casually as if she doesn't have a care in the world. A blaster fills her hand, pointed in our direction.

She's also wrong. A henge is a circle of stones. She might know that if she'd come home and finished school instead of embracing a life of crime. I don't know what a hemisphere of stone is, but not that. Maybe a honge. I'm going with honge.

Maybe trawlertown school wasn't that good for either of us.

"You always were such a good student," I effuse, glancing over my shoulder. No sign of my family.

She *wasn't* a good student even before she left early. She was adequate but conned most of her teachers into allowing extra-credit opportunities. She wouldn't have passed basic math if I hadn't tutored her. If they did experiment with plankat, it gave her the crazy without the smarts. How disappointing. Micah's mouth twitches with my lie.

She shrugs one slender shoulder in a carefree manner, as though she expects the praise. "You looked chummy with this crew the last time I saw you. What caused the sudden change of heart?"

"You betrayed us," Micah growls. He's a pretty good actor. His hands ball into fists and he steps closer to me.

"Chummy?" I blurt, careful not to let the blaster go wide. Wider. "This idiot tackled me, and it was all I could do to keep them from shooting me, because they thought I was working with you. I figured, if they're going to treat me like that, I might as well do it, you know? Not like they're going to pay me what I'm owed. No one ever pays me what I'm owed."

Now for the last piece. I have to play it just right. "When we got back, and I saw you had the fam, I had to come. You aren't the only, um, person like yourself, that I've tracked. Going after those close to them is usually either a starting maneuver or an ending one. You certainly aren't starting. Don't tell me you're giving up—asking to be caught?"

"There isn't anyone else like me. I'm unique," she snaps, carefree walk sliding into a stalk for a moment like a glitch in a coms. "I don't want to get caught. I just needed to motivate you, Bella."

I almost throw up in my mouth, which would really destroy the illusion I'm trying to maintain. "Consider me motivated."

"Are you though? Are you really?" She makes a *tsk* sound. "I think you're still lying to me."

Micah makes a quick lunge toward me, designed to distract, and I level the blaster more steadily at his chest. "Don't."

I carefully move around him, like I'm trying to find better ground. I want him between me and Aymbe. The next time he makes a move, I'll fire right past him, thumbing up the intensity enough to at least stun her. I can't bring myself to kill her, even now. If it *was* plankat poisoning that twisted her mind, maybe there's something that can be done to treat it. I'll restrain her and deliver her to the Escajedas, which will probably be a fate worse than death, but she'll have a fair trial and maybe some screening for insanity.

"You're supposed to stun them first, Bella. A lot less complaining that way."

"You see the size of this chunk of manhood. You expect me to drag him all the way myself?"

Micah, his back to Aymbe, mouths the words "chunk of manhood" at me with a raised eyebrow.

So I'm bad at improvisation.

"I have so much to teach you. Children, like the little Escajeda that finally got your attention properly, can be carried around easily. This one will be traced directly to you because you were last seen with him and were hired to be on his crew. You can try to ransom him, but they'll know it was you. It will ruin the game." She's keeping carefully to the side, blaster still in hand. "You're so bad at this."

"Oh. I didn't even think of that. I was so excited to bring something to the table." This is getting away from me and she's not at a good angle. I just need an opening.

"Cynbelline? Cynbelline, is that you? Run! She isn't what you think." My mother's voice emanating from the honge distracts me for a perilous instant. Just long enough for Aymbe to lunge past Micah and shove my blaster down.

I start to wrestle her for it until another sound breaks through our scuffle. Boots on rock. Lots of boots.

A group of soldiers in dark-blue armor with blond hair have appeared over the crest of the hill, like they've been waiting for this moment. The one at the lead is looking right at me with murderous glee in his eye. Not a soldier. Carmichael Pierce. Fuuuuuuuck.

"We have other uses for your little friend. As you know, Bella. That coms you had . . . so interesting. Especially when the first call came in, and it was a caller I already knew." Aymbe's hand is still holding my own down, and the soldiers' blasters are drawn.

"You didn't," I breathe. No. Oh no. A hot flash shoots through my body. My missing coms, just after our scuffle in Poison Green. She took the call. She set this up. She traded Micah to the Pierces. To face trial for crimes they well know he didn't commit.

Carmichael's presence tells me this has only a little to do with Micah and his warrant, and a lot to do with Pierce finally figuring out a weak spot of mine. I definitely should have let him put pants on before I turned him in.

"You're welcome. A bounty is like a ransom. You're already halfway there." She turns to Micah, alone and unarmed in the middle of the stones. "Did sweet Bella tell you she took a bounty for you? Did she tell you how much you were worth? Guess she decided to take you for a test drive first. Gotta admire a girl for taking what she wants." She eyes him up and down. "Maybe taking adults does have some merit. . . ."

Micah's dark eyes lock with my own, looking for the game. I desperately wrestle with Aymbe for the blaster, and she laughs like we're playing. I see the moment when he realizes she's telling the truth—at least a form of it. His gorgeous emotive dark eyes go flat and dead. His face droops in betrayal before it hardens in resignation.

I'm one more person he shouldn't trust. One more bad decision.

"I didn't—" Too late to explain. "Micah. Run. *Run.*" I try to activate the coms—we went silent because we thought Aymbe might hack the signal. Now, when I need to warn Caro and Itzel, she grabs my other hand. I tug ineffectually at the blaster, wondering how Aymbe got so fucking strong. I stomp on her instep and twist as hard as I can.

Micah doesn't get a chance to run because Carmichael shoots him with what I can only hope is a stun shot from his own blaster. Pierce has impeccable aim because it hits right in the joint of his armor, and Micah collapses like a puppet with cut strings. I pull my own trigger as we vie for my weapon. The beam hits Aymbe's leg, but I haven't adjusted the intensity yet and she laughs at the shock from the blow. She's still laughing when I punch her in the eye. Her fingers loosen enough for me to retrieve my blaster, thumbing up the intensity. It's fucked. It's all fucked. I fire my weapon past Micah at the approaching soldiers.

A hard fist collides with my jaw. "No *hitting*."

"No being a fucking lunatic." I stagger away from her, trying to place myself between Micah's stunned form and the Pierces. I address my medic despite the ever-growing clusterfuck around us. I don't even know if he's conscious and immobilized or out cold. "I wasn't going to do it. I didn't know you when they called, not really."

And it wasn't exactly an offer I could refuse. It's stupid to tell him. I could still salvage my play here. Could pretend to enjoy Aymbe's game. But I can't, because the idea that he thinks I was in on this, that I betrayed him, is too painful to comprehend. He finally trusted me enough to tell me his story. A stupid tear straggles down my face. I fire at the soldiers, and Aymbe's arms go around me from behind in a bear hug, limiting my range of motion.

"Play nice, Bella-girl. Our game isn't over yet."

Except it is, because Carmichael's next shot hits me right in the gut and I topple beside Micah. Pierce weapons. Powerful enough to stun even through armor. Rocks press into my body. I can't move. I can't even blink.

Aymbe crouches next to me, pulling my face shield up to study my expression. "I've been doing this for ages. Did you really think I only kidnapped one every four years? The Pierce Family has a market for people and I'm happy to procure for them. In return, they're happy to turn a blind eye when I do a little procuring of my own. They have a need for invisible people, you know. And invisible farms."

The plankat. She admits it. Which means that she completely

intends to kill me. The mineral-thick tang of blood coats my tongue. I must have bitten it when I fell.

Aymbe roughly pets my face with a flat hand. "It'll wear off in a bit. It's much more satisfying when you're fighting, but I can't let you ruin things for me."

Carmichael Pierce finally approaches Micah's body, kicking him to his back with a heavy boot. They all study his mark of banishment.

"Fits the profile. He's going to be a great scapegoat—a public disgrace. That's just what Sunspire needs." He smiles as he turns to address Aymbe. "You tell me she seemed fond of him?"

She chuckles. "My mother told me she took him to eat with the family. More than fond."

His laugh is chilling. "Good. Consider the contract closed. We'll be in touch." He finally spares time to study me, prone on the ground at his feet. "How does it feel to be stunned and help-less?"

Um. Awful. Is that his idea of a one-liner? Clearly, they aren't wasting plankat on the Family heirs.

As they hoist Micah over their shoulders and carry him away, I try to yell, to move, to do anything at all. My eyes are getting dry, but I can't even blink. All I can do is stare at his departing form. Aymbe pats me on the shoulder in mock consolation. "Don't worry, little Bella. You won't be far behind him."

I watch the retreating backs of the Pierce soldiers until Aymbe grabs me by the ankles, dragging me across the rough rock toward the stone structure that contains the rest of our family.

▪ ▪ ▪ ▪ ▪ ▪ ▪ ▪ ▪ ▪ ▪ ▪ ▪ ▪ ▪ ▪

CHAPTER 23

At some point, I lose consciousness. I don't know why. Maybe the weapon. Maybe a particularly hard rock to the back of my head. When I wake, I've been stripped of my armor and tied to a metal camp chair with hard plastic ties holding each wrist and ankle in place. The honge arches around me and cold water from above drips down on my shoulders and legs. The thin bodysuit I wear under my armor isn't doing much to keep the water from being an annoyance.

Not my biggest one. My biggest annoyance has wandered off. Somehow that worries me more. Clearly there's no one around to pay all our ransoms, which means her plans for us are darker than that. An escalation. Like she's bored with her current evil deeds and is off contemplating more. Or maybe getting paid for more. I can only hope that Caro and Itzel are aware this has gone underwater. Maybe they have a chance of freeing Micah before the Pierce ship takes off.

I know exactly where Carmichael will take him.

Sunspire. He can't resist showing off his imagined triumph in front of the citizens who probably already know better. Temper and Estella were probably right. If Aymbe was working with Pierce, they wouldn't have let her give Boreal back. They would have loved to have a hook into Escajeda. I gag, bent over as far as I can in the stiff metal chair, stomach rebelling everything at the same time.

"Cynbelline?" My father's low voice comes from behind me.

I roll my head back at an awkward angle and see both of my

parents, tied to their own chairs. My aunt is behind them, separate. She looks devastated. I'm sure we all do. "I have good news and bad news about Aymbe."

My mother sniffs. She's in surprisingly good shape. A little bedraggled, one bruise marring her high cheekbone. "Do you think this is the time for inappropriate jokes?"

I may not have any additional time, so might as well get all my inappropriate jokes out now. "Are you okay? Has she hurt you?"

"Has Aymbe hurt me? You mean the girl who was practically a daughter to me? The one who helped me make keft at firstday, to energize us for the day ahead?" My mother's voice is climbing beyond a whisper to an indignant hiss. "Do you mean when she showed up at our home and told us we had to follow her because you needed help and the connies couldn't be trusted? When we weren't fast enough, she held weapons on your grandparents. *Her* grandparents. Or when she knocked us out and tied us to chairs in some sort of cave-bubble to tell us the history of all her abduction or *murder* victims?"

"No, I mean like with a knife or a sock filled with rocks or something, actually." "Cave-bubble" is probably a better name than "honge." "It may not seem like it, but the fact that she's only employed psychological torture is good, because it means that all of you are in shape enough to run away if we plan our escape well."

"Cynbelline, we're tied to chairs on an island." My father says it helpfully, as though I've perhaps failed to notice our current situation. The downside of never sharing the true shit that I've been through is that now, apparently, my parents think that I'm utterly incapable of handling a crisis.

I strain down with my nose, folding over until I can brush it against the small glyph on the inside edge of the interface tattoo on my right wrist, shaped like a knife. The subdermal blade in my wrist slices its way through a thin layer of skin as it pokes out. I grit my teeth to keep from whimpering like a baby from the pain, because it won't help anything and might worry my parents. I take a deep breath through my nose as blood drips to the floor in a steady stream.

After the *Iceberg*, I promised myself that I'd never be defenseless again. Only deeply paranoid and desperate people get subdermal blades—for obvious reasons—but it was necessary. You can't be restrained if you can cut yourself free of most standard restraints. I remember my first encounter with Carmichael. I suspected he had one.

Of course he doesn't. He's never been in a position to be truly helpless. He'd be too much of a baby to handle the surgery.

I move my wrist back and forth, as much as I'm able within the restraints, slowly sawing through the hard plastic. It hurts because subdermal blades are embedded in the bone, which is a hard substance but not exactly created for sawing. Also because a blade just cut through my skin. When that tie gives, I wrench my wrist around to get the correct angle on the other side, then go for my ankles. If I survive this, I'm putting blades everywhere under my skin, despite how fucking much it hurts. You touch me wrong, and I'll turn spiny as a deep-space mine.

I can hear excitement in the slight movements behind me, when it becomes obvious that I'm working my way free. When I stagger out of my chair, lightheaded and dizzy, because while Micah and Itzel appear to be lab-grown killing machines, I'm just a normal person when it comes to fighting. Pierce certainly didn't waste their time giving me any combat mods. I wouldn't mind some extra strength right about now. Blood dribbles from my wrist, and I do my best to capture the stream using the sleeve of my bodysuit, so I don't leave little trails around the cave-bubble.

There's still no sign of Aymbe, but also no sign of weapons or anything that could be used for a decent ambush. My chair is in full view of the only viable entrance to the cave, which means she'll know I'm out of it and she'll expect a trap. Our only hope is to escape before she wanders back, because I suspect my backup has already scampered off after the Pierce Family and Micah—as they should have.

I don't have time to think about Micah. To dwell on that look of betrayal he gave me when it became clear that I had, in fact, betrayed him—although perhaps not in the way he believed. To play over the multitude of ways in which I could have handled the moment better.

I guess I do have time.

I saw at my mother's bindings first. My father wouldn't let me free him before her, and although he has the size, my mother has always been the one with the viciousness within her. I don't know if he'll be able to strike out at someone who was like a daughter to him, even knowing exactly what she is. My mother, however, will take a rock to Aymbe's head even if it breaks her own heart to do it. She's broken glass. Fragile but sharp.

My aunt is a wild card. She just got her daughter back. I have no idea what she'll do.

"I'm cutting the bottom of the line so that it isn't obvious I've tampered with them. If I don't get a chance to finish, if you stay still, she might think you're still restrained. It might give you an opportunity." I work at my mother's wrist ties, wincing when a few drops of blood leak out and stain the rock beneath her. I wipe my knee in the blood, smearing it so it isn't quite so obvious.

"Do you think I'm a fool?" she asks after I've freed one wrist.

I've been her daughter long enough to know that question is a trap. "No."

"Apparently you do. You assumed I couldn't handle the truth about her."

"Maybe this isn't the best time for it, but actually *I* had no idea of the truth about her until a few solar days ago, when I was out of coms range. So no, it's not that I don't think you can handle it. I'm just that stupid." I saw the tie harder, because the sooner I'm done here, the sooner I can leave.

She's quiet, like she's considering whether a daughter of hers could plausibly be that stupid. Aymbe, who was *almost* a daughter to her, could be the Abyssal Abductor, so anything is possible.

I manage to get her freed without any other recriminations.

"Aunt Mygda, how are you doing?" I still don't know if I should go for her next.

"She's alive—" Her voice is wonderingly joyful but turns bitter-sharp. "Despite all your fuckups. She survived it all and came back to me."

All righty. I won't be untying her until I have more backup.

I move to my father while my mother picks up a heavy rock and creeps around the edge of the cave-bubble, peering out the gaps between the stone shards.

"We know you did your best," my father reassures me, which maybe isn't the reassurance he thinks it is, because my best got everyone tied up in a cave by a crazy woman.

I squeeze his arm with my free hand as I keep sawing at his wrist bindings.

"She's coming back," my mother hisses from the south side of the cave.

The south side. The invisible zone. Which probably housed a Pierce retrieval vessel alongside Aymbe's ship. So she just finished her deal with them and they're on their way off-planet. Taking Micah. I saw harder, bleeding freely on the ground now, because time is more important than subterfuge. Both of my father's wrists are free and I get to work on his left ankle.

"She's close!" My mother's whisper is closer.

"I'm working on it!" I saw so hard it feels like the blade is cutting at my own skin as much as it is the plastic binding and finally sever it. The binding. Not my skin. Only one more leg to go.

"I'm going to take care of this." My mother says it in the voice usually saved for addressing a swindling vendor or an unworthy boyfriend of her daughter's. I don't know what she means, but I know I can't saw any faster.

"Do not take care of this, Mother!" I hiss at her. "She is a *killer*. Not just a ransomer. It's more than a hobby, it's basically a vocation."

She sniffs again, lip curling up as her fist tightens around the rock.

"That's where you get your stubborn look," my dad whispers to me. "It was always my favorite expression of hers."

I'm halfway through my father's last leg tie when a blaster beam shoots between us, scorching a rock at the back of the cave. I fall backward instinctively, rolling across the rock as more shots follow me.

"You ruin everything!" Aymbe approaches the cave from the outside, blaster out already, too far away for us to ambush yet. "I had a plan."

Our only chance is for me to make myself a target and lure her inside. "Oh, yeah, as good as the plan that got yourself kidnapped in the first place?"

Generally, I'm opposed to victim blaming, but in this case, it seems forgivable.

"I killed him first!" she screeches. I clearly struck a weak spot.

"You were a victim, Aymbe. That's how everyone knows you. That's how I knew you. My poor murdered cousin."

She fires again and I remember I'm not wearing armor anymore when a hot sizzle of pain lashes over my shoulder. I drop beneath an angled spike of rock. Not like I wasn't already bleeding. At least this wound is probably already cauterized. "Missed me!"

"Did not!"

My mother rolls her eyes at me from her position beside the entrance to the cave-bubble, heavy rock hoisted in her hand. I give her my innocent eyes and mouth "she shot me" at her while pointing at my shoulder. "You're a pathetic kidnapper. I always wondered why the Abductor lost all his style halfway through."

Lie. She definitely added more flare than the original Abductor—or maybe at least more financial savvy.

She bursts into the cave, blaster already firing at my feeble little stone shield, and I duck down just as my mother swings the stone for Aymbe's head and my aunt yells, "It's a trap!"

That's right.

My aunt has evaluated the situation and decided to help out the woman who tied her up and made a living terrorizing people. The woman who thought it would be a delightful life choice to let her own family think she was dead. Who didn't even bother to show at her own father's wake.

There's a dull thump, a scuffle, and an outraged squeal that sounds far too conscious. It's enough to have me out from behind my rock and running full tilt at them as Aymbe's blaster falls from the hand that my mother hit with the rock. She grabs my mother's hair with her free hand.

That's why you don't hit someone's *hand* with a rock. They have a spare.

This time I succeed with my tackle, largely because it is unexpected, driving her down to the rocks beneath me. She half drags my mother with her, refusing to release her hair. For a moment, my whole life is narrowed to visceral sensation. The cave water that drips in my hair from above as I struggle with her. My father yells something. The scrape of sharp rock on my shins where my bodysuit rides up. The catch of Aymbe's hands against my collar. The violence of my knuckles hitting her cheek. The viciousness of her knife as it slashes against my ribs, narrowly deflected by the twist of my body.

I cough out a bark of pain, doing my utmost to keep Aymbe in place. My mother growls—actually growls—as she wrestles Aymbe's knife-hand flat on the stone. She's strong. Either Aymbe's been lifting rocks to keep in shape or Pierce gave her all those mods they forgot to give me. Plenty of strength, very little training. Not that she's any less dangerous.

The faster I get her subdued, the sooner I can get off this rock and after Micah. She's wasting my time. She's wasting *his* time. I grab a fistful of her hair and use it to batter her head against the rock.

With a shriek, she wrests her hand away from my mother's grasp, backhanding her hard across the face, and rolls me like an angry eel, driving me into the stone wall. "Why won't you just give up?" she yells, hands tightening around my neck.

"I'm not a child!" I yell back, with what little air I have left as her fingers dig into my throat. "It's a lot harder when you try to subdue people who can fight back."

I knee her between the legs. Not as effective against a woman as a man, but no one likes getting hit where all their nerve endings live. Nails dig into my neck, but she doesn't release her grip. I can't breathe. My mother yells something.

A dull electrical charge runs through me out of nowhere, and suddenly Aymbe's body goes limp. I stare dazedly over her shoulder as her grip on my throat relaxes. My father stands like a hero in the middle of the cave, Aymbe's dropped blaster in hand, chair still tied to one leg and a sick look on his face. I roll her floppy body off my own and stagger to my feet, looking for anything to tie her up.

She's stunned, not dead.

Aunt Mygda is screaming at everyone. That seems like a future problem. I have too many now problems.

My mother hands me a cluster of plastic ties from a small pack at the side of the cave that I didn't notice earlier. I'm surprised she fought Aymbe so viciously, even with her steely core. I never stopped to think about who she became after I left. Just as I never stopped to think that maybe my father trained with a blaster just as hard as I do.

I don't know them. Not anymore. I knew who they were and who I *wanted* them to be. They don't know who I am. They know what I thought they'd want to know. Which doesn't come close to being the actual me. We fucked this up so royally between us three.

I'm just finishing binding Aymbe's ankles together, after wrists and elbows, when Caro and Itzel burst into the cave-bubble, blasters drawn and deadly looks on their faces.

How many people are going to try to shoot me before the day is over? Without me to guide them through the shoals, it was probably a long trip. Then they had to avoid the traps. By the dust on their coveralls, they didn't avoid them all.

"What did you do to Micah?" I don't have to look at Caro's blaster to know that it isn't set to stun mode.

I mean to answer. I want to answer. I was just strangled for a bit and it's hard to bounce back quickly. When I finally try to speak, it's a wheezing sound. I swallow. Try again. Wheeze again.

"She called the Pierce Family." My mother points at Aymbe's restrained form at our feet. "There was a bounty on him."

She casts me a meaningful glance. It says to shut up about how, exactly, Aymbe knew there was a bounty. Apparently our screaming altercation carried enough that my mother realizes there's more to Micah's capture than meets the eye. She probably also realizes that infuriating the two blaster-armed women is a bad idea. I press my hand to my ribs, hot blood slick against my palm.

"No, Cynbelline took the bounty. That's what my Aymbe said," Mygda helpfully pipes up. Apparently she's forgiven the whole kidnapper-killer thing. On one hand, I admire that level of familial commitment. I wish she'd applied that same grace to me when I failed to miraculously retrieve her daughter by myself back when she was taken.

I kind of wished my dad had stunned her, too. Sympathy will probably return with my ability to breathe like a normal person.

"Carmichael gave me the bounty." My voice is hoarse and ragged. "Threatened to reveal my true identity if I didn't take it. Means a lot of bad guys after my family. I lost the Pierce coms at Poison Green, and it was a relief. I didn't plan on delivering him. She got it somehow. Figured out who they wanted."

It wouldn't have been hard. There was only one banished man with us. My fingers clench against my ribs. My mother looks at me like I'm an idiot for telling the truth, but I'm going to start this whole radical thing where that's what I do now. My father drags the chair forward with one leg, still holding the blaster, now loosely pointed at Itzel and Caro. He shakes his head but puts his free hand around my mother's shoulders. "Of course she told the truth, Cygna. She's the daughter you raised. The same one who told the truth when she realized what the constables were up to. The one who does the right thing even if the wrong one is easier."

Which is a generous way to put it. Itzel huffs out a breath and crouches by my father, freeing his ankle from the chair with a sharp slash of a blade.

They both watch my aunt dubiously. Which is a good call.

"Where is he?" Caro gestures at me with her blaster. It goes a little wild and we all flinch away from the barrel. Itzel winces and lifts the weapon from the engineer's fingers with the delicacy of a bomb disarmer.

"*They* didn't hurt him, Caro." The biologist looks troubled. I mean . . . obviously. All of us look troubled. It's a troubling time.

"You arrived too late." I spit a mouthful of blood on the rock. I bit the inside of my cheek during one of Aymbe's blows. My mother winces slightly, because it's trashy to spit. I feel like getting punched in the face is a loophole. "But we still have a chance. The

Pierces just launched. They'll go to Sunspire Way Station—that's where his warrant originated, so that's where they'll try him. He's a medic, so could be they send him somewhere swanky like Shiki-gami prison to do medic stuff."

"What do you expect us to do, unarrest Micah?" Caro practi-cally cries. Now that she's not pointing a blaster at us, I can see the tension in the corner of her eyes, the quiver in her hand. She's terrified for Micah, and just like that all my hostility drains away.

"I expect us to rescue him."

CHAPTER 24

We take Aymbe's ship, the *Mimic*, because it's closest. And because it's fucking *nice*. A Pierce-made invisibility shield perches on its chassis, sending a signal large enough to blank out a quadrant of the island. According to Caro, this tech only works on-planet. Something about being in space fucks with the invisibility optics and signal warpers.

We also take every single other person along for the ride. The ship requires Aymbe's retina to power up, so she's presently locked in the hold. I suggested that we could pop an eye out, but no one found that funny. My aunt refused to be parted from her crazy daughter, which means that *she's* locked in one of the bunks because we can't trust her not to free Aymbe. My parents refused to be parted from me, once they found out my grandparents are okay, so now they're occupying the other bunk.

Which means that Caro, Itzel, and I don't have a bunk.

"This is what a spaceship is supposed to feel like," Itzel points out to Caro when we finally escape the pull of the planet.

"I know what a spaceship is supposed to feel like." Caro sends her side-eyes before returning to her datapad with jaw clenched.

"Then how come our ship does that rattling-vibrating thing?"

"Because it likes to," the engineer growls. She unbuckles from her seat in the helm and storms out, shouting over her shoulder when she hits the door, "I'm going to see how we can get real speed out of this pleasure craft."

"Touchy. She chafes at our budget." Itzel says the words under her breath, dancing her fingers over the console of the weapons panel. "She chafes at most things, to be honest."

"You have a son of the Escajeda on your ship and a phydium engine. You have a budget?" I force a jovial tone as I set coordinates for Sunspire, staring into the black as though I can still see the path of the Pierce ship with Micah in it. Itzel snorts in response. My hands twitch with adrenaline, built during my confrontation with Aymbe and never fully settled. I don't think it can be settled until I get Micah back. Until he knows that I didn't mean to turn him in. Until he lives.

He said he trusted me.

Something in the back of my throat quivers in a sound that's almost like a moan, and I swallow it, because now is not the time to break down. Now is the time to decide what I'm going to do when we get to the way station. "I need to make a call. Ensure we stay on track?"

The biologist hums an acquiescence, stroking a finger back and forth over what appears to be a particle-beam-weapon targeting system and I leave the helm before she decides to pockmark the closest moon. Just beyond the helm is a narrow hall with the two private bunks on one side and a bathroom with a toilet and particle shower on the other. Farther down the hall is another split: tiny galley stocked with a nutrient printer and across the hall seems to be a miscellaneous storage space containing a large collection of what can only be referred to as "murder tools." If anyone intercepts us, those will be difficult to explain. At the end of the hall, a staircase upward leads to the engine room and a ramp downward leads to the entrance hatch and small hold.

I return to the galley and thumb on my coms, hoping there are enough relay stations in this region to connect the call. I have no clue what time it is in the Burren. Luckily, Madrigal doesn't sleep. She picks up almost before my coms unit registers that the call has gone through.

"Do I get to identify your body yet?"

"It was Aymbe."

A pause. Some rustling in the background as she repositions herself. "I need context, kid. What's an Aymbe?"

"The Abyssal Abductor. She's Aymbe. My—my cousin. She killed the original. Took over because it seemed like a good way to get out of the trawlertown." I perch on the edge of a metal chair with one leg bolted to the floor, elbows on my knees and head down because it suddenly feels like a whole planet is pressing down on it. I wish Vuur was here, its hot breath warm against my neck.

"It's almost like the logic of crazy people doesn't make any sense."

"They took Micah."

"Who are they and who is Micah? You're getting worse at storytelling. He the one with the arms? Shouldn't have let anyone take the one with the arms. Arms like that are about as common as a nanoprinter in a machine shop."

Right. The last time I spoke to her, I was being circumspect. I explain Micah, as much as I'm able. Explain the warrant and my decision not to fulfill it. Which leads to explaining who I really am. Finally, I tell her about the truth of his time on Sunspire and Pierce's surprise appearance.

Something crunches.

"Did you just hear me pour my heart out to you about how a man I care for has been captured and will be put to death—about how he thinks I planned to betray him—even though he's innocent, and think 'Bored now, it's time for some chips'?"

"You don't expect me to take news like that on an empty stomach, do you?" More crunching. "I thought you were too hard-hearted to fall prey to nonsense like this. Wish I was right."

"I should add, we left the planet chasing the Pierces. We're on their tail now."

"Sounds like you didn't get me those extra chips you promised."

"*Viall*, Madrigal, is that all you care about? You told me I'd never regret not trusting but I would regret trusting foolishly. The problem is, I'm not the one who trusted foolishly. He did. Tell me you know something about the Claw. Something I can use." My hands are in fists. I didn't even mean to do it, I'm just carrying so much tension that I can barely force my fingers to straighten.

There's an extended silence. If one was being generous, one might assume she's washing off her hands. I'm not generous and I know it's the sound of scheming. "Might have. Might not. I want something in return."

What an excellent time for negotiations. "What? What do you want?"

"I want out. Out of the Burren. Out of this home. I want you to take me to Sunspire."

"I can't get you out. Only your next of kin can do that." What I assumed was her son dropped her off at the retirement home and left her there. He doesn't visit.

"That priap isn't even my kin. Was my second-in-command and got greedy."

I'm starting to think that running with a gang isn't good for one's overall well-being. "Oh, so we're being honest about who we are now, are we?"

"I don't know. *Are* we?" *Crunch crunch crunch.* Touché. "Look. I went along with it for a while. Things got hot and I needed to lie low. Now, though, now I see some opportunity."

"Fine. I'll get you out. But so help me, Madrigal, if you're taking advantage of a moment of weakness . . ."

"You won't do a fucking thing." She sounds pretty certain. "You're a softie, Cyn Khaw. You talk big but you feed the cats your leftovers every night."

"You know I'm a killer." I keep my voice quiet.

"You're a survivor. A killer is different. I'd know. *I'm* a killer." She sounds proud, which is how I know it's probably the truth.

"Fine," I grit out, feeling like my ability to threaten is undone by someone who appears to be entirely unintimidated.

She ends the connection abruptly, but I don't read into it. Madrigal's like that. She doesn't waste time with things like goodbyes.

. . . . .

Aymbe's galley doesn't come with anything but a nutrient printer, so I focus on creating the very best printed dinner of artificially colored slop possible. It's heavy in fake butter, which is the key to any excellent dinner. Second only to real butter. My mother finds me there, holding herself slightly rigid because she's never been on a spaceship before and it's a natural reaction to feel like the little metal box is about to jettison you to space at any moment. Her face is a mixture of concerned, horrified, unsettled, and disgusted. I hand her a plate of something smothered in pseudocheese. "How are you?"

That covers a lot of territory. How are you postkidnapping? How are you being off-world for the first time? How are you doing with learning the girl you thought was a victim is much more complicated? Any regrets about taking your sister's side so hardcore now that it turns out she's totally *fine* with Aymbe being who she is?

I saw a side of her in the cave that I don't recognize—somewhere during the point where we were both rolling around the floor wrestling Aymbe. The same with my father. Maybe a side that's always been there but I never noticed.

She sits at last, wrapping an arm around me like she's just remembered we both almost died. It's nice. We aren't a particularly touchy family, and I'm generally quite happy to keep my personal space, but nothing compares to your mother hugging you. She smells like saltwater soap and flowers. She mutters that she's as good as can be expected, which means "not very."

"How's Aunt Mygda?" Maybe she'll want to talk about her sister more than herself.

"Scared."

Perhaps this is where I inherited my loquaciousness. "Seems a touch more than scared."

Mom huffs out a breath, but her lips relax into a smile instead of a frown. "She's recovering. She's been in a bad mental state for a very long time."

I nod. We can find her a therapist. I don't know how much experience they'd have in this particular instance, but it'd be something. Now that she's started, it seems like my mother has much more to say.

"Instead of talking about that, let's talk about why you lead the kind of life where you have a subdermal blade embedded in your arm and why you never spoke a word of that to any of us?" In all the answers that I thought my mother would demand of me, this one catches me completely unprepared. I stare at her, mouth open, for a moment while I desperately search for an answer that isn't horrific.

Not giving me much of a chance to actually answer, she continues. "You think I never heard the stories about you? You're a boogieman vigilante. People speak your name in a whisper."

I . . . actually hoped she *hadn't* heard the stories about me. Or had thought it was some other Cyn Khaw. Khaw isn't that uncommon as names go. Especially in Pierce space. More importantly, the trawler doesn't get a lot of news from outside their own little bubble. She never mentioned it before. I guess we never mentioned a lot of things to each other. Our family has been surface-level as we try to protect each other from our truths. It was unfair. They deserved to be my first call when I woke up on the *Iceberg*. Deserved to be trusted with all of me instead of only the nice parts.

Winnowing it to the nice parts didn't leave much of me for them to know. I clearly don't know many parts about them, either. I don't know why my father bought his first blaster—or how.

I knew my mother had a wild side, but I didn't expect to see it myself as she slammed a rock into someone else's body.

My father joins us, collecting his own plate of butter-cheese goop. There's something off with the printer and all the food is going purple. It's probably fine.

With no other way to delay, it's time to do the right thing. The thing I should have long ago. I tell them the story of the *Iceberg*. Of what I suspect Pierce did to Aymbe. Of what I suspect they did to me. When I'm done, I'm met with silence. I wonder if I didn't explain it right. If they don't believe me, like I always worried they wouldn't. "I didn't go there to kill them for being human traffickers. I was just green enough that I didn't realize they'd already sold the cargo when I snuck on the ship. They weren't supposed to. It was supposed to be a supply stop. One of their victims reportedly looked like Aymbe. A trusted source told me it was her. That she was still alive. It wasn't. Obviously."

They stare at me like they don't know quite what to believe. It's a lot, I understand.

"Those Pierce priaps." My father's voice doesn't even sound familiar. He shot someone not long ago. Not to death, but the act of pulling a trigger is the act of intent. And the part where our medical care in the Pierce clinic was something else entirely. It's something of a turnabout. "You were so healthy once you came home, we didn't ask questions. *Viall*. We sent them a thank-you note. We sent them updates on your health."

"Hm. Robust, certainly." I can't be too upset about it right now. I might be some sort of void-surviving creature, but the surviving part is all that really matters. It's the others who worry me. The people we don't know about. The children who didn't survive their treatment. The question of if they really were playing around with plankat nibarat with their mods, leading to Aymbe's evolution. She spoke about farming and flowers. It wouldn't hold up in a Family tribunal, but it's confirmation enough for me.

The overarching concern, then, is what the Pierce Family gets out of creating people who can survive in such extremes, who heal quickly. Maybe they're creating the next generation of asteroid farmers. I doubt it.

"The average mods never would have allowed Aymbe to swim up from the bottom of a trench. They never would have allowed me to survive being spaced."

"You never told us." My mother is still hung up on the dishonesty rather than the trauma. Her face is stricken and drawn. I haven't seen it look like that since Aymbe was taken. It breaks my heart that I'm the cause. I never wanted her to be upset. I thought that by keeping it from her, I was protecting her.

Which was a very selfish way to consider things, now that I actually think about it.

"We didn't talk about bad things. Not since Aymbe. Bad things almost ruined us, so I tried to keep them away. All you cared about was if I'd gotten married . . . if I was having kids. If I was coming home anytime soon." I try to explain, forcing myself to maintain eye contact. My father's jaw is hard. Like he's biting back words. My mother's face is drawn. "I didn't want the life you all had planned for me, and I thought that without me at home, without the reminder of me, you might return to something like normal." All of us wanting to go back in time and ignoring who we are now. What a fucking waste. "As it turns out, none of us are normal people anymore."

"What made you think we wanted normal?" Some of her usual steel remains in my mother's voice. Just enough for it to flay.

"You wanted babies," I point out. "I gave my whole life to finding Aymbe's killer. I had no time for babies. For finding a partner. For any of that."

"We never wanted that for you," my father interjects, as though I somehow did this all to please them.

That last little tendon holding me together snaps. "*I wanted it for me. Just like you wanted to learn to use a blaster. Just like how Mom—"

Danger. Time to shut up.

"Just like I what?"

I glance frantically at my father, as though he'll save me from this mess I've made. Gloriously, he does. "You turned into a bit of a dictator, petal. You were always organizing and planning so that there wasn't a sliver of free space. As though a rigid schedule could forestall anything frightening."

She looks even more stricken. Like she didn't even realize what she was doing. Like we stabbed her. Well, we're all bleeding right now. Leaking our protective disappointments on the deck.

"Maybe we should meet who we really are." My father reaches his hand across the table, and I clasp it reflexively. My mother braces her hand over both of ours. "And stop trying to dwell on who we won't ever be."

"It wasn't even all that good before," my mother offers. "The house smelled like rotten algae in high summer, and I was bitter because I settled down before I got to see anywhere but the trawler."

My father exhales a laugh—almost a gasp. "I was bitter about that, too! I never thought you'd want to leave, so I didn't say anything."

Ah, so being stupid-uncommunicative runs in the family. Fantastic.

"I didn't really think that story about your prized houseplant was as interesting as you thought it was," my mom tells me, eyes bright with unshed tears. We aren't a crying people. There's a saying on the trawler: "Salt is better kept inside, lest the ocean steal it."

"That plant was fabulous!" I protest. "Dad asked so many questions about it!"

"Because you told me it was alive. Darling, I love you, but the only reason you keep *yourself* alive seems to be luck and happy accidents. It was the same when you were a child."

I decide not to tell him that I managed to kill it less than one standard week after I bought it.

"I'm proud of you, Bella." My father sets his rough-calloused hand on my shoulder. "You're a survivor and, more importantly, you're honorable. That's everything we could have ever wanted in a daughter."

Somehow that's what I've always wanted to hear, but I never knew it. I bite my tongue, the sharp pinch a distraction from the upswell of emotion. I realize that my mother is still half hugging me. I wrap one arm around her and lean back toward my father. They both embrace me. I missed this. I'm not sure I ever even had it, and I miss it.

"I still want a grandchild." My mother just has to have the last word.

CHAPTER 25

Everyone gazes about my office in the Burren with prurient curiosity. Running counter to my expectations, Caro's focus is on my Abductor board on the wall, and Itzel's is on the safe room–bedroom. For some reason, I assumed Caro would be into both the locks and also the evidence of my clear lunacy.

"This is a great idea," Itzel enthuses, running a finger over the locks. "It would take me quite a bit of time to get through it. If more people slept like this, my jobs would be much harder."

I try not to linger over what exactly she means by "jobs." I shoot a worried gaze at Caro, who I thought was against things like murder. She either hasn't noticed or doesn't care. Her finger traces the edge of a picture of Carmichael Pierce that I hung up as a reminder that he's always watching me. Her mouth twists down.

When we arrived, I did a quick scan for anything missing from my break-in. Nothing I could see. I took all my tech with me, so unless they took hastily drawn notes, they didn't get much. Maybe they figured out my locks? Or maybe Pierce was worried that I'd bailed on my mission and returned home.

My mother looks appalled. I don't know if it's because of the lack of the sunlight that keeps the trawlertown so bright, the steady coldness of the rock that surrounds us, or the general bleakness of the Burren itself. Or the room that Itzel is still inspecting. Could be that, too. My aunt pokes at the dusty crafted flowers that Aymbe made me. My cousin, tied to my office chair, smirks at me.

"You've really made something of yourself." My father attempts positivity, perhaps forgetting how vague the word "something" is. He stops and gasps, pointing at the dead houseplant still perched on the edge of the sink. "You said it was thriving!"

"Of all my lies . . ."

"It's on the edge of the sink! It's so close to water. How could you kill it?"

I count out on my fingers. "I'm underground. I've been away from home for weeks. Also, and this is the rough part . . . I don't actually care about houseplants."

He shakes his head sadly, entertaining visions of withering grandchildren perched next to the sink, no doubt.

I plant my foot on the edge of the office chair and shove Aymbe away from the desk, where she was slowly maneuvering herself. "We can't take her with us. Estella Escajeda's people are on their way, but they won't be here before we have to leave."

"I'll watch her," my aunt blurts just a little too soon. She isn't restrained but she probably should be. Twice, on the way here, we caught her sneaking down to Aymbe's prison in the hold, wire cutters in her pocket.

"We'll watch both of them." My mother glares at her sister.

"Ah, actually, I need you for the next part of the plan." She probably won't appreciate that the next part of the plan involves using her to gain access to the retirement home next door. "I also need Caro."

Itzel throws a slight arm around my father's elbows. It would be around his shoulders, but she's not quite tall enough to achieve that. "Looks like it's you and me, Parbel. Wanna learn how to throw knives?"

My father smirks a little bit. This feels like a mistake.

They end up locking Aymbe and Mygda in my safe room, which, as it turns out, works both ways. Something I didn't realize until Caro figured out the work-around.

So I guess I'm never sleeping there again.

I thought my mother would be upset at being elderly bait. She isn't. She hurls herself into the role with the dedication of a holo-star given one last chance to restart her career. She musses her perfectly quaffed hair. She paints on her cosmetics like a clown face, smeared near her mouth. She affects a high-pitched giggle. She exaggerates the slight stumble she has on solid ground after a lifetime at sea. She peppers us with questions about knitting, per-haps assuming that it is a necessary skill for her character.

If Madrigal ever found a knitting needle, she'd probably use it to stab the orderly who limits her chip stash.

"This isn't a long-term con, Mom. We go in, go on a tour, snatch Madrigal, and make a run for it once Caro checks her for trackers."

It never made sense to me how someone as vibrant as Madrigal would be locked in the home and wouldn't try to set out on her own. She's sharp as a tack and she may have slowed down, but she doesn't have any inability to provide for herself. She wouldn't have remained for so long if they didn't have some way to force her to stay.

Caro tucks a pouch of electrical equipment in the pocket of her cargo pants and gives my mother an assessing gaze. "You're going to want to look wealthier to get in the door. Clearly, they don't care if someone needs actual help. They want a payout."

I dig into the side drawer of my desk, flipping the small panel in the back that opens a side compartment, and remove a pair of etamarine earrings. They were given to me by a former client in lieu of payment. Apparently the client thought I was the type to wear a generous waterfall of precious stones from each ear. I prob-ably wouldn't make it twenty steps in the Burren without a thief trying to snatch them.

Luckily, the retirement home is only about ten steps. My mother clips them in her ears, and the pale-blue stones sparkle against the dark fall of her now-tangled hair.

"Why are you living in a dive if you have jewelry like this?" The woman really misses nothing, although the smear of lipstick by her mouth damages her sense of authority.

"I have more important ways to spend my credits." Like secretly paying back the debt my family incurred on Aymbe's ransom. And spending more of it trying to find her killer.

I glance at the picture of Carmichael. I hope Micah's okay. He's too valuable just to execute, surely, and trails take time. They must have a use for him. All we need is a little time to get all our pieces in place.

When we're ready, my father kisses my mother goodbye, smearing the lipstick even more. Itzel hands him a small light blade. Oh no, she was serious about the knife-throwing. She tosses a grin my way. "Don't worry, we'll aim for the Abductor board."

Fair, I guess.

. . . . .

I've never been inside the retirement home. It's . . . both better and worse than I anticipated. The lobby is clean, which is the better part. It's populated by three burly guard types and one hawkeyed receptionist armed with a scanner. That's the worse part. My mother freezes momentarily and then throws caution to the wind, muttering slightly to herself.

"Good morning!" I cheerfully announce to the receptionist. "After a long discussion, my mother has agreed that it's time to move to a home that can provide her more care. You're the best spot in the Burren."

And by "best" I mean "only."

The receptionist looks from me to Caro, back to my mother. "And who is this?"

Caro crosses her arms. "I'm her sister."

The receptionist takes in Caro's dark-brown skin, my mother's bronze, and my own light tan. The complete lack of resemblance of any other features.

"Different dads." I keep the smile pasted on my face.

My mother, who never loved anyone but my father, stiffens slightly. Then develops a twitch that somehow ends up with her elbow in my ribs. I cough.

The receptionist shrugs. "Sure, we can take her. Here are the forms. The fee is nonnegotiable."

"Oh, I couldn't just drop her off without seeing your facility."

The receptionist sighs and waves a hand to one of the guards. "Take them on the loop." She returns her attention to me. "She'll have to share a room. We're full right now."

"She loves sharing. So social." Caro taps her interface tattoo, activating something or other. "Do we get a discount for a non-private room?"

My mother's twitch switches sides. Caro huffs out an "oof."

"Nonnegotiable means nonnegotiable." The receptionist lifts her scanner and waves it over Caro. Nothing goes off, even though I happen to know that the engineer is carrying enough machinery to build a blaster from scratch if she felt like it. She also scans me.

She does not scan my mother. Rookie mistake. My mother has a blaster taped to her thigh under her skirt and a knife in her bra. I didn't even give her the knife. She just carries one there. And because she has voluminous breasts that she selfishly did not pass down to me, the hilt of the blade is obscured. I have so much to learn.

The guard leads us through the door. The space behind aligns with my expectations much better. It's less clean than the lobby. Not dirty, exactly, more like dingy. The hallway loops in a circle through the building. None of the rooms have windows, because windows require extra security and also because the home is embedded in the rock of the Burren just like my office is.

"This is the hallway." The guard points at the floor. I get the impression that he doesn't offer tours often. Madrigal's room should be around the corner on the right.

"Could we see a room?" I give him my best innocent eyes.

He sighs, clearly hoping that pointing out the hall would be sufficient. "Fine."

When he reaches for the first door on the left, clearly not caring about what the resident is doing right now, Caro yelps, "Not that one!"

"It's too close to the entrance." I make sure to have my hand looped through my mother's elbow. "She likes to escape. We need something farther from the front door. It'll make your job easier."

"We chip our residents." The guard shrugs, tapping something on his interface tattoo. "They feel an electrical signal if they get too close to the edge of the property. If they keep going, it stuns them. Kinda funny to watch. Ow!"

My mother's twitch has morphed into a fairly powerful round-house kick. I edge myself between them. "Oh no, do you have a cramp?"

She glares at me and raises an eyebrow. Caro hides a snicker in a cough. "As you see, she can't be controlled easily. She might hurt a roommate."

Now, this is a risk, but I'm betting that Madrigal is a thorn in this guard's side, because she's the opposite of easy. The hope is that between saying we need to be deeper in the building and that she might be a bad roomie, he'll take advantage of the fact that Madrigal is a pest and stick them together.

The guard nods and leads us down the hall. Limping slightly. Go, Mom.

We pause near door 109, which should lead to Madrigal's room. He opens door 110. Fuck. "This client is in a coma. Your mother won't bother them, and they won't bother her."

Why couldn't we get a vindictive guard? I glance at Caro. She looks back with a grimace.

My mother shoots the guard in the back, one side of her skirt hiked up where she retrieved her blaster. Caro yelps. I might yelp, too.

A quick glance indicates that she stunned him.

"We don't have time to waste, do we?" she asks.

No. No, we don't. Caro slips out the door and across the hall to 109, fidgeting with the door until she releases its lock. Madrigal is waiting just behind the door, a rucksack slung over her shoulder, a bag of chips in her hand, and a smile on her face. Also, a trace of purplish chip dust.

My mother braces in the hall like she's making a last stand, blaster at the ready. I hold out my hand. It's mine, after all. The plan was that she would smuggle it in for *me*. She huffs out a sigh and passes it over as Caro withdraws a scanner from her pocket and runs it over Madrigal. It beeps in two spots: the back of her neck and her hip. Madrigal braces a protective hand over her hip.

"This one is my own."

Now, I wonder what she keeps in that? Something that I'm sure is none of my business. Caro goes to work on the one in her neck.

"Should we try to get everyone out?" I ask my mother as I cover one side of the hall and she watches the other. "I don't like the idea of chipping people like wayward pets."

On the trawler, we keep our family close. If someone needs extra care, they may go to a nursing home, but they're constantly visited by friends and relatives. We have nothing like this, where people are placed to be forgotten.

My mother doesn't answer for a while but then reaches back and pats my elbow. "Leave it to me, sweetie. You have a lot on your plate."

I don't know what leaving it to her means. Maybe I don't want to. She's right, after all. My plate is full. Caro makes a soft exclamation of victory and follows Madrigal into the hall. "Got it. It's inactive for the next few minutes. Once she's out of range, it won't activate anywhere."

"What if there's a tracker?"

"You really think they're going to track me off-moon?" Madrigal crosses her arms. "You're smarter than that."

My mother eyes her. Only family's allowed to talk to me like that. Madrigal eyes her back, jaw hardening. "Madrigal, Cygna. Cygna, Madrigal."

"So you're the one my daughter's been calling." My mother's voice is cold.

"And you're the one she's been avoiding calling." Madrigal's is mild.

Both are super-dangerous states. I brace myself for what's sure to come next.

"Thank you," my mother says, and I almost drop the blaster.

Madrigal looks for the angle. Tilts her head. "You're welcome."

A soft scuff from room 110 alerts me to the guard's return to consciousness. Caro reaches past me and shuts the door, waving her interface tattoo over the door. The lock flashes red. "We're running out of time."

My mother pulls the knife out of her bra and holds it aloft. I pinch my eyes shut. Madrigal eyes the blade. "That's fine craftsmanship."

My mother accepts the compliment. "Thank you. My father made it."

My grandpa is making bra knives in his smithy. A concern for another day.

"Two more guards and the receptionist," Caro runs down what we have to get past on the way out. "I can pull at least one of the guards away with a security alert to a room down the hall."

I nod in agreement. She works her magic, and we wait for the guard to come. My blaster is set to stun and level with the hall.

He never comes. Clearly, the services here are not to be recommended. "We definitely have to come back for the others."

"I told you, I'll take care of it." My mother's words are implacable.

Madrigal smiles. I know that smile. It's the one right before she does something particularly devilish.

"Maybe I'll join you in that."

Are—are they friends now?

"We don't have time to wait," I redirect. "I'm going out the door first, since I'm the one with the blaster."

Madrigal shrugs, like this escape has grown boring. My mother's grip on her knife tightens. Caro waves her hands in the air, clearly doing something with her augmented lenses.

Who could ask for more from a crew?

I burst through the door to the front, blaster up. The two guards are tied to a support beam, unconscious. The receptionist is sitting motionless at her desk, Itzel's knife pressed to her throat, gentle as a kiss.

"Weren't you supposed to be watching Mygda and Aymbe?" I lower my blaster.

She grins. "Your father is excellent at knife-throwing already. He didn't need my training or my help handling them. Besides, they're all locked up."

My mom slips her knife back into her bra. "My father made him his first set of throwing knives. He treasures them."

He *what*?

Madrigal laughs, a bright unexpected sound. "Looks like it runs in the family."

"What does?" Caro feels the pulses of the guards. Itzel looks offended that her work is being second-guessed.

"Militant affection." Madrigal eats a purple chip shaped like a tube. Glances down at the bag. Then she offers it to my mother. My mother gives the dust a dubious look but dredges a chip out.

"This is pretty good." She licks her fingers clean.

I've created a monster of some sort, but I'm not sure what.

CHAPTER 26

The ship approaches Sunspire one standard day after we left the Burren. I wear a space suit because Sunspire's docking bay's atmosphere is only questionably maintained. Their equipment fails all the time and I'd rather not experience that pallid void again. Ever.

It's almost enough to set my heart pounding in my ears and shorten my breath, except there isn't time for that. When my pulse starts to throb, I distract myself with yet another of my endless list of tasks. Sunspire doesn't permit blasters, so I sort through my arsenal for weapons that aren't energy-based. We're dealing with a Family. There's no way I can outshoot the Pierces.

Caro, Itzel, and Madrigal stand beside me in the helm. My parents insisted on staying in the Burren and watching Mygda and Aymbe until Estella's people show up. She might be there already. I hope she is. I'll sleep better when she's under official custody.

Sunspire is a wheel station, rotating around a central spoke to create artificial gravity out at the rim of the wheel. It's old, which means that sometimes there's a hitch in the rotation that throws that gravity off.

"He has a chip," Caro breaks into my thoughts, standing in the helm and staring at me like she's maybe said that more than once. She's been looking more and more drawn as our journey has gone on. Like she saw something that haunted her. She chews on her lips like she's forcing words to stay in. It started after I told them what Micah discovered with the algae at Poison Green. The fact that there may be a compound that counteracts the negative side effects of plankat nibarat is probably scary to us all. Moreso to everyone except me, because I barely know what it is and I'm full up on fear.

"Locational?"

"No, financial." She rolls her eyes. "Yes, a locational chip. As soon as we enter the station, my drones can triangulate his location."

Drones are a loophole. So long as they aren't weaponized, the station's deterrent system won't detect them. A space station requires a lot of maintenance drones just to say aligned and spinning. It can't parse them too closely.

I shift awkwardly in the space suit. Madrigal stands beside me in my spare. It is far too big for her, even with the contractors all actuated. Itzel and Caro wear Aymbe's spare suits. We're lucky she had two. Clearly, Aymbe does not want for credits.

Which makes me think that not only are the Pierces turning a blind eye to her hobby and profiting from her procurement, but that they're actively paying her for the flesh trade. Maybe even setting her up with the tools to do it. Showing her locations that are already under the radar, like the Poison Green setup, so close to their little farm. A problem for later. My only problem for now is Micah.

We dock and exit the *Mimic*, helmets locked in place. The atmosphere is up in the docking bay of sector four at the moment, but safe is always better than sorry. Caro's small swarm of drones disperses, finding hatches and halls and eventually the open air of the station. The space-suit helmets don't interface with the drone heads-up display—some proprietary software nonsense—so Caro tracks them using her augmented-vision mods and keeps us updated through the coms as the drones clear sectors of the station.

Madrigal leads us from the docking bay, through a small decontamination stream, a bioburden test—which requires us to remove our helmets and breathe in a sensor—and finally out into the station itself. She swore that her connection will only answer questions if she's there. I'd give that a 50-percent likelihood of being true.

The ring stretches before us with a slope so gradual that you almost don't notice that the horizon only ends where the ceiling hits it. It's far enough away that it could just be perspective playing tricks. The rim of the station is only a few blocks wide—it's the length that counts. A joke that I've made more times than I care to enumerate.

The windows of the quadrant hall are broken and boarded up, and holographic paint has been slashed across the walls. FUCK PIERCE. Succinct. I guess it's not just the Burren.

Geoff, Madrigal's contact, resides in a tenement apartment, on a floor that's high enough you can tell the gravity is slightly heavier. The apartment is run-down, with graffiti on the walls and rust at its edges, but when we reach Geoff's floor, we find that he has possession of the entire level. The man who answers the door looks nearly Madrigal's age, with a neatly trimmed white beard, a broad nose, no hair on his scalp, and crinkles by his eyes that indicate he smiles just as much as he frowns.

He's wearing one of those synth-fabric fast-fashion trends that go around stations quickly because most stores are really just recyclers—spinning old designs into new with the same materials. The new designs never last quite as long as the first iteration, and the more you recycle the shorter the half-life of your fashion.

It appears that Sunspire is currently wearing narrow-legged pants with a wide stripe down the side of the leg and militaristic jackets over loose-draped undershirts. Geoff's ear is pierced with a large claw, likely showing his affiliation to the gang. The narrow end of the claw spikes the hole, and it can be pushed through over time, gaging the piercing. It's nearly all the way through.

Now, how does Madrigal know a Claw? I wonder if her gang interfaced with the old leadership. Smuggled goods. I don't get a chance to introduce myself to Geoff, because he's so busy sticking his tongue down Madrigal's throat. She does not protest. Unless protest looks like wrapping a leg around his waist. She's remarkably limber.

I clear my throat.

He squints at us, like we aren't what he expected. Or maybe like he forgot we were here. More likely that. We probably aren't. The three of us hovering in his foyer, dressed in space suits with our helmets clipped to our belts, probably look like we're exploring a strange new world, not traveling over a well-trod station street.

"Let us in, Geoff." Madrigal pats him on the behind when he turns to precede us into the apartment.

"Was this whole jailbreak so you could get laid?" I hiss at her.

"It had many purposes." She keeps her bland face. I wouldn't want to be one of the people who betrayed her in her own gang.

"Please prioritize mine. A man's life may be on the line."

"There's no way they're executing a medic. If he knows how to be smart, he's hunkering down being useful in some holding block, treating bedbug bites and lice. Even if they trot him through some sham trial to try to dredge up improved public sentiment." She waves away my concern with one queenly hand.

But like a woman of her word, she broaches the subject with Geoff the tongue-happy as he hands her a cup of steaming orange beverage. "Have you heard anything about Micah Arora? The medic I spoke to you about earlier. Where they're keeping him, for instance."

Even if the guarda are keeping this quiet, gangs thrive off the trade of confidential information, and Geoff is an old-timer.

He faces the rest of us. "I know Micah. From back in the day. He wasn't here long but he was a good man. They were keeping him in the station down the street. Just sent a shipment to Shikigami but kept him back. They delayed his trial because he was useful."

Madrigal shoots me a sharp glance that says, "I told you so." But then she seems to decide a glance wasn't enough and she actually verbalizes the sentiment. "I told you so."

"Is he still there? Do you have schematics?" What exactly is Geoff doing for us beyond making out with Madrigal? Micah needs our help. Just because he isn't dead doesn't mean he isn't in grave danger. My chest feels tight and I run my knuckles over my sternum, remembering that day not so long ago when his hand was pressed there by the net. "We need to make a plan."

"That's the thing—" Halfway through his response, Caro hiccups an excited breath and interrupts.

"Drones found him. Sector four. Outer edge. It looks like it's below us, right against the rim." She's speaking so rapidly that her words run over each other.

There's something wrong with the location. Prisoners aren't held at the rim. Nothing is. It's too risky out there and citizens kick up a fuss if you accidentally kill someone you didn't mean to. They don't seem to care when you do mean it. It's the incompetence that irks more than the violence.

Geoff breaks through the rush of Caro's words. "Something changed, and it changed fast. Carmichael Pierce dragged a judge out of bed for the sentencing. Everyone involved signed nondisclosures. The only reason I know is because I have bugs in the courthouse."

"Sentenced?" Itzel breathes the question. I can't breathe at all. My throat has closed. Something cracks behind me and Caro curses, picking a small fragment of plas-glass from her newly crushed datapad out of her palm. "How can he be sentenced? He hasn't even had a trial. He was just in holding."

Geoff gives us a look that's something like pity. "To death. It was arson. You know how they treat arson. They disappear you. Especially if you're no longer useful. He was asking questions. Questions about plankat nibarat."

Fuckity fuck *fuck*.

Micah's been sentenced. He's at the *rim*.

I run.

■ ■ ■ ■ ■ ■ ■ ■ ■ ■ ■ ■ ■ ■

"Tell me exactly how to get to his signal," I demand of Caro, as though she isn't doing exactly that. I can't help it. My blood thunders in my ears, deafeningly pulsing as I tear around a corner and into an alleyway. We were supposed to be doing a careful prison break. We were supposed to have schematics and plans and allies. Our allies, Madrigal and Geoff, are back in the apartment, probably naked by now.

Manholes lead to the sewers under the station streets and, beneath that, to the no-man's-land on the rim. The manholes run down the centerline of the station and that's my goal until told otherwise. We have to get *down* before we can get to him.

"He's under subblock seven. We're currently in five. The hatch to the rim from the sewer is in six, the next subblock over. If we hit the sewer, we can break out to the rim there and approach directly." Caro pants the instructions, keeping up but clearly ill-equipped for the chase.

"Can you keep their hatch to the outside closed?" It's a wild shot, but that would save a lot of problems. Can't space a man if you can't access space, and that's how they execute people in a ship. It's efficient. No body disposal because the method of execution *is* body disposal.

"Given the right amount of time and access, sure. I doubt we'll have that. I'm barely getting to the schematics now."

Fuck. Fuck. Fuuuuuuuck.

We arrive at the main street, nearly get hit by a hover bike, and I skid to a halt in the middle of the road, levering at a thick insulated manhole cover.

"There's a tram heading right at us." Itzel reaches for the edge of the cover.

"I suggest we lift more efficiently, then," I snap, which she doesn't deserve but there isn't any nice left in me. Caro joins us as the tram barrels in our direction and we slip down to the sewer just before it races over the manhole, its roaring engine echoing throughout the sewer like it's about to devour us.

"We maybe can't shut the hatch," I reiterate into the darkness. I need to think. Why can't I think? If ever there was a time when having a plan was critical, it's now, but all I can see behind my eyes is Micah's face. All I can hear is him foolishly saying that I'm worthy of trust. "No hatch. All right. What about the *Mimic*? How close can you get it to Micah's location on autopilot?"

Caro pauses and I wonder if I've asked for something deeply stupid for some reason before she finally replies, "Pretty fucking close."

"Get it closer." The sewers are dry, water being precious in a station, but filled with compost in various levels of breakdown. Also, stench. They are absolutely filled with stench. A thin line of pale-white lights runs along the roof of the tunnel, allowing enough illumination to navigate but not enough to see what exactly we're navigating through. Probably for the best. "If it's at the rim, then ship-to-ship weapons might be able to break through. We can cause a standoff."

"You have a plan for getting *out* of the standoff?"

"I don't hear either of you coming up with any plans!"

"Killing everyone who isn't Micah is a plan," Itzel mutters under her breath.

I'm not Micah. I don't love Itzel's plan. Mostly because it sounds even more wishful than my own.

I twist an ankle in a pile of especially soft compost. "Why do we keep chasing people through trash?"

"It must be the special something you contribute to our crew," Caro says sweetly.

Calling me part of the crew is such magnificent progress that I can't even complain.

"Entering six."

A stitch cramps in my side and I flail my arms to balance. Space suits were not made for running. They were made for slow careful movements while performing ship repairs. The helmet rattles against my thigh as it dangles from the strap around my belt. Itzel passes me in the dark, a slim shadow moving with such grace you'd believe that she regularly trains by running through refuse. The dark silence presses in around us as we struggle through the waste.

"Hatch coming in three . . . two . . . here." Caro flashes a quick strobe that illuminates nothing at all.

"Where?" I practically scream it.

Caro points down. At the guck. We drop in unison, shoveling away at it with our hands until a thin-lined grate is revealed. This one is easier than the manhole to remove. It's passing through it that's the trick. The station uses its rotation to create gravity, which means that we and the trash are standing on what would be considered the floor. The outer rim is plasma-lined, meaning they use artificial gravity on the other side of our current floor, flipping the expected gravity. So instead of dropping a whole level due to gravity, the gravity on the other side pushes against us like we're pushing up through a ceiling.

After a little wobbling due to the unexpected nature of it all, I push up and through, straddling the hatch and helping Caro and then Itzel through. Only when they're through do I look up. There's no ceiling. Not really. A thick layer of plasma functions like one, but it's ephemeral as a cloud, and every single hair on the back of my neck stands at attention.

There's no hatch. The outer rim has a plasma wall. Some ships have them, especially when they want drones to be able to go from atmo to vacuum easily. The plasma generates oxygen and offers insulation, but a drone can push from one side to the other fairly easily.

Pure momentum keeps me going, because my feet want to stumble to a halt. My body wants to curl in on itself. I clench my hands into fists and push forward. I'm not there. I'm not in the void. I'm void-adjacent, not void-immersed.

It's an awful thin line of distinction.

We sprint past the first two guarda, taking them by surprise. One attempts to hail ahead on his coms, and Caro's gleeful chortle when he's greeted with static tells me that she's blocked the message. I really do like her. Even if she hates me.

As we pass the border to seven, a swinging fist comes out of nowhere and I skid beneath the guarda in question, barely keeping my balance as I jab a punch up to her jaw. Her head snaps back and I capture her wrist, twisting her over my shoulder until she crashes to the artificially created floor with a curse and a thud. I hurdle her and keep running.

The guarda presence increases. Three now, forming a line along the rim. It's like they all came out to watch Micah be spaced. Itzel darts around us, fighting so quickly and so efficiently that I barely have to raise a fist before she's already dispatched my opponent, leaving me to focus on the task of running. Since the populace is forcibly kept without blasters, most of the guarda are not equipped with energy-based weapons. Something that seems fantastic until the first baton cracks into my shoulder, making my hand go limp and numb just long enough for a second swing. I manage to dance backward, delivering a left hook with my good hand as I shake the other limb until feeling returns to it. Caro yelps from behind me, but I don't have time to react, because two more guarda approach from in front.

How many are here? Too many. At least five but it's hard to tell because the rim is narrow and full of struggling bodies. One grabs me by the space suit and attempts to drag me backward. We should have had a plan. A better plan, that is. I always have a plan, or at least a strategy, but instead I'm running headlong through what might be a literal cadre of guarda—if only I knew how many a cadre were—to Micah, my only allies a woman who hates me and an assassin who hates killing. Oh, and my worst nightmare is hovering an arm's-length over my head, dispassionate, empty, and somehow so ravenously hungry I imagine I can hear its cavernous gullet rumbling.

Itzel is cornered against the wall by seven guarda who have clearly and correctly deemed her the critical risk.

My cheek throbs, and my lip is split, spiking a sharp little pain in my face when I grimace. Some priap tries to pull my hair until I punch him in the jaw. He makes the saddest little squeak when he stumbles into the person yanking at my suit, buying me time to wrench myself free. Suddenly the hall is open and Micah is right in front of me, flanked by two guarda with spotless uniforms and spit-shined badges edging their collars. He's gagged. Carmichael is between the two guarda, looking disgustingly pleased with himself. He catches my eyes over the other's shoulders and grins like my presence is the best surprise he's ever received.

"Freeze!" I scream, as though I have any authority. I don't have time to look behind me, to see if Caro and Itzel are free or captured.

Carmichael laughs, as though I'm making a joke.

"I have your pocket kidnapper in custody. She's about to be turned over to the Escajedas. I wonder what she's going to tell them about you?"

He seems remarkably unworried. "The Abyssal Abductor is a

lunatic and a criminal. She has no proof. Why would her word mean anything?"

That was dispensed with quickly. I thought he'd balk. That Aymbe would be worth something to him. "I know about the plankat nibarat. And I have proof. Proof that will be sent directly to the press if I don't walk out of here with Arora."

My big threat. Also a lie. Micah's subtle grimace around the mask tells me that he recognizes it as such. I want to tell him it will be okay. That I'm trustworthy. That I have him.

The guarda on the far side, gray hair cropped close and droopy mustache tickling his jaw, reads something aloud from his datapad. I can't make it out over the sounds of fighting that continue behind me. When he finishes reading, he folds the datapad and stores it in the breast pocket of his uniform.

Carmichael studies me through hateful eyes. "I don't believe you."

I bare my teeth, bluffing with all I have. "Try me."

They both grab Micah's arms. His wrists are restrained in front of him. His legs are loosely tethered by a thin chain. He's still wearing the space suit they probably dragged him in wearing—which seems like a waste of resources, except it appears that it's so old it may not be reliable anymore. I guess his prison experience didn't come with a handy change of clothes.

His eyes catch mine over the nearest guarda's shoulder. There's a warning in them. I don't know what about. Everything happening right now is ill-advised. There's also a kind of deep quiet stillness behind the manly resilience that he's trying so hard to project.

My heart breaks.

One guarda says something to his compatriot. I start running. The plasma lining the roof of the rim dips down to the floor directly in front of them, a glowing doorway to nothing at all. Carmichael Pierce steps forward behind him, eyes never leaving me. With one hard strong motion he shoves the helmetless Micah through the plasma wall to the void beyond. I know exactly what I see in his eyes then, because it's lived in my own. I screech something unintelligible and sprint forward as hard as I can. Carmichael laughs as I run toward him, drawing his blaster.

I put one last burst of speed on before I dodge past Pierce and throw myself directly through the plasma wall after Micah.

■ ■ ■ ■ ■ ■ ■ ■ ■ ■ ■ ■ ■ ■ ■

CHAPTER 28

The bone-numbing emptiness hits me like a bomb to the face. I force my eyes to stay open, using my momentum to float closer to Micah, because there's nothing else I can do. Tears freeze on my cheeks. The *Mimic* hovers right in front of us, close enough that even my stunned brain is able to work out a plan. More of a plan than I had when I followed Micah into the void, at least.

I collide with his body.

He's already motionless, face rigid as stone and eyes coated with a rime of ice, his facial skin just beginning to swell. My own vision blurs and I fumble at my waist for the strap that affixes my helmet to my belt. My fingers are thick and useless, but I manage to release the helmet, nearly losing it as it starts to drift away. I slam it down over Micah's head, locking it in place on his suit and completing the activation circuit that should start pumping recycled air from the small reservoir that runs along his spine. He's been inside an atmosphere long enough for it to refill.

He might wake up. He must wake up. It's only been seconds. People can survive longer than that in the void. So long as the air works. So long as I got here in time.

The helmet attaching to his suit probably makes a noise, but without any actual air, the noise never travels to my ears, which are probably frozen already anyway. My fingers won't bend. My hand is swollen, pressed against the glove of the suit. I stab it numbly at Micah's stiff body, trying to snag an arm, a leg, anything. Every movement is slower. Stiffer.

Less.

We drift closer to the *Mimic*. Not quickly enough. Enough time for my ever-more-sluggish brain to catch on the jagged sharp edge of where exactly I am. My mouth works, trying to swallow air that isn't here. My tongue is stiff and icy, a slab of frozen meat.

A sharp spike stabs my lungs. It's unfair that pain travels in the void and sound doesn't. I can't blink anymore but I can't see either, the tear film frozen solid on my eyes. Panic finally breaks through the ice around me. Desperation.

Familiar.

But different. Because Micah is here, too. He has air. Insulation. I just need to get him to the ship, because there's no telling when he'll wake up and that oxygen won't last forever. He needs me. I got him here. I have to get him out.

We hit the *Mimic*. Literally. Bounce off the chassis. I can barely move. One arm is looped around Micah. The other skids over the slick surface, desperately fumbling for a grip anywhere. Nothing.

There must be something. We bounce awkwardly off the ship on our way toward the docking hatch. My vision collapses to gray. Then black. I have to save him.

I am worthy of trust.

I'm slow. So slow. I make one last grasp for the ship. My numb fingers finally latch. I can't feel the cold anymore. I can't feel anything at all. I depress the manual lever on the hatch. Just like the one on the chassis of the *Mirror*, so long ago. I pull us inside. I strain for the air-lock lever, blind and numb. He trusted me.

I am worthy of trust.

I am worthy. . . .

CHAPTER 29

A heavy weight pumps at my breastbone. Hard. It hurts. Everything hurts. It feels like pins are being jabbed into my skin. That same skin is too tight for my body, stretching taut over bone.

"Wake up, Cyn," an anguished voice roars above me.

I *am* awake. I wish he'd stop pounding on my chest.

Guess I need to do something about that myself. I try to take a breath. It's ill-advised. Some sort of reactive spasm rolls up my throat and down to my lungs, shakes my stomach. I gag around air like it's water, like I don't even know how to breathe anymore. Maybe I don't. I manage to wheeze in a breath. Another. Hard arms wrap around me, half lifting me from the floor, and something presses against my cheek.

A face. Micah's face. With so much effort I nearly pass out again, I lift my hand, pausing for a moment to marvel that it moves at all. I press my fingers against his cheek. His banishment tattoo is dark, no longer glowing gold. His skin is crosshatched with angry red. His eyes are frantic.

"You okay?" I breathe the words more than say them. Mostly because I'm still getting the hang of the breathing thing, and actually speaking seems like a step too far. Luckily, my lips are pressed right against his ear.

He tightens his grip on my shoulders and pulls me away to study my face. My head flops backward like a baby, and he curses and props me back on the floor, looming in a way that's very satisfying but also that I can't take advantage of until I can figure out how to move. Or at least until I can catch my breath. And those pins stop their jabbing.

"Am *I* okay?" His previously beautifully smooth voice is raw and incredulous. He looks angry. I can't imagine why. "I didn't voluntarily space myself like a lunatic without a plan or a hope of survival."

Unfair. I had a sort of plan and a sort of hope for survival. Mostly *his* survival. "You . . ." Nope. That sentence is going to be too hard to properly articulate. "You spaced." Now that I'm slightly more aware, I realize that we're lying in the cargo bay of the *Mimic*, just past the air-lock entry. "You woke up."

"Yes, I woke up. I woke up with you nearly frozen solid and unmoving in my arms. You got us to safety and then died. You *died*."

"Stop whining. I saved you. You saved me." Those are full statements. I'm improving.

"And then," he continues as though he hasn't even heard me. His fingers dig into my skin like he's afraid to let me go. "I couldn't even properly perform CPR because you were frozen so stiff that compressions didn't work. Do you have any idea how terrified I was? You don't get to throw away your life for mine."

It finally registers that I'm alive. We're alive. This isn't some improbable afterlife. I smile. It hurts, so I stop. "Sure I do. Wasn't taking bounty." It's important he knows. "Didn't know how to get out of it."

"That conversation can wait until after a whole lot of triage. And also after we get to safety."

Right . . . they'll probably notice the ship hovering dangerously close to where he was spaced, unless they merely assume we're retrieving his body.

"Itzel and Caro." Don't have the energy to tell the whole story. "With me. Danger."

I pause. Catch my breath. Say the two words that matter. The two that matter more than anything else. The two that I've owed for a while. "Thank you."

He makes a strangled noise deep in the back of his throat, full of emotions that I can't even identify, and as his hands grip me even more firmly, everything gets dark again. Well, shit. If I went through all of that just to die now, I'm filing a complaint.

· · · · ·

When I wake again, everything hurts a lot less. I'm on the bed in Aymbe's bunk, some sort of goopy salve drenching my skin. It smells like tropical fruit and antiseptic. The two scents don't blend well. I scrape some off and rub it between two fingers. Sticky. Doesn't seem likely to absorb. Probably either a painkiller or a regenerator.

I sit, swing my feet over the side of the bed, and stumble over Micah, who's sleeping on the floor right next to me. I almost go down in a tangle of limbs, but he catches me as I land, clumsy as a newly birthed mammal. Then again, landing on his splayed body is not the worst way to hit the floor.

"You have a habit of tackling me when you wake up," his voice rumbles beneath me. "I could get used to that, Red."

Guess my flags haven't grown any less bloody. "You have a habit of lurking nearby while I'm sleeping."

His hands gently brace the flare of my waist. "Can you blame me? When left to your own devices, you voluntarily jump into the void."

Not for anyone but him. Preferably never again. I can't say it gets better with experience. "Here I thought you just liked being near me."

His calloused fingertips press in tighter. A shadow flares across his vision. When he replies, his voice is rough with emotion. "You need someone near you. Your back desperately needs watching. Try to get rid of me."

Clearly, I don't want to get rid of him. "Caro and Itzel?"

He gentles his grip. "It took about ten of them to finally restrain Itzel, but then Caro threatened to bring down the plasma wall if they didn't let her go. Apparently she even could have. She was quite proud of it. There will be no living with her. The two of them got away and are lying low in the station with your friend Madrigal. She's a treat, by the way. She threatened to castrate me if I didn't return you in one piece."

Everyone is safe. I'll ignore the "for now" part. "How long?"

"It's been a few standard days. Luckily, your cousin has a rapid-regeneration pod collecting dust in the hold. I ran us each through a cycle."

RRPs are insanely expensive. Most hospitals only have about two. Families hoard them. An RRP can take a blaster shot to the heart and turn it into a bad memory. I hold up my arm, peel back a bandage. My skin is new. Unscarred. No familiar crosshatch of pale flat marks. I almost miss them.

I take a deep experimental breath. My lungs don't scream. I don't cough. I feel vital. Healthy. I finally notice that the lurid red marks on Micah's face have also smoothed to clear brown skin. His voice is back to its previous velvety texture.

"I have to make a call."

He raises an eyebrow. "Just because you went through an RRP doesn't mean you're up for a call."

"Two calls."

"Can you even stand up?"

"Three calls."

Micah lifts me as he stands and deposits me back on the bed. "I'm bringing you a coms before we get to ten."

While he's gone, I do my best to not fall asleep. Rapid healing takes it out of a person. Last time I was spaced it wasn't for as long and I spent most of my recovery unconscious. It's easy to lose track of time when one is in a ghost ship. When Micah drops the earplug coms in my hand, he presses a kiss to my forehead and retreats to some other part of the ship.

I call my parents. Micah kept them informed, but knowing isn't the same as speaking to someone.

"What the hells were you thinking? You jumped into space?" My mother doesn't waste time with salutations.

"They spaced him." I can't come up with a better excuse than that. It certainly wasn't strategic. I didn't tell them much about Micah. They guessed plenty. That's how my family communicates: vague statements and intuition. "I knew I had a better chance of surviving than most."

I have her full attention. Sort of like talking to a viper on a coms. I'm not sure I like it. "Parbel, your daughter is on the coms."

"He saved me, too. I barely made it to the ship after I gave him my helmet. He revived me."

"You gave him your *helmet*?" she screeches.

I wince. "I didn't mention that part?"

"You absolutely did not." Her voice redirects somewhere in the room "She gave him her *helmet*, Parbel."

I hear the soft mumble of his response.

"It all worked out, though. I'm good as new. How are you? How are Aymbe and Mygda?"

My mom makes an angry sound of disbelief, and the coms is passed to my father. "About that. Five constables showed up at your office the other day. They demanded we release Aymbe into their custody. They all wore Pierce badges. We showed them your credentials and the bounty, but they said they'd take it from here. Mygda insisted on accompanying her."

Oh, she wasn't frustrated by me—my mother just didn't want to be the one to deliver the bad news. Pierce has their girl back. I flop my head on the pillow. Micah appears in the doorway, looking curious. I mime my head exploding. "You did the right thing."

"They didn't seem happy with her," he adds. So there's a chance

Pierce will lock her up as a liability. Nobody likes a loser. "We figured out how they knew later: there was a camera hidden in the
frame above your door. They saw everything."

That break-in. I was looking for something to be missing. I
didn't think of something added. I'm lucky they didn't take my
parents into custody.

We chat for a while longer, but sleep threatens, and eventually
I have to terminate the connection.

"Aymbe's out," I mumble to Micah. "Pierce got her."

"Fuck," he mutters.

"Fuck," I agree.

But then he leans over the bed, his lips brush my own, and I
find that I don't care about Aymbe quite so much.

CHAPTER 30

■ ■ ■ ■ ■ ■ ■ ■ ■ ■ ■ ■ ■ ■

A standard month later, a balmy ocean breeze ripples through my hair, sun-blocking clay cracks on my cheeks, and Micah stands beside me as we race over the deep-blue waters of Ginsidik, Poison Green rising in the distance. The sun sets on the horizon, casting the sky in a pale purple.

We took Mom and Dad home. Or, more specifically, Temper and Arcadio picked them up and *then* we took them home, since Micah and I are both officially deceased. I sold Aymbe's ship, and the proceeds went to finally bringing my family back in the black. A tiny part of me hoped that they'd want to stay in space, have some adventures, but home is home, and to them, the trawler will always be home. The good news is that they understand that it isn't *my* home.

In turn, I understand that it's my daughterly duty to visit on occasion. We're rebuilding and, with their new nest egg, they're getting to do some of that exploration they always wanted. For the first time in a long time, I have hope. Also, Etolla has apparently reevaluated and decided I'm going to have one child. That's not as horrifying as I thought it would be—some day in the future.

Aymbe left me a note, scrawled on a scrap of paper and shoved under my mattress. Probably only had time to do it when she heard Pierce outside the door. No apologies. No remorse. All it said is "Children are boring. Thanks for showing me adults can be much more fun. It's time for a new challenge."

Nice to know that I made a difference. Temper and Arcadio commed to let us know that Boreal reached her mother. Estella went public, causing a fervor that lasted in the holos a full week, up until Maria Flores revealed a hidden child of her own, likely jealous of all the good press the Escajedas were getting. In each and every holo, Boreal clutches Vuur, its head nuzzled under her chin. It's nearly twice the size it was when I last saw it. Clearly Boreal can source the good metal.

So here we are, with one last thing to wrap up.

"How many people did they say were on guard?" I ask, adjusting my body armor.

"No one from the Family. Too easy to trace. They hired local pirates to keep an eye on things. If there are any suspicious activities, connies from your trawlertown go on leave and check things out. Then, come harvest time, the Pierces send some lackeys to collect the goods."

Micah went from useful prisoner to next in line for execution when Carmichael caught him asking questions about the plankat practices. The night before he was almost executed, Micah went beyond asking questions and broke out of his cell. He got caught hacking into their system. They had to shut him up. Couldn't risk that information leaking.

We're both still dead, as far as official records go. Micah Arora and Cyn Khaw, an outlaw love story that ended with an execution and a suicide. I don't mind being off the books. I've had too many names over the years. Stepped into too many skins. I look forward to trying something new.

"So we probably already tackled their pirates."

"Stands to reason," he agrees. "And there's no reason to anticipate the connies would be present."

There is not. We dock outside the green and travel the rest of the way on foot. The sunset has deepened, from dark violet at the far horizon to a pale soft fuchsia near the setting Axios.

Micah hands me one of the packs and shoulders the other. "Are we going to talk about it?"

"About what?" I respond intelligently.

"What comes next. For both of us."

Ah. That. Maybe not. Because I don't know, and I'm terrified to consider it. "All right, what comes next?"

He gazes at the sunset before snagging my hand, tugging me gently toward the hollow basalt column. "I've had gangs and crews, flops and ships, but never anything that I considered mine. Never a home."

I've mostly had things that are exclusively mine. But that doesn't mean I've had a home lately. I screw up every ounce of courage I possess. "Would you consider sharing something of *mine*? Ours?"

"What did you have in mind?" His smooth voice washes over me like hot water. He lifts the trapdoor and drops into the plankat nibarat cave. I follow.

"I don't know. My old life is gone. Even Madrigal's in the ether, probably pitting herself against your old friend Regan as we speak to head the Claw, or at least restart her smuggling empire. I don't want to stay on Ginsidik, but my family and I want to try to root out the corruption in the constables. Do something to relieve the pressure put on them by Pierce."

Micah fires a shot directly into the irrigation lines. Water spills out, pooling on the far side of the room. It slopes down that way, so that a leak doesn't drown any of their crop. I spray the plants with the liquid in my bag.

"I have a place on the *Calamity*. The closest thing I have to family is there. I can't walk away." His words send a spike of dismay through my heart.

"I understand." I pull myself away, carefully taping over all the gaps in my psyche that might cause me to do something truly humiliating, like bursting into tears. We never made any promises, but I got used to having him around. To having support. To being trusted. To trusting, in return. So instead, I carefully walk through the field of flowers, being sure to spray every single plant.

He grunts out a sigh and follows, spinning me around and tugging me closer. "Clearly you don't, so maybe you should let me finish. I can't walk away forever. They need me. They might need *you*, too, if your rates are reasonable."

They might need *me*.

"My rates aren't reasonable," I blurt, a slow smile blooming on my face. "But I could make an exception. Maybe we can split our time."

I can feel his smile where his cheek is pressed against my forehead. My arm wraps around his waist. "That sounds good."

He slips his hands behind my thighs and scoops me up so quickly that I make an embarrassing squeaky sound as I find myself straddling his waist. I link my ankles behind his back automatically, fingers curling against the back of his armor.

I kiss him, reveling in the feeling of my body wrapped around his. Without the weight of unanswered questions pressing on my shoulders. Instead of a life focused on the worst parts of the past, I suddenly have a future that's huge and undefined and encompasses the stars. And even more amazingly, I have someone to walk it with me. "What's next?"

"Long-term? Take it as it comes. Short-term?" He hoists me higher, one hand migrating to my rear as he turns the kiss into something far deeper. "Short-term, I suggest we finish what we started here and then you show me that romantic island I never got to see."

I take a nip of his lower lip, drawing it out slightly as I lower my feet to the floor. "I guess we'd better be fast, then."

Once each flower is coated with accelerant, Micah lights the fuse. We stand near the exit pillar, watching the flowers wilt and curl as fire rages through the field. I link my hand with his again. "You always plan the best dates."

Micah laughs.

The flowers burn. Hopefully the first crop of many that we'll be able to destroy. There's a list. It isn't short. Once we're clear of the cave, we deploy the fuse on the algae processor. The basalt rumbles beneath our feet as it blows.

. . . . .

Later, but not much later, the boat approaches Opal. It's much faster than that old tugboat. Above us, the ionosphere performs its final act, ribbons of light dancing in the sky as the secondday sun begins to dawn. The sand refracts a prism of color, afire with the morning light. Rainbows float in the air, above and below. Micah's coveralls are unzipped before we reach the beach because I'm impatient by nature.

He sits on the glowing sand, me perched on his lap, hands roaming up my back, shoving my brown synth-leather jacket off my shoulders. I'm greedy for the feel of him and I slip my hands between the fabric of the coveralls and his chest, tracing the subtle ridges of muscle that adorn his skin. Our scars are nothing but a memory, constellations in the daytime, invisible to the human eye.

And he's already plotting a course of his own as he pulls my shirt over my head and traces a line of kisses down the side of my neck, across my collarbone, and down my sternum. His tongue edges a delicate pattern of its own, activating a trail of nerves in paths drawn by the void. The warm water laps at our legs.

I wrestle his coveralls half-off and now, instead of only the thin gap of skin exposed through the open zipper, I have all of it. He pulls me closer, and our breaths mingle, lips a hairsbreadth from each other. His lips crash into mine with a feral intensity that leaves me breathless for a reason that has nothing to do with anticipation and everything to do with appreciation.

I frame his face in my palms, soaking in the intensity, that warmth that he always outputs like a furnace. Slashes of light dance over his skin. I'd say he makes me see stars, but I see those every day and it's nothing as mundane as stars. It's the feeling of going into faster-than-light drive, where your stomach drops out and your eyes roll back and you can't quite comprehend where you were, where you are, and where you will be.

The restrained pressure in his hands as they explore my skin reminds me of his innate strength. Of the way he fights, clean and bloody and precise. Defending those he loves. That shouldn't turn me on, but it does. Competence is attractive, no matter its form. His body is hard beneath me—some parts harder than others. I melt atop him, hand delving down to stroke him as our kiss deepens.

The soft rush of the surf rolling over the shore fills my ears. The scent of the kelp flowers floating in the lagoon, the glow of light all around, and the insistent pressure of Micah's body against my own is overwhelming. I stand, pulling off his coveralls and shimmying out of my own pants, before returning to our previous position.

"You're always so impatient," Micah chuckles, dragging a knuckle over my cheekbone.

"Always, as though we've done this more than a few times. Maybe I just want to see if you're really as good as I remember or if I just signed on for a very disappointing future."

"Is that intended to be motivational?" He tweaks a nipple, and a spark of pleasure zips right to my core.

"Was it?" I return the favor, tracing the broad length of his shaft, dragging my thumb over its head.

The breath catches in his throat. "I'm deeply motivated."

My fingers wrap a little tighter around him, barely brushing together on the other side, and I shift off his lap to kneel between his legs, pushing his shoulders to rest on the sand. "As I recall, you did something pretty fantastic the last time and I didn't get a chance to return the favor."

He swallows, watching me like I'm the most beautiful thing he's ever seen, which can't possibly be correct but perhaps he's blinded by my red flags. Maybe that's why I brought him to a location that's so bright. "Fairness is important."

My smile is broad as I trace my fingers over his thighs, drag my teeth along the divot of muscle that shoots its way down his hips like an arrow toward his shaft, which is bobbing at attention and waiting to be recognized. I dig my nails into his legs, reveling in the helpless fascination in his gaze as I lower my head and lick a long hot line up the length of him.

I take my time, learning exactly what makes him squirm, what makes the breath choke in his throat, what makes his hands clench in fists. Finally, Micah gasps out a sort of inarticulate growl and grabs me under the arms, yanking me up his body until I'm draped on top of him, dopey grin plastered on my face, because it's fun to make this carefully controlled man lose it.

"We'll revisit that more, later. A lot more. Now, I need to be inside you before I explode, Red."

That sounds fantastic. I reach back down, and he chuckles under his breath, pushing my hand aside and running his fingers over the center of me, smiling when he feels exactly how wet I am. How turned on I was purely by the act of turning him on. One thick finger delves inside, and he traces slow circles with his thumb over the eager little bundle of nerves that's begging for attention. He curls his finger and my breath catches.

"Now. I want you now." I grab his shoulders, almost shaking him. "*Now.*"

He shakes beneath me as he laughs. "Happy to oblige."

I straddle his lap and he notches his shaft into me, thrusting up slowly, and my head falls back at the thick slide of sensation as he fills me. A guttural moan escapes when he finally hits home, and I wriggle slightly atop him as my body grows comfortable with the invasion. It doesn't take long. I rock my hips gently, gliding on top of him. Micah lets me take my time, his hands starting at my hips but roving up along my ribs, thumbs tracing the sensitive underside of my breasts, until he finally cradles them in his hands, gaze roving over my body while I move.

I pick up the pace as the blood pounds through my body, glorious heat drenching me from head to toe. My nails curl into his shoulders, dimpling his skin. A flush warms his chest, the high arc of his cheekbones. His eyes watch me with the intensity of a hunting bird. They *see* me with that same intensity. A trickle of sweat traces its way between my breasts and he watches its path avidly. Light showers our skin as the sun rises higher in the sky, colors dancing over every part of us.

A throbbing vital volume starts to build within me, pumped louder with every motion, every stroke. He moves beneath me, thrusting up as I plummet down. One arm bands around my waist and the other grasps the back of my head, pulling me near until my mouth meets his in a kiss.

"I'm so close," I gasp, overwhelmed with sensation, overwhelmed with him.

He picks up the pace, adding a little twist to each thrust of his hips, pillaging my mouth with his tongue until all I can think about is the energy coursing through each part of my body. That satisfied growly noise he makes when he's really proud of himself rumbles over me, and suddenly all that energy shoots to just one spot and my back bows with the power of my orgasm, ripping my mouth away from his as I gasp for breath.

Micah loses that controlled rhythm, slamming up into me as I ride him, his arms latched over my back and around me. The waves of pleasure just keep on crashing down, like whatever rhythm he's found is their perfect counterpoint, stretching a moment into an eternity. I barely maintain enough sense to feel him go stiff and rigid beneath me, and then a wall of water collides with us from behind.

Laughter bubbles between gasps for breath as I push myself slightly up from where I crashed down on Micah's broad chest.

Water sluices down my body, dripping onto Micah's. I watch the trailing sandy drops, fascinated. "You didn't have to make me feel *real* waves of sensation."

"I really did." He stretches his back, arms straining over his head before they return to their proper position, which is around me.

He looks like he belongs here. In my life I haven't been very accepting of people sharing space and time with me. I haven't made room for them either emotionally or physically. But here, in one of my favorite places, light dances over his skin and illuminates his eyes. I drag my fingers through his hair, pulling him into a hard short kiss. "I love you, you know."

"You leapt into space without a helmet for me. I figured it out. This will be the second time I said it, because the first time I was screaming it to your unresponsive body, but I love you, too."

"I haven't ever said it to anyone else. I defined love by what it leaves in its absence. That bitter cold emptiness like the depth of the void. Something that leeches away everything you are." I bask in the light of a million rainbows. Watch them play across his skin. "I didn't realize it's the *vessel*, not what fills it. Sometimes its contents are deep and sometimes shallow-thin, but the vessel is what matters. Building it up to be safe and solid, so that it can catch whatever falls."

"Like always, you're making it much harder than it has to be. Love is oxygen. Vital. Necessary. Natural."

I glare lazily at him. "Are you arguing with my romantic epiphany? Oxygen is useless without something to contain it. A ship. A tank. An atmosphere. I'm right."

"Fine." His fingers trace my cheek, calloused and gentle. We breathe the same air for the moment. "I'll be your oxygen if you'll be my atmosphere."

And together, we'll be a whole world. Solid and stable and filled with life. I bite my bottom lip, listening to the drugging lull of waves battering against the shore, smelling the thick heady mix of salt and skin and the blooming flowers. Feeling the solidity of the man wrapped around me.

"No wonder I woke up." I rest my head against the curve of his shoulder, skin alight with rainbows in the seconddawn sunlight, and bask in the fact that, somehow, I've gone from isolation to community, from vengeance to rebirth, from loss to love. I have something to dream about now. A future. A whole world, built from our love.

"Everything I didn't dare to want was only a resurrection away."

ACKNOWLEDGMENTS

We made it to book two! For anyone not following the math, that's double the books. Probably the only time I'll ever double my output in a year, so it's an important milestone. And one that absolutely wouldn't have happened without a figurative army of people working behind the scenes.

Thanks to Caitlin Blasdell of Liza Dawson Associates, who gave advice that allowed the story to become what it was meant to be and who has an intelligent answer for any question.

Thanks to the entire team at Bramble/Tor. Monique Patterson and Mal Frazier for deft editing hands and enthusiastic support throughout the process. MaryAnn Johanson for copy editing and Megan Kiddoo for production editing. Caro Perny for publicity and Jordan Hanley for marketing.

Thanks to a fantastic narrator, Paige Reisenfeld, who has brought this series to life in audiobook form.

Long before the book reached any of them, thanks to Frank Harris, who read the rough early chapters. Thanks to the Blue Badgers—Allison King and Mike Meneses—the best writing group a gal could ask for, who generously reviewed a draft in record speed. Thanks to Liz Hersh-Tucker, Sarah McIntosh, and Katie Hossepian for support, cheerleading, and group-chat availability. Thanks to both of my parents, Carolyn Fay and Jack Fay, for their encouragement and for listening to me yammer on for hours on end about the tiniest details in this process.

And finally, thanks to the readers. Whether you started with *Calamity* or *Fiasco*, I'm glad you're here. Welcome to the worlds of Uncharted Hearts. I hope you stay on to our next adventure.

ABOUT THE AUTHOR

CONSTANCE FAY writes space-romance novels and genre-fiction short stories. Her short fiction can be found in *The Magazine of Fantasy & Science Fiction*, *CatsCast* podcast, and other publications. She has a background in medical device R&D and lives in Colorado with a cat who edits all her work first.